P9-DOC-061

ALSO BY CYNTHIA HAND

UNEARTHLY

HALLOWED

BOUNDLESS

RADIANT: AN UNEARTHLY NOVELLA

(available as an ebook only)

THE LAST TIME WE SAY GOODBYE

MY LADY JANE

(with Brodi Ashton and Jodi Meadows)

CYNTHIA HAND

An Imprint of HarperCollins*Publishers*

HarperTeen is an imprint of HarperCollins Publishers.

The Afterlife of Holly Chase
 For information address HarperCollins Children's Books, a division of HarperCollins Publishers, 195 Broadway, New York, NY 10007.
www.epicreads.com

Library of Congress Control Number: 2017943434
ISBN 978-0-06-231850-3

Typography by Ellice M. Lee
17 18 19 20 21 PC/LSCH 10 9 8 7 6 5 4 3 2 1
❖
First Edition

For Leslie and for Tess.
Elf power forever.

"Man of the worldly mind!" replied the Ghost, "do you believe in me or not?"

"I do," said Scrooge. "I must. But why do spirits walk the earth, and why do they come to me?"

"It is required of every man," the Ghost returned, "that the spirit within him should walk abroad among his fellow-men, and travel far and wide; and if that spirit goes not forth in life, it is condemned to do so after death. It is doomed to wander through the world—oh, woe is me!—and witness what it cannot share, but might have shared on earth, and turned to happiness!"

—*Charles Dickens,* A CHRISTMAS CAROL

ONE

THE FIRST THING YOU SHOULD probably know is that Yvonne Worthington Chase was dead. It was all over the news when it happened, the entertainment shows, the newspapers and magazines, even the trashy tabloids. *A sudden tragedy*—that's how the media described it, because she was only fortysomething when it happened, plus Yvonne was famous, so her death was considered a much bigger deal than an ordinary person's.

Yvonne was a fashion stylist. Anybody who was, like, anybody in Hollywood hired her to make sure they were always looking fabulous. She had an uncanny ability to match the right item to the right person and situation, a way of finding that perfect gown to wear on the red carpet of the Golden Globes, or the correct shoes for that *Vogue* photo shoot on Zuma Beach, or the most infallible bag to take to lunch in Beverly Hills. Her obituary claimed that she died after complications from foot surgery, because her feet were screwed up from all the years she spent in stilettos. A believable story. But the truth is, Yvonne died getting your run-of-the-mill plastic surgery, which involved a breast lift, neck lift, and butt lift. It was during the neck lift that things went horribly wrong.

The obituary went on to state that Yvonne was survived by her husband, the well-respected film director Gideon Chase, and her sixteen-year-old stepdaughter, Holly.

That's me. Holly Chase.

I didn't cry at Yvonne's funeral. She wouldn't have wanted an emotional display. The whole time, I wore a pair of Bulgari Flora sunglasses, which hid my eyes and took up most of my face (these had belonged to Yvonne, actually—a huge perk out of Yvonne dying was that I finally got to raid her closet), and when it was all over, I took my phone out of my purse and snapped a selfie in the graveyard with my amazing new sunglasses. And posted it for all my followers to see.

I was a bad person back then. Seriously, I was. I would have backstabbed even my supposed best friends if I thought I could squeeze any attention out of it. I mocked everyone who I perceived as having even the slightest imperfection—that geeky girl in second period who clearly had no idea what the word *antiperspirant* meant, that boy in the cafeteria with the disgusting mole on his cheek, that cheerleader who really needed to do something about the hideous fat roll poking out from under her bra. I gossiped and spread rumors like it was going out of style. I knew I was being mean. I didn't care. All I wanted was to be like Yvonne. Rich. Fashionable. Famous. I already had fifty thousand followers, and that was only the beginning. Eventually, I just knew it, everyone was going to know my name.

So that was me. Holly Evangeline Chase. Sixteen—almost seventeen—years old, five foot seven, 115 pounds, brown eyes, blond hair, killer fashion sense, and a perfectly horrible human being. That's all you need to know about me for now, outside of the fact that, like I mentioned, Yvonne was dead. And she'd been dead almost exactly seven months the night this story truly begins. The night everything changed.

Christmas Eve.

I hated Christmas back then. Like, really hated it. I had my reasons, but I won't go into those just yet. That particular Christmas Eve, I'd spent the afternoon at a holiday runway show for Calvin Klein, which had given me a mega headache from all of the bright lights and the fake snow and the cheerful exclamations of "Merry Christmas!" that seemed to be coming at me from every direction. I'd worn this amazing pair of lipstick-red Charlotte Olympia shoes, but by five o'clock they felt like they were like two sizes too tight. So when I got home that night, I was in a mood. And I did what I usually did.

I took it out on the housekeeper.

"Why is it so hot in here?" I complained as she served me dinner.

"Hot?" she repeated in that voice she used when she was trying to act like she didn't understand my English. She put a plate in front of me—risotto or something. It smelled amazing. One thing I will say for Elena—the woman could cook.

"I just got home, and it's, like, over seventy in here," I said. "It's practically balmy."

"I turned on the heat today. It was chilly."

"But I haven't been here all day," I pointed out. "So why would you turn the heat on?"

We stared at each other for a few long seconds.

"It was chilly," she said again.

I had her right where I wanted her. "Oh, so you turned on the heat for *you*," I said crisply. "You think my dad wants to pay an astronomical heating bill to keep *you* all cozy and warm?"

I knew perfectly well that my dad would have no problem paying any amount of heating bill. But for me that wasn't the point. The point was that while my dad was out of town—and he was, like, always out of town—I was in charge, and Elena was not. In my opinion she took far too many liberties around the house. She needed to be put in her place.

"It's like you're basically stealing from us," I said.

"I'm very sorry, miss." She looked down at where her hands were clasped together in front of her. She had the worst hands—small and red and chapped. Maybe I should require her to wear gloves, I thought. Then she'd be warmer, too, and I wouldn't have to look at those hands every day.

"Whatevs," I said with a roll of my eyes. I took a tentative bite of the risotto, and it was delicious, so I took three more quick bites and then pushed my plate away. "And what is this stuff, anyway? This isn't low cal. Obviously. Do you want me to get fat? Is that it?"

"No," Elena said steadily. "I know. But I thought, this is a special meal for a special night."

"A special night?" I repeated. "What special night?"

"Christmas Eve. And I made plenty for you to warm up for yourself tomorrow."

I stared at her, my mouth opening in disbelief. "Wait, tomorrow? I'm supposed to eat this tomorrow? Where are *you* going to be?"

"I was going to spend the day with my daughter."

"And who gave you the day off?"

"It's Christmas." She was looking at her hands again.

"So what if it's Christmas?" I gasped, completely outraged. "I'm all alone here, and my dad pays you to attend to me. We didn't discuss you having Christmas off."

"But your father said—"

"I'm going to expect you to be here tomorrow." My headache pounded more fiercely than ever—I hated having to deal with the hired help. "And if you're not here, in the morning, on time, then maybe I'll have to find someone else to fill your position. Someone who will take this job seriously."

She glanced up, her jaw tightening, her eyes bright with all that she wanted to say to me, but of course she wouldn't dare. I almost wished she would—it'd been a while since I'd gotten someone fired. But then who would make my dinner tomorrow? It'd be too much of a pain to get someone else on such short notice, on Christmas Day no less.

"Tomorrow I want salmon for dinner. With lemon. Maybe some asparagus," I informed her like the matter was settled. "And pancakes for breakfast. And freshly squeezed orange juice."

She nodded stiffly. "All right." She took the plate of risotto. "Can I get you anything else?"

"No," I said. "I'm going to bed."

She scurried back to the kitchen. I'd been hard on her, I knew I had, but I didn't feel bad about it. *If you push people,* Yvonne always used to say, *then sooner or later they'll start to push themselves.* She'd be better for it, I thought. She'd work harder.

That took care of that, I thought with some satisfaction, and then I took a sleeping pill and went to bed. I was completely out, like, dead to the world, until a noise woke me in the middle of the night. It was loud, like a giant fist pounding against a door.

Bang.

Bang.

Bang.

And then silence.

"Dad?" I called, although I knew he was still on location in New Zealand or New York or somewhere. "Dad? Elena?"

No answer.

I checked my phone. The time was exactly midnight. No texts or emails. No other sounds in the house. I was, as usual, alone. I was about to slide my sleep mask back into place when something in the corner of the dark room caught my eye.

A shadow. A shadow that became my stepmother, standing at the foot of my bed. My stepmother, who, as I mentioned, had been dead for seven months.

Yvonne was still wearing the black Diane von Furstenberg

dress she'd been buried in. Her face was a nasty yellow, covered in a heavy layer of funeral-home makeup. Her ice-blue eyes had clouded to a dull gray. Weirdest of all, she was wearing pearls, string after string of perfect white pearls, around her neck, her wrists, wrapping around her always-dieting-skinny waist, snaking down her legs to her ankles and her Jimmy Choos like strings on a deranged marionette.

I squeezed my eyes closed, then opened them again, but Dead Yvonne didn't disappear. Instead she sat down at the edge of my bed and took my hand. Her fingers were cold. There was a jagged incision in the side of her neck, crudely stitched closed with black thread. As she leaned closer, I got a powerful whiff of formaldehyde and rot mixed with her 24, Faubourg perfume.

"Hello, darling girl," she rasped, the caked powder around her lips cracking as she spoke. "I've come to warn you."

I opened my mouth then, and screamed, and screamed, and screamed.

You know how the story goes, right? There's this old banker type named Ebenezer Scrooge, who shuffles around saying, "Bah, humbug." One Christmas Eve he's visited by the Ghosts of Christmas Past, Present, and Future. In the morning he wakes up, like, completely terrified, and says to himself, *This is my chance. I can change my future,* and starts handing out all of his money and buying a Christmas goose for a crippled kid and shouting, "Merry Christmas!" from the rooftops. Then he supposedly lives happily ever after. It's a nice story. I guess. But that's not how it happened for me.

My version's a little more complicated.

I'm going to skip ahead now to the part with the Ghosts. The first Ghost, specifically. Because that's what this story is really all about. The Ghost of Christmas Past.

My Ghost was just a girl. It was hard to tell, what with the glowing robes and the whole human-lamp effect, but even then, I noticed there was something weirdly normal about her. Something about the way she stood with her head tilted to one side and her hands clasped behind her back, as if she were listening to someone talking, only there wasn't anyone else there. You could almost believe, looking at her, that she was your average twelve-year-old, like this was just her job—playing the Ghost of Christmas Past—and the rest of the year she was playing with dolls. She kept bringing me to different memories from my past—this time I got left alone at school, a sad conversation I had with my dad, a Christmas party I'd actually enjoyed once from before my mom died—and every time she brought me to these scenes she kept staring at me with these huge, dead-serious blue eyes. Like she knew me.

"We can rest for a while, if you need to." The Ghost turned to look at me and smiled. Her teeth were oversized and a little crooked. "Are you okay?"

I wasn't even a little bit okay. Seeing my mom again, even if I knew it was just a memory, felt like having the wind knocked out of me. But I shook my head.

"Let's just get this over with," I said, and the Ghost grabbed my hand again to take me to the next place. The fog around us thickened, and the air took on a chill. There was something else in it, too, tiny particles of white swirling past. Snow. Which wasn't something I was used to seeing in California.

"Come on," the Ghost said, leading me forward through the flurry. We walked for a while—I couldn't have said how long—until the Ghost finally stopped and parted the fog like a curtain, and on the other side I saw Rosie Alvarez. Ro, I'd always called her.

My ex-BFF.

We were standing in my bedroom from before I had it redecorated, back when it was still robin's-egg blue and still had posters up on the walls and pictures of Ro and me taped to my mirror. I knew before the Ghost even said anything that she'd brought me back to the night Ro told me she didn't want to be friends anymore. I remembered that night perfectly. It'd only been last year.

"I don't want to be here," I told the Ghost.

"But you have to," the Ghost said. "You have to see it with new eyes."

Whatever that meant. I yanked away from her, but in spite of my intention to act cool and uninterested, I found myself taking a step toward Ro, then another and another, until I was standing next to the younger version of myself: the clueless Holly who was about to get dumped by her best friend.

I'd told everybody at school that *I'd* dumped *her*, of course, not the other way around. *I outgrew her* is how I'd spun it, like Ro was last year's designer jacket in the bin at the Salvation Army—not that I ever gave anything to charity. *I outgrew Ro a long time ago.*

In a way, this was true. That's what Ro herself was saying at that very moment, but I wasn't actually listening to her talk. I was staring at that splattering of freckles across the bridge of her nose. I'd forgotten that Ro even had freckles, or that her hair had been so long, when sometime last year she got this pixie cut that I wished I could say looked terrible on her, but actually it made her look streamlined and more put together, somehow.

"I don't even know why you still want to be friends with me," she was saying to the old Holly, the one who'd been staring at her phone during this entire conversation. Who was wearing the most gorgeous pair of silk Olivia von Halle pajamas, by the way.

The old Holly glanced up, surprised. "I never said I didn't want to be friends."

"You never said that," Ro agreed, "but let's be honest. If we met today—if I bumped into you at school—would you even let me sit with you at lunch?"

No, I thought. *Of course I wouldn't.*

But the old Holly didn't answer right away. She smoothed her hair over her shoulder and said, "Maybe. You don't know."

Ro frowned. "Come on, Holly. I know you think I'm not good enough to hang out with you. You've got your designer bags and your expensive clothes, your 'fifty thousand followers,' and I'm just a regular T-shirt and sneakers sort of girl."

Old Holly was still looking at her phone. "Well, I mean, not everyone can be fabulous, right?" she said distractedly. We'd had versions of this fight before, where Ro whined about how materialistic I was becoming and how everything shouldn't be about a person's wealth or social status. Of course Ro had to think that way, because she was poor. "But seriously," Old Me said, "why am

I supposed to feel guilty about having money? The world runs on money. That's just how it is."

"It doesn't have to be like that," Ro argued. "Do you remember what it was like before, Holly? When we used to watch TV with the sound turned off and make up the dialogue? Or we'd go to the pet store and name all the fish. We'd hang out on the beach and build weird sand creatures. We'd write songs. None of that was about money, remember? It was about us. What happened to that Holly?"

I remembered that Holly well. The one with the mousy hair and the braces who nobody noticed in a crowd. I'd been glad to get rid of her.

"I liked that girl." Rosie reached and took the phone out of Old Holly's hand. "I need you to hear this. Please."

Old Holly sighed. "I get it, Ro. I've changed, but so what? I haven't changed toward you."

"It's not the same. You're not the same." She bent her head and laughed, but it wasn't a happy sound. "Last week, I watched you making fun of a girl in the hall just because she was wearing leggings as pants. And her face when she saw you laughing at her, her face—" Her eyebrows pinched together. "We can't be friends anymore, Holly. I can't."

That hurt, even a year later. I still felt that tightness in my chest, that jolt when I realized she was serious. Ro and I had been, like, joined at the hip since we were three years old, inseparable, so much that I hardly had a memory that didn't include her. But with one little sentence our entire relationship was over.

I didn't want to watch what happened next. I knew exactly how this scene ended. She walked out of my life and never came back. She just *dumped* me.

"Why are you showing me this?" I asked the Ghost.

"I told you, these are just the shadows of things that have been," said the Ghost. "If you don't like them, don't blame me."

There was something so familiar about those words. The entire night felt like the worst case of déjà vu ever, all the way back to when Dead Yvonne had showed up in my room. Even then, after I finished screaming long enough to hear her warn me about the visit from the three spirits—even then, I thought, *I know this. I've seen this movie before.*

But I didn't know I was a Scrooge.

Still, one thing was perfectly clear: I was the villain here. They thought I was a bad person. They—and who was they, anyway, who was orchestrating this?—thought I needed to change who I was.

The room had gone foggy again. The Ghost was talking—something about Ro and what the future had in store for her, something amazing, no doubt, since Ro could obviously do no wrong. But again, I wasn't listening. I was thinking, *Hey, there's nothing wrong with me. I may not be nice, exactly; I may not be all sunshine and rainbows all the time, but I'm not a bad person.*

I'm not that bad, I thought. *I'm just a realist.*

That's what Yvonne used to call herself: a realist. Since she'd died I'd always listened to what I thought of as my Inner Yvonne, the voice in the back of my mind that told me how Yvonne

Worthington Chase would have reacted to any given situation, as if my stepmother were still there grooming me. *It's about survival of the fittest, my darling,* the Inner Yvonne said, *so you have to be the fittest. That's life.*

And then I started thinking about tonight's Yvonne, Yvonne-back-from-the-dead, moaning about how she should have been nicer, she should have been kinder to her fellow man. But the real Yvonne didn't apologize to anyone. She didn't compromise. She didn't look back.

So there was no way that tonight's Yvonne had been real.

The Ghost pulled at my sleeve. "Holly?"

None of this was real, I decided. It was all a dream, and when I woke up I would totally laugh at myself for how freaked out I'd been.

Take control of the dream, whispered the Inner Yvonne from the back room of my brain. *That's what we do in any uncertain situation. We take control.*

Right. Take control. Starting with how I was apparently supposed to be feeling guilty about Ro. I pulled my shoulders back and stood up straighter.

"Ro wasn't anything special," I said, turning to face the Ghost. "I was only friends with her because her mom was friends with my mom, and she wanted us to be besties. We clearly didn't have anything in common. I don't care that we're not friends anymore. I'm glad, even."

I was so good, I was almost believable.

The Ghost cocked her head again and stared at me. "She was

like a sister to you. You loved her."

I scoffed. "Did not."

"Did so," the Ghost shot back, like this disagreement was about whose turn it was on the swings. "You loved Rosie, but you let her go because she didn't fit in with the image you'd built of yourself."

"I did not love Ro," I insisted. "But that doesn't matter. We're not friends anymore. It's in the past, and there's nothing we can do to change that. So big freaking deal. Take me home. I am so done with playing this stupid game."

"But—" For the first time the Ghost looked hurt.

I didn't care. "Also, can you turn down your light thing? It's giving me a migraine."

"It matters," argued the Ghost, but she didn't look at me. Her light dimmed a few degrees. She reached for my hand again. "It matters," she said softly. "We should go."

I was different after that. I stopped taking it seriously. I mean, I laughed at the Ghost of Christmas Present—just point-blank laughed at his silly green robe and the wreath on his head. I even made fun of his beard. Then I stood there mocking everybody when he tried to show me what the other students at Malibu High School were saying about me behind my back. I sort of knew all that stuff anyway. Deep down, I always knew the truth—people despised me. It was because they were jealous, I told myself. They didn't matter, because I was the real deal.

Next the Ghost tried to show me how I was messing up Elena's life. Like I could really be responsible for someone else's total lame factor. It was all so Hallmark Channel: Elena trying so hard to do what I asked of her, making my meals, ironing my clothes, keeping the house spotless, and then her sweet little daughter, Nika, having a terrible accident. All supposedly my fault. It was only a dream, I reminded myself again and again. A stupid dream based on a stupid Christmas movie I'd seen as a kid. So I kept laughing, snickering, rolling my eyes.

Eventually the next Ghost showed up. He wore a hood so I couldn't see his face, and he didn't talk. He pointed with his long, skeletal fingers. I didn't laugh at him, because he was, like, mildly terrifying, but I also didn't believe him when he tried to show me the future: that I was going to die soon, apparently. Even when he brought me to Westwood Cemetery and presented me with the white marble slab with my name on it, I refused to take him seriously.

"Is this the best you can do?" I said with only the tiniest quiver in my voice. "Because this is such B-movie material. I'm practically Hollywood royalty, you know—my mother was a famous TV star, and my dad is a director, so I know the business. And this whole thing is obviously fake."

The Ghost opened his cloak. Inside it I saw only blackness, like he was made up of nothing but an empty void, and without warning, the void swallowed me. I lost the feeling in my feet. Then the numbness moved to my legs. My fingers. My arms. My face. All at once I felt a terrible pressure in my chest, like my lungs were being pressed flat by some tremendous weight. I could feel my heart struggling to pump, slower and slower, slower and slower, until . . .

This is what it's like to die, I thought. *This . . . nothingness.*

I couldn't move. I couldn't call for help. I couldn't even blink. The Ghost put his bony arms around me, and I felt something like cold and burning at the same time, like dry ice, and then everything went dark.

But the dark only lasted a few seconds. Then I woke with a jolt, choking for air, clutching at the bedpost. It was my bedpost, I realized. My room. Light streamed through the filmy curtains, and beyond them, a familiar palm tree swayed gently in the breeze.

I was home.

Somewhere in the house Elena was whistling a Christmas song.

I groped on the bedside table for my phone. It was 9:00 a.m., on the dot, December 25. Sixty-eight degrees in Malibu, and sunny. I laid a hand on my chest and felt my heart beating, fast but steady.

"Oh. My. God," I laughed. "That was the most psycho dream ever."

I stretched my arms over my head. My stomach rumbled.

"Elena!" I screamed. "Where are my pancakes?"

That day I didn't wish anyone a merry Christmas. I lounged around the house in my pajamas and watched TV and had Elena paint my toenails. When my dad called I barely said two words to him. I posted some photos, I texted my so-called friends, and I did some online shopping. For myself. I tried to put the whole troubling dream about Yvonne and the Ghosts of Christmas Whatever out of my mind.

So, to summarize: I didn't rethink my life choices. I didn't change.

Six days later LA experienced a freak cold snap. It sleeted

one night—not exactly snow, but colder and more solid than rain. Which formed a small icicle on the eaves of the Hot 8 building on Wilshire Boulevard in Beverly Hills, which is where on the morning of December 31, I was engaged in my Tuesday morning yoga class.

At precisely 8:58, the icicle fell. It caught the sun as it plummeted to the sidewalk, a gleam that temporarily blinded a bicyclist, who suddenly deviated into traffic, which caused a Hollywood Tours double-decker bus to swerve into the next lane, the people inside yelling and cursing, which caused a silver Bentley Continental GT, driven by a famous actress my dad had directed on three separate occasions, who was just slightly hungover and also talking on her cell phone, to veer toward the sidewalk at the exact moment that I, Holly Chase, stepped out of the yoga studio.

At 8:59, as I was lying on the sidewalk with a crowd gathering around me, I thought, *I know this. I've felt it before.* I remembered the ghosts. And finally, I believed that all of it might have been real. But by then it was too late.

By then it was 9:00, and I was dead.

This time when I woke up, I didn't recognize where I was. Not a hospital, I quickly figured out. I was lying on a weirdly shaped green velvet sofa with a crocheted blanket tucked around my legs. I sat up. I wasn't injured, which was weird. The horrible pain I'd felt on the sidewalk was gone. The bones that had been broken were whole, and all of my blood seemed to be back inside my body where it belonged. I was still wearing yoga pants and a tank top, but not the ones I'd been wearing in the accident—these were bright, just-bleached white.

I stood up carefully and looked around. It was an office, clearly, although the interior design of the place was horrible. One wall was lined with glassed-in bookshelves packed with rows of faded books. The floor was covered in a busy black carpet patterned with red, pink, and blue flowers, the kind of design you might find in an old hotel. A water cooler burbled in the corner. On the far wall was a huge, obviously antique mahogany desk with a slanted top, which held, along with a computer, several stacks of papers and folders and a mug full of freshly sharpened pencils. In the other corner sat a worn leather armchair and a little table with an old-fashioned record player. I walked over and read the label off the gleaming black vinyl record that was resting there quietly.

From Them to You, it read. *The Beatles Christmas Album. 1970. Free of charge to members of the Beatles Fan Club.*

Ugh, Christmas, I thought. *I'm so sick of Christmas I could puke.*

The office had a window, and I went over to it. I struggled for a minute with the curtains, but I finally managed to draw them back. Then—quite understandably, I think—I gasped. Because there were no palm trees. No endless blue sky. No ocean. No sunbaked stucco houses or gleaming swimming pools.

I wasn't in California anymore.

The window looked out onto the side of another tall building. All I could see were windows. I stepped closer to the glass. The sky overhead was a pale, yellowish gray, even though it was the middle of the night. It was snowing lightly. There was a layer of grungy snow on the window ledge. Hundreds of feet below, rows of red and white lights—cars—were moving slowly along the streets.

I recognized where I was immediately. New York City. I'd been there twice for Fashion Week, and I'd hated it both times, even though I knew as a fashion junkie I was supposed to love it. But back then I thought New York was like the opposite of LA. Dirty. Crowded. Gross.

The door behind me made a beeping sound—a lock being engaged. A man came into the room. He was old, like my dad's age, with floppy brown hair and a goatee, wearing a brown suit jacket with patches on the elbows. God.

"Havisham," he greeted me warmly in an English accent. "Delighted to meet you in person. Well, maybe not delighted. But glad."

"That's not my name," I started. "My name is—"

"I know. But it's tradition here to rename people after Dickens characters. A bit of an inside joke. I picked Havisham for you. It's catchy, right? Holly Havisham."

O-kay. I blinked a few times. "Who—who are you?"

"Oh, I'm Mr. Sikes," he said, as if that explained everything. "But people around here call me Boz."

He was holding a manila folder, and he tucked it under his arm so he could shake my hand. I noticed that the word HAVISHAM was printed in big black letters on the edge of the folder. I did not love the name Havisham. Plus I was beginning to feel a little woozy. Something unpleasant had just occurred to me.

"Am I . . . dead?" I whispered.

"Yes." He didn't sound too broken up about it. "And no."

I stared at him. "What does that mean?"

"It means," he said matter-of-factly, "that while you are working for us, for however long that may be, you are flesh, and not spirit. You are alive. But to everyone outside of this company, you are very much dead. Dead as a doornail, as they say."

"I think I need to sit down," I said.

He guided me back to the sofa, then fetched me a paper cup of water from the cooler. I sipped at it.

"Am I dreaming?" I asked him hopefully.

"No. There's no waking up from it all this time, I'm afraid."

"Did you say that . . . I'm going to be working for you?"

He smiled. "Yes, you are, my dear. Welcome to Project Scrooge."

FIVE YEARS LATER

TWO

"TWENTY BUCKS SAYS THE KID actually speaks the words," said Marty.

"No way," said Grant.

"Why don't you put your money where your mouth is, big shot?"

Grant pulled out his wallet. "You're on. But it has to be the exact words."

"Or the modern equivalent of the exact words," Marty clarified. "I mean, of course he's not going to say 'God bless us, every one.' This is the twenty-first century."

I'm surrounded by morons, I thought. They were like twins, those two, even though Grant was black and Marty was Korean—they were both completely dorky and determined to mess up my day. Tweedledumb and Tweedledumber. God.

"Cheater," Grant said. "You didn't say anything about the 'modern equivalent' before."

Marty crossed his arms over his beanpole chest. "I win if he says the word 'God' or the word 'bless'—how about that?"

"Fine." Grant grinned. "But *I'll* bet *you* twenty dollars that she buys the family a big turkey."

"She's a vegetarian," Marty pointed out.

"Are you going to take the bet or what?" Grant tapped the face of his watch. "Time's running out."

"She won't buy a turkey. She thinks that's murder."

I turned my attention back to the set of monitors that covered the wall at the front of the Go Room. The current Scrooge, number 172, had just woken up to find herself back in her own bedroom, alive and well.

Everybody leaned forward to see what she would do next.

For a few seconds the old lady just stood there in her silk nightgown (*people that age should not wear silk,* I thought) and looked around.

Then: "It's not too late," she whispered, tears in her eyes and everything. "It's not too late. I can still make things right."

"Bingo!" some idiot near the front of the room shouted. "We have reformation, people."

The Go Room exploded in applause. The receiver buzzed in my ear, reverb from all of the commotion going on, and I pulled it out and let it dangle on my shoulder. The mood was instantly lifted—if this Scrooge was truly changing her ways (which remained to be seen, I guess, but hey—this was the critical first step), then the operation could be counted as a success. People were already passing around champagne.

"No, thanks," I said as a newbie from accounting tried to offer me a glass. I didn't even bother trying to sneak any booze this year—according to Boz I was still technically a teenager, and therefore not old enough to partake in that part of the celebrations. "It's true that some of aging is about life experience," he always said whenever I tried to argue. "But a great deal of it is physiology, and in that way, you are still very much seventeen years old."

I was apparently going to be seventeen forever.

"Great job tonight, by the way," said the noob from accounting.

"Thanks," I answered, but the girl had already moved on to somebody else.

I always felt self-conscious at this stage. Everyone in the room knew me as the Ghost of Christmas Past—the Lamp, they called me—but I didn't know how many people here also knew that, not so long ago, it'd been me up on the monitors.

A failed Scrooge.

The current Scrooge was now dancing around her room like a schoolgirl, gleeful in the knowledge that she wasn't dead. The excitement transformed her into someone that I, even after spending months inside this woman's head, wouldn't have recognized if I'd met her on the street. Already she looked like a completely different person.

Nonsense. People don't change, the Inner Yvonne said matter-of-factly from the back of my brain. *They are who they are. What changes is only the way they allow us to see them.*

My feet hurt. I wished I could escape to my dressing room, get my makeup off and pack up my costume for the dry cleaner's, but Boz always insisted that everybody, from the lowliest analyst at the company to the tech guys (like Grant and Marty) to the major players (me and the rest of the Ghosts), stay for the big ending. I found this wildly hypocritical, because he was, in essence, forcing his staff to *work on Christmas*. But nobody argued with Boz.

Speaking of the illustrious Mr. Sikes, Boz had finally caught on that there was gambling taking place on the floor. Which was against another one of his rules.

"We don't wager on them," he was saying to Marty firmly. "This is not a game, young man."

Marty looked put out. "I wasn't betting on the big stuff—just the details. You know, to keep it lively."

"No wagers," Boz repeated.

Buzzkill.

On the monitors, Scrooge 172 (whose real name was Elizabeth Charles, CEO of one of the largest and most corrupt health insurance companies in the country) was making a few phone calls. "Merry Christmas!" she kept exclaiming. "Merrrrrrrrrry Christmas!"

Then she called and ordered the Brown family (this year's equivalent of the Cratchits) a giant Christmas turkey.

Marty covertly passed Grant a twenty.

We kept watching throughout the morning, until Scrooge 172 ended up visiting the Brown home personally to tell Mrs. Brown that her son Todd's medical expenses were going to be covered after all. Everybody started sniffling at that point. Everyone, that is, except me. I never did the crying thing. It would have ruined my makeup.

"Thank you, ma'am," whispered the little boy on the monitors. "God bless you, Mrs. Charles."

Grant passed the twenty back to Marty.

The screens went black.

"Good work, everyone." Boz came up to the front of the room. "We were a well-oiled machine tonight. Which means that the world is a better place, thanks to us. And, of course, merry Christmas!"

The room filled with a chorus of *Merry Christmases.* Even I found myself mouthing the words.

"Go home. Rest up. Enjoy your holidays," he continued, "and I will see you all back here next year, ready to start on Scrooge 173."

The team began to disperse. I hurried toward the door.

"Oh, Havisham," Boz called. "Before you go, I'd like to see you in my office, please."

Sigh. "Now?"

"You can get cleaned up first," Boz said charitably. "Just see me before you leave."

Double sigh. "Okay." I turned and trudged off toward my dressing room.

I ran into Dave—the Ghost of Christmas Present—in the hall. He'd taken off his robe and his wreath, but he still reminded me of the Jolly Green Giant. Dave was, like, six foot four and bearded and had probably died in his late thirties, and all I could really think when I looked at him was how I probably should have been nicer to him the night I was the Scrooge. He knew exactly who I was, but in five years he'd never acted like I was anything but a vital part of this company. Dave was the very definition of a nice guy. Which made me wonder how he'd ended up working here. What was he being punished for?

"It's a good thing," he said.

At first I wasn't sure he was even talking to me. "What?"

He stopped outside of his dressing room door—the one marked *Copperfield*—and gave me a goofy smile. "Working here. It's a good thing."

FYI: Dave could read minds. It was part of his job description. Most of the time he kept that ability turned off, to be polite, I guess, but on Christmas it always kind of overrode his system.

"We help people," he said. "We change the world."

"Yeah. I know." Cue the company motto.

"For the record, I like working with you, Holly."

"Thanks."

"I'm going to miss it."

Okay, so that was a strange thing to say. But before I could ask what he meant, he went into his dressing room and closed the door.

I changed into my regular clothes and reported back to Boz. When I got to his office, I found him standing at the window looking out at the city while big, fluffy flakes of snow danced past the glass. Boz just loved New York. He loved the lights of Times Square and the bustle of Broadway. He loved the subways and the hot dog stands, the honking cars and the brush of shoulders on the street. He even loved the cold. He was always going on about it.

I tapped on the door nervously.

"Oh, Havisham, come in," he said. "There's someone here I'd like you to meet."

I wasn't even two steps inside his office when a girl jumped out at me. For a second I thought she was going to attack me or hug me. Either way, I stepped back fast.

"Oh, wow," the girl breathed. "You're the Ghost of Christmas Past."

"Yeah, that's me," I admitted.

"Havisham, meet Dorrit," Boz said. "She's a sophomore at NYU—isn't that fantastic?"

The girl didn't look a day over fifteen, in my opinion. I mean, she was wearing a green sweater with a polar bear on it, her platinum-colored hair was in one of those messy half-falling-out ponytails, and her purple glasses were much too big for her face, but not in the cool hipster sort of way.

"Wow," she chirped. "You're the biggest celebrity I've ever met. Well, I did see Taylor Swift in Central Park once, but I didn't actually meet her."

Boz cleared his throat. Project Scrooge wasn't a place for fangirls—Boz never let people from the outside see what went on inside the Project, never ever. "Well, Dorrit," he said awkwardly, avoiding my questioning stare, "it's Havisham's job—not Havisham herself—who's famous. Holly's only been with us for a short while."

Oh, thanks, Boz, I thought. *Thank you so much.*

"What's it been now, Holly? Four years?" he asked.

"Five."

"Yes, that's right. Five."

"Wow," the girl said again. "Five years as the Ghost of Christmas Past. That's so—wow."

I didn't know how many more wows I could take.

"I've wanted to meet the Ghost of Christmas Past ever since I found out about this project," the girl said. "So cool, by the way, so totally noble, what you're doing here. You're changing the world."

"How *did* you find out about the Project?" I asked carefully.

"Oh, Dorrit is our new intern," Boz answered for her.

I frowned. We didn't use interns. PS wasn't the kind of company that did its headhunting through the normal channels. For obvious reasons. Not all of the people who worked there were dead—that was just me and the other Ghosts, I thought, and possibly Boz, but he never talked about it—but there was enough top-secret stuff going on that Boz was super careful about who we hired. People around the office joked that it was harder to get a position at Project Scrooge than it was to get recruited for the FBI. The process apparently involved Blackpool's power to see the future and rigorous tests and interviews and layers and layers of confidentiality agreements.

"I've decided that she's going to be your assistant," Boz continued.

The girl gave a suppressed squeal of excitement.

My mouth dropped open.

"But . . . I've never had an assistant."

"You've never had an assistant *until now*," Boz corrected cheerfully.

Dorrit's smile was almost a supernova.

"But I don't need an assistant," I protested.

"I know you don't need an assistant," Boz said. "But I thought it might be nice to have someone else around. A fresh pair of eyes. Someone to help you, someone to bounce ideas off of, someone to look after you and give you more personalized attention."

This set off a bunch of alarm bells, obviously, but Boz had that freakishly stubborn glint in his eye. I'd seen that look on his face a few times before, and it had never turned out well for me.

I decided to go with it.

"Um . . . awesome." I extended my hand for the girl to shake. "I guess this means welcome aboard, Dorrit," I said in my very best Boz impression.

The girl simply exploded into a puddle of goo. "Thank you, Miss Havisham," she said, pumping my hand up and down. "I won't let you down, Miss Havisham. I promise. Thank you. Thanks."

Suddenly I got a flash from when she was a kid, which happened sometimes when I touched people—the way Dave could hear the present and Blackpool could see the future, I felt the past. In that moment I could feel what this girl had been like as a toddler, snuggled up in her bed in a dark room, awake and waiting.

A light went on. A man's voice said softly, *Come on, sweetie. It's morning.*

Is it Christmas yet? she asked.

Freaking Christmas. I gritted my teeth and firmly pushed this girl's past out of my mind. I walked her to the door. "All righty," I said. "I guess I'll see you later?" Then I pried my hand away from hers and closed the door right on her cute little button nose. I turned to Boz. "Are you trying to kill me?"

"You forgot to wish her a merry Christmas," he said from where he was sitting at his desk. He straightened a stack of papers and gazed longingly at the record player.

"Or maybe you're trying to kill *her*," I concluded. "You think after a week with Little Mary Sunshine I'll go crazy and rip her tiny blond head off. Because I will do it. I swear, Boz, I don't deal well with her type."

"I think she may surprise you," he said, smiling in an annoyingly mysterious way. "All I ask is that you give her a chance."

"Fine. Can I go now?"

"Just one more thing." He opened his desk drawer and took out a small wrapped gift, about the size and shape of a ring box. "Merry Christmas, Havisham."

I stared at him. We'd never exchanged gifts before, not once in five years. "I didn't . . . I don't have anything for . . ."

He shook his head and pushed the box into my hand. "It's all right. Take it. Open it when you get home."

"Uh, thank you?" I didn't know what else to say.

"You're welcome," he said. "And I'll expect you at eleven sharp on your start date—what is it this year?"

"April first," I answered. Boz always gave the entire company the month of January as vacation. Then Blackpool spent February and March deciding on who would be the new Scrooge. And then we were all back in business. The Scrooge business.

"Of course, April first," Boz agreed. "Don't be late."

I never was. Even though I didn't know why it would make a difference if I showed up on time.

The subway was almost empty on the way back to my place, apart from the few disgusting Christmas-morning types: lovers who couldn't help their PDAs, smiling families on their way to their grandmother's house, the odd guy in a Santa suit. I picked a seat at the end of the car and slumped there in my Hoodie the whole ride.

The Hoodie was one of the big perks that came with the Ghost of Christmas Past job. To the outside observer, it appeared to be a normal black hoodie, but when you zipped it up and pulled the hood over your head, you became completely invisible. It had saved my butt lots of times while I was sneaking around a Scrooge's house. I wasn't supposed to use the Hoodie for anything but company business, of course, but I wore it all the time. It was comfortable.

It was four stops between 195 Broadway, where Project Scrooge's headquarters was located, and my stop downtown. Then down three blocks to my apartment. Then up four flights of stairs, because, of course, it was a walk-up. Then home.

I was legally deceased, which made regular things like credit checks impossible, so the company paid the rent for this place, plus the utilities and the furnishings: a twin bed and a lamp and an ugly-but-comfortable plaid sofa, a tiny kitchen table that could seat two (but never did, because I never had anyone over), the basic refrigerator and stove and all the necessary pots, pans, and dishes (but no dishwasher), a chipped pedestal sink in the bathroom, and an old claw-foot tub with a shower attachment. I also received a hundred dollars a month for food and miscellaneous expenses. That was it. One hundred dollars. No money for decent clothes. No internet. No smartphone. No frills of any kind. I had to get by with less money each month than what the Old Holly had spent on manicures.

I'd worked at PS for almost a year before I got over the sense of total outrage that flooded me every single time I opened the door to my closet-sized apartment—like I was stepping into a horror flick, complete with the occasional cockroach. I'd even tried to run away once, but I hadn't gotten very far before my arms and legs went numb and I passed out in the middle of the airport. I'd woken up right back on the green sofa in the PS building, where Boz had gently explained to me (again) that I didn't have a life outside of the company. I was there because they wanted me to be there, until they'd decided I'd been there long enough. In other words, I was stuck.

When I got home I flung myself down on the couch and sighed. I hated this part. There was nothing to do now for three whole months. It was supposed to be a nice thing for the employees of Project Scrooge—time to spend with your family and friends after months of hard, unrelenting work—but I didn't have family. I didn't have friends. I didn't have money to shop or do anything cool. I couldn't go anywhere.

Ten minutes into vacation, and I was already bored.

Next door, through the paper-thin wall, I could hear the neighbor lady watching *It's a Wonderful Life*. My dad and I always used to watch that movie together, before Mom died and Yvonne came along to take her place. Dad loved it, for some reason. I always told him I thought it was the cheesiest cheese.

"What is it you want, Mary?" Jimmy Stewart was asking Donna Reed through the wall. "You want the moon? Just say the word, and I'll throw a lasso around it and pull it down."

Dad was such an incurable romantic.

I'd told Dad that the movie was lame, but I'd secretly loved it, especially the romantic parts, the parts where it's like George and Mary can't help but fall in love with each other. That's how it felt like love should be—inevitable. Irresistible. Written in the stars.

Not that I would know.

I sneaked into the hall with my Hoodie to "borrow" the neighbor lady's newspaper. To check the movies section. To see if one of Dad's movies was playing.

He didn't make a film for two years after I died. Then he did a couple of big blockbusters, one about robots and one about aliens. That wasn't his style at all, but it paid the bills, I suppose.

I saw those movies, like, fifteen times each. They were both pretty good if you like that kind of thing, grand adventures, full of bright colors and sweeping music and all the feels in the key moments. Of course they both had happy endings, too. The hero wins. The villain loses. The end.

Anyway, so I checked to see if there was a new movie from Gideon Chase. There wasn't. I returned the paper to the spot outside my neighbor's door and went inside. I was about to hang up my Hoodie when I felt something stashed in the pocket.

The present. From Boz.

I opened it. Inside was a pocket watch—silver and a little tarnished. It was pretty, in an antique sort of way. Vintage. It was still going, but the time it showed was three hours behind.

An old watch. *Weird,* I thought. *Why would Boz give me a watch?*

Why, for that matter, would Boz give me an assistant?

What was he up to?

It probably wasn't anything good. But maybe I didn't care. After five long years, five Scrooges, five Christmas Eves performing the same old show, I was just so tired of it all—the same people, the same tasks, the same script, the same paperwork afterward—and what did it get me, I thought, what did this crap job ever do for me?

Nothing.

It was just a job. A job that—if I was lucky, right?—I was probably going to be doing for decades, if not centuries. Over and over and over again. Lather, rinse, repeat.

I'd figured out a long time ago that Project Scrooge was my own personal version of hell.

THREE

I'M GOING TO FAST FORWARD again, past the three months where I basically lazed slothlike around my apartment, or aimlessly wandered the streets of New York looking in store windows at stuff I didn't have the money to buy, or used the Hoodie to sneak into movie theaters for free and spend hours sitting in the dark with a bunch of strangers who never even knew that I was there. Let's pick up on the first day back at Project Scrooge. Where my new assistant was waiting right inside my office door the moment I arrived, a cup of coffee in hand.

"Good morning, Miss Havisham!" she bubbled.

Oh good, she's a morning person, I thought. And today she was wearing a yellow polka-dot sweater and orange capris with black ballet flats. The girl needed serious help in the fashion department.

I took the coffee, drank a sip, then spit it out. "This is cold!"

She grabbed the cup back from me. "Oh, I'm so sorry! I've been waiting here since nine. I didn't know you didn't have to come in until eleven." Her head tilted to one side like a curious puppy's. "Why don't you have to come in until eleven, when everyone else has to be here at nine? If you don't mind me asking."

I could have given her the truthful answer, which was that I had died at exactly nine o'clock in the morning, so that was when my body "reset" itself. Sometimes I barely felt it, like a ripple that started at my head and worked down to my toes, but other days that moment felt like dying all over again, a flicker of the cold and the dark. It was mildly disorienting, to say the least. I preferred to be sleeping when it happened, and therefore unaware.

But I didn't mention this to the annoying blonde.

"I work a lot of nights on this job," I explained instead. "The only time I have to be here during the day is for department and company meetings. So today it's eleven."

She nodded. "Eleven. Check. And what do you like in your coffee? Sugar? Milk?" she asked. "I thought I saw a few of those flavored sweeteners in the break room, too."

"You know, there's a great little coffee shop about four blocks away from here," I answered brightly. "I'd love a large vanilla latte. *Extra* hot. Whole milk."

She stared at me with her huge eyes from behind her huge glasses for a minute, surprised by my order. I could tell she wanted to ask me if there was a company account to pay for said latte (there wasn't), but she didn't want to look stupid.

"Large vanilla latte, extra hot, whole milk," she repeated.

"That's it." I estimated that I had about three days before Boz caught on to this fancy coffee thing and shut me down, but it would be worth it while it lasted. "Okay, now off with you."

She blinked. "Off with me?"

"To the coffee shop." I took her by the shoulders and guided her out of my office.

"But isn't there a meeting with your team in a few minutes, like you said? I don't want to miss that," she protested as I walked her to the elevators.

"The sooner you go, the sooner you can return." I pressed the button for down. "Oh, and what's your name?" I asked.

She hesitated. For a second, it looked like she couldn't actually remember her name. "Um, Dorrit?"

"No, not the stupid Dickens name Boz gave you. Your real name."

"Stephanie," she stammered. "My friends call me Steph."

The elevator dinged and the door opened. She got in. I waved. She waved back, her face a little crestfallen.

"Bye, Stephanie."

The doors closed.

I smiled and headed for Conference Room B. For the staff meeting, which was about to start. Without her. Which was exactly how I wanted it.

"Hey, did you see the new chick?" Marty asked before I even had a chance to say hello to everybody and get comfortable at my place at the head of the conference table. "Who's she?"

I rubbed my hand over my face and exhaled sharply. "Don't use the word *chick* in reference to women, Marty. It makes you sound like a jackass."

"Yeah, jackass," Grant added. He turned to me. "Who is she, though?"

I'd been hoping to skip over this whole topic, but obviously that wasn't going to happen. "She's my new assistant."

"You've never needed an assistant before," Marty observed helpfully.

"That's what I said."

"Well, I say it's awesome. Are the other Ghosts getting assistants, too?" Grant grinned. "Are we in for a wave of attractive new women in the near future?"

Come to think of it, Dave probably could use an assistant. He always seemed to have more to do than he had time in the day. I couldn't even conceive of an assistant for Blackpool. "I don't know," I admitted. "But knock it off, you guys. Can we get started, please?" I glanced around at the other members of my team, who'd been waiting quietly. "How was your break?"

They answered with a weak chorus of *goods.*

"Good." I opened my debriefing folder on Scrooge 172. "So let's talk about how it went this year. Fairly smoothly, I thought."

"What's her name?" Marty asked.

"Who?"

"Your new assistant? And why isn't she here, anyway? Shouldn't she be 'assisting' you?"

"I sent her on an errand."

"And what's her name?" Marty persisted. "You never told us her name."

"Oh my God, Marty, enough with the questions!" I exclaimed. "Her name is Dorrit."

There was a collective cringe around the table.

"Dorrit, as in Little?" Marty shook his head. "Somebody's got to talk to Boz. Like an intervention. This naming thing is getting out of hand."

I remembered that the name Boz had given Marty was Claypole. After some character in *Oliver Twist*.

"Her real name is Stephanie. Now that's all I'm going to say about her, okay? Let's move on."

Right then the door to the conference room opened and Stephanie burst in. "I'm here!" she panted. She crossed around the table to hand me a slender white cup with a cardboard sleeve around it. "Large vanilla latte with skim milk. Extra hot."

Whole milk, I'd asked for. Whole milk. But whatevs.

She glanced around the table at all the faces staring up at her. Her cheeks went pink. "Um, hi, everyone."

"Hey, since when do you get fancy coffee?" Grant asked.

"Since I got an assistant to get it for me," I said primly. "Sit down, Stephanie." I gestured to an empty chair at the end of the table.

"But Boz said my name is supposed to be . . ."

"It doesn't matter what Boz said. Sit."

She sat. "Wow. It's wonderful to meet you all," she said breathlessly.

So, of course, now I had to waste my time making the formal introductions. "Okay. Welcome, Stephanie. This is my team at Project Scrooge. We each have a team, the other two Ghosts and I, and we each have a code name. I'm called the Lamp, the Ghost of Christmas Present is the Clock, and the Ghost of Christmas Future is the Hood. Don't ask why. It's a Boz thing."

"Hi, there," Marty said to her in a low voice I'd never heard him use before. "How are you doing? Can I get you anything?"

"This is Marty," I explained. "He's on quantum mechanics. He's also great with all things IT, so if you ever have a computer problem, he's your man."

"Yes, I'm your man," Marty said in the supposedly sexy voice. "I'd be glad to look over your hard drive any day."

Mortifying. I kept going down the table before he had a chance to say anything else. "And this is Grant. He's a mechanical engineer, and he and Kevin over there make sure that all the machinery is functioning properly."

"My lady." Grant pretended to tip an invisible hat at Stephanie, who smiled and nodded.

I rolled my eyes and went on down the line.

"This is Tomas, Larry, and Lin, who work in research and development"—they waved politely—"and Tox at the end there. She's on OM. She's also the handler for the Jacob Marley."

"What's OM?" Stephanie asked.

Marty leaned forward and lifted his eyebrows mysteriously. "Otherworldly matters," he whispered. "It's where all the magic happens."

Her big eyes got even bigger. "Oh."

"So that's all of us," I said. "Team Lamp."

"Wow." Stephanie looked slightly dazed. Or maybe that was just her normal expression. "I would just like to say that I'm honored to get to be part of this group—go Team Lamp!—and I will work hard for you guys. What you're doing here is so important. You're saving souls." She smiled. "I like to think of you as angels."

"Amen," said Grant.

"That's so true," agreed Marty.

Someone had consumed a little too much of the company Kool-Aid, if you asked me.

"So what's your clearance?" Tox asked, because she was probably suspicious, the way I was, that suddenly this new person without much in the way of credentials got to be part of our super-secret company. Tox had been around even longer than I had—she'd been transferred from downstairs a couple years ago. So she would know how strange this was—an intern at Project Scrooge.

"My clearance?" Stephanie asked.

"How much are you allowed to know about what goes on around here?"

Stephanie frowned. "I don't know. Boz just gave me this." She pulled out a laminated badge. It had a red-and-green stripe along the top.

We were all surprised. Why would an assistant need full security clearance? Even I didn't have privileges that high. My badge would only grant me access to the areas I specifically needed: my office, the conference rooms, the Transport Room, and the Go

Room. Her badge would, in theory, let her go anywhere in the building. It didn't make any sense.

"Is there something wrong with my badge?" Stephanie asked.

"It's nothing. Let's move on." I flipped through the notes in my file. "On Christmas Eve I noticed that there was a bit of a lag between scenes two and three."

"It was a power surge in the mainframe," Grant explained. "I'm all over it. Shouldn't be a problem this year."

I went on for a few more minutes, pointing out the high and low points of our performance for Scrooge 172. Then Marty decided we were done being productive and leaned over to talk to Stephanie again. "After this I could totally show you around the office," he practically drawled.

"That'd be super," she said.

"Moving on," I said more loudly. "I think this year we should—"

"Does Boz know you're getting fancy coffee?" Grant asked, frowning.

"And, hey, if you ever want to go out to dinner sometime," Marty continued.

"I want fancy coffee," Grant said.

I knew when I was beaten. The meeting was just a formality, really, a welcome-back type deal, and I'd said what I needed to say. I closed my folder and forced a smile. "All right, go do your jobs, people. I'll see you all at three o'clock in the Go Room."

"Wow, that was so exciting," Stephanie exclaimed as the team began to rapidly disperse. "What's next?"

"Uh . . . Marty will show you around," I said.

Marty stepped forward and actually offered Stephanie his scrawny arm with which to parade her around the office. She giggled. They wandered off down the hall together.

Then the room was empty except for Tox and me. I took a deep breath and let it out.

"Steph seems nice," Tox observed. Tox was the jaded one of our group, the one who didn't take crap from anybody. So it seemed odd that she'd appreciate the new girl. Especially this particularly annoying new girl.

"Oh, she's nice, all right. A little vague, maybe." I gathered up my stuff.

"You know, she'd make a good GCP," Tox said thoughtfully.

I froze. "I'm sorry—*what*?"

Her eyes widened. "I don't mean instead of you. You're a good Lamp, Holly. Decent, anyway. I just meant that she has that look, you know? That agelessness. That purity thing. Put her in a white dress and light her up, and maybe she could pull it off."

Well, then I couldn't help but picture Stephanie in my dress and my robes with my shining wreath on her naturally blond little head. I immediately felt like someone had punched me in the gut.

Because Tox was right.

That girl could totally pull off my job.

And maybe, I realized, that was exactly what she'd been brought on board to do.

***

"So you're replacing me?" I didn't bother knocking on Boz's office door. I just charged in. "'Fess up, Boz. Is that what this is all about? A new girl all ready to step into my shoes? Am I supposed to be training her to replace me? Because I won't do it, Boz. I won't."

"Nice to see you, too, Havisham," he replied calmly. "Did you have a good holiday?"

"I can't believe you would replace me!" Sure, I hated this job—I'd always hated it—but deep down I knew that it was a lot better than the alternative.

"That would bother you, if you were replaced?"

I swallowed hard. "I'm good at my job. Don't tell me that I'm not good at my job, Boz. I've always done everything you've asked."

For some reason I was about to start crying.

"Sit down, Holly," Boz said.

Oh God. He almost never called me Holly. I sank into the red leather armchair near his desk.

"I can do better," I whispered. "Please. Don't send me . . . wherever it is that you'd send me."

He looked at me with solemn eyes. "Are you finally afraid of hell, then?"

Well . . . yes. Of course I was. I felt that darkness every day. I'd seen Yvonne and her strings of pearls, and since then I'd interacted with five more Jacob Marleys, each equally miserable in their eternal punishments. "Doomed to wander through the world and witness what they cannot share, but might have shared on earth, and turned to happiness." Something like that.

"Relax," Boz said. "Dorrit is not your replacement, Holly.

That's not how it works here."

"It isn't?"

He handed me a tissue.

"Traditionally, the roles of the Ghosts are filled by former players," Boz explained as I twisted the tissue into pieces between my hands. "People who are already deceased, I mean. Like you. So it's the truth when you say *I am the Ghost of Christmas Past*, because you are, indeed, a ghost."

"Yeah, except I'm technically like a zombie," I said.

His mouth twitched. "Yes, technically."

"So Dave and Blackpool were failed Scrooges, too?" I could believe it with Blackpool, but not Dave. I didn't think Dave would be capable of a genuine *Bah, humbug* if he tried for a million years.

"Blackpool was Scrooge 130," Boz said. "He's been an employee of the company ever since."

I did some quick math. That meant forty-three years in the Project. Forty-three years. Like a prison sentence. "And Dave?" I was almost scared to ask.

"Copperfield's only been with us for seven years." Boz cleared his throat. "I'm afraid he's leaving us after this year, moving on to his final destination. Which means we'll need to find a new Ghost of Christmas Present."

My mouth opened and then closed without me getting any words out.

"Your job is safe for now, Havisham." Boz chuckled and patted my arm. "Good gracious, child. You should see the look on your face."

I tried to glare at him and failed. I was still too completely freaked out. "So you're saying I'm not fired."

"You're not going anywhere anytime soon." He smiled. "But it's true that I did hire Dorrit because your performance has been slipping."

He angled his computer screen so that I could see it, and then clicked at his mouse a few times. A video began to play—footage from this past Christmas Eve. There I was, standing in all my shining glory in front of a terrified Elizabeth Charles. Boz turned up the volume.

"How did you get in here?" she demanded, clutching her duvet to her chest. "Are you . . . one of the ghosts I've been warned about?"

"I am," I answered on the tape, my voice almost a monotone. "I am the Ghost of Christmas Past. Your past. And I'm here to help you."

Boz paused the video and turned to me.

"What? I said my lines," I pointed out.

"You sound bored. Your heart just wasn't in it this year," Boz said.

What did he expect? It wasn't like I was working here voluntarily. My heart was *never* going to be in it.

There was an uncomfortable silence. Then Boz cleared his throat and said, "Anyhow, we're going to try harder this year, aren't we? I trust that you had a restful vacation. And I hope you were pleased with your gift."

It took me a second to get what he was talking about, but then I remembered the watch he'd given me for Christmas. I'd stuck it in my pocket this morning in case he'd meant me to use it for something, but I hadn't been able to figure out how to set it to the right time. I took it out. "Yeah, it's neat. Thanks."

"I thought you'd like to have it," he explained. "It was—or is, I should say—your father's."

I froze. "Wait. What?"

He reached over the desk with his hand held out, and I put the watch in it. He opened it carefully, then turned it to show me an inscription I hadn't noticed before. *To G,* it read, *I love you more every second. Love, A.*

Gideon and Ariana. My parents. I gulped in a breath. "Oh. Thank you."

He put the watch back into my hand. "You're quite welcome."

I blinked a few times and stared down at it, resolving to never, ever go anywhere without it. I didn't have anything else from my old life. Nothing to remember my dad by but his movies. Nothing of my mom's, not even an old photo. This watch was suddenly kind of everything. I closed my fingers around it and swallowed down the lump in my throat. "I'm sorry about my performance, Boz. I just—"

"No need to apologize," he said. "People get burned out. It happens to us all from time to time."

"Even you?" I joked. "The Great and Powerful Boz?"

"Even me, Holly." He laughed and rubbed his hand across

his goatee-covered chin. "Pay no attention to the man behind the curtain."

For the rest of the day I pondered the meaning of the words *final destination*, and the fact that Dave was "moving on." As in, going somewhere else. As in, leaving Project Scrooge. Dave was like a fixture in this place. Losing him seemed . . . intense. I would never have guessed he'd only been here two years longer than I had. And now he was going somewhere else. What did Boz mean, his "final destination"? What was *that*? I was still getting my head around it when we all gathered in the Go Room for the 3:00 p.m. meeting.

Little Dorrit had been by my side since after lunch, like a blond leech. Marty and Grant of course beelined right for her the minute they entered the Go Room. It was pathetic, really, the way they were fawning all over her. She wasn't even that good-looking.

"How's your first day going?" Marty asked her, bumping her shoulder the way goofy guys do to try to get a girl's attention. He lowered his voice. "The Lamp's not being mean to you, is she?"

"No," Stephanie murmured back. "She's been quiet all afternoon. Is she always so quiet?"

I put my hands on my hips and turned to stare at them. "*She's* right here, you know. And for the record, I happen to have a lot of things on my mind at the moment. Because my job is difficult. So shut it."

They didn't speak again for all of two minutes. Then Stephanie said, "So what's going to happen at this meeting?"

"It's like the opening ceremony," Grant replied. "Boz comes in and introduces the Big Three. Then he'll give a shout-out to the teams. And then they'll bring out the Board."

"The board?"

"The Board," explained Marty like it was the coolest thing ever, "is where they pin up the information on the new Scrooge."

"Wow—how do you find the new Scrooge? How do you decide?"

"That's up to Blackpool," Grant said. "He chooses the Scrooge. He can see into the future."

"It's all very otherworldly," said Marty.

"Wow," said Stephanie. "So what happens then?"

Marty waggled his eyebrows at her. "Then the real fun begins."

I may have thrown up in my mouth a little.

Thankfully, Boz appeared at the front of the room and everybody stopped talking.

"Welcome back," he boomed. "Are you ready for another Scrooge?"

The crowd cheered. Everyone, it seemed, but me.

"Good," Boz said. "Then let's get started."

The next half hour played out almost exactly the way Grant and Marty had described. I had to go up to be recognized as the current GCP, which to me always felt like being singled out as the leader of the school marching band—not exactly something you want to own up to in front of a crowd. It was awkward.

"The Ghost of Christmas Past: Havisham!" Boz shouted.

Clap clap clap.

Of course it'd been a huge relief when Boz told me he wasn't replacing me.

But the way he'd said it. *You're not going anywhere anytime soon.*

"The Ghost of Christmas Present: Copperfield!"

Dave stepped forward, smiling as if he wasn't going anywhere. Like the words *final destination* didn't even exist.

"This is going to be Copperfield's last year with us," Boz continued smoothly, "so let's make sure it's the best one yet."

Nobody else looked particularly surprised by this announcement. I guess I was the last to know. Dave, for his part, seemed fine. He kept glancing in my direction, though, with this partly sad smile on his face. As if he was really going to miss me, like he said. Once again I wished I'd been nicer to him the night I'd been the Scrooge. His beard was fine.

"And last, but certainly not least, the Ghost of Christmas Future: Blackpool!" Boz shouted like this was a baseball game and Blackpool was the MVP.

Blackpool lifted his hand in an awkward wave. He wasn't wearing his robe of death (that was only his costume on Christmas Eve), and without it he appeared to be a regular guy: tall, black, with a shaved head, smartly dressed in a dark gray suit and tie, maybe as old as fifty. He was nothing super impressive to behold, Blackpool. But when he turned to look at me I couldn't help the chill that ran down my spine.

I remembered the numbness. The suffocating dark. Like I was a light that he'd snuffed out once.

"All right, now let's see who we've got for a Scrooge this year,"

Boz said, clapping his hands together.

They wheeled out the Board.

Blackpool took a pair of reading glasses out of his breast pocket, unfolded a simple sheet of yellow legal paper, and began to fill us in about this year's Scrooge: he lived in New York, which was good news because it would make things easier for us working locally; he was some kind of real estate tycoon; and he was of course rife with all the predictably bad qualities that make up your typical Scrooge—hard-hearted, obsessed with money, that kind of thing. It was the same shtick every year. Find a really rotten person. Change him, change the world.

Yawn. At this point, all the Scrooges essentially felt the same to me. They were all like reincarnations of the original Ebenezer Scrooge, which made sense, I guess. Sometimes it kind of blew my mind that I'd ever been one of them. Outside of the money thing (and yeah, okay, maybe I'd been a tad materialistic) I had nothing in common with all those shriveled, ugly old geezers.

It still felt like some kind of colossal mistake.

"Scrooges tend to be Caucasian males in their seventies, statistically speaking," Grant said to Stephanie matter-of-factly.

"You're full of crap. You know that, right?" Marty told Grant. "We're equal-opportunity at Project Scrooge. Our last Scrooge was a woman, remember?"

"She was clearly an exception to the rule," countered Grant. "An anomaly. Most Scrooges, if we're just talking the numbers, are—"

He didn't get to finish his sentence, because that's when one of

Blackpool's team tacked an eight-by-ten photo of the new Scrooge up on the Board, and everybody in the Go Room started talking all at once.

"Wow." Next to me Stephanie slid her glasses up on her nose. "Who is *that*?"

"Now *that's* an anomaly," said Marty.

"Whoa," breathed Grant. "What the—"

I pushed forward to get a better look at the Board. A crowd was gathering around the photo, pointing and saying things as eloquent as "Whoa!"

It was easy to see why.

This year's Scrooge was no shriveled old geezer. He couldn't have been older than eighteen.

And he was totally hot.

FOUR

"I DON'T KNOW ABOUT YOU, but I don't like him," Marty said loudly as he scarfed down his microwaved macaroni and cheese a few days later. He'd been saying that to anyone within earshot since Blackpool had first announced the new Scrooge's name. Ethan. Ethan Jonathan Winters III, to be exact. Of course he was all the employees of Project Scrooge had been talking about in the break room. Ethan Jonathan Winters III—eye candy.

"I don't like him, either," Grant said.

Jealous, sniffed my Inner Yvonne. Which was probably true.

"He's a Scrooge, so isn't he supposed to be unlikable?" Stephanie asked.

"Oh, sure, they're all unlikable," Marty said with a shrug. "But you always end up rooting for them. You hope things work out for them in the end. I'm going to have a hard time rooting for Ethan Winters, is all I'm saying."

"I think he's too young to be a Scrooge," Grant added.

I could have argued this point, of course, but then I came to the Scrooge situation from a unique perspective. And I didn't think Ethan Winters was so bad. He came from a good family, and by *good* I mean rich. He was the heir to one of the biggest real estate dynasties in New York, a family legacy that stretched back more than two hundred years, practically a Rockefeller. He had stellar taste in clothes. And then there was how he looked, oh, how he looked, coming in at six foot two—a little tall for my taste, since I didn't like to crane my neck in order to look at a guy, but otherwise perfectly proportioned: not too beefy, not too skinny. Hair: dark brown and always neatly cut and meticulously styled. Blue eyes, but in some pictures I noticed they appeared a steely gray. And a face that could have been chiseled by Michelangelo.

Oh yeah, the new Scrooge was like sunburn. Like lava. Like the heat of a thousand suns. The universe was doing me a favor, putting this boy up on the Board.

"But he's as rotten as the rest of them," said Marty.

Okay, reports were coming in from Dave's team about our Scrooge 173 doing some not-good stuff to his fellow man, the way he spoke to the people who worked for him, the maid and the cook and so on, the way he treated the other boys at his exclusive all-male prep school, the way he jumped into cabs that someone else had hailed, for instance, or showed up to fancy charity events without actually doing anything for the charity.

But who was I to judge?

Stephanie took a sip of her chocolate milk. "So what happens now?"

"Now we get to break inside his head," Marty said wickedly. "And take over his mind."

From the next table over, I checked my watch and gathered together the remains of my half-eaten lunch. Stephanie noticed me getting up and told the tech guys that she had to go. She followed me out of the break room and down the hall to my office. Even though there were still ten minutes left of her lunch hour.

She started yammering as soon as my office door closed behind us. "Um, Miss Havisham?"

I winced. "Do me a favor and call me Holly. Havisham was a crazy old spinster in *Great Expectations*."

"The one who never takes off her wedding dress?"

"That's the one. So . . . Holly, please."

She smiled. "Holly. Okay. The paperwork for last year is all finished, and I filed it with the records department. I also made you a copy for your office. I color-coded it pink. It's in your filing cabinet," she informed me.

"I have a filing cabinet?"

She pointed behind me, where, yes, what do you know, there was a filing cabinet tucked against the back wall. It looked freshly dusted, too.

"Great." I sat down at my desk, which was now neatly organized. No papers or work orders or anything, and the paperwork that usually took two or three weeks to get all squared away was apparently done. All thanks to my perky new assistant. It didn't totally suck. But today she was wearing a navy-blue T-shirt with sailboats on it that read, "Not all who wander are lost." That would have been okay by itself, but she had paired it with a bright red cardigan and a white eyelet skirt. Happy Fourth of July in April, everyone. It physically hurt me to look at her. Plus she was just so in my face with her big glasses and her cheerful smile and her squeaky little voice.

I had to get rid of her. I tried to think of a new errand to send her on. I'd come up with a few good ones in the past week. More expensive coffee. A wild-goose chase after a file that didn't exist in the records department. A two-hour journey to an office supply store halfway across the city to pick up a specific type of pen—the only kind I could work with, I told her. But she always came back sooner than I'd hoped.

Stephanie sat down across from my desk, perched on the edge of her seat like she might take flight at any moment. "Is there anything else I can do for you today?"

I stared out the window at the building across the street. I was out of ideas. It was Friday. Maybe I could just tell her to go home early.

"If not, I was wondering if you might finally have time to answer some questions I have about the company," she said in a hopeful voice.

I spun my chair back around to find her waiting with a pen and a notebook. "Didn't you get a kind of briefing when Boz hired you?"

She shook her head. "Boz just gave me a copy of *A Christmas Carol*. He said you'd explain everything to me when you had time."

I sighed. "Did he tell you *anything*? Anything at all?"

She chewed on her lip guiltily. "I mean, I understand the general concept of the company: saving people, rehabilitating them one soul at a time. Changing the world. But how it all happens—I don't know much about the actual process." She positioned her pen on the paper. "So. I'm ready to learn. Tell me everything."

O-kay. Everything seemed like a lot. "Well, as you may have noticed, this company revolves around one particular day of the year." Start with the obvious, Yvonne always said.

"Ooh, ooh, I know this," Stephanie squealed. "Christmas! I just love Christmas. When I was a kid I used to stay up all night on Christmas Eve. I couldn't sleep, I was so excited. And then I would—"

"Stephanie." I stopped her.

"Yes?"

"There's a lot to go over here, and if we're going to make it through it all before quitting time, I'm going to need you to focus."

"Oh, I'm sorry. I'll be quiet." She made a motion like she was zipping her lips together.

I sighed. "There are different branches of Project Scrooge all over the world—in London, obviously, where the whole thing began, but also in Tokyo, Sydney, New Delhi, you get the idea. We here in New York City cover the entire United States."

"What about Canada?" she asked. "Who does Canada?"

"I don't think there's ever been a Scrooge in Canada," I

answered. "At least, not that I've heard of."

"No Scrooge in Canada, eh?" she said out loud as she wrote that down in her notebook. Then she giggled at her own joke.

I soldiered on. "Every year at Project Scrooge is broken up into five staves."

She frowned. "Staves? Do you mean stages?"

"No, I mean *staves*. It's a musical term, like part of a song. Because the company is based on—"

"A Christmas Carol!" she burst out. "Staves! That's so neat."

Or totally corny, but okay.

"Stave one is the Generation part—that's where Blackpool comes up with the name of the new Scrooge. Which he does in the first few months of the year, while the rest of us are on break, so we're technically into stave two now—the Identification part of the process."

"Identification," she wrote. "What's that?"

"Blackpool tells us who the Scrooge is, because he can see it, somehow—I'm not sure how that works, actually, except that he can see the future. Then it's our job to figure out how the person Blackpool picks fits into the Ebenezer Scrooge narrative. That's the big task for us. It takes most of our time leading up to Christmas." She looked like she was going to ask another question, so I talked faster. "It's our responsibility, as Team Lamp, to filter through the Scrooge's memories. We determine the turning points in his life, the important moments, the game changers. That's so we can decide what scenes from his past to show him when we come to him on Christmas."

Stephanie's pen paused against the paper for a moment. "And how do you get his memories? Do you really take over his mind?"

I shook my head. "It's a delicate process. One part science, one part . . ." I didn't want to say the word *magic*, because that sounded too Disneyland. "Supernatural . . . stuff." I kept going.

"Anyway, so that's Identification. Then comes Preparation—where we come up with a detailed plan for the night we're going to kidnap the Scrooge—what we're going to show him and what we're going to say. After that comes the actual Performance—December the twenty-fourth, although we don't enter the Scrooge's bedroom until midnight—so it's technically the twenty-fifth. Christmas."

Stephanie grinned. "I can only imagine how thrilling it would be to perform a new version of the *Christmas Carol*—but for reals—every single year."

"Yes, thrilling." Boz had assured me that Stephanie wasn't there to replace me, but I still didn't love hearing her gush over my job. She could get her own job.

"And then what? What's the fifth stave?"

I shrugged. "That's called the Evaluation. It's like maintenance, as I understand it. Keeping an eye on the past Scrooges, making sure that they don't backslide."

"Do they? Backslide?" She seemed disappointed by the idea.

"I don't know." I didn't know much about the successful Scrooges—I just knew about one particular failed Scrooge: me. "The Evaluation people hang out in the lower levels of the building. I don't go downstairs, like, ever."

Stephanie looked over her notes. "So, Gippy."

"Huh?"

"The five staves are Gencration, Identification, Preparation, Performance, and Evaluation. G. I. P. P. E. Gippy."

I held in a sigh. "Right."

"I've got a few more questions."

Of course she did.

"I'm still unclear about the Identification part. What exactly are we trying to identify?"

"We're trying to match up our current Scrooge's life with the *Christmas Carol* story, basically," I explained. "We need to figure out—'identify'—all the major characters, like the Freds and the Fezziwigs and all the others."

"Fezziwigs?" She looked confused.

"It's all in that book Boz gave you—*A Christmas Carol*. You should read it cover to cover. Each Scrooge has a series of characters that are meant to represent something important in his life. The Fezziwig, for instance, represents an early role model the Scrooge had who was kind and generous. In the book he was an old chubby guy, but with our Scrooge, the Fezziwig could be anybody—it could be a skinny woman or a little kid, just so long as that person represents the spirit of giving and openheartedness that the Scrooge needs to see. Get it?"

"Identify the characters." She wrote that down. "So who are the other characters? Besides Fezziwig, I mean?"

I was about to run down the list, but then I figured it'd be easier just to show her.

"Come on," I said. "Follow me."

We headed down the hall toward Conference Room A, Little Dorrit on my heels like a happy Labrador. The room was much bigger than Conference Room B, with a large table in the middle surrounded by chairs. I flipped on the lights.

The big corkboard that had been in the Go Room, the capital-B Board, had been moved to the head of the table, with Ethan's picture still stuck to the top of it. The walls around the perimeter of the room were set up with large whiteboards each labeled with a name, starting with one that read MARLEY on the far left: MARLEY, FAN, FEZZIWIG, BELLE, CRATCHIT, PORTLIES, FRED, TINY TIM.

"Wow," remarked Stephanie.

I crossed over to the board that read FEZZIWIG.

"This is the room where we have all of our monthly meetings on the Scrooge situation. In the time between these meetings we're supposed to identify an equivalent for each of these characters," I said. "We as Team Lamp are responsible for the Jacob Marley, the Fan, the Fezziwig, and the Belle—the important people in the Scrooge's past. And then Dave's team handles the Cratchit, the portly gentlemen, the Fred, and the Tiny Tim, since those are all people in the present. We focus on one of these characters every couple of months, so from now until the end of June, we'll work on the Marley, and Dave's team will work on the Cratchit."

"So what does the Ghost of Christmas Future do?" Stephanie asked.

"Blackpool? Mostly he just sits around looking like Grumpy Cat. But apparently while he's doing that he's seeing visions of the

Scrooge's future, so he helps with the Identification thing, too, since he can tell what's going to happen to people."

The door to the conference room opened, and Dave and Boz waltzed in. They looked momentarily surprised to see us in there.

"Oh. Havisham. Dorrit. Hello," Boz said.

"Hello," Stephanie replied cheerfully. She even waved at Dave.

"Uh, as I was saying, we've got at least one feed on almost all of the central locations," Dave reported to Boz. "It's not as many as last year, but I think it's good coverage for now."

"Excellent," Boz replied.

I had an idea. "Can we take a peek at what we have set up? I'm showing Dorrit here how the company works, and that might be nice for her to see."

Dave and Boz exchanged glances. "Of course," Boz said at last. "We'll go have a look right now."

We went back down the hall toward Dave's office. Dave had to swipe his badge to open the door. Inside was a fairly regular-looking office with a desk and filing cabinet and so on, a lot like mine. But on the other side of the room there was an oversized bright red door, and through that door there was a large room filled with television monitors and a bunch of other fancy-looking electrical equipment.

The Surveillance Room. I'd been in there only a few times myself. It was pretty cool.

"Wow," breathed Stephanie. "This is like a spy movie."

Dave picked up a remote and pressed a button, and suddenly all of the monitors turned on, each one showing a different location.

"Before we really get started on our work with the Scrooge, Dave's team has to set up extensive surveillance." I nodded at Dave. "The company monitors his house, his job, the places he goes out to eat, anywhere where we can observe him interacting with the world. That way, wherever the Scrooge goes, we can watch him."

"In the bathroom?" Stephanie grimaced.

"No, not in the bathroom! Ew."

"We don't monitor bathrooms," Dave said gently.

"We don't have cameras in churches, either," I added. It was Boz's weirdest rule.

"Yes. We allow privacy in the presence of the Maker," Boz said, like that explained it.

"Not that a lot of Scrooges like to hang out in churches," I pointed out, which was why I found the rule so completely weird. "Though we did have this one a few years ago who was a church deacon. He was the you're-all-going-to-hell type. But then he used to swipe money from the collection plate. A total cliché."

Boz coughed. I realized I was getting off topic.

"Anyway." I gestured around the room. "This is how the company knows what's happening with the Scrooge."

"Indoors, that is," said Dave. "We never have great coverage outside. But most Scrooges are homebodies anyway. So it works."

Stephanie and I walked around from monitor to monitor and peered into the rooms of Ethan's penthouse apartment (his bedroom, the kitchen, the multiple living and dining spaces, and the elevator), his school (several classrooms, the library, the dining room, the main foyer, and the stairs), and another building I wasn't familiar with.

Ethan was in the school gym at the moment.

He was playing tennis, wearing black gym shorts that hit him about six inches above the knee and a simple polo, and he was sweating a little.

Thank you, universe.

I watched as he gracefully backhanded the tennis ball at his opponent, his biceps flexing, his legs shifting position in sync with his arms. He raised his non-racket arm and wiped the perspiration from his perfectly shaped forehead, and I could have swooned.

Gorgeous. Everything about him. Spectacular.

"You can tell he's not very nice," Stephanie commented, her nose wrinkling. "He's trash-talking the other player—watch how his lip curls up. He's sneering at him."

Dave pressed another few buttons on the remote, and suddenly we could hear him.

"This is an all-boys school, Murphy," Ethan panted as he moved across the court. "No girls allowed."

"Shut up, Winters," his opponent huffed, and swatted the ball back to Ethan's side.

"Except your mother," Ethan continued without missing a beat. "We all know an exception gets made for her around here."

Dave muted it again.

Okay, I could concede that Little Dorrit was right about Ethan being not very nice. Not like that was a big surprise. I mean, he must be the Scrooge for a good reason. But boys trash-talk when they play sports, right? That's just what they do. And seriously, he was so insanely attractive it was hard not to forgive him everything. It was not lost on me that I'd be inside Ethan Winters's bedroom at least once or twice a week for the next six months. Sifting through his dreams, his memories. Hovering over him as he slept.

"Are you quite all right, Havisham?" Boz came up to me. "You look feverish."

"Oh, I hope you're not getting sick," said Stephanie with genuine concern. "There's a bad bug going around at NYU. Don't you live near there?"

I didn't get sick, of course. Another plus that came with being technically deceased.

"I'm fine," I murmured. "It's just warm in here."

Boz followed my gaze to the screen and Ethan. "He's a novelty, I'll admit, not the normal selection, but I think he has real potential."

Yes. Hot, hot potential.

But there was more to it than that. From the moment they'd tacked Ethan's picture to the Board, I'd felt a zing of recognition. He was the first Scrooge I'd ever encountered who was anything like me, younger than fifty and at the start of his life, totally unaware that it was all about to go up in smoke. I found the very idea of Ethan fascinating—would he do what I'd done? Would he doubt, would he laugh it off, would he refuse to let it get to him? Or would he do what I should have done? Would he change?

"So, er, Dorrit," Dave jumped in with his usual jovial voice, breaking me out of my introspection, "how are you finding your time at Project Scrooge this year? Enjoyable, I hope, and not too overwhelming."

"It's been everything I could have possibly imagined and more," Stephanie said.

Kiss-up.

"And Havisham here is treating you well?" Boz prompted.

I glanced up and met her eyes. Now would not be the best time for her to tell him about all the stupid errands I'd been sending her on.

"Best boss I ever had," she answered.

Total kiss-up.

Boz nodded. "I'm so glad to hear it. I knew that you and Havisham would hit it off."

And then they were all smiling weirdly. God.

"Apparently this is Dave's last year as the Clock," I said, to change the subject to something that wasn't me. "So you're lucky to be here to get to witness him in action."

"Your last year, wow," said Stephanie softly. "I bet you're going to miss it."

"More than I could ever express," Dave replied.

"What do you think was the best part about the job?" she asked.

"The people," he answered immediately. "I will miss my coworkers. Some more than others."

They did that weird smile thing again.

"So it looks like we're all set," Boz said. "We've got eyes on Ethan Winters."

I turned my attention back to the monitors. Ethan wasn't on any of them anymore; he'd finished his match and gone into the locker room, where tragically there were no cameras allowed.

"Almost," Dave corrected. "I have a few bugs to work out, and a few more places to set up a feed, but then we'll be ready."

"Ready for what?" asked Stephanie.

"Ready to break inside Ethan's head," I said with a grin.

For once, I couldn't wait to get started.

FIVE

"TESTING. ONE. TWO. TESTING."

I pressed the receiver deeper into my ear and instantly regretted it. "I can hear you, Grant. God. You don't have to yell."

"Righto, boss," he said, softer but still annoyingly loud. "We're almost ready for you."

"Wow. This is crazy." Stephanie was practically jumping up and down, she was so excited. "Grant's just going to push that little green button, and then this door"—she gestured to the shiny metal door that stood by itself in a frame in the center of the Transport Room—"this perfectly normal-looking door, is going to open up into Ethan Winters's bedroom?"

"That's how it works," said Grant. "Neat, huh?"

"The neatest!" Stephanie gazed at him admiringly.

"If we can ever confirm the guy's asleep." Marty sounded uncharacteristically irritated. "What is taking so long, Grant?"

"We're waiting for his heart rate to drop to the appropriate levels," Grant informed him, watching the set of monitors that showed a darkened bedroom from several different angles.

Right on cue, Ethan began to snore.

"Oh, come on, he's sleeping!" Marty said. "Let's do this already!"

"It has to be a deep sleep, moron. We don't want him to wake up in the middle, do we?" Grant retorted.

I sighed and walked back and forth across the Transport Room, stretching my arms and legs. I'd been in the minds of five Scrooges in my time at PS, week after week, month after month, year after year, more than a hundred memory sifts, if I stopped to count, but this time, this first time inside Ethan's head, it felt different. I had butterflies flapping around my stomach.

Get a grip, I told myself. *He's just another Scrooge.*

"Are we there yet?" Marty complained.

"Shut it, Marty." Grant was sure taking his sweet time with the monitors. Then finally he smiled. "Okay, Holly. We're live in five. Four. Three. Two."

He pressed the green button.

The gateway door started humming, and then glowing.

I zipped up the Hoodie.

"Holy wow!" Stephanie gasped. "Holly?"

"Yes?"

"I can't even see you at all!"

"That's the point."

She reached out toward me blindly and caught my arm. She

gasped again. "You're completely invisible! Neat!"

I sighed. "Stephanie?"

"Yes?"

"You've got to let go of my arm now. And get back so I can, like, open the door."

She released me, and I stepped up to the silver door and put my hand on the knob. It had a kind of electric energy that made all the hairs on the back of my neck stand up.

"Lights going out," Grant said, and the room went black. "Now everybody needs to be absolutely quiet while the gateway is open."

"That means you, Stephanie," I added.

She didn't answer. It was too dark to tell, but she was probably making that zipped-lips motion.

"Let's do this," I whispered.

Very, very slowly, I turned the doorknob.

There was a tiny click, and then the door swung silently outward, revealing Ethan's bedroom. Another step and I'd gone from 195 Broadway to Sixty-Fourth Street, almost a hundred city blocks in the blink of an eye.

In other words: neat.

I shut the door carefully behind me. My heart was pounding in my ears. I always felt like a total criminal when I was in a Scrooge's bedroom for the first time. A cat burglar. I loved every minute of it. Call me an adrenaline junkie, but the memory sifts were like the only time since I'd been dead that I felt truly alive.

Moonlight was leaking through the window, enough that I didn't need the night-vision goggles I always wore around my neck.

I crept toward the sleeping figure on the bed.

Hello, Prince Charming, I thought as I stared down at his peaceful face. Although right now he was technically more of a Sleeping Beauty type.

"Do you read us?" I heard Grant's small voice in my ear.

"Yes," I whispered.

Ethan was sleeping on his back, but he wasn't snoring anymore. I took a small aerosol can out of my pocket and sprayed the air around his face. It smelled like lavender air freshener, but it was actually a mist that would make him sleep more deeply. Just in case.

"His heart rate's still good," Grant reported. "Proceed with the mind meld."

I dug into my other pocket for the transducer, a delicate line of thin, almost translucent wire attached to a small silver electrode. This I stuck gently to Ethan's forehead.

"He lives here all by himself," Grant said. "Not even a goldfish. Now that is sad, in my opinion. Everyone needs a pet or something. Remember that little spaniel that Elizabeth Charles had? She freaking loved that dog. I had a good feeling about how things would turn out for her, seeing that. Nobody can be all bad if they like dogs."

I didn't like dogs. I wasn't much of a pet person of any kind. Early on after I'd become the GCP, when the isolation of the whole thing was killing me, I'd gone to a pet shelter. I thought I might get myself a cat.

Cats, as it turned out, are not too fond of well-preserved zombies.

"It was a really cute dog," Grant said, and I got the idea that he was talking to Stephanie, not me. "White with tan spots, big floppy ears, huge brown eyes. What was its name, Marty? . . . Oh, that's right. Berkeley. The dog's name was Berkeley. Which was funny because Mrs. Charles's ex-husband was a Stanford man."

"If you haven't noticed, I am trying to work here," I hissed.

"Roger that," Grant said. "Sorry."

Carefully I unspooled the wire until I reached the other electrode, which I placed against my own temple. Then I took Ethan's hand in mine. That's how it worked. I needed the electrical impulse and the skin-to-skin contact.

Science and magic.

His hand when I took it was warm, his fingers long and slender, nails neatly trimmed. I leaned closer. God. Even in the dark, he was wildly attractive.

Focus, Holly. I closed my eyes, and almost immediately I was sucked into his dream.

He was dreaming about . . . swimming?

I knew from Dave's reports that Ethan spent most of his free time at the New York Athletic Club, swimming and playing racquetball and squash, fencing and boxing and running around the track. There'd already been an argument inside Project Scrooge about whether it was ethical to videotape the inside of what was essentially a gym, which was only a step up from a bathroom in some people's—cough, Boz's—prim and proper eyes. In the end it'd been decided that there would be no video in the athletic or dressing areas of the club, just the dining and sitting rooms. It wasn't likely that Ethan was going to be doing anything significant or exciting in those off-limits places anyway, Dave had reasoned. He just went there to work out.

We'd never had a Scrooge who'd been into fitness before. Usually they tended to stay at home and count their money.

Anyway, in his dream, Ethan swam up and down lane three of an old-fashioned indoor swimming pool. I could feel him in the dream, the water sluicing off his body, the coolness of it, the light wavering under the surface. It was like that when I was connected with the Scrooges. I saw what they saw. I felt what they felt. I could feel the way Ethan used swimming to quiet his thoughts, pushing himself relentlessly through the water, one stroke after another.

As dreams went, it was pretty boring stuff. It was definitely time to move on. I squeezed his hand gently, strengthening the link between us, and guided his consciousness away from the dream and into the storehouse of his memory.

For the first few seconds I was swamped by the sudden onslaught of sensation—tastes and smells and sounds popping up everywhere, images flashing through my mind.

A giant, long-necked dinosaur made of bones.

A little girl in a tiara.

The sensation of being small and riding on a man's shoulders through a crowd.

Watching my parents ice-skate at Rockefeller Center.

The sound of a phone ringing.

The feeling of a crisp hundred-dollar bill in my hand.

A policeman at the door, frowning.

An old man with cold blue eyes.

A man with warm blue eyes I didn't want to think about.

A diamond bracelet in a velvet box.

A ring.

I struggled to keep us separate through it all—what was Ethan and what was me—but it was hard. It was always hard, especially at first. You could get lost in the other person's mind, forget where you ended and the Scrooge began.

Find a Christmas, I reminded myself. *Get your bearings in his life.*

When I first started working on the Project I couldn't understand what Christmas really added to the situation. Why the Ghost of *Christmas* Past, I wondered? Why not just the Ghost of the Past in general? But five years of sifting memories had shown me that a person's memory was keener on special occasions. It didn't matter if a person loved or hated Christmas (and I for one still hated it); their emotions always ran deeper that time of year. And when you're rummaging through thousands of memories, it's easy to pick out the Christmas trees and the twinkling colored lights and the stupid Christmas carols, and that's how you can mark the progression of time, one Christmas after another.

Plus, there was that whole "spirit of Christmas" thing that Boz was always going on about. Which I didn't buy.

The first Christmas I picked up with Ethan was one when he was very young. At first all I could see was his snow boots. I felt them, too, on little-kid Ethan's feet as he ran along some sort of path through a blanket of fresh snow. There was snow in the air. The path was lined with a wire fence and black lampposts every few yards, each post adorned with a red bow to celebrate the season. On the other side of the fence was a forest of leafless trees, their branches black and snow-laden. It was almost dark, the way it sometimes gets during a storm, and the sky and the ground were both muted shades of blue.

I could feel Ethan's nose like it was my nose—it was cold, and his legs were tired, but it felt good to run after being cooped up so he didn't care—he loved being the first person to make tracks in the new snow. He was smiling as he ran.

"Hey, buddy, come back!" came a voice from behind him. "Don't get too far ahead."

He stopped and turned around, breathless. Two figures came toward him up the path—a man in a gray wool jacket with a red plaid scarf and a girl in a puffy purple coat.

The man was his dad, I felt. He was the man with the warm blue eyes.

The girl was . . . Jack—that was the name Ethan labeled her with in his mind. His sister. She was older, maybe ten or eleven. Her cheeks were rosy, and her eyes were blue, too, bright with mischief. She reached down and grabbed a handful of snow and lobbed it at their dad, who roared in good-humored outrage and bent to scoop up his own snowball.

"Oh, you are going to pay for that," his dad panted, and then he tried to tackle her, but she danced out of the way, laughing, and Ethan joined in the fight.

They went on playing in the snow—running and dodging and hurling snowballs at one another, completely destroying the serenity of this winter wonderland. The blue of the sky grew deeper. Suddenly the lamps went on, and then the trees lit up, too, each tree along the path wrapped in thousands of tiny white lights, like entire galaxies of stars against the backdrop of the snowy park. For a minute, Ethan and his dad and sister just stood there, spellbound by the sight. Then from somewhere in the distance came the muted sounds of a Christmas song played on a saxophone.

Ethan's dad put his arms around his children and sang along. "*Have yourselves a merry little Christmas. . . .*" The words almost seemed to float in the air around them. "*Let your heart be light. . . . From now on our troubles will be out of sight.*"

Jack checked her watch.

"We should go, Dad," she said. "Mom will be wondering what happened to us."

I knew through Ethan that they'd been at the Museum of Natural History all afternoon. Ethan had liked the dinosaurs more than anything else. And his mom had promised to make spaghetti for dinner. His favorite.

"All right, we can go home," his dad fake grumbled. "Let's get you warmed up." He tousled Ethan's hair and pulled him into his chest. Ethan remembered exactly the way his dad had smelled that day—the mixture of deodorant and shaving cream and wet wool from his snow-sodden hat. That smell reminded him of happiness.

He hadn't felt that way in a long time.

His mind jumped to another memory, which happened sometimes—one memory leading to another without me directing it. I tended to follow the Scrooge's train of thought in those instances.

It was usually connected, somehow, to something important. Like with this memory with the same little boy, a few years older, standing in front of a coffin.

Ethan didn't linger there. He didn't like to remember, even in his subconscious mind. He pressed the memory deep down inside him and moved on.

In the next memory his dad had been dead for more than a year. His mother was out working late, and his sister was at a friend's. There was a nanny now, but she was in another room on the phone with her boyfriend, by the sound of it. Ethan was alone in the glow of the television. He was watching a commercial that showed a family having breakfast together before opening their presents around a beautiful Christmas tree. A coffee commercial playing a familiar song.

Have yourselves a merry little Christmas. . . .

Ethan's teeth clenched. I could feel the hate welling inside him, like a bitter taste in his mouth. He detested that family and their breakfast table and their stack of French toast and their steaming cups of supposedly delicious coffee. He loathed their Christmas tree and their presents and their matching pajamas. But most of all, he despised their smiling, happy faces.

He didn't say the words, but they were there just the same.

Bah, humbug.

I knew exactly how he felt.

"Good sift tonight, Holly," Grant said after I came back through the Portal.

"Yeah," said Marty. "You're a pro."

"Thanks," I said absently. Of course, Grant and Marty couldn't know how the sift had actually gone. They could only see what the cameras saw—a dark bedroom and me standing over Ethan while he slept. I was the only one who truly knew what had been going on in the Scrooge's mind.

"Now you're supposed to fill out some sort of report?" piped up Stephanie.

Right, the report. If Project Scrooge was really my own personal version of hell, my hell was made up of never-ending paperwork.

I nodded and made my way back to my office. I told Stephanie to go home, I'd see her at the meeting in another few days. I didn't want her pacing around while I wrote this dumb report, checking my grammar or highlighting all the important passages or something equally Stephanie-like. So then I was alone, finally, and I could think.

I spent ten minutes staring at my computer screen.

Ethan's dad had died. It was so obvious that it was this single event that had put Ethan on the path to Scrooginess. And this I could totally understand.

My mom died when I was thirteen. It was like her death split an uncrossable line down the middle of my life, a before and an after.

Before, we lived in Beverly Hills in a house painted all warm, bright colors and filled with antiques and special flea-market finds that my mom had painstakingly collected and refinished, so every piece of furniture we owned was personal, she said. After, we lived in a pristine, sprawling place in Malibu, and the furniture and walls were mostly gray and white. Clean. Modern. Yvonne's.

Before, Ro and I spent hours together, playing games by the pool and making the most elaborate paper dolls you've ever seen and dressing up in all my mom's outrageously cool Hollywood clothes. After, we started hanging out at the beach, just watching the waves. And then hanging out less. And then not hanging out at all.

Before, my dad cracked jokes. After, he threw himself into work. He wanted to talk to me, sometimes, get involved in my life when it suited him to try, but he was never home. We didn't talk about Mom.

Before, I was what you might call happy. After, it was like happy people became the enemy. Happy people were weak. They were clueless. They did stupid things like die on you.

Before, I thought Christmas was a day my mother had created entirely for my benefit. After, Christmas felt like a black hole that would suck me into it for weeks. It made me think of my mom when I didn't want to think of her. Which understandably made me cranky, but you're not allowed to be cranky on Christmas. You're supposed to be all merry and bright.

After, I convinced myself that Christmas was just another day, an excuse to spend too much money on gifts people don't really appreciate and go to lame parties where people wore Christmas sweaters—an affront to good fashion everywhere—and drank too much eggnog—possibly the grossest beverage ever to have been invented. After, when people said, "Merry Christmas," I thought,

Whatevs. Which was, I suppose, my version of *Bah, humbug.*

I shook my head, trying to clear out my crowded thoughts. I had to finish my work. I dashed off a quick report about the details of the sift and headed home, still thinking about Ethan's dad and my mom the entire time. Like when Ethan was looking at that TV family all snug in their pain-free, insufferably content lives, hating them so much, how I felt like I instantly got him. I knew him.

That night I had a dream about my mom and Charlie Brown.

It was the last Christmas before she got sick. We spent that one in Hawaii, because my dad had to film there at the beginning of the year. We used to go with my dad on location all the time. Before, I mean. Anyway, in my dream/memory my mom somehow got this little tree to put up in our hotel room. A Charlie Brown tree, she called it, because there was this Charlie Brown Christmas special where Charlie is sent to get a tree and comes back with this stunted, tipped-over shrub, but when they decorate it, it magically becomes beautiful. So this Hawaii tree of ours was kind of pathetic, but it still deserved someone to care about it, Mom said. We didn't have ornaments, so Dad made popcorn, and he and I sat on the bed threading it piece by piece onto a long strand of dental floss. Mom cut some napkins into odd little snowflakes. And we found some grocery store candy canes to hang on the branches.

"You see, you don't need much to make Christmas," Mom said after we were done decorating. The tree wasn't pretty, but it was nice. It was ours. She planted a kiss on the top of my head. "All you need is love."

In the dream, I wanted to say, "You're wrong. We need

you," because somehow I knew it was only a dream, and I knew that she was dead—she'd been dead such a long time, it felt like forever—and I wanted to tell her that her dying had really screwed up everything for me. I was a freaking Scrooge now. I was dead, too, and where was she? If we were both dead, why couldn't I find her? Why wasn't she here? I wanted to ask her, but that's when I opened my eyes.

I was back in New York City. Cars honking on the street below. I smelled peppermint.

I closed my eyes again. "Bah, humbug," I said out loud to the empty room. "Whatevs. So what?"

SIX

"SO WHAT HAVE WE LEARNED about Ethan Winters?" Boz asked when the other Ghosts and I, along with several members of all three teams—Past, Present, and Future—were gathered in Conference Room A for our initial Scrooge meeting. "Havisham?"

Stephanie slid a folder over to me. I opened it and scanned through my report of the memory sift and the notes my staff had put together from their research into Ethan's past so far.

I cleared my throat. "Well, Ethan's had kind of a tough life, it turns out." Next to me I heard frantic scribbling. I turned to see that Stephanie had taken out her notebook and was jotting all of this down. Like this meeting was a class she'd have a test on later.

"Indeed. A tragic past is quite normal for a Scrooge," Boz said, way too cheerfully.

This, I would argue, is why Scrooges are so messed up. It wouldn't be hard to avoid becoming a bad person if your life had always been full of ice cream and apple pie. But we'd been given rotten apples. It was monumentally unfair, in my opinion.

"His dad died when he was twelve," I said. "After that he was left on his own a lot."

"A history of isolation, yes. That's typical."

Scribble scribble scribble, went Stephanie.

"Have you identified a Marley?" Boz asked.

It was early in the game for that—the Marley was our starting point in April and May, but I'd been in Ethan's memories only the one time. At this stage I was expected to do sifts once a week, unless getting the right details out of Ethan proved difficult—then I'd get approved for twice a week, although more than that was apparently not great for the Scrooge's brain. But right now I was still trying to find my way around Ethan's mind, sort the flashes I'd seen that meant something from the random, insignificant ones. No one expected me to have the answers yet. Still, I thought about the old man with the cold blue eyes I'd seen during those first moments in Ethan's memory. He was old—which Marleys tended to be. Obviously rich, from the impeccable three-piece suit he'd been wearing, another Marley quality. And scowling.

"It's too soon to tell," I said, "but I do have a hunch."

"Follow it," Boz ordered like this was his idea. "It's like I've always said: follow your instincts." He turned to Dave. "Copperfield, tell us about the present."

Dave scratched at his beard. "Ethan's been easier than most Scrooges to get our eyes and ears on, since he's in the city. He recently became legally independent even though he's not eighteen yet—'emancipated,' they call it, and now he resides in a penthouse apartment on the corner of Sixty-Fourth and Third, which used to belong to his grandfather. His mother lives in the Bronx with her second husband. She calls Ethan once a week, but otherwise he has no family interaction. He lives alone. He attends the Browning School on Sixty-Second, where he's a straight-A student and the captain of the tennis team, but I wouldn't exactly call him popular. He has friends, but no close friends, as we'd expect in a Scrooge. And outside of school he spends most of his time at the New York Athletic Club."

"So he's a—what's the word?—jock?" Boz said.

I pictured Ethan swimming, the way his arms had sliced through the cool water in his dream.

Dave shook his head. "I think he focuses on athletics only because he wants to perfect himself. It's very important to him to have the best of everything. The best equipment, the best scores, the best body. He simply wants to be the best."

An admirable quality, if you ask me, sniffed my Inner Yvonne.

"Any ideas on the Cratchit?" Boz asked. That was always Dave's first assignment after he set up surveillance: find the Bob Cratchit, who was usually an employee of the Scrooge's or someone he had a kind of authority over. It'd be interesting to see how this worked out in Ethan's case, seeing as he was only seventeen and unlikely to be anybody's boss.

Dave flipped through his notes. "I've got a good candidate. Daniel Denton is his name, but the students refer to him as 'Dent.' He's a scholarship student—a hilarious, sweet kid, actually—only obviously lacking the wealth and advantages the other boys at the school enjoy. Ethan Winters seems to take personal offense that this kid is at Browning, so he's always playing cruel jokes on him. Right now he has Dent believing that there's a secret society at the school—the Eucleian Society. Dent wants to join, of course. So Ethan has Dent doing all of these initiation stunts. First it was sticking a raw egg in the back of the desk of an unpopular teacher. Then he made Dent come to school in a toga and recite a poem at the top of the school stairs just as class was getting out. That sort of thing."

"But there is no Eucleian Society, right?" I asked.

"Not at Browning. So Ethan has Dent doing all of these humiliating things for nothing. Anyway," Dave summed up, "he exerts a kind of power over this boy, which is consistent with a Cratchit. I'm not certain yet, but like Holly said, I've got a hunch about him."

"Oh, I love hunches," Boz said. "How about you, Blackpool?" He turned toward the other side of the table, where the GCF was brooding. "What does the future have in store for our Mr. Winters? Any hunches there?"

"I have seen the Scrooge's death," intoned Blackpool. That was grim, but it wasn't surprising. Every Scrooge we encountered had less than a year to live. It didn't matter how they old they were—they were all fated to die sometime in the next twelve months. I'd asked Boz about that once, and he'd said it was one of the criteria Blackpool used to choose a Scrooge—his "imminent demise," he called it. "They have to run out of all the other chances that life has given them to change on their own," Boz had explained. "So our chance will be their last chance."

"When will it happen? How?" asked Boz.

"Struck by an automobile," Blackpool answered, "on Christmas morning."

Wait, *what*?

"On Christmas Day, *this year*?" Stephanie sounded as shocked as I felt. "You mean that if we don't succeed, if Ethan Winters doesn't see the error of his ways and change his present course, he won't even make it through one day?"

"Six fifty-six a.m.," Blackpool said with an air of grim satisfaction. "On Broadway."

There was a moment of silence. I shivered. I knew exactly what dying after you got hit by a car felt like, after all. Not fun.

"But that's what we're here to do, right?" Of course Dave, with his endless optimism, was the first to recover from this morbid news. "We're going to make sure that doesn't happen. We're going to change the Scrooge's fate."

"Well said, Copperfield," Boz agreed. "That is exactly what we're here to do. We are going to save this Scrooge. Or at least we'll give it our very best try."

Right. I suddenly noticed that everyone in the room was smiling. It was a strange expression that'd been going around the office lately, this knowing smile that made me feel vaguely like I was missing something. Not to mention that everyone was staring right at me. I guessed Blackpool had made the announcement, and Dave and Boz had expressed their enthusiasm for the project, and now it was my turn.

"Yeah," I said awkwardly. "That's right. We're going to do this thing. We are totally going to save this Scrooge."

The Jacob Marley was usually pretty easy to identify. He was always a type of role model, but never in a positive way—he encouraged the young Ebenezer Scrooge to put blind ambition above everything else; he nurtured the Scrooge's flaws, year after year, until they became equals and people had a hard time even telling them apart. Then eventually the Marley died and left the Scrooge to carry on for both of them.

I knew what had happened to my own Marley—Yvonne Worthington Chase. She was doomed to forever wander the earth, invisible, watching all the people come and go in all the wrong clothing choices, but never being able to do anything about it. Probably still wearing her Diane von Furstenberg and smelling like a corpse and dragging around her chains of pearls. It wasn't the kind of ending I would have wished for her.

Yvonne wasn't a nice person—I knew that. But all these years later, even after I understood her part in my own screwed-up fate, I was still grateful for what she did for me. Because before Yvonne, everyone used to say I looked like my mother. They always meant it as a compliment, being that my mom was drop-dead gorgeous. She and my dad met at one of those crazy exclusive parties in the Valley. By then both of them were already famous in their own right, but my dad didn't watch a lot of TV, so he didn't recognize her as *the* Ariana Jackson, and my mom had heard of Gideon Chase but never met him in person. He wore board shorts and flip-flops, or so the story went. She wore a white sundress and a magnolia in her hair. "I couldn't keep my eyes off her" was how my dad always told it, and I knew exactly what he meant. There was something mesmerizing about her, something that made you want to keep staring at her face. Her beauty was completely effortless, too. Even without makeup, she could light up a room.

I did look like her. Sort of. My eyes were the same shade of golden brown, my nose was long and straight with the small bump at the end, my bottom lip was much fuller than the top one, and my chin came to a point that was nearly too sharp, just like hers. But Mom's hair was a shiny chestnut color and fell in perfect waves down her back. My hair was dull as muddy water, half curly, half limp. My teeth were crooked, and my ears—the only thing that I could clearly tell I inherited from my dad—stuck out horribly from my head. I was all angles, where Mom was gentle curves. She kind of floated when she walked. I slouched. Mom was luminous, amazing, charismatic. I was frizzy. Awkward. Shy. I was like a bad photocopy of her, which made it even worse, because people couldn't help but compare us.

But Mom's beauty didn't last. She lost her hair and was left with a few little fuzzy strands that clung damply to her nearly bare skull. Her skin became sallow. Her face puffed out from all the drugs they pumped into her. Her lips chapped. Her eyelashes and eyebrows fell out. Her body withered away so much she started to look like a gruesome stick figure—her head abnormally large, bobbling on top of an intersection of straight, indefinable lines. She was ugly by the end. It was the thing that made her the angriest, I think—the cancer stealing her beauty. It wasn't enough that she had to suffer so much and die so young. She had to die ugly, too.

That's how we ended up with Yvonne. She was just Yvonne Worthington then, well established as a fashion stylist but not über-famous yet. She was in the middle of her first season of her fashion reality show. She'd worked with my mom a few times before the cancer, done her up for the Emmys one year. But when Yvonne heard she was sick, she pressured my mom to be on her show. So one day she showed up at our house with her camera crew, bringing with her a series of glamorous wigs, clothes that would disguise how frail my mother had become, products like organic bath soaks and soothing lotions and makeup that would hide the circles under Ariana Jackson's bloodshot eyes. I remember that day like it was yesterday.

"This is so kind of you," my mother kept saying, but she didn't really want the attention. She'd only said yes to the whole thing because it was impossible to say no to Yvonne.

"I just thought you might want to feel human again," Yvonne said sweetly.

"That really is amazing of you," said my dad. He smiled at her. He genuinely meant it. "Thank you so much."

After she'd talked to my parents for a while, got some good footage, made my mother look less like Gollum, Yvonne took me aside. "And let's see you, my little darling," she said, pulling me out to arm's length to give me a once-over. "Well. You look just like your mother." She tapped her chin thoughtfully. "Though I really think we should do something about that hair."

I stared up at her. Having this reality-show-personality in my house felt a bit unreal, like there was a lioness stalking around the living room. I could see that Yvonne had carefully constructed every part of herself—her long platinum hair, her perfect makeup, her form-fitting black clothes. Even then I understood that her appearance was like her armor, her shield against the world. She looked tough and smart and capable of anything.

I thought, *She's not going to get sick. She's not going to die.*

And I wanted to be just like her.

That's how it began. My dad married Yvonne about a year after Mom died. Yvonne was like a different person around my dad—she laughed at his jokes and hung on his every word and was always kind of petting him. He didn't figure out what she was really like until it was too late to back out. Then he started disappearing into his work. And I started dyeing my hair blond and straightening it, so when I looked in the mirror I didn't see my dead mother anymore. I saw Yvonne's strength. I saw a fighter, a survivor, a realist. I saw a version of myself that I could live with. And that's what got me through. So, in her own horrible way, Yvonne saved me.

Anyway. That was my Marley. I had a hunch that Ethan's was his grandfather. The old man with the cold blue eyes. I'd seen only a flash of him during my first memory sift with Ethan, and he had the right look, as I mentioned, but most of all it was the feeling I'd gotten when that image had flitted through Ethan's mind—a kind of hard reverence that I recognized, a mix of dislike and admiration. So during the next sift, I went hunting for Ethan Jonathan Winters I. Ethan Senior.

He wasn't super difficult to locate. He hadn't been around much when Ethan was little—I got the impression, sorting through the past here and there, that he and Ethan's father hadn't exactly seen eye to eye about most things. But after Ethan's father died, the grandfather started popping up all over the place like a cantankerous old penny.

I picked one of the keener memories and honed in on it: Ethan knocking on the door to his grandfather's study. If I had to place us in time, I'd say this was after his dad had died (there was just that particular tang of grief in Ethan's awareness that I was so familiar with myself—the terrible ache), but not long after. Ethan and his mother and sister were staying at what was then Ethan Senior's penthouse until his mother could get her feet under her. At least that was what the old man kept telling everyone. Kid Ethan thought this was strange for him to say, because his mother had never been off her feet, that he knew. But the apartment had plenty of room, and Ethan felt safe there. Like the bad things that happened in the world couldn't happen in that place. Grandfather had so much money that nothing could touch him.

Ethan knocked on the study door. A sharp voice told him to come in.

His grandfather was on the phone. "I don't care whose fault it is," he was saying. "Fix it." He waved Ethan inside. "You've got until Monday, or you'll be looking for another job. Good-bye." He slammed the phone down and glared at little Ethan. "What do you want?"

Heart beating fast, Ethan handed him a report card. His

grandfather scanned it quickly.

"It's acceptable," he said.

The last time Ethan had given his report card to his dad, he'd received a high five and a rough hug and a "what a brain you're becoming," before his father had whipped out his wallet and given him ten dollars—one for every A he'd earned. Then they'd gone to get ice cream.

His grandfather frowned. "I suppose you expect some sort of congratulations, but you'll get no such thing from me. If you want a trophy, go join Little League."

Ethan straightened. "I don't care about a trophy, sir. Mom's out of town until Tuesday, so I need you to sign it. To prove that you've seen it."

"Oh." The old man hastily scrawled his signature at the bottom of the paper. He pushed it back toward Ethan. "There you are." Then he picked up his phone and dialed. "Mary," he barked when the person on the other end picked up. "Call HR and have them start processing Hopkins's termination. Have them deliver his pink slip on Tuesday."

He hung up again.

Ethan didn't say anything, but his grandfather explained anyway. "I don't give second chances," he said. "Second chances make you weak. He'll be better off if I fire him. This way he'll learn."

His grandfather had apparently said a lot of that kind of thing to Ethan over the years. This was the first time, though, that Ethan paid attention. He'd been listening closely ever since, and now he could flip through these tidbits of advice like songs on a playlist.

Never give anything away unless you know it will benefit you somehow in the long run.

Never settle for a woman who isn't beautiful. But take care that she's not stupid, either. Beautiful, stupid women have been the undoing of many a great man.

Don't let anybody get to you, and if they get to you, don't let them see it. Never let them see you weak.

It was just like the way I heard my Inner Yvonne. Pure gold Marley-type stuff.

I looked for another memory of the old man and pinged on a particular Christmas morning sometime after the report card moment. The Winters family was still living in the penthouse, gathered in the living room opening presents that were piled neatly on the coffee table—no tree in the old man's place, no other decorations, no Christmas spirit evident anywhere. Ethan was in a better mood than the Christmas with the family in the coffee commercial—he'd just received that new gaming system he'd wanted, so he was kind of happy. And he wanted to make his mom feel better, because he knew she was hurting, too.

"Thanks, Mom. This is awesome," he said, and tried to give her a smile.

There had been kindness in him, I thought. *Once.*

"Rots your brain," Ethan Senior muttered from his overstuffed leather chair in the corner. He was practically scowling the entire time the present opening was happening. "That's why this generation is made up of morons—because their parents just plug them in and let the television do the raising."

I felt Ethan's smile fade. His mother tried to act like she hadn't heard the insult. His sister, though, who seemed about seventeen, looked at her grandfather and smirked. "Whereas you just left the raising to the hired help, isn't that right, Grandpa?"

Jack kind of rocked. Ethan thought so, too. There was a fearlessness to her. She'd never cared what other people thought of her. If she wanted to dye her hair neon pink, she did it. If she wanted to wear combat boots with a plaid miniskirt, she wore them. She'd told Ethan that her nickname at school was Honey Badger. He had no idea what that meant.

"Don't be impertinent," snapped Ethan Senior.

"I can't seem to help myself," she shot back with a falsely sweet smile. "It must be my terrible upbringing."

Ethan's mother raised her hand. "Let's try to get through this peaceably, please." She bent to pick up another present from the table, a long silver-wrapped box. She read the tag and then handed it to Jack.

"Who's this from?" Jack asked, frowning.

"From me. And it's more than you deserve," answered the old man.

Jack unwrapped the package, revealing a velvet box. She opened it. Inside was a diamond bracelet, which was totally familiar—I'd seen that bracelet the first time I'd been in Ethan's mind. It was important, I felt. A key image that he carried with him. A turning point.

"Well?" the old man demanded after a minute. "What do you think?"

"What is it, exactly?" Jack asked, staring down at the glittering string of jewels.

"It's a tennis bracelet. Isn't that what the young girls like to wear? It cost a pretty penny, I'll tell you that."

"And what am I supposed to do with it?" Jack clearly wasn't as impressed as she was supposed to be. "I'm not really into tennis."

"Wear it. Show your friends. That way they'll know you're a Winters."

She shut the box. "No, thank you, Grandfather." Her tone was surprisingly polite.

The old man's face was slowly turning a beet red color, but his expression was calm, collected. "You don't want it?"

"It's not my taste," she pointed out.

"As if you had any taste. Fine." He held out his hand for it. "Give it back to me."

She did. He immediately held the box out to Ethan. "This bracelet is worth twenty-five thousand dollars," he said coldly. "If your sister's too stupid to accept it, I want you to have it. Keep it. Sell it, when you're old enough. It will be part of your inheritance."

"Don't call her stupid." Ethan's mother had a protective arm around Jack now. "We're here because you wanted us to be here. If you treat us this way, we won't come back."

"In what way have I treated you? I've paid for the children's school, shoes, clothing. I've kept you out of the poorhouse after my son died," scoffed the old man.

"I didn't ask you to do any of those things," said Ethan's mother. "Get your coats, kids. We're going."

That was clearly the moment when Ethan's mom officially got her feet back under her.

Jack went out to the hall to fetch her jacket, but Ethan hesitated. His grandfather was still holding out the box. Still looking at him with eyes that were like chips of ice.

"Ethan, come on," his mother urged from the doorway.

"Take it," the elder Ethan Winters urged.

"Ethan, now."

"Don't let them make you soft," Ethan Senior said softly. "It ruined your father, and it will ruin you, too. And never pass up an opportunity to gain an asset."

"I'm coming, Mom," Ethan said. He didn't really know what the word *asset* meant, but he understood twenty-five thousand dollars well enough. He glanced over his shoulder, and his mother wasn't looking at him—she was messing with Jack's scarf—so he reached out and took the velvet box from his grandfather, who smiled. Ethan opened the box quickly, and then he slipped the diamond bracelet into his pocket.

"Good boy," he heard his grandfather whisper as he walked out with his mother.

Oh yeah, I thought. *This guy has Marley written all over him.*

I spent a few minutes perusing the moments surrounding his death—his stroke, the series of hospital visits, his funeral. Then I watched from fifteen-year-old Ethan's eyes as he took the urn of his grandfather's ashes into the study and set it on his grandfather's desk. He stood there for a minute looking around at all of the items that had belonged to Ethan Jonathan Winters I—books and papers, mostly, an antique clock ticking on the wall. And he actually missed the tough old bird.

"He was a bad man." Jack came into the study. She was a senior in high school now, and she'd dyed her hair blue to match her eyes. "Don't you remember how he used to talk down to Dad?"

"What are you talking about?" Ethan asked sullenly.

"Dad quit the company," Jack said. "He left to go back to school for something besides business. That never sat well with Grandfather. They fought about it all the time before Dad died."

"Grandfather was a great man," Ethan said, his throat tight. "Dad was a screwup."

Jack's eyes filled with hurt and surprise. "You look just like Dad, you know?" Her expression hardened. "But now I think maybe you're more like dear old Grandfather, after all."

After she'd gone, Ethan thought about the diamond bracelet. He'd kept it hidden in an envelope at the back of his desk for two years, and he hadn't told a soul about it, ever. He looked again around his grandfather's office. He'd been told, just that morning, that the old man had left everything to him. His fortune. The business, as soon as he was old enough to run it. This very building. *It's all going to be mine,* Ethan thought.

"Hey, Holly, he's starting to move into a lighter sleep stage," came Grant's voice in my ear. "You should head back soon. Or give him a second dose of the lavender, if you need to keep working."

It was late, and I had what I'd come for. Slowly I untangled myself from Ethan's mind until we were fully separate again, him lying on his side in his near pitch-black bedroom, muttering in his sleep, me standing over him. I detached the transducer carefully and made my way back to the closet door, which was glowing around the edges. I opened it, stepped through, and was instantly back at Project Scrooge. The lights went on. Grant and Marty, both looking bleary-eyed, gave me a thumbs-up and started to gather their cards. They had apparently been playing poker all night while I was slaving away. Slackers. Stephanie bounded over to me with a vanilla latte. I sipped at it blissfully as she and I walked back to my office, our footsteps echoing in the empty hallway. The building was quiet this time of night. Deserted. I liked it so much better that way.

"So, did you get the Marley?" Stephanie asked as I plopped down at my desk. I put my arms over my head and stretched, rolled my neck from side to side. I was so exhausted it was suddenly hard to keep my eyes open. Sometimes the mind melding took a lot out of me. Especially those times when the Scrooge really reminded me of, well, me.

"I got the Marley," I said with a tired smile.

SEVEN

"SO THE DAD'S THE FAN, right?" Grant asked.

"I mean, the dad's obviously the Fan." Marty turned to mansplain this to Stephanie. "In the book, Fan is Ebenezer Scrooge's sister. She's the one good thing in Scrooge's life—the only person who loves him unconditionally, who believes in him, who's on his side no matter what." Stephanie already knew this, as over the course of the past few weeks she'd practically memorized *A Christmas Carol*, but she nodded politely.

"And then the Fan always dies," Grant added. "Total bummer."

It was July. We were all sitting around the table in Conference Room B for a Team Lamp meeting. We'd just listened to Tox lay out her strategy for how she was going to wrangle up the spirit of Ethan Jonathan Winters I from wherever he'd wandered in the afterlife. That was how it worked: I found the Marley in the Scrooge's memories. Tox found the Marley, like, literally. She was kind of a Ghostbuster—she located the spirit and brought it in to Project Scrooge. It was also her responsibility to convince this unhappy spirit to play his part on Christmas Eve—warn the Scrooge, be repentant, that kind of thing. I didn't know why, since Tox handled the negotiations and I pretty much stayed out of it, but we never had any trouble convincing the Marleys to cooperate.

So now, with finding the Marley checked off, we were on to the next step: the Fan.

"Ethan's dad does seem like a good Fan," Stephanie said. "But that's almost too easy, isn't it? Why do we need all this time to figure out the Fan if we already know who it is?"

"Okay, no. Maybe we've *identified* the Fan," Tox said, "but that doesn't mean this next couple of months is going to be some kind of cake walk. What we have to do now is decide on the perfect Fan moment to show Ethan, the one that will affect him the most without sending him into a grief spiral or making him shut down completely." She laughed. "The situation is delicate, clearly. So you see, now is when we actually have to *figure out* the Fan."

"So we sift for Fan moments," Stephanie assumed. "Find the best ones."

"But it's not that simple, is it, Holly?" Grant said.

I sighed. "Yes and no. The problem is that Ethan doesn't want to think about his father. He's resistant, especially with stuff that has to do directly with his dad's death. I still haven't been able to access any of that."

Tomas, who worked in research and development, flipped through his folder, where I could see a copy of a newspaper clipping.

"We know most of the details," he said. "Ethan's dad was killed five years ago on the morning of December twenty-ninth, in a freak accident on the sidewalk at Lexington Avenue. He was just at the wrong place at the wrong time, and then bam—he got hit by falling construction debris. At least it was quick."

I doubted that made a lot of difference to Ethan. That sounded bad.

"I thought you could look at any memory you wanted to," Stephanie said, frowning.

I shook my head. "What I'm doing during a sift is basically remembering something with the Scrooge. He experiences it as a sort of dream, and I can direct it, in a way, but he has to cooperate. If he doesn't want to go there, I can't make him."

"So what do we do if he won't go there?"

"We look for ways in. Find memories to connect to that aren't as painful, and hope to be able to catch a glimpse at the more important stuff. I did get that one initial memory of Central Park in the snow, so it's possible. But it'd be better if I could see the dad's death and know exactly how to approach the subject with Ethan."

"Like I said," Tox harrumphed, "it's delicate. Sometimes it's easier to catch a real ghost than a bunch of emotional baggage. I'm glad my job is the ghost."

"And you're *sure* the dad's the Fan?" Stephanie asked.

I closed my eyes and sighed. "Ethan was a normal kid until his dad died. He was fine."

And just like that, I wasn't thinking about Ethan anymore. I was thinking about me.

"Okay, maybe he wasn't exactly normal-normal," I admitted. "But he wasn't the way he is now. He had a family and a life and hopes and dreams like every other kid, and then . . ."

I remembered the door to my mother's hospital room. Pushing it open. Seeing my mom lying there hooked up to all her tubes and wires. She'd looked like she was sleeping, but she wasn't sleeping.

"And then?" Stephanie said gently.

I opened my eyes and blinked away the image. "And then one day all of that stopped. His dad was gone, and everything changed. He changed. Anyway. I'm, like, ninety-eight percent certain that Ethan's dad is the Fan. As for the rest, we'll get there. Ethan might not want to mull over a bunch of sad memories, but it'll happen eventually."

Because I knew: You can try to keep the worst things down inside you. You can shove them away, not think about them, not deal. But they bubble up to the surface. They always do.

I was right. Of course I was. The Fan stuff did come, eventually. Every week I chipped away at the smaller, unobtrusive memories of Ethan with his dad, tiny moments like walking to his first day of school, or that time they tried to make a cake for his mom's birthday but ended up almost burning the apartment down, or his dad teaching him how to tie a tie. I still hadn't experienced anything directly related to his dad's death, not the funeral or the moment when he'd heard the news or any of that—Ethan still kept that completely suppressed—but by August I'd settled on what I thought was the right moment to show him on Christmas Eve. It was this bit about

Ethan losing at the school science fair and his dad helping him cope with the failure. It was good because it showed the unconditional love the Fan always has. It would do.

Frankly, I was on a roll at work, a model employee, some might say, checking off those Scrooge boxes left and right. And finally, after a lot of trial and error, Ethan let me see a memory about his dad that he really felt something about, which I considered progress.

It involved first grade and a boy at school. The kid (whose name Ethan didn't even remember at this point) kept pushing Ethan—like literally pushing him. He did it every time they passed each other in the hall, in the line at lunch, waiting for their parents at the end of each afternoon. And then one day Ethan was in the cafeteria, and he was kind of sulking at the prospect of there not being any tator tots, which was Kid Ethan's favorite thing, when the bully pushed him from behind.

It made Ethan spill his chocolate milk, and he, like, snapped. I could feel the blood rush to his face, his little fists clenching, his lip curling up in a snarl, his vision clouding with fury. He turned around and pushed the kid back, and not just a little push. Ethan put his hands on the kid's chest and shoved him out of the line and right to the end of the connecting tables that half of the school was sitting at, eating. Ethan hurled that troublesome kid against the edge of the table until the kid fell, and then Ethan heaved with the strength of a much bigger person and slid the kid down the entire length of the table, through all the plates and silverware and glasses, like a fight in an old Western movie where the hero slides the villain down the bar.

Ethan ended up in the headmaster's office. He was suspended for a week. Which he thought was super unfair, and I tended to agree. The kid had it coming.

"That's not the point," his dad said that night when they talked about it.

"But the kid pushed me!" Ethan said. "He's been pushing me every day."

"So you tell somebody," his dad said. "You don't push back."

Ethan scoffed. "Who would I tell?"

Ethan's dad pressed his hands to his chest. "Me! You tell me! And then we figure out what to do together, okay?"

"But you're not at school," Ethan argued. "You're not there."

"So you tell me the second you get home. Or you ask to make a phone call." Ethan's dad slung his arm around Kid Ethan's shoulder and hugged him. It felt good, being squeezed. Being loved. Being safe. It made him feel better.

"I'm always going to be here for you, buddy," his dad said then. "Always always. I promise."

Even asleep, Ethan's body tensed when he remembered those words. Ethan knew now that if someone pushed you, you had to push back. Anything else was weak. His father, he thought, had been weak—soft, just as his grandfather had told him. And his dad had been a liar. *I'm always going to be here for you,* he'd said. But he wasn't. Which was the biggest lie of all.

I swallowed down the lump that had jumped up in my throat. My dad once said those words to me. It must be a parent thing. After

Mom died, when I was slumped in an empty pew at the church waiting for her funeral to start, he'd sat down next to me, and put his arm around me that same way, and he'd said, "I'm always going to be here for you, Holly."

Which turned out to be a lie, too.

People lie, the Inner Yvonne said matter-of-factly. *It's what they do.*

It's what they do.

"Are you okay?" Stephanie asked when I came back through the Portal.

"Why wouldn't I be okay?" I said tightly.

"You seem upset," she observed.

I took my latte from her. "I'm fine. Just tired." She looked tired herself. Her hair was piled up in a messy bun on the top of her head, random strands falling out. She was wearing a wrinkled NYU sweatshirt and jeans. It was the best outfit I'd ever seen her wear. Which, sadly, was saying something.

"How's school going?" I asked her as we walked back to my office.

She glanced over at me, startled. She'd been working at PS for months, and this was the first time I'd ever asked her about her life.

"School? Oh, it's . . . fine."

"When do you even go to class?" I asked. "It seems like you're always here."

I waited for her to start chattering, to tell me about her classes, her professors, her roommate, something, but she just handed me the folder to file my report into. Then she rubbed the back of her neck and sighed. "It does seem that way, doesn't it?"

It totally did.

That night I had another one of those annoying dreams about my past. It was a side effect of the memory sifts, I thought. I delved into someone else's past, which got my subconscious working on my own. Another reason why this job was a form of punishment.

This dream was about my dad. Our last real conversation.

"Come with me to New Zealand" was how it started. "It'll be fun."

"No, thanks." I was sixteen, just weeks from my death, tweezing my eyebrows at my vanity mirror. I stopped to look at him in the mirror. His face was so hopeful. "New Zealand's cold."

"December is summer in New Zealand," he said. "It's practically tropical."

"There are sheep in New Zealand," I said, wrinkling up my nose.

"Sheep are cute," he argued.

"They're smelly."

He changed tactics. "There are hobbits there, too. I have it on good authority."

This was one of my best memories—going to see *The Hobbit* with my dad when I was younger. He was so excited. Like he wasn't some big, famous director. Like he was just a kid, and I was a kid, and the movie was the coolest thing ever. But I was sixteen—almost seventeen—now. I wasn't a kid anymore.

"Dad," I sighed. "There's a runway show for Calvin Klein on

the twenty-fourth that I want to go to."

He didn't give up. "Afterward I have to go to New York for a bit. You could come. New Year's in Times Square."

I hated New York. It was a well-established fact. "I have stuff."

"Bummer," he said. "But, hey, I miss you, Hol. I want to spend some time together. I feel like since Yvonne died, we've been . . ."

". . . since Mom died, actually," I corrected him. "But whatevs. It's no big deal. You're busy. I'm busy. It's fine. We're good."

"It's not fine. Come hang out with me," he urged, almost pleading with me now.

"I can't."

"You can."

"I—"

"You totally can. You're a high school student. You don't have any real obligations. You can do anything. Especially go to New Zealand with your father."

Adults always loved to tell you that your life wasn't actually real. I threw the tweezers down and turned to look at him. "Dad, I'm not going to New Zealand, okay? Or New York. Or anywhere. I don't want to go."

"All right. So in March—"

"I'm not interested in your movies," I burst out. "I don't even like them."

He stepped back. "Okay, ouch."

"It's just . . . they're not my thing," I murmured. I knew I'd gone too far. I'd hurt him. But part of hurting him felt good, because it was a little taste of how I'd felt when he just kind of abandoned me after Mom died. How he *wasn't* there for me.

Even though he was trying to be, right now.

He tried to smile. "I could make a movie about robots. Would you like that kind of movie? Killer robots. I had a robot screenplay on my desk yesterday."

"Dad . . ."

"How about aliens?" His eyes widened like this was the best idea ever. "I've been dying to make a movie about aliens. We could shoot it in London. There are no sheep there. We could hang out with the queen."

"Why can't you ever be serious?" I glared at him. "I said no. Leave me alone. I have my life, and you have your life, and we should just keep it that way."

He nodded stiffly. "Okay. Okay. I hear you."

"Okay. Can you . . . ?" I gestured toward the door.

"Sure." And he was gone.

It was the last time I ever saw him.

"Dad, wait," I said, realizing all of a sudden that this had been it—more than the night with the Ghosts and the travels through time—*this moment right here* had been my last chance. If I'd gone with him I would never have been standing on Wilshire Boulevard that morning after yoga. Maybe I wouldn't even have been picked as the Scrooge. If I'd just said yes to that simple little request, I'd be alive right now. But I hadn't known that. I couldn't have known. "Dad, wait!" I called again. But it was too late. I was waking up.

I opened my eyes. My heart was beating fast. I was back in the crappy walk-up, it was still crappy, and the air conditioner was apparently not working, either, because it was sweltering in there, even at ten o'clock in the morning. I threw off the covers. I'd never gotten used to summer in New York. The heat. The humidity. In California I'd never been hot like this. I was sweating, like literally damp with sweat. I smelled lavender and realized I was wearing my Hoodie. I must have gone to sleep in it.

I fiddled with the air-conditioning unit in the window, which was blowing air, but not cold air. I called the super. Voice mail. I stripped down to a tank top and shorts. I drank ice water. Stuck a damp washcloth on the back of my neck. Nothing helped. Then I did the only other thing I could think to do: I stole neighbor lady's newspaper. I fanned myself for a minute and then scanned the movie section, not finding anything good, not really expecting to see anything, but theaters typically have AC, I was thinking, and that's when one of the titles totally jumped out at me.

There it was. Like it was waiting for me. Like it was destiny.

Evangeline's Well.

A new film, it read. *From acclaimed director Gideon Chase.*

EIGHT

I SAW DAD'S MOVIE THREE times in a row. It was Friday, and since I'd just done a sift I had the night off. The film was playing at the Angelika, which just happened to be my favorite movie theater in all of Manhattan, and, not so coincidentally, it was super close to my apartment, and it had an air-conditioning system that worked, hooray. I went to the earliest two showings of *Evangeline's Well* back to back. The first time I watched it like I was receiving a message straight from my dad—I sat with my eyes wide open, not wanting to blink and miss a single frame. The second time I relaxed and enjoyed the story more. I noticed the finer details and formed opinions about the actors' performances and the costumes and the music that played behind their words. I watched it like a movie, the way it was meant to be watched. Then my back was stiff, and I went out to get some newspapers and read the reviews while I had dinner. Then I planned to return for the evening show.

Evangeline's Well was about a man who saves his daughter from a monster. The critics likened it to those dark, imaginative films like *Pan's Labyrinth* where you feel like you're becoming part of some vivid, intense nightmare. And it had more heart, the critics said, than Gideon Chase's other recent films.

The story goes like this: There's an old well in the center of town, and at a certain time of day, when the sun is overhead just right, a person can see the future in the reflection of the water in the well. The daughter of the town's mayor goes to look at her future more than anyone else. She's a pretty girl—a life-of-the-party kind of girl—and when she gazes into the well she sees herself on the arm of the richest boy in town or something equally promising. But one day as she leans over to peer at her reflection, a monster reaches up from the depths of the water and pulls her in. Then her father must go after her into the well, which turns out to be a dark and mystical world underneath our own. He fights his way through a tangled maze and defeats the shadow creatures that run wild in the forgotten land, all to rescue his missing daughter.

If it sounds lame, well, I guess it should have been. But the critics were right—it was beautifully imagined and horribly, horribly sad.

When it was over the third time, I wiped my eyes and looked around. I was wearing the Hoodie and nobody else could see me, but I was still embarrassed by how hard I'd been crying at the end, even this third time through. The theater was about half full—a good turnout, I thought, for a lower-budget film like this, and the audience was made up almost entirely of people on dates.

There's nothing like being surrounded by couples to call attention to the fact that you're alone.

One couple two rows behind me caught my attention. The woman was sitting back with a thoughtful expression, tears on her face but also a quiet smile, still watching the credits move up the screen.

"So was it as good as you thought it would be?" the guy sitting next to her asked.

She gave a satisfied sigh. "It was better."

It felt like time stopped and then started again with a heave, and then the theater was spinning all around me. I knew that mouth forming those words, that voice—although her voice was slightly different now, lower. I knew those freckles across her nose, visible even in the dim theater. She was older, so much older than the last time I'd seen her, but I would have known her anywhere.

The woman sitting two rows behind me was Rosie Alvarez.

Ro.

My ex-best friend.

She was on a blind date, it turned out. After the movie they walked around for a while, making small talk as I followed in the Hoodie. Then they stopped at a frozen yogurt shop. I sat one table over and shamelessly listened to everything they said.

Ro loved my dad's movie. That was the first thing they discussed.

"My favorite part was how the man offered up his own soul to save Evangeline," she said. "Even though he knew the Shadow

King would trap them both, he couldn't just leave her to her fate. He still sacrificed himself, knowing how things would end. There's such a beauty in that. Choosing love, no matter what it costs."

She'd said the L-word, which kind of flustered her date, because they'd never been out together before, and here was this girl talking about beauty and love with such passion in her voice. He was sort of cute, this guy, blond-haired and blue-eyed and extra super dull. But he knew how to dress at least—a simple button-up black dress shirt and dark-wash jeans. Nice watch. Quality shoes. She could do worse.

"So you actually know the director?" he asked.

Ro nodded. "My mom was his first wife's makeup artist for years. I was over at his house all the time when I was a kid."

I waited for her to tell him about me.

"I owe that man a lot," she said instead.

I'd never thought about my dad and Ro even knowing each other that well.

"He has a huge study where he keeps all his own books and the ones people send him when they're trying to get him to make their novels into films," Ro continued. "When my mom was working, getting his wife ready for some event, I used to sneak inside the study. I had trouble with reading at first, dyslexic, you know, but here was this . . . feast of wonderful, exciting books, right within my reach. One time he caught me in there, all curled up with a novel. I was scared, but he just laughed and told me I could go in anytime, borrow any book I wanted."

I didn't remember anything about that. I knew Ro was

sometimes in the house while my mom was getting ready, nights I usually spent at my grandma's so my parents could go out together. I knew that Ro had dyslexia. She had a favorite tee that read, "Dyslexics of the world untie," that she wore, like, once a week when we were freshmen. And I knew she loved books, and she was always reading something or other, but I never knew where her books came from. She never told me.

"He'd ask me about the things I read, too," Ro said. "Later, there was a period at the end of high school when he became a bit of a shut-in. I'd go and visit him, and we'd have these amazing conversations. About philosophy. Religion. Art. Once he said something about the nature of stories that I never forgot. He said, *Without stories, we're all just lonely islands.*"

Her date looked at her blankly.

"Stories let us see and hear and feel what someone else does," she explained. "They build bridges to the other islands. That's why stories are so important. They create true empathy."

She glanced away for a second, embarrassed to be going on and on about this. "Anyway. Gideon Chase is a big part of why I wanted to become a writer. He made the telling of stories sound like a sacred calling."

Wait, Ro wanted to be a writer? When had that happened?

Wonderful, said the Inner Yvonne wryly. *Just what the world needs. Another writer.*

"It must have been inspiring to get to know him," said Captain Bland. "It sounds like he was a good mentor to you, for sure."

"He's more like my friend than a mentor. I talked to him on the phone last week. He's a quiet man, but he's really funny, actually. He's just very private now, especially after . . ." She stopped.

After his daughter died, I filled in for her. Again, I waited for her to say it, to tell him all about the daughter of Gideon Chase, her best friend in the world for years and years, and how she'd died in a tragic accident. Or for her date to bring it up, because if he knew anything about Gideon Chase, he'd probably heard of me. I'd been famous, after all. A little bit famous, anyway. I had fans.

"Like I said, I owe him a lot," Ro said. "He wrote me a letter of recommendation for USC." She took a bite of her frozen yogurt. "But I've been talking way too much about me. Tell me about you."

Blah blah blah, said her date. Blah. Blah. Blah. He clearly loved to talk about himself. It took forever for the conversation to come back around to Ro.

"So, you're a writer," he finally said. "What kinds of things do you write?"

Plays, she told him. Short stories. Poems. The occasional screenplay. And then she talked about how she was a bartender, which she enjoyed because she got to hear so many interesting stories. She liked New York, but she missed California. The beach. Her parents and her friends. She missed the sunny days.

She talked and talked, but she never mentioned me.

Not one word.

You expect her to talk about her dead friend when she's out on a blind date? asked the Yvonne in my head. *She probably barely remembers you. You should go home now. What happens to Ro doesn't concern you anymore.*

Yvonne was right. I knew she was right. But Ro had been my very best friend, the person I used to think knew me better than anyone else.

I had to see what her life was like without me.

I followed Ro home and then came back and spent the rest of the weekend basically stalking her.

She lived in the Bronx with her great-aunt, a sweet old lady who went to mass at a church down the street twice a day. Ro called her *Gran Tía*, and she washed the dishes and took out the trash and carried groceries into the house, ever the dutiful niece. Her room was on the top floor of her aunt's house, and once I saw her up there at her desk in front of the window, writing.

I wondered if she ever wrote about me. If she still thought about me sometimes, and felt sad that I had died.

Her date's name had been David, by the way. When she'd gone home that night, her aunt had come out to meet her in the yard and asked her about how her date had gone, and she'd said (and I quote), "It went fine. David's fine," and when her aunt laughed and poked her in the ribs and asked, "So you'll be seeing more of this fine guy?" she'd shrugged and said, "I don't know. Maybe."

I couldn't stop peeking in the windows at her—I couldn't stop staring—noticing all the ways that she was different and all the ways that she was exactly the same. Her hair was long again, for instance. It was black and wavy and she wore it braided over one shoulder most of the time. Her face was slightly longer and leaner than it had been, but her body had filled out. She actually had breasts. And hips. She was so . . . old. Twenty-three, I calculated. A college graduate. Old enough to hold down a full-time job and be out there in the city on her own.

She'd grown up.

Still, her laugh was the same, and I recognized the scar above her left eyebrow from where something had flown out of the lawn mower one time and clipped her, and she had needed stitches to close up the gash. Her freckles were still there. Her dark eyes still had that sparkly quality, that mischievous expression that always used to make me giggle.

She was still Ro.

So many times that weekend I thought about showing myself to her. It would have been so easy to slide the hood off, step out from the shadows where she could see me, and call her name. I imagined over and over what would happen then. She'd stare at me, her face all disbelieving, and she'd come closer, and she'd say, "Holly? Oh my God, Holly?" And I would smile and nod and maybe cry, and then she'd probably hug me.

But then what? How could I tell her what had happened to me? How could explain why I still looked like a seventeen-year-old girl when I was supposed to be in my twenties? How could I make her understand why I wasn't actually buried in the Forest Lawn cemetery?

It was Sunday morning when I finally tore myself away, when I made myself face the truth. I was dead to Ro. There was nothing for me to give her, or for her to give me. Besides, she'd dumped me long before I'd died. She had a life, a life where she could apparently just call up *my dad* and talk to him anytime she wanted. A life filled with people to meet and places to explore. Where she had a future.

She had a life. I didn't.

I almost got all the way home before I decided I couldn't stand to be in my apartment, so I walked. I walked and walked and walked. Alone. I was always alone. I was always going to be alone, I realized.

Not going anywhere anytime soon.

Stuck, forever.

Lost.

I could see them, right there in front of me—the people and places and things that other people saw. But I couldn't touch their world. I couldn't be a real part of it. I was just a ghost.

Eventually I stopped walking. I'd been wandering for hours, not paying attention to where my feet were taking me. I didn't even know where I was.

I turned in a slow circle, looking around. On one side of me was Central Park, the south end. I recognized the rows of horses pulling carriages and food vendors and foot taxis. God. My apartment was at Eighth and Third. It was going to take me forever to get home. I glanced across the street. The building on the corner with the black awning looked familiar. There was an American flag posted on the left side of the door, and a red-and-white flag with a winged foot in the center of it on the right. This, too, felt super familiar.

I squinted to read the gold lettering on the awning.

New York Athletic Club.

That's why it was familiar. That's where Ethan's pool was.

The pool.

The one I'd seen only in his dreams.

NINE

I SHOULDN'T BE HERE, I thought.

And yet there I was, standing in my Hoodie just inside the entrance to the New York Athletic Club. It was an impressive room: marble floors and ornate wood paneling and a row of gorgeous chandeliers that made you feel like you'd stepped back in time. I'd been standing there invisibly for five minutes, learning the pattern of the doorman's walk back and forth across the lobby and trying to make a decision about what to do.

I should just get out of here, I told myself. *This is crazy.*

But instead I waited until the flood of guys going in and out of the club slowed to more of a trickle, and I could slip into an elevator alone. From there it wasn't too hard to get to the athletic part of the building. I kept telling myself that I was just going to take a peek at the pool. I wanted to see what it looked like in real life, and what was so awesome about this particular pool that it made Ethan want to go back there in his subconscious mind. I mean, he dreamed about this pool constantly. I'd just get a look, see for myself, and then I'd go.

In the empty women's locker room, as I pulled back my hood and became visible again, my heart started slamming into my ribs. I knew Boz would lose his freaking mind if he saw me here on Dave's monitors. But there were no cameras in the athletic areas of the club. Not the locker rooms. Or the pool. I took a deep breath and let it out slowly. I couldn't remember the last time I'd been to a swimming pool. Not since I'd been dead, anyway.

On the way out I stopped and surveyed myself in the long wall of locker room mirrors. I was kind of a mess, wearing the Hoodie with black skinny jeans and cheap black-and-white-checkered canvas flats. Minimal makeup—a bit of concealer and mascara. My eyelids were slightly puffy. I frowned at the small pimple below my mouth. Every single morning I had to cover up this same tiny little zit that I'd had when I died. Since my body reset itself every day, I was stuck with a perpetual pimple for the rest of eternity. An unfair thing to do to a teenage girl, if you asked me.

And you could stand to lose five pounds, said the Inner Yvonne, even though that'd be impossible. *But your hair looks amazing.* Fortunately, just before I died I'd also had a Brazilian blow-out, so my hair was a shiny, just-colored golden blond that fell almost to my waist. It did look pretty good, even loose and unstyled and a bit tangled.

But how I looked didn't matter anyway, since I was just going to pop in there and check out the pool. In and out. That's all. No big deal.

The room was smaller in real life than it had been in Ethan's dream. The floor was covered with thousands of tiny white and blue porcelain tiles, and occasionally they spelled out *NO DIVING* along the edges of the water. The walls were also laid with tiles, dark blue near the floor and then the pattern getting lighter and more sporadic as they approached the ceiling, which was white and high and arching, with chandeliers every few feet to light the room at night. Along one wall were four hazy eight-paned windows. A set of lounge chairs with navy cushions lined up against the other wall. There was a banner of red and white triangles across the pool, the red ones printed with the winged foot, which apparently was the logo for the NYAC. The water cast ripples of light onto the walls, and the air was heavy with the smell of chlorine.

So, there, I'd seen it. I should go. I should have gone right then, in and out just like I'd planned, but that's when I also saw Ethan.

He was swimming in lane three.

Of course he was. From the moment I'd realized that I was standing across the street from the club—Ethan's club—I'd known I would go in, and that somehow I'd find him there. I didn't let myself think about the rules I was breaking, approaching Ethan Winters III—Scrooge 173—in real life. I told myself I was only there for the pool. But I wasn't fooling anyone. Least of all myself.

I made my way carefully along the edge of the pool, picked an empty chaise at the far side, and sat down. There was an abandoned copy of the *New York Times* on the seat next to me, and I stole it. I unfolded the newspaper across my lap and pretended to read.

What are you doing? said a warning voice in my head. This wasn't Yvonne. It sounded suspiciously like Boz.

I want to see Ethan, I replied. When I was sifting his memories, I never really got a good look at him, after all. It was dark in his bedroom. The surveillance photos and videos that circulated around the office weren't the best quality. They couldn't do him justice. I just wanted to see this guy in real life. I'd sit for a few minutes and watch him, and then I'd go.

But that wasn't the real reason I'd come in here. Deep down, I knew that, too. It's why I hadn't worn the Hoodie.

Even though I'd never actually met him, Ethan was the person I felt closest to. I understood him—what he was going through. What he would go through. Maybe I just wanted to be around another person for a while. So I wouldn't feel so terribly alone.

"Hey, I haven't seen you in here before." Some guy put his foot up on the chaise next to mine and leaned toward me, dripping pool water on my pants.

Ugh. The pool obviously wasn't nice and deserted the way it'd been in Ethan's dream. It was populated with men: men with hairy chests and men wearing bathing caps and goggles and men who shouldn't be wearing Speedos, but were. Gross. I'd guess that this one was over the age of thirty. Double gross.

"I said, I haven't seen you here before," the dripping guy said. "What's your name?"

"My name's none of your business." I tried to focus on my fake reading.

"Ah, don't be like that," said the guy. "I'm just trying to make conversation."

I lowered the newspaper. He had slick dark hair and a farmer's tan, but it was easy to see that he thought he was a ten while he was actually more of a seven, and he was used to women being impressed by him. The kind of guy with a ten-thousand-dollar wristwatch.

"Do you have a good lawyer?" I asked him.

His cocky grin disappeared. "What?"

"I'm seventeen," I said loudly. "So I'll ask again: Do you have a good lawyer? Because you're going to need one if you get involved with me."

He took off. I glanced toward the pool. All I saw in lane three was a dark head bobbing in the water. I lifted the newspaper again, and started to read a fascinating article about Hollywood's new feminist treatment of women in the movies. Using a quote from Gideon Chase, no less. It was like my dad was following me around.

"Hello, sweet thing." Another guy. "I like your shoes."

"Not interested," I said. And seriously? My shoes were awful. "Go swim or something."

He muttered something that rhymed with the word *witch* and stalked off. I started to go back to my reading, but then I realized something very important.

Ethan wasn't in the pool.

Wait. Where was he? I put down the newspaper and sat up.

I didn't have to look far, because he was basically standing right beside me, drying himself off with a red towel that'd been folded up on the chair next to mine. I'd been sitting next to his stuff the entire time.

He didn't say anything. He didn't look at me. He gathered his things and started off for the locker room.

That's when I lost my brain entirely.

"Wait," I called.

He stopped. Turned back. The red towel was slung around his shoulders but otherwise his chest was bare, his hair wet and glistening. I blinked up at him.

Speak, Holly, I thought. *Anytime now.*

"Uh, can I ask you a question?" I asked.

He raised an eyebrow. "Yes?"

"What's a guy like you doing in here surrounded by these creepy old men?" Yes, I was stupid. I got this one chance to talk to Ethan, and the best I could come up with was a version of the old "What's a girl like you doing in a place like this?"

But the corner of his mouth turned up. "I could ask you the same."

A slow panic was starting to build in me that pretty soon would be a fast panic. I was *talking to the Scrooge.* Why was I talking to the Scrooge? And, more important, at least for the time being, what was I planning to say to him?

"Exactly," I said.

"Exactly?"

"You and I don't belong here," I said. "I'm . . . uh . . ."

I had to be someone else, I realized. I couldn't be Holly Chase, because Holly Chase was Havisham, and Havisham was the Ghost of Christmas Past, and Ethan was going to have a pretty intense date with the Ghost of Christmas Past for a few hours in late December. I had to be someone else. Someone who might actually be here sitting by the pool for a good reason.

My mind raced.

"I'm waiting for my . . . dad," I said, "who keeps insisting on dragging me to this stupid club while he drinks brandy with his business partners. I'm here under protest." Okay, that hadn't been a terrible explanation. It was pretty good, actually. I quickly thought up a scenario in which I was the daughter of some high-powered business exec. "What's your excuse?"

The side of his mouth hitched up again.

"What?" I asked.

"I'm just half afraid to talk to you," he said. "After seeing how you dispatched those guys who came up to you earlier."

So he *had* been watching me. I tilted my head back to look at his face, fighting a smile. His eyes were dark gray today, like distant storm clouds. God, he was hot. And now we were obviously going to have *an entire conversation*. If I was being someone else, I could do that. I was never going to see him like this again, obviously. Nobody else would ever have to know. Why not have some fun with it?

"Those guys were too old for me," I said. "Are *you* too old for me?"

"I'm seventeen."

"Then you may stay," I pronounced. "For now."

He hesitated. But then he said, "I'm honored," and slid into the chair next to mine. "So are you planning on actually swimming while you're here at the pool?"

I shrugged. "Never learned how." Ha, this wasn't even remotely true. When I was alive I'd never lived in a house that didn't have a pool. My dad used to call me his little fish. But, again, at that moment I wasn't Holly. It was kind of nice being not-Holly. Freeing.

"So you don't swim, but you wanted to sit by the pool. Indoors. With the creepy old men."

"It's the last place my dad would think to look for me."

"Ah, so you've got daddy issues."

"I have boredom issues." I smiled. "But now you're going to entertain me."

"Oh, I am?" he said wryly. "How?"

"You're going to pretend to be my boyfriend," I said casually. Even as the sentence came out of my mouth, I couldn't believe I said it. This not-Holly girl was kind of fearless.

He gave me an incredulous look. "And why would I do that?"

"To keep all the creepy old guys off me, of course. It's the only gentlemanly thing to do here." It was so easy, I was finding out, to turn on that part of myself who remembered how to handle boys. I hadn't had a real conversation with a real live non-Project-Scrooge-related boy in five years. You'd think I'd be rusty. But it was like riding a bike. I could still flirt.

It was quiet for a minute while Ethan thought about this. I waited.

"All right," he said finally. "I'm your boyfriend." He leaned back in his chair and looked around us. The pool area was almost empty now. No real threat of creepy old guys, obviously.

He reached for my hand.

"What are you doing?" I asked.

"I'm being your boyfriend. Sweet thing." His warm fingers enclosed mine.

I got an image from his past. Something with a little girl wearing a tiara. I pushed it quickly out of my consciousness. The last thing I needed right now was to space out because I was honing in on his past. Which I already pretty much knew.

"Hot lips," I tried out.

"Baby."

"Snookums."

"Sweetie."

"Sugar bum."

He exhaled in a breathy laugh. Then we sat there for what felt like hours, but was probably more like twenty minutes, trading pet names, holding hands. It was a familiar feeling, holding his hand, but it was also completely new. At one point I put my hand to his face like I was his adoring girlfriend, and he kissed my palm. Just like that.

I could have passed out, seriously. It was so hot.

"So?" he said after a while.

"Hmm?"

"Are you going to tell me your name? It seems weird that I don't even know my girlfriend's name."

"I'm H—" I stopped myself in the nick of time. I couldn't give him my real name. What if he googled me?

"What?" he said. "The suspense is killing me."

I was in way over my head. I sat up. "Do you know what time it is?"

He smirked and pointed to the huge clock on the wall almost directly behind us. It was nearly six.

"Dinnertime," I said. "No wonder my stomach is rumbling."

"We could have dinner in the club," Ethan suggested. "The chef here is one of the best in the city."

Oh my God, he was asking me out. I could have said yes—I wanted to, God, I wanted to, for both the food and the company—but then it would have become a real date, and the real date would have been in the real dining room. Which had Dave's cameras watching over it. And Dave's team would be expecting Ethan to leave soon. If I kept him much longer, they'd wonder.

I shook my head. "My dad will be ready by now. I should go."

"Wait," Ethan said. "Let me get your number at least."

"I don't have a phone."

His eyes narrowed. "You. Don't have a phone. Why don't I believe that?"

"I'm totally unplugged," I said. "My dad confiscated my phone. I'm being punished."

His frown disappeared, replaced by a curious smile. "That's too bad. Most girls I know would wither and die without their phones. How will I get in touch with you, then?"

"Oh, you want to get in touch with me, do you?" I laughed

nervously. "How about this—I'll find you again. You're a regular around here, right?"

"Have you seen me here before? I thought you looked familiar," he said.

"Maybe I've seen you. In passing."

"I'll be here tomorrow night," he said. "You can find me then."

"I have plans tomorrow night." This was true. I had to work from eight p.m. to two a.m. Which, incidentally, involved me sneaking into Ethan's bedroom around midnight and trying to read his mind. How crazy was that? "It's kind of hard for me to get here on weekdays. I have stuff, er, school-related stuff, you know. So how about this? When my dad brings me back here again some weekend, which he'll do because that's what he always does, I'll look for you."

"Okay," he agreed reluctantly. I could tell he didn't love this plan. "You're seriously not even going to tell me your name?"

I leaned in and kissed his cheek. "Bye, baby."

"Sweet thing," he murmured.

God, I was crazy. I was reckless. I was dumb.

But I was smiling as I walked away.

TEN

"HE'S OUT FOR THE NIGHT," Grant announced. "Proceed, Miss Havisham."

Roughly thirty hours had gone by since I'd met Ethan in real life. I was back at work like this was a perfectly normal night shift at the office. Like yesterday at the pool had never happened.

But it had.

It shouldn't have happened, I'd been telling myself for, like, the past twenty-nine hours. *It can never happen again.* But—sigh—it'd been fun while it lasted. That was the word for it: fun. It'd been so fun to talk to Ethan. More fun than I'd had in years.

"Working more on the Fan this time, right, Holly?" Grant said in my ear as I sleepwalked through the first part of the sifting process.

"Right." But truthfully I didn't have any desire to look into the death of Ethan's dad tonight. I wanted to see Ethan again, not that brokenhearted little boy he'd become after his father died. Besides, I already had enough Fan material to work with on Christmas. Normally in this situation I might get a jump on next month's assignment—the Fezziwig. The Fezziwig loved parties, so that could be a little more lighthearted, work-wise, but I wasn't really feeling that, either. What I wanted, under everything, was to go back to that pool and talk to Ethan some more.

Which I couldn't do. Ever again.

I sighed again.

Wait. Or maybe I could. It suddenly occurred to me that I *could* go back to the pool with Ethan, because he had a memory of me now. I could relive it, at least.

It took me all of two seconds to find it once I was back in Ethan's mind. The pool. The girl sitting by the pool. It was so bizarre, seeing myself through someone else's eyes, like watching a home movie I hadn't been aware was being shot. That blond girl, reading a newspaper by the pool—unbelievably, crazy as it seemed—she was *me*.

Ethan had seen her the minute she came into the room. He'd waited for her to shimmy out of her jeans and reveal a bathing suit, but instead she sat down on the chaise next to where he'd stashed his towel. Then she stole his copy of the *New York Times*. He considered right then that maybe he'd talk to her. It wasn't every day that a girl like that came into the club. Not a beautiful girl like that.

I'm serious, that was literally what he thought. I sucked in an excited breath. I suddenly realized I was doing what every single girl in the history of the human race would have killed to do right after meeting a cute guy—I was looking inside his mind and finding out exactly what he'd been thinking at the time.

So far it was awesome. I couldn't wait to see the rest.

Ethan watched as the first man from the club hit on the girl. "Do you have a good lawyer?" God, that was hilarious. He'd had to turn his face in the other direction in the pool so he could laugh quietly in the water. She had an evil side, this girl. He could appreciate that. Then she said she was seventeen. It just so happened that Ethan was seventeen. Which felt to Ethan like a happy coincidence.

Again he debated talking to her. He knew how to talk to women, or at least he thought he knew. Girls didn't intimidate him, even beautiful girls, but he didn't really seek them out for conversation. Still, a girl like that with her legs stretched out for miles might be worth a few minutes of his attention. He planned his approach as he took his final lap in the pool. He'd point out that the newspaper in her hands was technically his property? No. She might get defensive. He'd ask about what article she was reading? No. It'd seem like he was trying too hard. He didn't want her to think he was trying at all. He'd ask her what time it was? No, because there was a giant clock right above her head—he'd look like a moron. He'd compliment her shoes. Yes. Girls loved when you noticed their shoes.

He was pulling himself out of the water when he heard another guy say, "Hello, sweet thing. I like your shoes."

Ethan cursed under his breath. And who went up to a girl and called her "sweet thing" like that? Tool.

I totally agreed.

"Not interested," replied the girl, with an annoyed edge to her voice.

Ethan walked over to retrieve his towel. She kept reading. He took advantage of the closer proximity to get a better look at her. Nice. Even nicer up close. But a girl like that had a boyfriend, he told himself. She didn't want to be bothered. She wasn't interested.

So he dried off briskly and turned to head back to the locker room.

But then she said, "Wait."

He turned. She looked up at him, her eyes wide, her lips parted slightly, and something strange happened inside of Ethan's chest, a little kick of excitement.

"Can I ask you a question?" she asked. Which *was* a question, but he didn't point that out. There was something familiar about her voice, like he'd heard it before, but he knew better than to ask her if they'd ever met. He would have remembered a girl like that.

She asked him to pretend to be her boyfriend, which was unexpected. This was a no-brainer to Ethan. He'd play along any day.

So they talked. They joked. They flirted back and forth. She was smart, probably smarter than he was, which he found unsettling but cool.

She was funny.

She was gorgeous—he couldn't imagine a girl he'd find more attractive if he'd Photoshopped her together. Her lively brown eyes were regarding him with open interest. His heart was starting to pound.

He never had this kind of reaction to a girl, he thought. What was wrong with him? Or maybe it was something right with her. He felt like he'd known her for years, maybe, but then some part of him also felt like he'd been waiting for her to come along. Like he'd been expecting her, and now here she was.

There had to be a catch. Ethan had learned over the years that no good thing came without a catch. A price. Something. He was probably dreaming, he thought. He'd had the strangest dreams lately, so vivid, and this felt exactly like one of those. Maybe she was a dream girl, and now he'd wake up.

She lifted her hand to his face, caressing his cheek, and his nerves lit up like fireworks. The inside of her wrist smelled amazing, like lavender and something sweet, like candy. He kissed her palm (my palm, this was *me* he was remembering, *me* he was lighting up for, how was this actually happening?) and she shivered and goose bumps rose up on the back of her arm.

That's when Ethan blew it. (Or at least he thought so.) Because then he asked her out.

She immediately told him she had to go. She wouldn't give him her number—she gave some unbelievable excuse about not having a cell phone. She wouldn't agree to meet him again at any set time. She still wouldn't even tell him her name. She kept saying she'd "look for him" later, whatever that meant. And she left.

After she went he sat there by the pool kind of stunned, still smelling her perfume, for way longer than he should have. He wondered where exactly he'd gone wrong.

She had a boyfriend, he concluded. A real one. Even if she didn't, he wasn't in the mood to get something started with the opposite sex. Girls were too much trouble. They were always demanding that you pay attention to every little thing they say, and they wanted you to hold their hand and buy them things. Yes, they were definitely expensive. They were time-consuming. They were needy.

He'd be better off, Ethan decided, if he never saw that girl again.

But he still got that excited feeling in his stomach when he pictured her. His hour with the mystery girl had been the most fun he'd had in a while. He hadn't been bored. He hadn't felt any pressure to be anyone but himself. He'd felt . . . alive. Which was something he hadn't felt, he realized, for a really long time.

After the sift I stayed late in my office. I couldn't concentrate well enough to write my stupid report. Plus, I had to make the whole thing up, because I couldn't exactly report on where I'd really been in Ethan's mind. God, I couldn't stop thinking about him. The thing that got to me the most was that he saw me, he really *saw* me, and though I hadn't even been trying to look good, I'd been wearing no makeup and cheap shoes, he thought I was beautiful. I was more than just a ghost to him.

I was *a girl like that.*

It made me want to go back to the New York Athletic Club right this minute and talk to him. Prove to him that I wasn't your typical girl. That I hadn't blown him off. That I liked him, too. But he wouldn't be there, of course. He was sleeping now.

I had to go home. Figure some things out. I grabbed the Hoodie, put it on, more out of habit than anything else, and headed down the dark hall toward the elevator. I was passing by Boz's office on the way out when I heard the voices.

Raised voices.

Naturally I stopped to find out what was up.

"I don't like it," said a voice. "I've never approved of the idea. It's insulting for you to ask us to do this. It's just not how things are done here."

I recognized the hard edge of the voice right away. Blackpool. And what a shock—he didn't like something? I'd never seen Blackpool like anything. Ever. But what were they referring to?

"It's too late to back out now, my friend," said another voice, and I recognized this one too: Boz. "We're committed. We'll see it through."

"And it's going to work," came Dave's voice. "Haven't you seen that, Arthur? Can't you feel it? I can."

I slid the hood of my Hoodie over my head so I'd go invisible. Something about this conversation was making the hairs on the back of my neck stand up.

"I hope you know what you're doing," Blackpool grumbled.

"I do," said Boz.

"You realize that you're risking everything for this?" Blackpool asked him. "Everything we've done, everything we've accomplished—"

"But isn't that what we're about here?" Dave interrupted softly. "Every single time we open a portal to a Scrooge's bedroom, aren't we taking risks? That's what we do, Arthur. We risk everything. We put it all on the line."

Footsteps approached the door, and I took off as quietly as I could down the hall. It wasn't until I was sitting on the subway again, veering toward home, that my heart finally began to slow.

I didn't know what they'd been talking about, but one thing was obvious: something weird was definitely going on at Project Scrooge. Something weirder than usual, I mean. Something out of the ordinary.

But I had my own problems to worry about. I'd been telling myself that my afternoon with Ethan had to be a one-time thing, but seeing it through his eyes had changed my mind.

I had to see him again.

The question was, how?

ELEVEN

"ALL RIGHT, PEOPLE, LET'S GET started," Boz said as we all gathered in Conference Room A for the August meeting. "Let's hear more about our infamous Mr. Winters, shall we? Hopefully we're making some progress. Havisham, you go first."

"Why do I always have to go first?" I asked.

Boz seemed taken aback. "It's the natural order of things to go past, present, and then future, wouldn't you say? It's the way we always—"

"Yes, yes, it's the way we've always done it, so we always have to do it that way." I rolled my eyes. "Can't we just change things up a little? Start with Blackpool for once?"

Boz frowned, but then he nodded. "Very well. Blackpool. Report on Mr. Winters, please."

Blackpool glared at me. I smiled back at him. He glared some more.

"I've seen the Scrooge's death," he intoned finally. "That is all."

O-kay. Way to contribute absolutely nothing, Blackpool. I wondered if he was still upset about whatever it was that he and Boz and Dave had been arguing about. All week I'd noticed a kind of tension in the air between Blackpool and Boz. Like they were in a silent but serious argument.

"All right; if that's how it is, I won't push you." Boz frowned and turned away from Blackpool. "How about you, Copperfield?"

But Dave wasn't ready, either. He rustled through his notes like he'd forgotten how to read. "Well—" He cleared his throat. "Um, yes. We've got Ethan's schedule down—we understand his patterns fairly well by now. He goes to school, goes to the gym, goes home. He gets a phone call from his mother on Tuesday evenings. Plays indoor soccer on Wednesdays, that kind of thing. He goes to the occasional party on Saturday nights, usually with a different girl each time—no one steady."

I was trying to subtly take notes on Ethan's schedule. *Indoor soccer—Wednesdays. Phone call—Tuesday night. Parties—Saturdays.* But these were all places the company would be monitoring. All of that useful information about Ethan's life—the exact whens and wheres I was missing—was locked away inside of Dave's office. Which I didn't have access to.

"No girlfriend?" Boz said. "I assume there's a Belle lurking around somewhere in his life?"

"Not one that I've seen," Dave said. "But that's not really my department."

They looked at me. I shrugged. "I don't do the Belle until October."

"True enough," Boz said. "All in due time."

The Belle was the Scrooge's ex, the long-lost love, the happiness-that-could-have-been. I'd never seen Ethan goo-goo-eyed with a girl. In all the memory sifts I'd done, no girl ever stood out, but then, it didn't necessarily have to be a romantic connection with the Belle. My own Belle had been Ro.

My throat tightened, thinking about Ro all grown up, oblivious and happy with her life. The very definition of the words *alive and well.*

"Last time, Copperfield, you reported that you and your team had identified the Portlies as that homeless man on Sixth," Boz recalled.

"Yes, we have. That's all set," Dave said.

"So this month, have you worked out the details with the Fred?" Boz asked.

Dave scratched his beard. "We've been looking into the sister, Jack. She's family, and that's promising, but she doesn't seem interested in making any connection with her brother at this point. But that could change, I guess. Or it could be the mother, or the maternal grandmother. Both of them invite Ethan to family events fairly regularly. Of course, he never attends. But they keep asking."

It sounded like Dave had no idea who the Fred was.

"Hmm, I see. Keep watching it," Boz directed. He turned to

me again. "Are you willing to share with us *now*, Havisham?"

"Of course," I said. Except I still didn't have anything meaningful to share. I'd been what you might call preoccupied for the past week. I'd been trying to figure out how to see Ethan again without anyone at Project Scrooge knowing about it. So far I'd totally failed. I couldn't meet him at his apartment or at his school—Dave's team was watching both places practically every second. So I assumed my best option would be to go back to the New York Athletic Club—in fact, I'd already gone back and sat there stupidly by the pool waiting for, like, hours to see if he would randomly show, but he never did. I just didn't know *when* Ethan was going to be *where*. I'd been trying to piece it together from Ethan's memories, but that was also complicated, because we don't recall our schedules the same way we remember specific moments in our lives, and we don't exactly go into every memory thinking, *Oh yeah, this is Tuesday, at 10:53 a.m.*

I sighed. It'd been almost an entire week, and I still hadn't seen him again. By now he'd probably forgotten all about me.

"And what is it you have to share?" Boz asked. "Tell me you have the Fezziwig."

"I'm close. Any day now." I didn't care about the Fezziwig. I wasn't remotely close to finding one, but Boz didn't have to know that.

"Have you learned anything new?" he asked.

I'd learned lots of things. I'd been picking up all kinds of interesting tidbits of information in Ethan's brain while I was trying to figure out his schedule. For instance: his favorite food was spaghetti, but he also liked pizza, with mushrooms and olives and green peppers. He brushed his teeth three times a day. And used mouthwash. And flossed. He was, like, the most kissable boy ever. And he was a Yankees fan, duh. He liked reality shows. He also liked watching soccer and golf, but hey, everybody has flaws. I could get past it. He actually *enjoyed* shopping for clothes—he liked building his image, piece by piece and item by item. His favorite color was black. Mine, too. He was a snob about the coffee he drank. Same. He also liked Perrier. God, it was like we were soul mates.

And most important, he liked me. And I liked him. I liked him so much it was kind of killing me.

I shook my head. "This Fezziwig's a tough one."

"Look at parties. You know the Fezziwig loves parties," Boz advised.

I stared at him. "Yes, I know. This is not my first rodeo, Boz."

"It seems that everyone is struggling a bit this month," he said. Which, again, made me feel somewhat better. "We need to focus. Help each other. Work together."

The meeting dragged on. Boz and Dave started talking about Jack, and how she may or may not be the Fred. I was hardly listening at this point. I was still thinking about seeing Ethan again. It felt nearly impossible, because he was under such constant surveillance. There were holes, of course, pockets of time when he wasn't being watched as closely, but I didn't know where and when those pockets occurred. Which brought me back to this simple fact: I needed to know what Dave knew. But I couldn't just ask him, and it'd be suspicious if I started poking around in places I didn't normally go. Even the Hoodie couldn't help me, because I didn't have access to Dave's office. It required a badge swipe, and my security clearance wasn't high enough.

I sighed. I was out of ideas.

"Can I get you a coffee?" whispered a voice right into my ear, and I nearly knocked heads with Stephanie. "You look like you need a pick-me-up," she observed quietly.

"No. Thanks."

I sighed again. Gosh, she was always just so helpful, wasn't she?

And then I had an idea. A wonderful but maybe awful idea. It suddenly occurred to me that if I was going to do this—if I was actually going to pull off seeing Ethan in real life—I'd need help. Someone inside the company. A person I could get to do things for me so I wouldn't draw attention to myself. Cover for me. Someone to watch my back.

Someone who, I just remembered, happened to mysteriously have full security clearance. "On second thought, I do have something you can help me with," I whispered back to Stephanie.

"Sure. What is it?" she asked.

Boz stopped talking and turned to stare at me pointedly. "Wouldn't you agree, Havisham?"

I had no idea what he was asking about. "Yes," I said. "I totally agree."

Boz and Dave went back to talking.

"Later," I whispered to Stephanie. "I'll tell you later."

"Okay. I can't wait to hear what it is," she whispered back. "You know I'm always here to help."

Which was just what I'd been hoping she'd say.

TWELVE

I INVITED STEPHANIE OVER FOR dinner at my apartment. As in, I told her to bring me a pizza.

"Wow, your place is great!" she panted after I buzzed her in and she'd schlepped up the four flights of stairs. "So cozy."

I didn't bother to show her around. She could see pretty much all of it from the doorway.

Stephanie set the pizza on the middle of my little kitchen table. She was wearing a mint-green sweater with a cartoon hamburger on it, only the hamburger had a giant eye and possibly a pair of fangs, like it was alive and about to attack you. I couldn't stop staring at it.

"Do you have some plates?" she asked after a minute.

I broke out my stash of Diet Coke and a couple of mugs and got out two plates. I gave her the chipped one with the blue flowers. She acted like it was the finest china.

"I don't live far from here," she informed me as we sat eating the pizza. "About three blocks away, off St. Marks? So we're practically neighbors. We should hang out more often."

It was an unfamiliar feeling, having someone over at my place. It made me feel naked, in a way. Because if I showed up at work with my hair and makeup done perfectly, wearing the right clothes (black skinny jeans and a nice white button-up rolled at the sleeves was my typical look), nobody would really know how utterly shabby my life was. But now this girl was here to witness it firsthand, and she was trying to be nice and tell me how great she thought it all was—such a pretty plate, such a cozy place, such a nice view—but that made it all seem worse to me.

"So you're a Ghost, right?" she asked. "Does that mean that you're dead?"

I choked on my Diet Coke. Stephanie waited patiently for me to stop coughing. She didn't pester me, but her expression clearly said, *Well, are you?*

"Yes," I answered finally. "And no."

"What does that mean?"

"I died once. But clearly I'm still kicking, aren't I?"

She laughed, but she felt bad for me, obviously. Poor dead me. "I thought so. I was talking to Da—Copperfield the other day, and he was telling me about how it happened with him, and it occurred to me that you must be dead, too. So how did you die?"

The way I saw it, the less she knew about the circumstances surrounding my death, the better. If she knew I was a failed Scrooge, she'd never be able to trust me. And I needed her to trust me, or this new plan of mine was never going to work.

"Car accident," I sputtered. Which was not exactly a lie.

"I'm so sorry," she said, like I'd just told her that my grandma had passed away. She leaned forward with her elbow on the table and put her chin in her hand. "What's it like, being dead?"

I shrugged. "Boring. When you're alive—really alive, I mean—you change, a little bit every day. But when you're dead, nothing really changes. You're just the same, day in and day out."

Except that day with Ethan, I reminded myself, when it felt like everything changed.

"But you eat and sleep and use the bathroom like everybody else, right?"

"I can, but I don't have to," I explained. "If I didn't want to, I wouldn't have to eat or sleep. I couldn't starve to death or die of exhaustion, because in the morning my body would just start over again."

Her eyes were wide. "Your body starts over again every morning?"

"Uh-huh." I didn't know how to explain that to her, so I didn't even try. "There are definite advantages to being dead." I grabbed another piece of pizza. "For instance, I can eat anything I want and not gain weight."

She had the good sense to look envious.

"My hair never grows, so I never have to dye my roots," I said, twisting a golden curl around my finger. "And I won't ever get old."

Or be old enough to vote. I thought again about Ro and her

job and her date and the way she was following her dreams. Which made my chest feel tight.

Stephanie squinted at my part line. "What color's your hair really?"

"On the other hand," I continued, "every single morning I have to cover up this tiny little zit right here." I pointed at it. "I mean, every. Single. Day. It's like I'm stuck in never-ending puberty. It sucks."

"You can't even see it," she said.

She was nice. So freaking nice. Too nice.

"I can imagine how that would be hard, though," she said. "The unchanging part. It would make it tough to have normal relationships, I think. How would you make friends if you always stay the same, and everyone else just naturally moves on with their lives?"

Well, this was a depressing conversation.

Stephanie tucked a strand of corn-silk-colored hair behind her ear. "I'm sorry, that was rude. I'm just interested in this whole dead-but-alive thing. I'm a psychology major, can you tell?"

"Yeah." Sometimes she seemed like a little girl—sweet and clueless and likely to remain that way forever, no matter how old she got. But other times I was reminded that Stephanie was actually a college student, something that I would never be, and there were real, honest-to-goodness thoughts going on behind those big purple glasses of hers. Maybe she was smarter than I gave her credit for.

I only hoped she wasn't *too* smart.

"Anyway," she said. "You said you needed help with something?"

I took a deep breath. This was either my best idea ever or my worst one. "First off, I just wanted to say thank you for what a stellar assistant you've been these past few months. I know I was a little wary in the beginning, but now I totally feel like you're part of the Project Scrooge family."

Stephanie gasped and put a hand over her heart. "Oh, thank you, Holly. That means so much."

"I mean it. Really."

"So what can I help you with?" she asked. "Because you know I'd do anything to help you. I believe in you and all that you're doing at Project Scrooge."

"Great. I, uh . . ." God, this was nerve-racking. It was now or never. "I need access to Dave's office so I can get Ethan's schedule."

Boom. There it was.

Her head tilted to one side. She finished chewing a bite of pizza and swallowed. "Why?"

Here it was, my big confession. "I want to talk to Ethan in real life."

"You mean, when he's *awake*?"

"Yes. That's my plan."

Her mouth dropped open for a few seconds. "Why would you do that?"

"Because Ethan's not like the other Scrooges," I said. "Showing up with him on Christmas Eve isn't going to be enough to save him. He needs more direct intervention. He needs someone in his life to help him change. Someone young, who understands what he's going through."

Stephanie shook her head. "But that's not how we do things, Holly."

"I know. I know. But I think this is an extreme case here. Which is why I'd like to risk it. Because I really, really believe it's the only way we're going to pull it off this year. Someone has to go the extra mile."

Stephanie still looked doubtful. "So you would, what, just talk to him?"

I nodded. "Basically. And get him to talk to me. You can accomplish a lot just by listening to someone. And I'd try to provide him something positive in his life. I'd become his friend. Sometimes all a person needs to turn themselves around is one good friend."

I was getting through to her. I could tell by the look on her face.

"Okay, that might be true," she said. "I guess I've had my doubts about the 'just show them the error of their ways' approach, if I'm being totally honest. But then what would happen on Christmas Eve? We'd still have to go through the Performance part of the process, right?"

"Right."

"But when you went to show Ethan his past, he'd recognize you. He'd know something strange was going on. And that could undo everything."

I'd already thought this through. "He wouldn't recognize me," I said quickly. "The costume is pretty extreme, trust me. If I was wearing it right now, you wouldn't know it was me."

She bit her lip. "I don't know, Holly."

"You have to trust me," I said. "I've been doing this job for a long time. I just have this feeling about it. Sometimes that's something that happens when you're a Ghost—you sense things that ordinary people don't. And there's definitely a feeling I've had about Ethan Winters, ever since Blackpool first called his name. It's like a little voice in the back of my mind, telling me I have to do something big, something extra. So when that kind of thing happens, when I feel that . . . special intuition, I try to pay attention to it, let it guide me."

Stephanie was still biting her lip. Then she said, "You're right."

I hardly dared to breathe. "I'm right?"

"I trust you to know what you're doing. And if you say you're being guided by something—something obviously bigger than us, you know, you should do what it's telling you." She smiled bravely. "I'll help you. Whatever you need, I'll do it."

I poured her a little more Diet Coke. "You can't tell anyone at the office. They wouldn't understand. They're so stuck on the way they've always done things, you know."

She grinned. "This is kind of exciting. Like we're secret agents."

"Exactly like secret agents," I pointed out. "I'd get in big, big trouble if anyone at Project Scrooge ever found out what we were doing. We'd both get in big trouble."

"I'm like a vault." She made that lip-zipping motion again and then beamed at me. "I won't breathe a word."

"Cool," I said, and I couldn't help smiling myself. "I knew I could count on you."

"What do you need me to do first?" she asked.

"We have to get into Dave's office. We need to know about the surveillance shifts—who and when each member of his team is assigned to monitor Ethan. And we need a detailed description of Ethan's daily schedule."

"I know just how to get that," she said.

Her badge. Which for some crazy reason would work on Dave's office door when mine wouldn't.

"Cupcakes," she said. "Nobody can resist cupcakes."

"Huh?"

"You'll see."

"Cupcakes!" Stephanie called out in the middle of the hall at exactly 11:30 the next morning. Operation Cupcake, as she called it, was a go. "There are cupcakes in the Go Room!"

That got everyone's attention fast—heads started popping out of doors and people began shuffling down the halls just as fast as their feet would carry them to the free cupcakes. Pretty soon the Go Room was crowded with people stuffing their faces with cupcakes. Plus, we had chips and a veggie tray with dip and soda, and the song "A Holly Jolly Christmas" was playing on the loudspeaker. All Stephanie, by the way. I hated that song.

"I made one just for you. See, it has an M." Stephanie handed a cupcake to Marty, who was staring at her kind of glassy-eyed.

"Uh, thanks, Stephanie," he mumbled. "Thanks a lot."

It wasn't just the cupcakes attracting the attention, either. We'd stayed up all night baking, and somehow in the delirium of this morning, I'd decided to give Stephanie a makeover. So today she was wearing a charcoal-gray pencil skirt and a lavender Dolce & Gabbana top I'd found on the clearance rack at Bloomingdale's a few years ago. The lavender was a good color on her; it brought out the blue of her eyes. It'd be better if she were wearing contacts, but she didn't have any and she was as blind as a bat without her glasses, she said. Still, with the shimmery violet eye shadow and mascara I'd put on her, a dash of blush and highlight on her cheekbones, some mouthwash and a rose-petal-colored lipstick, she was looking much better than usual. I'd curled her long blond hair and pinned it into a simple updo that escaped down her back. She was a bit wobbly in my black suede heels—knockoffs, but more attractive than Stephanie's inventory of terrible flats—but the look rocked on her. She appeared to be a college-age business professional for once. Like a bona fide grown-up.

"Hey, where'd you get the cupca—" Grant shuffled into the Go Room and came to a full stop in front of Stephanie. "Whoa. What happened to you? You look . . . nice."

She frowned, revealing these cute little bumps on her forehead. "You don't like how I usually look?"

Grant scratched the back of his neck. "Oh, no, I love how you usually look. It's just that you look *extra nice* today."

"Thank you." She smiled sweetly. "Hey, could you do me a little favor?"

"Whatever my lady desires," he said.

She laughed. "Could you help me pass these out?"

She handed him a tray of the cupcakes. And off they went together, with Marty following behind hoping for another cupcake.

Out of the corner of my eye I spotted Boz cruising past the Go Room with his typical long-legged strides, but then he paused and came back to the door to watch Stephanie and Co. dispense their sugary goodness. He seemed momentarily confused. "What's going on in here? Is this your doing, Havisham?"

I raised my hands in mock surrender. "Don't look at me. It was all Stephanie's idea. They're French vanilla with fudge frosting."

Boz went over and got a cupcake. "This is delicious," he said between mouthfuls. "Now I need tea."

I pointed to the electric teapot in the corner. Stephanie really had thought of everything. I was going to get some myself, but just then Dave strolled in with a bunch of his people, looking both confused and delighted. Which was what I'd been waiting for.

"Cupcakes! Get a cupcake!" Stephanie sang out.

"I love cupcakes!" Dave exclaimed.

Time for me to go.

There were very few stragglers in the hall, and if I saw one I said something like, "There are cupcakes in the Go Room—hurry and get one before they're gone!" and then they'd start running. Just before I reached Dave's office door, I stopped and looked around. Nobody was watching. I zipped up the Hoodie just in case and pulled on the hood. Then I slipped Stephanie's badge out of my pocket and swiped it. The door beeped and swung open.

I was in.

I took a quick glance around. There was no one in the Surveillance Room. Stephanie was so right: people couldn't resist cupcakes.

I went straight to Dave's computer and searched through his files until I found Ethan's schedule. Then I went into the back room and wrote down a list of all the working cameras that were watching Ethan. Done and done. It'd been like fifteen minutes by then, so I hurried to locate the last piece I needed: the work schedule for Dave's team.

Only I couldn't find it. Dave didn't have it in his computer.

I went to search in his desk. And that's where I discovered a folder with my name on it—HAVISHAM in big black letters across the edge. I'd seen it before—under Boz's arm the first time I'd ever been in his office.

I opened it to a random page and started reading.

1. Excessive materialism, it read in careful familiar-looking handwriting—Boz's, I assumed. *PS: limit her access to money, make her work for what she has. 2. Narcissism, a focus solely on herself with no awareness of the people around her—*

I heard voices in the hall. At the same moment my phone buzzed in my pocket. It was a text from Stephanie.

They're coming! Get out of there QUICK!

I slammed the folder shut and stuck it back where I'd found it. I looked around in a panic, totally freaking out for all of five seconds before I remembered that they wouldn't be able to see me. Hooray for the Hoodie. I only had to be quiet and stay out of their way.

The door beeped, and some guy whose name I didn't know came in with Tox, which was slightly confusing, because Tox was on my team. She didn't belong in Dave's office any more than I did. "My favorite's the peanut-butter kind," she was saying. "There's a shop in Midtown that makes the best peanut-butter-and-jelly ones. I'm serious."

"I prefer carrot," the guy said. "But vanilla with fudge frosting is a close second."

I held my breath as they passed through Dave's office and into the Surveillance Room. Then I tiptoed to the door, turning the handle very, very slowly as I pushed it open. My eyes suddenly focused on the paper taped to the back of the door. It was labeled: *Scrooge 173 Monitoring Schedule.*

My work here was done.

Stephanie was waiting for me when I burst into my office, breathing hard. "Oh my gosh, I'm so sorry, Holly!" she cried when she saw the look on my face. "I did my best, I swear. There were so many people and so much noise and then when I noticed they were gone I ran out in the hall but they were already almost there and—"

"I did it," I managed to gasp as I flopped into my chair.

Her mouth dropped open in a way that reminded me of a cartoon character. "You got the files?" she squeaked. "The stuff you needed? Everything?"

"I got it." I laid the notebook in which I'd written down Ethan's schedule and the camera information on my desk and dug in the Hoodie pocket for the crumpled paper I'd snatched off the door. Finally the smile that had been slowly traveling from my brain to my lips arrived and turned up the corners of my mouth, and then I couldn't stop grinning. "It's all here—everything I need."

"I knew we could do it," Stephanie said. "We make a great team, you know."

We did. It was nice to have someone on my side for once. It

made me think, weirdly, about Ro. How we used to just sit around and make each other laugh.

"The cupcakes were freaking genius," I said.

"I saved you one." Stephanie opened my desk drawer and pulled out a little plate with a beautiful-looking cupcake on it. She set it on the desk in front of me. "Enjoy. You've earned it."

I took a bite. It tasted like sweet, sweet victory.

THIRTEEN

I WENT BACK TO THE pool at the New York Athletic Club that Monday afternoon. According to Dave's handy little schedule, Ethan was there every Monday from four to six.

I kept my Hoodie on this time and watched him for a while. Then, still invisible, I crossed to one end of the pool and waited until he was at the far side. I took the note out of my pocket. I'd written my message in red crayon so it wouldn't run when he picked it up with his wet hands. I folded the paper and left it so it was standing up where he'd be able to see it when he came back this way, on the edge of the pool just over the number three.

I hoped he was as smart as his straight As gave him credit for, because he'd have to figure out the message. I'd made it purposefully ambiguous.

MIDNIGHT, it read in big red-crayon letters. *MEET ME AT THE LEFT LION. LOVE, YOUR FAKE GIRLFRIEND.*

* * *

It was 11:55 when a cab pulled up to the New York Public Library and Ethan got out. His gaze went straight to me where I was sitting on the stone bench next to one of the huge white lion statues that guarded the stairs up to the library. The left one, of course.

"You're early," I observed as he approached. I bit back a smile. He remembered me. He was still interested enough to come out here in the middle of the night.

"I like to be punctual," he replied. "Especially when strange girls are involved. I'm just glad I picked here and not the Central Park Zoo."

"Wait. You think I'm strange?" I asked.

He looked at me hard, like he was trying to figure me out, and he could do that through the powers of simple observation. I was wearing a red tank top, skinny jeans, and black flip-flops. I'd curled my hair, put on a little eyeliner and red lips. This time I'd made an effort.

"How was your swim at the club this afternoon?" I asked him.

He sat down next to me on the bench. "How did you get in and out of there without me seeing you?"

"Maybe you weren't paying attention," I said.

"I was paying attention. I've been waiting for you to show up."

It was so hard not to grin my face off. Instead I arched an eyebrow at him. "What can I say? A magician never shares her secrets."

Or her secret Hoodie.

"So you're into magic?" he asked.

"Well, I do have a few tricks up my sleeve."

"What's your name?" Ethan asked.

"Why, so you can google me?"

"Maybe."

"If you want to find out about me, you'll have to do it the old-fashioned way. You'll have to ask me." I turned to him and clapped my hands together. "We could play Truth or Dare."

"Fine, you go first. Truth or dare?" he asked.

"Truth."

"Why midnight? Why here?"

Right on cue, the bells from one of the cathedrals farther down on Fifth Avenue began to toll.

"Because I'm like the opposite of Cinderella. My ball only starts after midnight."

He looked down at my flip-flops. "I don't see any glass slippers."

"Glass slippers are so last season."

"So you're expecting me to be Prince Charming?" he asked.

I put a finger to my chin like I was thinking. "Are you a prince?"

"No."

"Are you charming?"

"You tell me."

Yes. It was kind of weird, actually. I'd never met a charming Scrooge before.

"You still haven't answered my question," he said.

"It had to be midnight." I leaned close to Ethan's ear. "Because that's as early as I can sneak out." Or: I knew that the surveillance on Ethan was practically nonexistent in the hours between midnight and six, because everyone at the Project assumed that he'd be sleeping. Midnight was usually when I started sifting memories, the nights I worked.

"Did you put pillows and a blond wig in your bed?" he asked.

I laughed. "How did you know?"

"And why here?" He gazed up at the lion's face, which stared impassively across Fifth Avenue.

"I like him. His name is Fortitude. The other one is Patience. Me and Patience have never really gotten along. So is it my turn to ask a question? Or give you a dare?"

"Truth," he said.

"Why did you come? I'm a strange girl, you know. A stranger."

"I was curious," he said.

"You know what they say about curiosity."

"Are you trying to scare me off?"

"No," I said.

"Good."

I was suddenly aware of how little space there was between us. His pupils were so big in this light that his eyes looked black. He smelled like cologne, some amazing designer cologne, no doubt, but I could also detect a hint of chlorine from the pool. At the same moment, we looked at each other's lips, and then quickly away.

When I was planning this interlude I thought the left lion had been a more romantic spot. I'd imagined that it would be beautiful under the shadow of the statue and the branches of a tree that stretched over us, the moon dangling in the sky, the bright-lit buildings like tall lanterns towering all around us, the stream of traffic on Fifth Avenue rushing by like a river of light and noise. I could see the scene like it was being shot as a movie, me in my red tank top, Ethan in his black tee and jeans, creating our own little bubble of privacy in the heart of the city.

But in reality, my butt was sort of numb from the stone bench, and there was a nasty brown puddle at our feet with cigarette butts floating in it, and the scaffolding on the buildings across the street made me feel like we were in a construction zone. The tree looked scraggly, and I couldn't find the moon. The traffic was noisy in a bad way, full of sirens and horns honking and clouds of exhaust puffing out into the air.

"My turn," Ethan said. "Truth or dare?"

"Dare."

He grinned. "I dare you to kiss . . . the lion."

I lifted my eyebrows suggestively. "Okay." I jumped up and planted a kiss on the lion's stony cheek. "Truth or dare."

"Dare," he returned.

"I dare you to kiss . . ."

His expression was hopeful.

". . . my hand," I said, and lifted it up for him.

He sighed and then took my hand in his. Then he brushed his lips against the tops of my knuckles. My heart banged against my ribs.

"Truth or dare," he murmured.

If I said dare, I knew he might ask me to kiss him on the mouth. Lipstick or no lipstick. And I'd do it. "Truth," I rasped.

"Do you have a boyfriend? A real one, I mean?"

"No. I do not."

"How is that possible?"

"That's two questions," I pointed out.

"What's your name?" he asked with a grin.

"Hey, that's three," I laughed, but whatever. "Okay. Fine." I was prepared this time. "I'm Victoria." It was the classiest, most perfect name I could think of. Not Holly, a silly name my mother had insisted on giving me because I was born in Hollywood on December 26—her holiday Hollywood miracle, she used to call me. "Tori, if you want to go shorter."

"What's your last name?"

"Scott."

"Victoria Scott." I watched his lips form the words. "Interesting. My girlfriend is named Victoria Scott."

"Your *fake* girlfriend," I clarified.

"Tori," he tried out. "I'm Ethan Winters."

He left out the III and the part about him being the heir to one of the city's largest real estate companies. Because maybe he thought I would google him.

I smiled. "A pleasure to make your acquaintance, Ethan Winters."

"So tell me about Tori Scott," he said, abandoning the game. "Who are you, besides a single, beautiful, magic-loving girl who likes to run around the city in the middle of the night?"

"Uh, that mostly covers it." Fortunately I had the story for Victoria Scott all mapped out. "I'm an only child. I go to Brearley. I live near the Flatiron . . ." I'd deliberately picked a place not too close to where Ethan lived, so he wouldn't expect to randomly bump into me. "My parents are divorced, so during the week I live with my mom and on weekends, I'm stuck with my dad. So that's me."

I thought, *First off, I'd like to thank the Academy for this incredible honor. . . .* The acting gene that ran in my family was definitely paying off. It was fun, but it also felt . . . less than stellar, somehow, making stuff up to tell Ethan. I wished I could be completely myself. But it wasn't possible, not with the people at Project Scrooge working around the clock to know every move he made. If he started talking about a girl named Holly, I'd be finished. So Victoria it would have to be.

Before Ethan could ask any follow-up questions, I turned the spotlight on him. "What about you? Who is the elusive Ethan Winters?"

"Elusive? That's a stretch, I think. Also an only child," he said. "I go to the Browning School, and I live on the Upper East Side."

"And your parents?"

"My parents are still, relatively speaking, happily married," he said, not quite looking at me as the lie slipped so easily from his lips. "They're boring. My life is pretty boring, actually."

For all of three seconds I imagine I looked pretty surprised. Add the word *liar* to Ethan's list of Scroogey flaws. But I'd just lied for five minutes straight. I was lying about almost everything. I could see why he'd lie about his parents, too. To save me the sob story. To avoid going there.

I recovered. "Your life was boring until I came along," I corrected him.

The corner of his mouth lifted. "Yes. Until you came along. So . . ." He turned to face me. "Truth or dare."

"Truth."

He grinned. "When can I see you again?"

"Hmm. Are you free around New Year's?" I teased.

He grabbed my hand. "You know you want to go out with me."

"Oh, I do?"

"Why else would you go to all this trouble? I must have made an impression last time."

"Maybe."

"Come on. I can show you the world. Shining, shimmering, splendid," he sang. Which totally shocked me. I would never have pegged Ethan as the singing type. Or the Disney type. It was kind of adorable.

I laughed. "You look like a prince," I observed. "But you know that guy Aladdin turned out to be a fraud."

"I'm the real deal," he said softly. "You'll see. Go out with me."

This was everything I'd been fantasizing about all month, this simple thing: the guy asks the girl out, the girl says yes. "I don't know," I said. "Boys, they're so much trouble. They're always so needy, always demanding that you hang on their every word and stroke their ego all the time. Not to mention time-consuming." I gave a little shudder. "Ugh. And it's expensive to go out in the city. Let's face it, a decent meal costs so much these days."

Ethan looked baffled. "That's no problem. I have money."

I gasped like I was shocked. "Do you? I never would have guessed."

His eyes narrowed slightly, looking at my face, and then the tiniest smile appeared on his lips. He'd figured out I was messing with him.

"I don't like to let the guy pay for dinner," I continued cheerfully. "It can give them unreasonable expectations."

"Who said anything about dinner?" he countered.

"I'm not generally available for lunch. I'm a night owl."

"Go out with me." He was still, through all that banter, holding my hand. He put his other hand on top, trapping it. "Come on, I dare you."

This whole thing could rapidly get out of hand, I realized. I wanted to keep seeing Ethan, as much as I possibly could, but every time I saw him in real life I was taking an enormous risk. Still, as long as we stayed outdoors and kept out of his usual patterns, I'd be safe. Probably.

"Okay, okay," I said like I was doing him a big favor. "I'll go out with you. But I get to pick the place."

FOURTEEN

"YOU SEEM LIKE YOU'RE IN a good mood." Stephanie handed me a bottle of sparkling water with a straw in it. I took it and drank a sip, then handed it back. She lowered her voice so Grant and Marty couldn't hear us. "Did you have good luck making contact with you know who?"

"We had a very good conversation." I pulled my hair back into a tight ponytail and then stuck the earbud into my ear. "I'm sure I'm going to be able to help him this way."

This was true, actually. I'd put a spin on what my real motivation was in order to get Stephanie on board with this whole see-Ethan-in-real-life plot, but I did want to help Ethan. And what could be better for a Scrooge than a new, exciting relationship? In fact, even though I'd only seen Ethan twice while he was awake, already he seemed about twenty percent less Scroogey.

"Anything else going on?" Stephanie asked. I was still smiling,

I realized. I straightened out my face.

"Nope. Same old boring afterlife as always." It was Friday night, and I'd been thinking about nothing but Ethan since Monday. It'd been torture waiting for the weekend to come around, when we'd planned to meet up again.

"You ready to see Ethan?" Stephanie asked.

"What?"

"Grant says Ethan's almost in the REM stage," she said.

"Oh. Right. Okay, I'm ready." Of course I couldn't wait to see Ethan again.

"Hey, boss!" Marty and Grant jogged up to me. They were both grinning from ear to ear—never a good sign. "We've got a surprise for you," Marty said. "You'll never guess what it is."

They were staring at me like they expected *me* to give *them* something.

I hated surprises. "So? What is it?" I asked.

"You're supposed to guess."

I also hated guessing. "But you said I'd never be able to guess."

"Yeah, but—" Marty wiped a hand down the front of his face and sighed, but he was grinning again when he put his hand down. "All right, fine. Here." He grabbed my hand and put something in it.

"You're welcome," said Grant.

It was a familiar coil of fine silver wire connecting two electrodes.

"It's the transducer," I said, confused.

"It's the *new* transducer. We've made some improvements."

Marty grabbed the transducer back from me and unrolled it. Then, without even asking for permission, he stuck one of the electrodes to my temple.

I didn't feel anything different. "Okay. Thank you?"

"Just wait until you see what it can do." They took my hands and pulled me over to the monitoring station.

There, on one of the screens, was Ethan, lying on his back with one arm thrown over his head.

"Here." Grant pointed to another monitor.

It was, as far as I could tell, a video feed of the monitor itself. Which showed the monitor, and a little monitor inside of that one, and an even tinier one inside of that one, and back and back. An eternity of monitors.

Marty and Grant high-fived each other. "It works!" Grant said. "Well, I mean, at least the visual part works. We'll still have to test the other part."

"The other part." I was starting to get a bad feeling about this little invention, whatever it was.

"Let's test it real quick," Marty said. "Close your eyes, Holly."

I frowned. "I don't think I—"

"Come on, boss! You're going to love this," Grant pleaded. "Trust me."

"Do it in the name of science," said Marty.

Stephanie looked at me and smiled. "I bet it's going to be neat."

She was back to wearing her own quirky clothes—a blue top with little gray foxes all over it, black pants, and a gray button-up sweater. My gaze went instantly to her feet—her ballet flats had rabbit ears sticking out of the fronts.

My makeover hadn't stuck. So very sad.

"Whatevs." I closed my eyes.

"Now, no matter what happens, don't think about an elephant," Marty said.

Which of course made me instantly picture an elephant.

"Oh, wow!" Stephanie gasped from beside me.

"How about a pink elephant?" Grant said.

Then the three of them, Marty, Grant, and Stephanie, all burst out laughing.

"That's amazing!" Stephanie said. "So, what, you can read what she's thinking?"

Uh-oh.

"Yeah, if she's thinking about an image—it only reads what she sees and hears, not her actual thoughts," said Marty.

"What that means," explained Grant, "is that now we can actually see not only what's going on inside of the Lamp's head, but what's happening inside of a Scrooge's brain when she connects with him. We'll be able to see everything Holly sees, and we can even record it so we can analyze it later—maybe show clips of it at the weekly meetings, et cetera."

He and Marty high-fived again.

This was bad. The last thing I wanted was for the entire company to be able to see what was going on inside of my head. Or Ethan's head, for that matter. I opened my eyes and tore the electrode off my head. "You know, guys, I don't think this is a good idea. . . ."

I trailed off. Because Boz had just entered the room.

"Hello, Team Lamp," he greeted us with his usual deadly cheerful smile. "How are we today?"

"What are you doing here?" I asked.

"I came to witness this new gadget these two geniuses have come up with." He shook hands with Grant and Marty. "Won't that be something, to see what you see?"

"That will be something," I agreed faintly.

Grant checked Ethan's vitals on a monitor. "Ethan's ready."

Terrific.

Boz patted me on the shoulder. "You don't mind if I watch you work, do you, Havisham?"

I plastered a smile on my face. "Of course not."

"Splendid." Boz took a seat behind the monitors.

Stephanie handed me the Hoodie, and I put it on. Grant checked the sound levels for my earbud. We dimmed the lights and fired up the Portal, I put up the hood, and then I was in Ethan's bedroom.

I was understandably nervous. I was also pretty disappointed, like crushed, at the idea that I wasn't going to be able to dig up any more of Ethan's memories of us. Not so long as everyone could follow along. Stupid Grant and Marty. Inventing things. I never asked them to invent things. Why couldn't they just do the bare minimum at their jobs like everyone else?

Good mood gone.

I took my time getting over to Ethan's bed. He was sleeping soundly, one arm still curled around his head. It was quiet except for the deep, rhythmic chuff of his breath.

I sprayed him with the lavender deep-sleep mist.

"You're good to go, Holly," said Grant in my ear. "He's ready."

I took out the new transducer and applied it, first to his head and then to mine.

A few minutes ago I'd hoped that Ethan might be dreaming about me, but now I was praying he wasn't. Then I'd have some serious explaining to do.

The minute I touched his hand, I saw the pool, but I didn't let us stay there for more than a split second, on the off chance that we'd come face-to-face with Victoria. I hurried us right into the stores of his memories and started to move past the barrage of images and sensations that flooded through my brain.

There was the little girl in the tiara.

The smell of rain on a hot city sidewalk.

A landscape of barren red rocks—Mars? Why was he thinking about Mars, of all things?

"Whoa, this is so awesome," came Grant's voice in my ear. "We can see everything."

Yeah. Awesome. Right.

"Um, this is all good stuff, Holly," said Grant a little hesitantly, "but Boz says that you should seek out the Fezziwig."

Oh good, now Boz was going to be telling me how to do my job. As if I didn't know I was supposed to be looking for the Fezziwig—that was this month's assignment, as usual. But if Boz wanted the Fezziwig, I'd find the stupid Fezziwig.

This time I thought I'd check out Ethan's mom as the Fezziwig.

From what I'd seen in Ethan's memories, his mom had been pretty cool, before his dad had died, anyway. Then she'd essentially had the same reaction to losing her spouse that my dad did. She'd found a replacement—a new husband and an entirely new life, which wasn't fair to Ethan, but still, she'd tried to be a good mom. She was kind. Generous with people. Talented at what she did—she was a world-class photographer, Dave had informed us once. All of these were qualities of a good Fezziwig. And I also knew that Ethan's mom liked a good party. Because when he thought of the word *party*, he immediately connected it to his mother.

I went back into Ethan's memory bank, looking for a Christmas party with his mom, and almost immediately I stumbled upon a great one.

Christmas music blared from a stereo in the corner of the living room. The air was full of good smells: trays of roast ham and turkey, fresh-baked rolls, and pumpkin pie. Ethan's mom was wearing a white apron with holly leaves embroidered around the edges, and she was singing along to the music.

Ethan, however—the seven-year-old version—was not in the best mood.

"Oh my God, he's, like, adorable," came Grant's voice in my ear.

"Do I have to wear this?" Ethan complained loudly, shuffling into the kitchen struggling to pull a red sweater vest over his head. Even back then, Ethan had the good sense to oppose sweater vests.

"You look very handsome," his mother insisted, tucking in his shirt and then smoothing down his hair.

"Come on, Mom," he bellyached. "I hate this. It's lame."

"And . . . there he is," Grant observed. "That's Ethan, all right."

I wanted to tell him to shut up, but this time it would be on tape. And in front of Boz.

The doorbell buzzed. Ethan's mom turned back to the stove. "Ethan, sweetie, can you be the doorman for this party? Let people in for me? Take their coats?"

He made a face at her.

"That's my good boy."

His dad entered the room buttoning up a red-and-green plaid shirt. He smelled like soap and aftershave, and his hair was still wet from the shower.

"Do I have to wear this?" he asked, frowning.

She produced a sprig of mistletoe from her apron pocket and dangled it over his head. "Come here, you."

"Well, if I must," he said with a sly smile.

"You must. You simply must."

They kissed. When they came apart his dad was holding a square silver box. He waggled his eyebrows up and down and put it in his wife's hand. "I feel the need to decorate you this fine evening," he said.

Inside was a ring with a set of blue stones across the top. Ethan's mom gasped when she saw it. "Baby! This is beautiful." She put it on the ring finger of her right hand and then pulled it in to her chest. "This is too much. We can't afford it."

"We can't afford this party, either," he said. "But some things are worth sacrificing for. That's what you said, right?"

"Yes," she agreed. "We should spend money on things that bring us together. I'm not sure this brings us together, but thank you."

"Sure it brings us together," said Ethan's dad. "Look." He pulled her in for another kiss, a deeper, much more passionate kiss this time.

Kid Ethan thought the kissing was disgusting. Mostly Grown Up Ethan, who was reliving the moment with me, like a dream, missed his dad and his mom so much in that moment that both he and I felt it like a physical pain, a phantom limb that was severed a long time ago and could never be reattached. As usual, I knew that feeling all too well.

The door buzzed again.

"Is anyone going to get that?" Jack materialized from the hallway. Her gaze landed on her kissing parental units. "Gross, you two. Get a room."

I never thought it was gross when my parents kissed. I'd gone to the set once when I was four or five, when my mom was shooting her TV show, and I'd seen another man kiss her while they were filming a scene. I'd ruined the take by running up and kicking that guy in the shin. Hard.

A stranger kissing my mother—that was gross.

But when my parents kissed, it always looked like what they should be doing.

"Uh, Holly?" Grant said in my ear.

My mom loved parties, too, only she hadn't been my Fezziwig: that honor had gone to my great-aunt on my dad's side—Sonja, who never met a party she didn't like and often invited all the area's homeless to the celebration. But my mom . . . my mom used to throw parties regularly at our old house in Beverly Hills, which was where we lived before she died and my dad moved us out to Malibu. I remember going downstairs in my pajamas on the mornings of those parties and seeing her already at work preparing for the night's festivities: the glasses laid out sparkling in row after row, the mounds of plates and bundles of napkins and silverware piled high, the gardener stringing lights up around the back patio and dropping floating flowers into the pool, the smell of the most mouthwatering food on the planet wafting through the air.

She loved Christmas parties most of all, I think. Christmas had been a big deal in her family—she'd grown up back east and hadn't moved to California until she was fifteen, and some part of her never left my grandma's big white house in snowy Vermont. Her family would start celebrating the holiday season the day after Thanksgiving and wouldn't stop until the first of January. There was a special sausage soup they'd eat on Christmas and a special eggnog-like drink with coconut and rum, and let's not forget the turkey. My mother freaking loved turkey. She was a vegetarian for most of the year, but not at Christmas. She loved Christmas so much.

"Uh, Holly," said Grant. "I think you've lost the memory. I don't know what we're getting here, but it's . . . something else. Not the party."

Except that last Christmas. My grandma came to take care of her that last Christmas, and she cooked up all my mom's favorites: sweet potatoes and mashed potatoes and a three-bean salad that'd been my great-grandmother's recipe, stuffing and green bean casserole and homemade rolls, and she'd made my favorite: cinnamon rolls, which we also ate on Christmas morning. But my mother refused to eat any of it.

"What, you want me to be a cow?" she spat, which was ridiculous because she had to weigh only about seventy-five pounds by then.

My grandma kept trying. Kept offering. Kept cooking and bringing the meals to my mother in bed.

"I can't even taste anything!" my mother screamed, and then she threw the plate of gingerbread cookies against the wall, where it shattered.

She knew she was going to die by then. That was all she could taste.

"Stop it," my grandma said. "You're feeling sorry for yourself."

"Why shouldn't I feel sorry for myself?" she cried. "What, you want me to just lie down and make my peace? Say I'm ready to go, and thank God for it? No!"

"You need to think of your daughter."

Her eyes flitted to me, where I was standing near the door. "I can't bear to think about her. I can't."

I ran out of the room when she said that. Later Dad found me sitting at the edge of the pool with my legs in the water, crying silently. He sat down beside me. He'd probably heard about what happened. I mean, she'd been screaming so loud, everybody probably heard her. Everybody knew.

He didn't say anything, but he sat with me until the sun went down and I got cold, and then he said I should go in.

"Sometimes I hate her," I whispered.

"It's okay. She didn't mean it, you know. She loves you. She's just scared."

I shook my head. "No. It's not okay. Sometimes I wish she would die already."

It was the worst thing to say, but it was true. I did mean it, which was the unforgivable thing about this memory.

Memory. I was in a memory. Wait.

"Holly! Come in, Holly!" Grant was almost shouting at me. I blinked a few times.

Oh crap. Where was Ethan? I'd totally lost my connection.

"I'm sorry," I gasped.

"Boz says you should come on back, Holly," Grant said in my ear. "Just come back."

When I came through the Portal, everyone was quiet. Stephanie was clutching a tissue, her eyes red-rimmed and her face all blotchy. Grant and Marty both looked faintly embarrassed. Even Boz was solemn. I expected him to give me a kind of lecture on how I should have stayed focused on Ethan, but instead he just said, "That was . . . vivid. I didn't know it would be like that."

He didn't know the half of how vivid it could be. He hadn't felt what Ethan felt. What I felt. He didn't know anything about what that was like.

I nodded. "I keep telling you, you should pay me more to do this job."

I went to pass by him, but he put a hand on my shoulder. "Holly . . ."

I coughed to clear my throat. "Look, I screwed up. I'm sorry. But we've got the Fezziwig on the books now, right? That's all that matters, isn't it?" I glanced around. "Can we all agree that his mom is the Fezziwig?"

"Yes. The Fezziwig. It would seem so." Boz let me go, and I fled to my office.

It took a while for me to calm down. I sat at my desk and turned my dad's watch over and over in my hand, remembering. I hadn't thought about that day for a long time—the day my mom went half crazy and threw my grandma's cookies at the wall. The sound of that plate shattering. The look on my grandmother's face when she said, "Stop it."

There was a light tap at the door. Stephanie.

"I brought you some tea." She handed me a mug. The heat felt good on my hands, which were like ice.

"Are you okay?" she asked as I sipped at it slowly. "That was intense for me just watching. I can't imagine how it would be for you."

"All in a day's work."

She bit her lip and looked at her bunny shoes. "My mom died, too, you know. I was little, and I don't remember much, but . . ."

I didn't want to talk about it. "Everybody's mother dies," I said. "It doesn't make you special." I was referring to myself there, not her. But hurt flashed in her big blue eyes.

"You're right. Of course, you're right. Anyway. I thought maybe you might want to do something this weekend," she said. "Maybe go shopping or see a movie . . ."

For a second I was actually tempted by her offer. Movies almost always made me forget myself. But then I remembered.

"I can't this weekend." I sat up a little, finding a hint of my smile again. Okay, so tonight had been a disaster, and totally not what I'd been hoping for, but Ethan wouldn't remember it—it was locked away in his subconscious brain. I still had Ethan in the Real World to think about. To look forward to.

"Sorry," I said to Stephanie. "I have plans."

FIFTEEN

"THIS IS A DATE, RIGHT?" Ethan turned to grin at me. We were standing against the bright orange rail on the bow of the Staten Island Ferry. It was past four in the morning. The breeze was blowing Ethan's hair around in the most adorable way. His eyes were deep blue tonight, and I kept finding myself staring into them.

"Yes," I answered. "Why, does it not seem like a date to you?" A few hours earlier, we'd had dinner on the roof of the Kimberly Hotel under a canopy of little white lights with the Midtown cityscape looming in the background. Which in my mind definitely felt like a date, except for the two-minute ride in the hotel elevator, where I caught sight of the surveillance camera on the ceiling and considered whether or not Dave could have possibly been watching us. Which was silly of me, because of course Dave wouldn't be watching some random elevator in a random hotel. Still, I felt much safer when we were outside in the open. Like there on the boat, where it felt like we were setting out on some big adventure. Which, in some ways, we kind of were.

"It's not like any date I've ever been on," Ethan said.

"Have you been on a lot of dates?" I arched an eyebrow at him.

He smiled like he was almost afraid to tell me. "A few."

I put my elbow against the rail and leaned my chin into my hand. "And where did you go, on these few dates you've had?"

"Dinner. Movies. Concerts. I took a girl to a Broadway show once."

I gasped like I was so jealous. "Which one?"

"The one with the witch?" He obviously couldn't remember the name.

"Oh, the deeply misunderstood witch, the one who's actually the good guy even though we've been taught to think she's the villain," I clarified. I'd sneaked into that one with my Hoodie once. I'd liked it, for obvious reasons. "And was she impressed, this girl you took to the theater?"

"I guess."

I turned to look out at the city. The water along the edge of the river seemed gold, there were so many lights reflecting off it, and in the distance, where the water was black and absolutely empty, we could see the faint blue pillar of the Statue of Liberty. New York was starting to grow on me. Finally. The air was cool and tinged with salt. I felt alive, so completely alive again, just standing there with Ethan as the boat skimmed over the water, looking out at the glowing city.

But Ethan was looking at me. "Are you cold?"

I was fine, but I said, "Why, are you going to offer me your jacket?"

"No. I was just curious," he said, and I laughed, and he laughed, and when we stopped laughing he had his arm around me.

"This is better," he said.

"Much better," I agreed. "And warmer."

"Tell me more about you," he said. "I want to know."

I couldn't help the little wrinkle of a frown that popped up for a few seconds. There was not much I could tell him, not much in my life that was normal or real. But I made up some stuff about the situation with my overbearing "dad," who started to sound more and more like Boz the more I talked about him.

"He sounds pretty frustrating, your dad," Ethan said after a while.

"He is. But he cares." I tucked a stray piece of hair behind my ear. "At least there's that."

Ethan nodded, his eyes suddenly distant, and I realized the idea of a dad out there caring about you must be painful for him. I tried to backpedal.

"Still. My dad's so freaking condescending," I said. "He always thinks he knows what's best for me. But he doesn't even really know me. He doesn't bother to find out who I am. He just tells me what to do."

"I get that," Ethan said. "Is your dad starting to blab on and on about the future, and how bright it is? I hate it when they talk about the future."

"College, you mean?" I asked. My dad—my real dad, not

Boz—had only talked college with me one time. He'd said he'd hoped I'd go to USC or UCLA or Pepperdine, somewhere local, so I wouldn't go away and leave him all alone.

"That's the point of college, isn't it?" I'd told him. "To get away from our parents."

Yes, I'd been a little brat. Or maybe even a big one.

"Not just college. The future," Ethan said, pronouncing the word *future* like it was in all caps. "My dad was—is—always talking about how amazing the future is going to be. How I'm going to grow up to be this supergenius, world-altering person. But I keep thinking, maybe not. Maybe I'm just a regular person. And maybe the future is going to suck. You don't know."

"So you're, like, a total optimist," I teased.

"I would say I'm a realist," he said. "I just think, we don't get promised anything good in this life. Bad things happen all the time. They're happening right now, somewhere out there. They'll keep happening. Who knows? Maybe this moment, right here, is as good as I'm ever going to be."

He leaned closer. His eyes dropped to my lips. I sucked in a breath. I was weirdly nervous about kissing Ethan. Like it was all fun and games until someone got kissed. And then it would be really real.

I pulled back. "So is this the part where you say, 'We don't know what will happen tomorrow, so we better live for tonight, baby'?" I laughed. "That's your big move?"

He made a production of removing his arm from around me. "Not anymore."

"Aw." I made a sympathetic noise. "I blew it, didn't I?"

"You did," he said, but he was smiling.

I turned to face him and put my arms around his neck, like we were going to start slow dancing to a song only we could hear. "Just so you know, I don't think you're a regular person."

"You don't?"

"I don't think you're a supergenius, either, though. But you're pretty cute."

He winced. "Cute."

"Very cute," I said.

"Well, I think you're downright adorable," he said.

"Hey!"

"Like a kitten," he added, his hands settling on my waist in a way that made my pulse pick up. "An orange and white stripy kitten."

"Oh, but you're cute like a puppy," I said. "A golden retriever puppy. Wrapped in a pink fuzzy blanket. With a bow around its neck."

"Oh, man." He pulled me a little closer. "That's horrible."

"Right? You're so cute it makes me want to—"

He was looking at my mouth again. God, we were like magnets pulling toward each other. We had been since the beginning. He leaned in. Our lips were inches apart.

"Puke," I murmured.

He sighed and closed his eyes. "Hey, Tori, are you ever going to let me kiss you?"

"Let you? Shouldn't it be kind of mutual?" I rasped.

"Isn't it kind of mutual?" His eyes opened and searched mine. I bit my lip.

"All right, it's totally mutual," I agreed. I leaned up and pressed my lips to his. Kissing him felt like falling, in a way. It felt like jumping without a net.

"Okay," he breathed when we finally pulled apart. "Wow."

I put my hand over my mouth, kind of shocked. I mean, I'd just kissed the Scrooge. There was no turning back now. It was happening. It was real.

He leaned in again but I stepped back.

"That was . . . amazing, but now maybe we could just get to know each other better?" I suggested faintly. "I'd like to talk."

"I love to talk," he said, which was funny because I knew that wasn't true, but he didn't know I knew that wasn't true. "I'll talk your ear off."

I laughed. "Please don't. I like my ears where they are."

"Me too." He pretended to inspect one of my ears. "You have very nice ears."

My ears? That had to be, like, the least attractive part of me. And his breath against the back of my neck was making me crazy. I shivered and pushed back from him. "Talk."

"Okay, talk," he agreed.

So that's what we did—we talked. For hours, we rode the ferry back and forth, and we talked. I invented some more nonsense about people at my school and class and my imaginary life, and Ethan complained about how much he hated all the hoop-jumping you had to do to get through school, and how maybe he wanted to take a year off before he went to college. We chatted about the music we liked and places we wanted to see in the world and politics and even a little bit about fashion, and then the sun came up, blazing over the water, coloring us both with gold.

Ethan yawned and checked his watch. "This was fun, but I'm going to have to sleep at school now."

"Dream of me," I told him, which was an inside joke. But that's also what it felt like with Ethan. Like I was living a kind of dream.

And also kind of like I was waking up.

"We're ready whenever you are, Holly," Grant said. "Holly? *Holly?*"

I blinked. I was standing in front of the glowing door in the Transport Room, about to cross back into Ethan's apartment. Back to work.

"Earth to Holly?" Grant said into the microphone. "Come in, Holly."

Stephanie touched my shoulder. "Do you need anything?" The big blue eyes behind her glasses were concerned.

I shook my head. "Sorry. I'm fine. I'm ready."

The lights in the Transport Room dimmed. The door started to hum. I opened the door slowly, padding silently into Ethan's apartment. I knew the floor plan so well by now I could navigate his bedroom easily in the dark, slipping silently around the edge of his bed to the side where he was sleeping.

He sighed and turned over to face me.

God, he really was the most insanely beautiful boy I'd ever seen. He smelled amazing, for one thing, even his breath, which washed over me as the air moved in and out from between his slightly parted lips. My head swam with it—his beauty, his scent, his heat. I felt like I could just stand there indefinitely, watching him, close enough to see every curving eyelash, the slight dent in his chin. All it would take would be for me to lean forward about two feet. I could be the Prince to his Snow White in the glass casket, and wake him with a kiss.

I couldn't stop thinking about our kiss on the boat. How amazing and right it had felt. How good.

"Geez, she's just standing there," came Grant's voice in my ear. "Holly?"

I coughed and moved back a little. *Act normal,* I told myself. *Do the job.*

I walked myself through all the usual business: the transducer, holding his hand, merging into his dreams. But when I arrived inside Ethan's mind, he was dreaming about me.

He was dreaming about me!

In the dream we were standing at the edge of the ferry. Only in the dream, Ethan was wearing a business suit. I was wearing a little red dress. I could see myself from his perspective, staring into my own brown eyes, rubbing a soft golden curl of my hair between his fingers, honing in on my lips. I could even see the stupid little zit, although Ethan didn't think anything of it.

"This is a date, right?" he murmured. He lowered his head to kiss me.

"What the . . . ," I heard Grant say in disbelief. Because Grant could totally see what I saw. Because of the stupid new transducer.

This was all being televised at the office. And recorded.

Everything happened very fast then. I yanked away from Ethan, both physically and mentally, and ripped off the transducer. Which totally woke him up.

He jerked upright in bed. I stumbled away from him.

"Who is that?" he called out, his voice sharp. It was dark—thank God it was dark—but he still saw someone there. A shadow. "What are you doing in my room?"

I pulled the hood over my head and vanished.

Ethan turned on the lamp next to the bed and leapt to his feet. The sudden light blinded me. I crept to a corner of the room and waited, hardly daring to breathe, as Ethan looked around. He checked by every large piece of furniture. He looked under his bed. He threw open the closet, which about gave me a heart attack, but there was nothing there but the neat line of his shirts. The closet door wasn't the Portal anymore, because Grant kept the Portal closed during the time I was in a Scrooge's bedroom, opening it only for the few minutes it took me to come in and out. Which was company policy because of situations such as these.

"Tori?" Ethan whispered.

Maybe he could smell me, I thought. Or sense me, somehow. I pressed my eyes closed. I didn't know what I was going to do. Without the Portal I'd have to get out the hard way. The elevator. The doorman. The street. Or I could just stay here and wait for Ethan to go back to sleep. Which, judging by the freaked-out look on his face, could be a really long time.

But then another door slammed loudly somewhere else in the

apartment. Ethan whipped around toward the sound and then strode out of the room.

I ran to the closet door.

"Now, Grant, now," I whispered fervently. "Get me out of here."

The edge of the door began to glow, and I opened it and tumbled back into the Transport Room. I shut the door and leaned against it, gasping for breath. The lights came up. Grant, Marty, and Stephanie all ran up to me.

"Holy crap, Holly!" said Grant.

"Dude," said Marty, his face almost green. "Dude."

Stephanie tried to smile, but her face was pale, too. "Well, that was a close one," she said with a nervous laugh.

Of course there had to be an incident report on the whole thing. It was a Code 2319, after all, which was shorthand for: HOLY CRAP THE SCROOGE IS AWAKE!

In the entire history of the company, it had only ever happened twice before. It was Stephanie's quick thinking (she'd had the idea to open a Portal in another room and then slam the door to draw Ethan out of his bedroom) that had allowed me to return to Project Scrooge safely. And I'd left the transducer on the floor. Which meant the team had to go back to get it.

It'd been a tough night.

"So do you want to tell me what happened?" Boz asked as I sat across from him at his desk the following morning.

"I don't really know what happened."

"The tape shows something I don't know how to interpret," he said grimly. "It appears as though Mr. Winters saw *you* in his mind. He was dreaming of you."

I thought up a lie, and I thought it up quick.

"It wasn't Ethan's mind you saw in the video." I rubbed my hand over my face like I had a headache. "It was mine."

Boz's bushy eyebrows were low over his dark eyes. "Yours."

"I was imagining that . . ." I trailed off guiltily. "I guess I just pictured . . . Ethan and me . . . together."

Boz's eyebrows lifted. "I see."

"I'm so sorry. It won't happen again."

He scribbled something down on a piece of paper. "The footage also shows that you didn't apply the deep-sleep spray when you first entered the room. Which explains why Mr. Winters woke up."

I was starting to feel slightly sick to my stomach. This was bad, so bad.

"I'm sorry," I said again. "I don't know how I forgot."

"You've been distracted lately," he said. "You're unfocused, Havisham, and you're making small mistakes, like that sift when you remembered your own mother instead of Ethan's. You were very late finding the Fezziwig. You're even filing your paperwork incorrectly. If it weren't for Stephanie, you'd be a total disaster."

He paused. I realized that he was waiting for me to explain myself.

"I'm sorry," I said again.

His frown deepened. "Are you developing feelings for Ethan Winters?"

The question seemed to hang in the air for several seconds

before I finally sputtered, "Feelings for Ethan? For a Scrooge?"

"It wouldn't be so surprising," Boz said. "You're spending a great deal of time with this boy."

I froze.

"You're inside his head, privy to his dreams, his fears and desires, his joys and sorrows, his most private inner thoughts and most treasured memories. There's a level of intimacy that comes with that. And you're a young girl, and he's a young man, and he's somewhat attractive. Under these conditions, it'd be easy for you to become confused about your feelings."

"Confused about my feelings," I repeated.

"What we do here at Project Scrooge is personal. There's no avoiding that. I come to love every single one of the Scrooges, in my way. Which is why it's so painful if it doesn't work for them, and why we all try so hard to make sure that it does work out. But you must try to remember that this is not about you, dear," Boz said. "This is about Ethan Winters. His fate. His soul. Not yours."

"Right. Ethan Winters."

"It's personal, but it mustn't become too personal."

If only he knew how personal it was between Ethan and me. It had always been personal. We were so alike, Ethan and I. I mean, the similarities were pretty crazy when I thought about it. Seventeen years old? Check. Filthy rich? Check. Dead parent? Check. Doomed to be killed by a car? Double check.

I shivered. Some part of me would always hear that noise in the back of my mind. The squeal of brakes.

"Havisham?" Boz prompted.

I tried to lighten the mood. "Maybe we should come up with a professional-detachment-in-the-workplace seminar for all the employees, like a Scrooge harassment training thing."

He stared at me. "What?"

"Joke."

"Oh. Ha-ha." He actually attempted to laugh. "A seminar. Yes. Now, as I was saying, it's very important for us to maintain a certain level of distance and objectivity. Is that clear, Havisham?"

"Crystal."

"Wonderful." He wrote a few more things down in his notepad. "I'm almost glad we had this little mishap. It gave us this chance to talk."

I suddenly felt tired. It was exhausting keeping up with it all, pretending to be someone else when I was with Ethan, pretending that Ethan was just an ordinary Scrooge when I was at work.

"Yeah," I said. "Great talk."

SIXTEEN

TIME STARTED TO FLY. THIS is the part where, if my life were a movie, there'd be a montage, and you'd see Ethan and me on a series of dates all throughout that fall: tasting our way through the delights of Chelsea Market, wandering the High Line slurping Popsicles, watching Shakespeare in Central Park. The trees started to turn red and the air finally cooled. At least once a week Ethan and I met at the left lion and wandered the city together, almost always outside, away from the reach of Dave's prying cameras. It was nice, being with Ethan. It was more than nice. It felt . . . normal. Like I was a normal girl, instead of a dead one. I was alive.

It was also complicated. I wanted to be with Ethan, but what did that mean for Christmas? For the Project? For me?

These were questions I didn't know how to answer. I just knew I had to keep seeing him.

Then one day I was in a meeting that was going just fine until

Dave said, totally out of the blue, "Oh, I almost forgot," and took a photograph out of his folder and slid it to the center of the table. "I think she might be Ethan's Belle."

The Belle was my job, not Dave's. So I was understandably surprised.

"What?" I grabbed the eight-by-ten and pulled it toward me. It was a surveillance photo from one of Dave's cameras. It was a bit grainy, but you could still tell that this girl was gorgeous. She was wearing a white Badgley Mischka gown that made my breath catch, with a high front and a swooping back, a jeweled belt at the waist. Her long dark hair was pulled back into a simple, sleek ponytail. Clean, minimal makeup. A breathtaking beaded handbag.

"Where is this?" I asked.

"A fund-raiser Ethan attended last week," Dave answered.

Well. I was of the opinion that you should never wear that kind of dress to a fund-raiser—not in white. Too bridal. And Ethan was meeting a girl at a fund-raiser last week? I'd seen him two days ago, and he had never said anything about it.

My stomach did this weird twisty thing.

"Who is she?" Boz asked.

"I was hoping Holly could tell me," Dave said. "I only know that when she showed up at the dinner, Ethan began to act strangely. Like they had a history."

A history. I swallowed.

"I haven't seen her in Ethan's head before," I said. I was reasonably sure, anyway. Not that I had been looking very hard yet for the Belle. I wasn't too eager to see memories of Ethan with another girl, even one who broke his heart. I guess that was because the Scrooge was usually still secretly pining away for the Belle. Which was what made her such an effective tool on Christmas.

I coughed. "So far it's been like you said: Ethan's got a different girl at every party. But no one special. No ex-girlfriend."

"Maybe I'm wrong." Dave smiled vaguely. "It was just intuition on my part, nothing solid. But I was thinking that it's possible that Ethan's relationship with the Belle is yet to come. Maybe he's about to fall in love."

The twisty feeling in my stomach got even twistier. Normally the Belle was in the past. She'd already broken up with the Scrooge well before we arrived on the scene. The idea that Ethan's Belle was yet to come, well . . . that could royally mess things up for me. That would be horrible.

"That would be ideal," said Boz. "Love can be an excellent motivator for change. Falling in love can help us to see the things in life that are truly important. It can make us want to be better people. It can teach us to sacrifice what is in our own best interest for the sake of someone else. I hope Ethan does fall in love with this girl. For his sake." He turned to me. "You'll need to go looking for Ethan's history with her immediately. Find out who she is. Where their connection lies. What's happened between them."

"I'll get right on that," I said faintly.

He turned back to Dave. "What's your progress on the Tiny Tim?"

Dave blew out an exaggerated breath. "This one is hard to pin down. I'm thinking Daniel Denton's mother. I'm still certain that the Cratchit is Denton—he continues to exert a Scrooge-like control over the boy—and Dent's only family connection is his mother, so she's the natural choice. But I'm not sure yet."

"Perhaps you should be paying attention to your own duties instead of Havisham's," Blackpool said from the end of the table. "Mind your own business?"

Everyone turned to gape at Blackpool, and then back at Dave, whose stubbly face was turning a deep shade of red. I usually didn't agree with Blackpool about anything, but this time he was right. Dave should do his job, and let me do mine. But wait, why was Blackpool suddenly speaking up for me? That was suspicious.

"Hey. Boz said that we should be helping each other," piped up Stephanie from her seat next to mine. "Da—Copperfield was just trying to help."

"Indeed," growled Blackpool. "You're so very helpful, Copperfield."

"No, Little Dorrit is right," Boz said. "We should help each other. There's always been some overlap between the Ghosts. We are working together for a common purpose, after all."

"And I've got the Tiny Tim," Dave said. "I just don't know what the TTF is yet."

"The TTF?" Stephanie asked.

Boz smiled at dear, dumb Stephanie. "Part of what we do here at Project Scrooge is not only to rehabilitate a wayward individual, but to seek to understand each Scrooge's potential to affect the world. When a Scrooge decides to change his ways, it can often make an essential difference in other people's lives, not just his own."

Stephanie whipped out her notebook and wrote that down, of course. "Can you give me an example?"

"All right," Boz said. "We once had a Bob Cratchit who was a housekeeper named Elena."

I froze.

Boz didn't look at me as he continued. "Elena had a young daughter named Nika, and very early on Blackpool got the impression that if young Nika grew up, she'd become a doctor. Not just a doctor, though. A world-famous surgeon."

At the other end of the table, Blackpool was frowning deeply again, like he didn't enjoy having his name drawn into it. Or maybe he just didn't like to be reminded of my case, which was probably the first significant failure the company had experienced in years. And also why he'd never tried to hide that he didn't like me.

"So the little girl, Nika, could grow up to save hundreds of lives as a surgeon," Stephanie said. "Which could have an enormous impact, like a ripple effect."

I was staring under the table at my shoes now.

"But what happened to Nika?" Stephanie asked.

"Well, one evening, as Blackpool predicted, this particular Scrooge kept Elena working late . . . ," Boz said.

It'd been the day before I died—I'd told Elena that she had to vacuum out my car before she went home, after she made my dinner and did the dishes and put fresh sheets on my bed.

"And then Elena stayed nearly an hour longer, instead of coming home," Boz continued. "She forgot that she was supposed to be home early to be with her daughter while her mother, who usually watched the child during the day, picked up another shift at the restaurant where she worked. So Elena was late. And Nika tried to cook dinner for herself. And there was a fire. . . ."

Stephanie made a distressed noise. I kept looking at my shoes. I hadn't even heard about the fire. I'd been killed the next morning after yoga. I mean, Blackpool had shown me what would happen when he came to me that Christmas. He'd even taken me to the funeral after, to see how Elena's family was so totally broken up, how Elena's life was essentially ruined by the death of her daughter. But I hadn't believed him at the time. I'd laughed it off.

"Do all the Tiny Tims die?" Stephanie asked quietly.

"Not all," Boz said. "But if the Scrooge doesn't repent, there is always a negative impact to the Tiny Tim. It's not just about the Scrooge, you see. It's about every person the Scrooge touches. A ripple effect, as you said. We call this the Tiny Tim Factor."

"TTF. So I guess it's really important that we figure all of this out," Stephanie concluded.

"Yes, it is. And we usually do," Boz said more cheerfully. "We have a fairly good track record."

A good track record, with a few notable exceptions. Just put a big fat *F* in the middle of my forehead. Right then I could have punched Boz for bringing up Elena and Nika. And Dave for smiling at me so sympathetically. And Stephanie just because.

"Do you have anything to add, Havisham?" Boz asked.

I glanced up at him, startled. What could he expect me to say? It wasn't like what happened to Nika was directly my fault. And even if it was, I couldn't change it now.

"About Ethan?" he added.

Oh. Ethan. "I'll investigate the Belle," I said. "And I could sift memories with this Denton kid and look for a Tiny Tim figure. If that would be helpful." I smiled at Dave.

He nodded. "Thanks."

"No problem," I said. "No problem at all."

That night I dreamed about Nika. I had only one memory of her, from a day that Elena's childcare had fallen through, and she'd brought her daughter to the house for a few hours. In that one memory I had, in the dream, Nika was a scruffy little girl with white-blond hair wearing a red-and-blue-striped jumper dress.

"Can I play with you?" she asked.

I was sitting at the kitchen table cutting out clothes for paper dolls. I was about twelve—the last year of normalcy. Before my mom died. Before Yvonne. Back when I was just a regular girl with a regular life.

If I was twelve, that would have made Nika about three or four.

"Can I play?" she asked.

"These scissors are too sharp," I said. "Only for big girls."

Nika ran off somewhere and came back with a pair of safety scissors—clunky and plastic and completely blunt. "Now can I play?"

I sacrificed one of the paper dolls to give to her, and it turned out to be a real sacrifice, too, because within five minutes the doll got ripped in half.

"Oops," Nika said. "But don't worry. I'll get tape."

That's all I remembered. *I'll get tape.*

I woke up and poured myself a bowl of cereal. I hated my dreams these days. It almost might be worth it not to sleep anymore. With the reset, I didn't need sleep, and I could do without the dreams.

I couldn't shake the image of Nika from my mind. The girl who died in a fire.

Because of me. I didn't turn on the stove in Elena's house, but I also didn't bother to save her. I didn't do anything. Elena was probably like that paper doll, ripped in half, and there wasn't enough tape in the world to fix her.

The next morning I went to a library with free internet and tried to look up Elena. She used to run a cooking blog, something called The Russian Chef, where she'd post all her best recipes. But when I looked, all Elena's social media had been taken down. She hadn't posted anything for five years. It was like she vanished off the face of the earth at the same time Nika did.

She was gone. And, as usual, I tried really hard to push her out of my mind.

I'd said I would get right on finding the Belle, so that's what I did. During the next sift I went to a party where something out of the ordinary, Ethan felt, had happened with a girl.

A girl. This still made me feel all twisty inside. I did not want to be investigating into Ethan's time with another girl—especially if it was the beautiful girl in the Badgley Mischka dress. I obviously wasn't feeling super motivated to find the Belle. She suddenly felt like competition. But looking for the Belle was what I was supposed to be working on, and I had to keep doing my job. So I concentrated on the stupid party.

A party was a good place to find the Belle—in many versions of the story, anyway, young Ebenezer Scrooge meets Belle for the first time at a Christmas party. This particular party in Ethan's memory was a big, loud shindig in another Browning student's brownstone in Brooklyn. Absentee parents. A lot of booze. People crammed in every nook and cranny. The music was turned up so high Ethan could feel the waves of sound bounce off his eardrums, the beat thumping him in the gut, the chest, reverberating through his entire body. He didn't like it. He didn't enjoy parties. But the people around him all knew his name—they said hello as he passed by—and he liked that they knew his name. Even if he didn't know most of theirs.

Then Ethan saw someone he didn't expect to be there—Dent. The kid was chubby and redheaded and had pretty bad acne, and he was hiding out in the corner of the living room all by himself. At school the day before Ethan had invited Dent to this party on a whim, but he hadn't really thought the kid would actually come.

"Hey, Dent," Ethan called out over the music.

"Hey, Ethan!" Dent stumbled toward him, banging his shin on the coffee table. He was wearing a slightly small navy-blue polo and cargo pants with his stomach poking out at the top. He tried to smile. "I'm here," he yelled.

"I see that. I'm glad you could make it," Ethan yelled back.

"Yeah. Me too." Dent wiped his nose. "Uh, what's up?"

"The next phase in your initiation, right here, right now," Ethan said.

Oh, that's right, I thought. There was something about a fake club that Ethan was making Dent try to get into.

"What do I have to do this time?" Dent asked warily.

"First you have to have a drink," Ethan said. "That's not an official requirement, but it will make the rest easier."

"Okay." Dent sounded pretty uncertain.

"And then you have to kiss the hottest girl at the party," Ethan shouted over the bass.

If it was possible for Dent's face to get an even pastier shade of white, it did. He actually grimaced. "You're joking, right? Me, kiss a girl."

"Not just a girl. The hottest girl."

That seemed extreme. And about as probable as snow in Times Square in the middle of July.

Dent's mouth fell open. "I can't *kiss* her. That'd be, like, assault."

"I have faith in you, buddy," Ethan said with a shrug. "The members of the Eucleian Society are known most for our guts. Besides, you wouldn't want to come this far and then strike out here, would you?"

He clapped Dent on the back and then left him to go find the aforementioned drinks. There was an entire line of suitably hot girls in the kitchen, waiting to mix up their rum and Cokes or something. One of them was easily the hottest of the hot—Kendra Cunningham, standing there in a black minidress with a cascade of dark blond curls piled over her shoulder. She broke into a flirty smile the second she laid eyes on Ethan. Which seemed to be a completely normal reaction from any red-blooded female. Myself included, apparently.

"Ethan Winters," Kendra said sweetly. "Nice to see you again."

"It's always good to see you, Ken," he replied.

"It's been a while." She fake pouted.

"And I've totally missed you." He hooked an arm around her shoulder. Kendra didn't exactly pull away. Because she liked him, probably. "Hey, can you do me a solid?" he murmured next to Kendra's ear.

"Sure," she breathed.

"There's this fat kid in the living room, and in a minute, you should go out there and offer him a drink."

She squeezed her perfectly shaped eyebrows together. "A fat kid?"

"Yeah. It's a prank. You take him a drink, and then he'll try to kiss you."

She pulled back. "A fat kid will try to kiss me. And then what will I do?"

Ethan was unable to hide his wicked smile. "Whatever you want. A good old-fashioned slap, maybe. Drink to the face? Use your imagination." He darted up to the front of the line for the alcohol. "Excuse me," he said politely, like he hadn't just cut the line. He poured something from a bottle into a red plastic cup, returned to Kendra, and held the cup out to her. "There you go. The fat kid awaits."

She frowned. "You're kind of a bad boy, aren't you?"

"It's why you love me."

She bit her lip and then smiled. She took the cup. "Okay, I'll do it." The flirty smile returned. "But you owe me."

He followed her from a distance as she went into the living room, his phone out to catch what happened on video. Kendra easily spotted Dent back in his hiding place in the corner. The boy looked shocked when she came up to him, but he did manage to talk to her. Neither I nor Ethan could hear what he said to her over the blare of the music, or what she said back, but she gave Dent the cup, and he drank one swallow and then scrunched his face up and stuck his tongue out and pretended to gag. She laughed. He smiled and shuffled his feet.

Ethan starting filming the scene. Here it came: the attempted kiss. The slap. The drama. It was all about to unfold. Ethan zoomed in on the scene. Dent's face was red, but he was obviously gathering up his courage. Kendra turned to go, and he touched her arm to stop her.

The music quieted suddenly—we were between songs. We could hear again.

Ethan leaned forward to listen.

"I know this is kind of unorthodox, but would it be all right if I kissed you?" Dent asked, straightening up to his full, unimpressive height of like five foot four and looking right into Kendra's eyes.

Asking permission. That was a surprise.

"You want to kiss me. Why?" she asked, glancing at Ethan again.

"You're the hottest girl at the party," Dent explained. "And I've never kissed a girl before, so I thought I'd try for the best. If you would do me this incredible honor of being my first kiss, it's something that I will carry with me for the rest of my life."

"Oh," said Kendra. "Well, when you put it that way . . . okay."

She leaned forward and Dent leaned forward and they brushed lips. Then Dent smiled and held out his hand like he wanted to shake hands with her. She laughed and let him.

"Thank you very much, miss . . . ?"

"Kendra," she said.

"Kendra. You've kind of made my year," he said. "Maybe even my life."

She laughed, embarrassed, and turned and headed back for the kitchen. She didn't say a word to Ethan as she passed. And the craziest thing about it was that people were already looking at Dent differently than they had just minutes before that, with a grudging kind of respect in their eyes. They started talking to him. Congratulating him.

Ethan scoffed. He was actually shocked by this turn of events. He had the strangest feeling now that maybe he was the one being pranked. And he was also secretly impressed with Dent, just asking her point blank like that.

The music blared again. I hung around in the memory for a while longer, although I was pretty sure I wasn't going to find the Belle here. By the end of the night Ethan had a girl hanging on each arm, giggling up at him, telling him how funny/smart/bad he was, but he wasn't into either of them. He was bored out of his skull. Parties were always the same—the same songs, the same boozy breath all around him, the same lame jokes and dares and guys getting toasted. He hated parties. Why did he go to parties? he asked himself. He didn't really know the answer. Because it was expected of him, he guessed. The guy he was supposed to be went to parties.

That was an interesting thought—the guy he was supposed to be. He even remembered it specifically from this night, thinking those words: *the guy I'm supposed to be.* That's the only reason I could be here with him, sharing his memory of this night as he recalled it. He clearly remembered the moment with Dent and Kendra, he hazily remembered the girls, the dancing, the music. But most of all, he remembered being surrounded by people, but feeling alone.

Back in his bedroom, I wanted to tell him that I understood what he meant. I felt it every single day, as I rode the subway, as I walked the city streets, noticing the people on every side of me chatting on their phones or hanging out together or on their way to connect with someone else. There were eight and a half million people living in New York City. It was one of the busiest places on the planet. And it was the loneliest place in the world. At least it had been. Until I'd started spending time with him.

SEVENTEEN

STEPHANIE WAS STILL TALKING. AND talking. And talking.

"It's November! We should know who the Belle is by now. It's not your fault—I'm not saying that. You're totally doing your best, Holly, with this Belle situation. I mean, I know Da—Copperfield said that it might be this girl in the white dress at that charity thing—but why would he think that? That's a pretty big assumption, really, just because 'Ethan was acting strange' when he saw her? What constitutes strange, anyway? Maybe he wasn't even reacting to her. Maybe he had a piece of pork that didn't agree with him. Maybe he didn't get a good night's sleep the night before. Maybe he was just tired. He's seventeen, I mean, when I was seventeen I didn't have a love of my life. Most people don't fall in real love before they're seventeen, I mean real love, I mean, the love of your life kind of love. Well, I guess some people do, but some of us don't even find that ever. Boz is worried, I can tell."

Obviously. I'd been sifting for the Belle for weeks, and we still had no clue who she was. I'd even been in Ethan's mind specifically looking for the girl in the white dress, and I hadn't found a trace of her.

"It's just so frustrating!" Stephanie burst out, and then flopped down into her chair.

"What's going on with you?" I asked. "Did something happen?"

She bit her lip. Today she was wearing a pastel-pink dress that had Boston terriers printed all over it, and a purple cardigan.

She looks like a unicorn just threw up on her, said my Inner Yvonne.

She also looks upset, I thought.

"We will figure out the Belle, okay?" I said. "That's what we do. It can't always be perfect. We're trying to match up someone's life with a template that was written in 1843. It's not going to be an exact match. It never really is, but every year we make it work."

"But how?"

"We make compromises and find substitutions. We—okay, so forgive me if I sound like Boz when I say this, but—we keep ourselves true to the *spirit* of *A Christmas Carol.* That's the beauty of it, right? Each Scrooge is different, and they all have completely different experiences and different significant people in their lives who affect those experiences. But in the end they all get to be a part of the same inspiring story."

She sighed. "You're right. That is beautiful."

"So the Belle might not even be a romantic thing," I said. "It isn't always. It could just be a friend." *Mine was,* I didn't say out loud. And thinking about Ro now put a lump in my throat every time. Talk about seeing the wonderful life I could have lived.

The trouble was, Ethan didn't have any close friends. For a guy as sharp and twisted and hilarious as I knew he could be, he was completely isolated from real relationships with people his own age.

Except me. I smiled.

"Now do you want to tell me what's really bothering you?" I asked Stephanie.

Her slump got even slumpier. "It's personal. Not exactly appropriate workplace conversation."

I stood up. "Get your jacket. I'm taking you to an early lunch. My treat."

Her eyes widened behind her glasses. "Your treat?"

"You don't have to act all shocked. I'm your boss, right? I can take you to lunch." I checked my purse, and I had exactly sixty-eight dollars left for the month, which would just about cover a nice lunch for two in Manhattan. I didn't have anything better to spend it on. "Just don't tell Grant and Marty," I said.

An hour later we were finishing up our meal at a place called Vintry on Stone Street, where Stephanie had just wolfed down a mozzarella and tomato panini, and I was still picking at the truffle mushroom cavatelli. It was amazing. Sometimes, in this un-life I lived now, I forgot about the way food can comfort you, the way the world seems like it can't be that bad if it can afford you this simple pleasure.

I ordered dessert. Because chocolate.

Stephanie seemed like she'd finally relaxed a smidge. So I said, "Now tell me what's up with you. Maybe I can help." I couldn't believe I was doing this—asking Little Dorrit to talk more than she usually did—but I was feeling good lately, better than I had in years, as a matter of fact. Ethan's presence in my life had brightened my outlook on the world considerably.

"Come on," I ordered. "Spill it. Tell me what's wrong."

She hesitated. But then she said, "Grant asked me out."

I blinked at her. "What? When?"

She bit her lip again. "This morning. After the meeting."

"Only this morning? God, how long have you worked at the company? I thought Grant was going to ask you out on day one. Well, he and Marty both."

"But that's the problem," she said.

"You don't like Grant?"

"I do like him!" she exclaimed miserably. "I like him so much. He's so nice, and he's so smart, and he's nerdy—I know he's nerdy, but I *love* nerdy—and he has these soulful eyes and this sweet smile and he's . . . wonderful."

O-kay. It made me a little uncomfortable trying to look at Grant through the sexy lens, but okay. "So . . . what's the problem, again?"

"Marty." The waitress arrived and set a milk chocolate crème brûlée in front of Stephanie, and the girl didn't even pause—she just picked up the spoon and dug in. Not that I could blame her.

"Thank you," I murmured to the waitress, and eyed my own dessert: profiteroles with vanilla ice cream and a warm chocolate sauce. "What about Marty?"

"Marty likes me, too, like you said, although he's been a lot more up front about it. He asked me out months ago . . ."

That was so Marty.

". . . and I didn't really know him very well then, and I wanted to focus on doing a good job for you, so I told him I didn't want to date anyone at the company." She sighed. "I rejected him."

"And now you want to say yes to Grant, but you've already established that you're against dating within the company."

She shook her head. "It's worse than that. Marty is Grant's best friend. They hang out together all the time even when they're not at work. They have this tabletop club that they put on with their other friends together every Wednesday. It's so cute." She took a huge spoonful of crème brûlée and swallowed. "What should I do?"

She should focus on what's important here, said the Yvonne in my head. *Her career. If she dates this silly Grant boy, it's only going to end badly and make her look unprofessional. There's no room for sentiment in business, and this is business. Intra-office romance is very ill advised.*

I wanted to argue that "this silly Grant boy" happened to have a PhD in engineering at the ripe old age of twenty-three, which made him like a child genius or something, but I couldn't argue with my Inner Yvonne. She always won.

Plus, her advice made sense if I looked at the situation from the point of view I was most familiar with, which was from the perspective of what was best for *me*. If Grant and Stephanie started dating, then Marty would probably be upset, and then things would get tense and awkward around the office, and all the tenseness and awkwardness would probably eventually break up Grant and Stephanie, which would make things even worse. It could wreck the dynamics of Team Lamp.

So what Yvonne said was the right answer: no, Stephanie should not date Grant.

But she liked him. A lot.

And I knew he liked her. He was more obtuse about it than Marty, but still. Whenever he was around Stephanie he'd start pumping out all these useless facts about things—quantum physics, something called SciShow on the internet, the theory of relativity. It was nerd flirting, showing his big impressive knowledge like a peacock flashing his pretty feathers.

It was kind of adorable. They'd be a cute couple. I could picture it.

And I was feeling optimistic about budding romances.

I put down my spoon. "You know what Boz always says?"

Her eyebrow bumps appeared. "Um, let's see. 'No one is useless in this world who lightens the burdens of it for anyone else'?"

"No, not that one. The other one. The one about love."

"I don't think I've heard that one."

I paused here for dramatic effect. "A loving heart is the truest wisdom."

I'd looked it up once. It was paraphrased from *David Copperfield*.

Boz said it constantly.

Stephanie's mouth opened, but she didn't speak.

"Food for thought, that's all." I finished my dessert and caught the attention of the waitress. "Check, please?"

Back at the office, there was a kind of uproar going on when we returned, people from Dave's team darting around the hallways shouting orders at one another like the place was on fire.

I suspected cupcakes were afoot. Too bad I'd eaten all that chocolate earlier.

I spotted Tox in the hall, just standing there watching the action all around her with an amused expression. Stephanie and I wandered over to her. I hadn't seen Tox since that day she'd been in Dave's office. She always made her own schedule. "Hey."

"I've got grandpa in the basement," she informed me.

"Huh?" said Stephanie.

"Ethan Senior." Tox jerked her chin in a weird nod. "It took me a while to find him, too. He's a wily little bugger."

"Oh. Good job, Tox," I said distractedly, watching some guy cross the hall with an armful of wires for some reason. "I knew you could do it. What's going on here?"

"There's been a tip on the Belle," she said matter-of-factly. She smiled. "Everyone's going insane. Apparently Dave thinks that the girl in the white dress is going to show up at this big Make-A-Wish ball tonight."

Grant and Marty came galloping up to me like two puppies

with a tennis ball. "Ethan's going to the ball! Dave got a copy of the guest list, and Ethan's on it. So Dave wants to get the venue bugged ASAP, so they can record any interaction between Ethan and the white-dress girl. This might be it. This could be when the Belle moment actually happens. Or maybe it's just when something starts between them. Either way, pretty cool." Grant finished his little speech and then glanced at Stephanie. His ears went red. "Hi."

"Hi," she murmured.

"Hi," said Marty loudly. "I think we've all said hi now." He frowned. "Let's go, Grant."

I took Stephanie by the shoulders and steered her into my office.

"I need you to do me a favor. Go figure out exactly what surveillance is already on Ethan between now and this evening."

She didn't even ask me why. "You got it, Holly."

I sank into my chair. This was terrible. Ethan going to a ball. A real dancing and bubbly drinks and tiny finger food sort of ball. With the girl in the white dress. He didn't even like the girl in the white dress. He didn't even know her. Not yet. He knew me. He liked *me. Screw the Belle,* I thought. *Ethan is mine.*

There was a knock, and Boz stuck his head in. "Hello, Havisham."

"Hey, boss, what's up?" I tried to sound cheerful.

"You heard our good news about tonight?"

"I heard."

"To think that we might actually uncover this mysterious Belle. It's so exciting."

"Thrilling," I agreed, my voice coming out a little strained. Crap.

He clucked his tongue. "Oh, don't be down in the mouth because Dave is working on the Belle when that's usually your job. It's a special situation, I think, with this particular Belle in the present more than she belongs in the past. We're just all pitching in to help each other this year. It shows real company unity."

I nodded. "I was supposed to be sifting Ethan's memory tonight, but I guess that's not going to happen now. Maybe I can have the night off?"

"Of course. You have the night free. A group of the staff thought it might be fun, though, to come in tonight, maybe dress up a bit, play some music, and watch Dave's feed of the ball. You should come. How often do you get to see a romance in the making?"

"I know, right?" I said. "I will consider that."

"Wonderful. See you there," he beamed, and pulled his head back out and closed the door.

I bent and put my head on my desk, facedown. It felt cool and steadying.

There was a knock on the door.

"Occupied," I mumbled into the desk.

"It's me." Stephanie popped her head in. "We have surveillance on him at the school, but you knew that. It ends about a block from the school building. And of course we're watching at his apartment."

I couldn't go to his apartment. I couldn't call him and tell him to meet me. I'd have to make it to the school when it was getting out. There were seven blocks between Browning and Ethan's apartment. I'd catch him there.

"Are you going to the thing?" Stephanie asked me. "The watching the feed thing?"

"Uh, maybe?" No, I was not. "You?" It'd be helpful if the staff was all distracted by setting up surveillance at the venue and having a little office party, instead of watching Ethan like a hawk. It would give me a chance to slip in unnoticed and grab him.

Stephanie shook her head. "Grant will be there. And Marty. It would be awkward."

"A loving heart is the truest wisdom," I reminded her.

She gave a dramatic sigh. "I'll think about it."

"Marty will be fine," I said. "He's a big boy."

She nodded. "It's not just Marty. I guess I'm just afraid if I said yes to going out with Grant, I'd be doing it for the wrong reasons. I'm emotional right now, so maybe I just want to be . . . comforted? Not alone."

I got it. Not alone was good. "Why are you so emotional right now?" I asked.

She squeezed her eyes closed for a second, like she couldn't believe she'd just said that. "Oh. It's this thing with my dad. I can't really talk about it right now. Do you need anything else? Coffee?" she guessed.

I sighed. "Coffee would be amazing."

She pointed at me. "Coming right up."

"You're the best," I said, and I actually meant it.

"That's why they pay me the big bucks," she said. "Oh. Wait.

Thanks for lunch, by the way," she said.

"Anytime," I replied. Well. Anytime that it was totally convenient for me. I glanced up at the clock. It was almost two. Ethan got out of school around three.

"Actually, I have to go," I said, jumping up and grabbing the Hoodie.

"Right now?"

"Boz gave me the rest of the day off," I explained on my way to the elevator. "I've got some things I have to do."

I had to go see about a boy.

EIGHTEEN

"HEY THERE, STRANGER." I POPPED out of an alleyway approximately three blocks from Ethan's school and gave him an impromptu hug from behind. He went completely rigid, but when he looked over his shoulder and saw it was me, he turned around to hug me, too.

"Tori!" His face was priceless. I'd caught him totally off guard.

"That's my name." I let the hug go on for a bit longer than I should have, considering the hurry I was in. It felt so good to have his arms around me. Like I was a solid, real-live person. I was tempted to just snuggle into his chest and stay put. Permanently.

He pulled back. "Where did you come from?"

"Heaven?" I tried.

"It's the middle of the day."

"I am aware of that."

"Where's Night-Owl Victoria?" he asked.

"I thought you might be getting bored with her," I said. "So I thought . . ." I gestured like I was pitching a movie title. "Victoria in the Afternoon."

"How'd you know I would walking by here? Are you . . . stalking me?" he asked, arching an eyebrow at me like the idea was super appealing.

"No, that would be wrong. Let's just say I can sense when you're nearby," I explained all wide-eyed. "Like a pigeon."

"What?" He laughed. "A pigeon."

"A homing pigeon! Okay, fine. I'd tell you how I knew you'd be here, but then I'd have to kill you."

He nodded like I was making total sense. "You're a spy. I always suspected as much. Which branch are you? CIA? FBI? Interpol?"

"Shh." I put a finger over his lips.

Someone behind us chuckled. I froze. For a second I thought maybe it was somebody from the company, and I was busted.

Ethan gave a little roll of his eyes. I peered around his shoulder. There, standing in the middle of the sidewalk staring at us, was a familiar chubby kid with red hair.

"Dent!" I exclaimed before I stopped to think about it. "How are you?"

His eyes widened. "I'm . . . good. Who—"

"Wait, how do you know Dent?" Ethan asked, frowning.

I'd really stepped in it this time. I nodded and then changed my mind and shook my head. "You've talked about him?" I said like this was a question.

Ethan didn't say anything. He must have been replaying our

conversations back in his head, looking for the part where he'd told me all about Dent. Which of course was nonexistent. He'd never said a word to me about Dent.

"I'm Danny," Dent said, stepping forward, smiling. "What's your name?"

"Danny?" I said. This I did not know. I'd forgotten that Daniel was Dent's first name.

"No, *I'm* Danny," the kid said with another chuckle. "But I guess you can call me Dent, too, since everybody does. And you are . . . somebody else. Whose name is . . ."

"Victoria," Ethan answered for me. "Tori, this is Dent. Dent, Tori. Awesome. You know each other." He glanced at me. "I'll see you tomorrow."

"She's prettier than you said she was," Dent said.

I stared at Ethan. "Have you been talking about me?"

"Pretty much nonstop for, like, two months," Dent said.

"Okay. So, see you around," Ethan said. "Bye-bye, Dent."

"He doesn't have to leave," I protested as Dent hefted his backpack onto his other shoulder and started to walk away. "You don't have to leave."

"Nice meeting you, Tori," Dent said. He saluted. Then he went down the subway entrance.

I turned to Ethan. "So he seems like a nice guy."

"He is. He's too nice, actually. It's going to get him hurt someday," Ethan said.

I was confused. Ethan was acting like Dent was his friend, a real friend, even, the kind you walk home with after school. The kind you talk to about girls. But the Scrooge was never friends with the Cratchit. Like, ever. He always looked at the Cratchit with disdain.

"How did you become friends with Dent—Danny?"

Ethan shook his head. "He annoyed me at first. I used to pull pranks on him, last year. And he'd fall for it. Every. Single. Time. He'd believe whatever I told him. But it didn't matter, really. I'd try to get him in trouble, but he always made it through, like, smiling and stuff. He still annoys me. But he's grown on me, too."

Kind of the way I felt about Stephanie. But not very Scrooge versus Cratchit.

"You could have let him stay with us. I wouldn't have minded," I said, smoothing the lapel of his jacket. "It's me who's intruding here."

"You were a welcome intruder." Ethan took my hands and spun me like we were about to dance. "I've been thinking about you all week. I was hoping you'd show up, actually, because there's this thing tonight I have to go to . . ."

"I'd love to go out tonight," I said. "That's why I'm here. I'm asking you out. Starting right now. Can I steal you?"

His eyes were blue today, blue like the flames in the little canisters that caterers use to keep food warm. "Right now?" he repeated. "Sure. But later I—"

"Good. I hope you're ready for some mega fun."

He nodded. "But I have this thing tonight—"

"Do you *have* to go to the thing tonight?" I asked.

"Well, no, but I thought maybe we could go together, if you

want. It's a ball. Like a ball with dancing. Would you like to play at actually being Cinderella?"

I would have loved to play Cinderella. So much it was kind of killing me. I'd missed prom, after all.

"I can't," I said.

He frowned. "Because . . ."

"I don't have a ball gown. Or a pumpkin. Or mice friends."

"We could get you a dress," he said. "This is Manhattan. There are shops everywhere. And I can get us a limo. It's no pumpkin, but . . . I'm afraid I can't help you with the mice."

God, he was really killing me. "I . . . can't go."

"Why not?"

"Because spy reasons. But I have something else for us to do. Way more fun."

I could tell he was holding on to the idea of me going to the dance with him. "But—"

"Trust me. This will be better."

He gave in. "Okay."

"Okay? Prince Charming will blow off the ball?"

"Balls are lame." He grinned. "I'd never be caught dead at a ball."

I hugged him again. I could have hugged him every five minutes for, like, ever. Then I took his hand and started towing him in the opposite direction of his apartment, away from where Dave's team at Project Scrooge would be expecting him any minute now. We had to move. "Come on, slowpoke."

"Wait, I should go home. Get out of this uniform," he said.

I grabbed his tie and tugged on it playfully. "Oh, no. You've got to stay in the uniform. That is hot." I lifted my hand to hail a cab. Miraculously, one pulled up right away. I followed Ethan as he ducked inside the car. Then I said to the driver, "Prospect Heights, please."

Ethan laughed and shook his head like I was the craziest girl ever, but he liked it. "Where are you taking me?" he asked.

"To the moon!" I exclaimed.

"Oh, the moon." He put an arm around me as we lurched away, officially off course from everything that was supposed to happen tonight. "I've never been to the moon. I hear it's lovely this time of year."

We spent the rest of the day roaming the Brooklyn Botanic Garden, which was never as crowded as Central Park. It felt secluded, sitting there in the grass surrounded by trees, looking up at the cloudless blue sky. You could forget you were in the city. And it was the last place that the company would ever think to look for Ethan. We'd escaped Project Scrooge, at least for the night.

"This is nice," Ethan said, leaning back and closing his eyes in the late afternoon sun. But I could tell he was thinking about how it wasn't nicer than a fancy ball.

"Just wait," I said. "The best is yet to come."

We explored the rose gardens and hung out watching the koi in the Japanese garden before hitting the gift shop, where Ethan bought me a tiny cactus to mark the occasion. I couldn't wait to stick it in the window of my apartment. "It's so cute!" I kept saying, and Ethan said, "It's just a cactus, Tori. It cost five dollars."

"But it's from you. I will think about you every time I look at it," I said. "So it's priceless."

"Hmm." He smiled. "If I'd known you'd like it that much I would have bought a cactus for every room."

"That would be excessive. And dangerous," I laughed.

Later we got ice cream cones and sat eating them on the swings at a nearby playground, watching the sky go a brilliant orange and then gray and then a deep, deep blue. When it was fully dark I led Ethan to the merry-go-round that was hiding under the bridge—Jane's Carousel, it was called. I'd always wanted to ride on it—it looked amazing, this fully restored carousel from the twenties. It was all lit up against the bridge and the dark river, blazing with lights and the bright colors of the horses. I picked a white horse with wings on its chest, and Ethan took the one next to mine, and we laughed and pretended to race as we went around and around to the music. Then we rode a second time, and this time Ethan stood next to my horse and I picked a stationary one, one that didn't move up and down, so we could talk.

"This is better than a stupid dance, right?" I murmured, staring down at him.

He nodded. "You know, sometimes when I'm with you it doesn't feel real."

I knew just what he meant. It made me sad a little.

I slid down and put my arms around him. The carousel whirled through the dark, but I felt like we were standing still. I wanted it to last. I wanted it to be love, the kind of love they make movies about. This was what love felt like, wasn't it? The way my heart pounded and my chest felt like it was being squeezed? The way his face had become everything beautiful in this world? The way his laugh made me feel like I could fly?

"Come here," I said softly. "I really want to kiss you right now."

Our lips touched, exploring gently, once, and then again. We'd kissed before—lots of times since that first time on the Staten Island Ferry—but this time felt different. The world became Ethan and the solidness of his arms holding me and the pressure of his mouth on mine. It was perfect. Then I could feel the ride slowing down, and I became aware that we weren't alone—that people might be watching. I opened my eyes and took a step back, suddenly dizzy.

Ethan brushed a strand of hair out of my face. "You sure know how to sweep a guy off his feet."

I wasn't capable of speech yet. I could only smile up at him.

We left the carousel and walked out in the park. The night was cool and breezy. I wore Ethan's suit jacket as we wandered along the edge of the river, my hand in his hand. I knew that somewhere—I didn't even know exactly where—the ball had started, it was in full swing by now, and the people at Project Scrooge were almost certainly freaking out because they couldn't find Ethan. He wasn't at the ball with the girl in the white dress. He was here with me. Looking at me like he really, really wanted to kiss me again.

I stood on tiptoes and pressed my lips to his. Then I pushed him back and walked us over to sit on a park bench overlooking the river. We watched the boats pass by for a while. "What about Truth or Dare?" I asked suddenly.

He leaned in. "I dare you to—"

I put my hand over his mouth before it could find mine again. It was like now that we'd started kissing, we couldn't stop. "Your turn first. Truth or dare." I moved my hand. "Go on."

He sighed. "Fine. Truth."

"Am I your girlfriend now?"

"Oh." He leaned back and smirked at me. "Okay. We're going to have this conversation."

"Am I?"

"Do you want to be my girlfriend, Victoria?"

The sound of the fake name jarred me. It reminded me that he didn't actually know who I was.

I stared out at the water. "I guess what I'm asking is, are we exclusive?"

He frowned. "You want to go out with other guys?"

"No," I answered. "But we haven't talked about it. For all I know, you've been seeing other girls all this time." Like a girl in a Badgley Mischka gown, for instance. Even though I was still fairly certain he didn't know her.

"Oh, sure," he said, raking a hand through his dark hair and raising an eyebrow at me. "I have a bunch of girls. A harem. Their names are, let's see—there are so many it's hard to keep track—Katy. Rihanna. Taylor. Adele."

I pushed at his shoulder. He laughed.

"No girls but you, Tori."

I kissed him as a kind of thank you, but I was restless all of a sudden. "Hey, let's catch a cab, go to the top of the Empire State Building. I've never done that." It felt reckless, since that would require Ethan and me to go indoors, and there were of course lots of cameras in the Empire State Building, but Dave's team would be watching the ball, wouldn't they? They'd never catch us.

I got up like I wanted to go, but Ethan grabbed my hand and pulled me around to face him.

"Just so we're clear, I'm fine with being your boyfriend," he said. "I was from the beginning, remember? That day at the pool, when it was like you just popped out of nowhere—the perfect girl. I said yes back then."

I sat down next to him. "So it's serious, then."

"As serious as it's ever been for me."

I grinned. "Does this mean you're going to take me to meet your parents?"

His smile faded, and he looked away. "My parents travel a lot, so it's difficult to schedule anything if I don't do it like months in advance."

I didn't know why I'd said that. It forced him to continue the lie that his parents were both alive and well. I just suddenly wanted to know exactly what I was to him. Or wasn't. I couldn't read his mind about it anymore.

"Have you ever brought a girl to meet your parents before?" I asked lightly.

"Oh God," he groaned. "Here we go."

"What? I'm just assessing the competition here."

"You're the first girl I've ever dated for more than, like, a week."

"Oh, I see. Players gotta play," I concluded.

"No, it wasn't like that. My school is boys only, and in that situation you have to go out and find girls to date, and that seemed like a lot of hassle. So I was really glad that day you walked into the club and stole my newspaper and started yelling about how you were seventeen and told me to get lost."

I put my hand over my mouth and gasped in fake horror. "Was I your first kiss?"

I could see his face getting red even in the dark. "No."

"Who was your first kiss, then? Come on, tell me her name."

"She was . . ." He stopped. "Wait. It's not my turn. That was like the longest truth or dare answer ever. It's your turn. Truth or dare."

"Truth."

"Who was *your* first kiss?"

For the first time, I didn't have an answer prepared for him. "I change my choice. Dare," I said.

"Oh, so you can dish it out, but you can't take it." He crossed his arms over his chest. "Okay. I *dare* you to tell me who your first kiss was."

"He was just a boy. The gardener's son," I explained.

He waited. I sighed.

"He kept trying to stick his tongue in my mouth, and I kept pulling away because I'd been chewing gum before and I didn't know what to do with it. It was kind of gross, actually."

Ethan was smiling again.

"Now you," I insisted. "Your first kiss. I want details."

In his memories, I'd seen Ethan kiss girls—I'd been searching through those moments in my halfhearted quest to find Ethan's Belle—but I'd never seen his first kiss.

"It was at a party," he said.

I'd seen him kiss lots of girls at parties. Like Kendra Cunningham. God, I really hoped his first kiss wasn't Kendra Cunningham.

"I was seven."

I gaped at him. "Seven. Years old?"

He laughed at my expression. "It was a birthday for this girl whose mom was a friend of my mom's. I didn't want to go, because I thought it'd be a bunch of little girls in princess dresses and stuff, and when we got there, it was exactly that—princesses everywhere. But then this one princess in a blue dress grabbed me and pulled me into the bathroom, and she told me, 'I'm the birthday girl, so you have to kiss me.'"

"Well, obviously," I said. "There are rules about these things."

"So I did."

I giggled. I couldn't help it. The image was too cute. "How romantic. Kissed against your will in a bathroom."

"I wouldn't say it was against my will," he mused. "It definitely made me a fan of kissing from that point on."

"So I owe this princess a big thank you."

"I still see her around sometimes." I glanced down at his hands like this was the part he found embarrassing. "She shows up at fund-raising dinners or charity benefits that my grandmother tries to get me to go to—like this ball tonight, for instance. She's probably there right now, even."

"You have a little crush on her," I guessed, a chill tingling down my spine at the words *she's probably there right now.*

"Maybe I did, once." He shook his head and took me by the shoulders to pull me toward him. Our faces were close—I could smell strawberry on his breath from the ice cream. "But now I have you, Tori," he said. "My official girlfriend, if you want the title."

"All right."

He kissed me.

"What's her name?" I asked when we came apart again. "The princess with the personal space issues?"

"Bella," he said.

I pulled back so suddenly I almost fell off the bench. "Her name is . . . Bella?"

"Isabella, formally."

I felt like I was on the carousel again, spinning, out of control. My face must have shown it because Ethan said, "Hey, don't worry, Tori. Nothing real ever happened between Bella and me. There's nothing there."

Bella. Her name was Bella.

You've got to be freaking kidding me, I thought.

It was two days before I was on the schedule to go back into Ethan's mind, but when I did, I went straight for his memories of Bella, and now that I had a name to go by, I found them. Easy peasy. It took all of five minutes for me to figure out that Bella was the only girl Ethan had ever been truly interested in—before me, that is.

She was definitely the one in the picture Dave had taken of the fund-raiser. The girl in the Badgley Mischka.

I located the moment—when Ethan saw her there, standing across the room at the Courage Award dinner, it turned out, which was some event that honored wounded servicemen.

He recognized her immediately. The second he laid eyes on her his stomach turned over, and his heart started to beat faster. He was staring like an idiot.

She glanced over her shoulder (she had great hair, I thought—long and shiny as a satin ribbon) and saw him. She was wearing white elbow-length gloves and she raised her hand to give him a shy wave, her face warming in a smile.

She didn't seem like the kind of girl who'd grab a boy at a party and demand a kiss. She had kind of an Audrey Hepburn thing going for her, actually. Large brown eyes and long lashes, framed by strong but striking dark eyebrows. A small, straight nose. High cheekbones.

Classic, said Yvonne. *She's classically beautiful.*

Bella. Her name was circling in Ethan's brain. *Bella.*

No was the word going through mine. *No. No.*

Dave's intuition had been right when he'd first passed around Bella's picture. Bella was probably Ethan's Belle.

I broke away from sleeping Ethan and tugged off the transducer. I drew the comforter up over his shoulder. Couldn't have him getting cold. "Hey, I'm tapped out," I said, rubbing at my aching temples. "Let's quit for the night."

"Okeydokey," Grant said, but he sounded—what, reluctant? annoyed?—that I was suggesting making an early night of it.

When I came back through the Portal, I saw why.

It was just Grant and Stephanie in the Transport Room. They were both somewhat disheveled. The collar of Grant's black polo shirt was mussed up, and Stephanie's hair was all over the place. She wasn't even wearing her glasses.

"Okay, I'm out," I said as I took off my Hoodie and headed for the door.

Stephanie bounded after me, tucking her hair behind her ears, which didn't really help. Her cheeks were pink.

"Sorry about that," she said breathlessly as I booked it down the hall.

"No, no. It's kind of my fault, right?"

She smiled. "Right."

She still wasn't wearing her glasses, which made her seem like a different person somehow. Her T-shirt was a depiction of a girl riding a bicycle—no, a *mermaid* riding a bicycle—underwater, with fish and bubbles, and strings of yellow hair floating all around her. Stephanie was also wearing jeans again today. And loafers.

Casual Friday. She looked pretty good, actually. "I'm happy for you," I said.

"What was going on in Ethan's brain this time?" She smiled excitedly. "Did you find the Belle? Because, believe me, after that whole mess with Ethan not even showing up to the ball, we could use some good news right now. Finding the Belle would fix everything."

"You weren't watching the monitors?" I asked.

Her face flushed pink again. "Uh . . . not exactly."

Nice. But I could make that work for me.

"I'm not sure about the Belle yet," I said.

After Stephanie went home I spent hours alone in my office thinking things over, trying to understand what it all meant. Because, okay, maybe Dave was right, but Ethan wasn't lying when he claimed that nothing of any real significance had ever happened with Bella since that day in the bathroom when they were seven years old.

They'd never had a relationship.

Which meant that they'd never broken up.

Which meant that I couldn't take Ethan to Bella on Christmas Eve to show him all that he'd missed out on—all the love and happiness that could have been. Unless what Dave had been saying lately was also true. Ethan was supposed to have been at the ball. Maybe that's when it would have started with Bella.

And I'd made sure that he hadn't been at that ball. I'd changed his future.

No going back.

I used the Hoodie to sneak into the Transport Room. The recording of me sifting Ethan's memory that night was cued up, ready for people to review later. By the morning the whole place would know that we'd officially found Ethan's Belle. They'd be strategizing for how to get him back on track.

I watched the video once, twice, three times, until I'd committed every detail to memory.

And then I deleted the file.

NINETEEN

IN THE DAYS THAT FOLLOWED, I concocted this little fantasy for myself, one where after Christmas Ethan and I would still be together. We'd be together more, even, because then the company would no longer be watching him. Not closely, anyway. According to Tox, who used to work downstairs, remember, the company checked in on their past Scrooges once or twice a year, tops. Just to make sure everything was still going smoothly. So in January, PS would move on to a different Scrooge. I could have Ethan all to myself.

That's assuming he succeeded where I myself had failed. He had to pass his Scrooge test.

But I wasn't really worried. As the days passed, Ethan seemed less and less like a Scrooge to me and more like a regular boy. Sometimes I'd forget that was why I'd met him. Except for the occasional lie he told me, which was usually about his parents, he wasn't like any Scrooge I'd ever known.

For instance: he bought me things, like chocolates and a fake ID. One day he presented me with my very own secret cell phone, so that we'd be able to speak freely. Of course, I couldn't actually talk to him on it, because Project Scrooge had his phone tapped and I was sure they'd recognize my voice. So I had to keep it down to ambiguous texts. But I made it work.

Still, that was the thing: Scrooges didn't buy people presents. They didn't spend their money if they could help it. They didn't smile as much as Ethan smiled at me. They didn't tell jokes. They didn't kiss.

It was like, whenever Ethan was with me (and he was with me more and more, in those days), he stopped being a Scrooge.

The company, of course, noticed that something out of the ordinary was going on. Their Scrooge 173 had this annoying habit of disappearing off the radar whenever their backs were turned, it seemed, and they didn't know where he went.

It was clearly driving Boz bat-crazy. I'd never seen him so worked up.

"It's a girl," he was saying during one of our November meetings. "He's met someone. I know it."

"How do you even know it's a girl?" I asked. "It could be anything. He could be playing poker or have a secret drug habit, for all you can tell."

"It's a girl; I know it. He has that love spring in his step," Boz said.

Love spring. Aw.

"I'm on it," Dave said. "I have my team working around the clock. We'll find out what's going on with him. I promise."

My time with Ethan was really making Dave look bad. It was making us all look bad, actually. It was mid-November, and the company still didn't have the Belle or all the locations where we'd take Ethan on Christmas Eve. I felt guilty about it, of course. It was all my fault. But I didn't feel guilty enough to stop seeing Ethan.

"There still isn't a Belle?" Boz said after I came up empty at yet another meeting. "Why haven't we found a Belle yet? The Belle is very important. The Belle is critical."

As if I didn't know.

I felt mildly guilty about Bella. What would Boz do if he knew that I'd erased her transducer recordings? I shrugged. "I have no idea who the Belle is. Ethan's never had a girlfriend. She just isn't there."

Boz frowned. "Or maybe you're not looking very hard."

"What?" I stared at him.

"Maybe you don't want Ethan to have a girlfriend," Boz added.

I actually gasped. This was the first time, like, ever, that Boz had questioned my ability to perform my job in front of the rest of the team.

"Why would I care if Ethan had a girlfriend?" I demanded. "Look. I've done what you've asked me to. I have sifted through Ethan's love life pretty thoroughly by now, and I haven't found anything. Nothing. Nada. I'm doing the best I can, Boz. So lay off."

My heart was pounding. God, I was such a liar. But what else could I do?

Dave cleared his throat. "Maybe Ethan's Belle isn't a romantic kind of love. We've had Scrooges like that in the past."

I put my hand up to stop him. "Don't even go there."

Boz sighed. "You're right. I shouldn't put so much pressure on you. I'm sure you're doing a fine job, Havisham. It's just . . . time is running out."

I knew that. I knew that not having the Belle was a huge problem, but I didn't know how to fix it without losing Ethan. And I couldn't . . . I couldn't lose Ethan. Not now.

Boz was about to close up the meeting when suddenly Marty—my Marty, from my team—raised his hand. "Um, sir?"

Boz stopped and looked at him. "Yes . . . Claypole, right?"

Marty winced at the Dickens name. "Right." He shook it off. "I just wanted to ask a question real quick."

Boz sat back. "Go ahead, young man."

"Why is Ethan Winters the Scrooge?"

"What?" Dave asked, like he didn't hear him correctly. "What do you mean?"

"Marty. . . ," I warned.

But Marty obviously had something he wanted to get off his chest. "I haven't been here that long, so I don't have a lot of experience with Scrooges, but it seems to me that the reason we're having a hard time finding what we need to with this Scrooge is because he's not, like, a real Scrooge."

It was totally silent in Conference Room A for a full minute. You could have heard a pin drop.

"What?" Marty looked around. "Come on, guys. I'm just saying what we're all thinking. Ethan Winters is no Ebenezer Scrooge."

"But why do you say that?" Boz said quickly.

Marty closed his eyes to say the lines from memory. *"Oh, but he was a tight-fisted hand at the grindstone, Scrooge. A squeezing, wrenching, grasping . . ."* He frowned. "Uh . . ."

"Grasping, scraping, clutching, covetous old sinner!" Grant finished for him.

Marty opened his eyes. "That's how Dickens describes Scrooge. Does that sound even a little bit like Ethan? I mean, he's mean-spirited at times, but he's not a covetous old sinner."

"He's also not a very nice person," Tox interjected.

Grant picked up where Marty left off. "He's not even really a miser. I see his room when I run the Portal, and the guy has some nice stuff. Expensive stuff. He's not pinching pennies. Isn't it possible that we have the wrong guy? Maybe it's supposed to be the grandfather?"

"The grandfather's dead," someone on Dave's team pointed out.

"Okay, so maybe not the grandfather. But somebody else."

"And what qualifies you to recognize a good Scrooge when you see one?" came a voice from the back of the room. I turned to see Stephanie standing up. She was wearing a violet-colored dress made out of sweatshirt material, but she'd taken off her big purple glasses, which made her look about a million times better than normal. She crossed her arms over her chest. "Ethan's obsessed with money. He's cold. He's greedy. He's oblivious to the human condition—he doesn't see the people in need around him. He's completely self-absorbed. That makes him just like all the other Scrooges."

Ethan's not, though, I thought. He wasn't cold or super greedy or self-absorbed. But that was Marty's point. He wasn't that bad.

But then, I never thought I was that bad, either.

"He *does* fit the classic definition of an Ebenezer Scrooge," Stephanie insisted. "His name even starts with the letter *E*. Coincidence? I think not." She took a deep breath. "And there's more to it than his flaws, clearly. We shouldn't forget that Ethan Winters has a future—an important future, right? And Blackpool could see into that future, which is why he chose Ethan in the first place. Has Blackpool ever led you in the wrong direction before? Has he ever been wrong?"

Nobody said anything, but the answer was obvious. No. Blackpool had always been right.

But Grant and Marty still weren't happy.

"Okay, let's say Ethan's got the right character deficiencies or whatever, which I still think is a bit of a stretch. The problem is that he's seventeen years old," Grant argued. "He's just a kid."

"He's still going to die within the year, like all of the others," Stephanie retorted. Her cheeks were red and her eyes had this scary light in them. I got the sense that she and Grant had had this fight before, about Ethan.

"But maybe it's not really about his qualifications," continued Marty like he and Grant shared the same brain. "Maybe it's about our chances of success. The people of Ethan's generation—and, okay, my generation, I'll admit it—don't believe in magic. We don't believe in the supernatural. We believe in special effects. We've been watching movies all our lives. Nothing seems new or shocking or awe-inspiring to us anymore. So when we show up in Ethan Winters's bedroom on Christmas with our dog and pony show, do you really think he'll take it seriously? No. He won't believe it. And because he doesn't believe it, he won't change."

Again, he had a point.

Some of the people in the room were looking at me now. Because they must know that's almost exactly what had happened in my case: I hadn't taken it seriously. They weren't saying anything, but I could tell what they were thinking.

My face felt like it was on fire.

Stephanie had been vigorously shaking her head the entire time Marty was talking, so hard her ponytail fell out and her blond hair tumbled down around her shoulders. "That's ageism," she said primly. "Pure and simple, that's prejudice. Just because someone's young doesn't mean that he can't be open to seeing the truth." She opened her purse and grabbed a little red book with gold-edged pages—the company-issued copy of Charles Dickens's *A Christmas Carol* Boz had given her. Stephanie held it up. "In this story, Ebenezer Scrooge starts out doubting that what he sees is real. He thinks the whole thing might be indigestion." She flipped quickly through the pages. "'There's more of gravy than of grave about you,'" she read, her voice totally confident and not the least bit squeaky. "Right? But it didn't take long for him to figure out that it's all really happening—because the details that he was being shown were all real, and they couldn't be faked, and he knew that. His dead partner showing up in his room. Scenes from his past that nobody else could have known about. The real people in his real life. The company convinced the Scrooge then, and we'll convince him now. Because that's what we do, and if society changes in a way that makes it harder, then we have to change, too. But we can't give up on a Scrooge just because it might not be easy."

"Well," Dave said at last. "There you have it. Well said, Steph."

Stephanie sat back down.

Boz gave a bemused laugh. "That was certainly a lively debate. And it's fine for you to have your doubts, and I understand why you have them, given that it's November and we're running behind schedule, what with our missing Belle, but Dorrit is right that it all comes down to Blackpool." He turned to face Blackpool, who'd been sitting at the conference table in complete silence for this entire brouhaha. "Blackpool, perhaps you could shed a little light on why you chose Ethan as our Scrooge this year. What do you see in store for our Mr. Winters?"

Blackpool looked at the door like he was considering walking out. "I cannot foresee his immediate future at the moment," he mumbled.

What? The rest of the staff in the conference room started to whisper among themselves. Was Blackpool actually saying that he didn't know the future? And what did that even mean? I for one had never figured out how Blackpool's gift was supposed to work. It was a chicken-or-egg kind of problem. Did Blackpool see what would happen because that's what was inevitably going to happen, or did things happen because Blackpool told us they would, and we all acted accordingly, which made them happen?

It made my head hurt to think about.

"I don't understand," Boz said. "Surely—"

"Mr. Winters's future has become rather hazy to me," Blackpool said gruffly. "There are unusual variables at play."

A shiver worked its way down my spine. He didn't mean me, did he? He couldn't mean me.

He was glaring at me again. But that was normal. He couldn't know I'd been meeting Ethan in real life. He couldn't know.

Well, obviously he *could* know. But if he did, he would have ratted me out by now, and I'd be on the fast track straight to hell. And it'd be real hell this time—I didn't doubt it. Anyway, Blackpool would take real pleasure in the idea of me getting fired. So he couldn't know, or he would have told on me already.

"So you have nothing to report?" Boz sounded disturbed. This never happened, at least not in the time I'd been with the company. Blackpool never said the future was hazy. He usually acted so certain, so unshakable in his assessment of the right course of action for us to take.

Blackpool made an aggravated sound in the back of his throat. "Sometimes a Scrooge presents a number of different possible variations for the future—the most likely option, and one or two alternatives. The path seems clear enough, but there are moments when the person could step off the path and change his destiny, so to speak."

"So Ethan has an alternate destiny?" I asked.

Blackpool cleared his throat. "Yes. More than one, in fact. I could see immediately that he has great potential."

That was the word that was always used to describe Ethan, I realized. *Potential.*

"What do you mean, potential?" Marty could not let it go. "What kind of potential are we talking here?"

Blackpool was staring at the table. "He could become an influential politician, for instance."

"A politician—what, do you mean like the president?" Stephanie asked.

Blackpool hesitated, but then he said, "It's possible."

"Of the United States?" gasped Marty.

Blackpool looked right at me then, his expression unreadable, and I wondered again if maybe, just maybe, he could see that I'd been spending time with Ethan. That I was involved in one of Ethan's versions of the future. But then why hadn't he told anyone?

Everyone was murmuring excitedly about the Ethan For President possibility. Now that would definitely constitute changing the world.

"All right." Boz took off his glasses and rubbed his eyes. "Enough speculation. It's enough to say that this Scrooge is very, very important, even if he is unconventional, as Scrooges come."

Then he promptly dismissed the meeting. The room cleared. But Boz asked me to stay behind.

"I just wanted to tell you I'm sorry," he said when we were alone.

"Oh. You're sorry." I waited. "For?"

"For insinuating that you . . ."

I raised my eyebrows. "Didn't know what I was talking about

because I'm just a silly girl?"

He looked away. "I apologize. Sincerely, I do. I don't think you're just a silly girl, Havisham. I don't know what came over me. I'm out of sorts myself, it seems."

"It's okay," I said. "We all get burned out sometimes."

He smiled. "Yes. I find that I often struggle during times of transition. I resist change."

"You? No. I don't believe it."

He snorted. "Thank you for that." He held the door for me, and we started to walk out together. Then we came around the corner, and there was Stephanie hugging Dave outside his office door. They were just . . . hugging. After a few seconds Dave pulled back and took her by the shoulders the way a coach gives his star player a pep talk. He said something that I couldn't hear. She nodded and smiled.

Boz cleared his throat, and they jumped apart. Stephanie gave Dave an exaggerated pat on the shoulder. "Thanks, Copperfield. I needed that." She turned to us and pushed her glasses up.

She took off down the hall and into the break room without another word. Dave went into his office and closed the door.

"Well, that was weird," I observed to Boz.

"I think you'll find 'weird' things happen around here every day," Boz said.

"Dave never gives *me* hugs," I sniffed.

"You should ask him sometime. He's quite the master of hugs," Boz said.

I held back a laugh at the idea. Dave the hugger. "How's it

going, finding his replacement? You have to find a replacement, right?"

His smile faded. "Indeed I do." He sighed.

"Does his replacement have to be dead?"

"We prefer that, yes," Boz said.

"But what if you can't find the right dead guy?" I added as we continued down the hall. "I mean, what if there's not an appropriately qualified dead person available to take the job? Doesn't the replacement have to be a former Scrooge? Like me, and Blackpool?"

"We have to properly time these transitions," Boz answered slowly, as if he were carefully considering each word. "Sometimes, if there's not a suitable replacement for the Ghost when we need one, we fill the position with a temporary stand-in for a short period. An interim Ghost, if you will. But usually we don't have a problem finding our Ghosts. One seems to become mysteriously available at just the moment one is needed."

Interesting. This made me wonder . . .

"Who was the GCP when I was the Scrooge?" I asked.

Boz's bushy eyebrows lifted in surprise.

"Your Ghost of Christmas Past was an interim," he said. "Before that, it was a lovely woman named Shirley. She was the Lamp for more than fifty years, that little old lady. Everyone just adored her."

How nice for Shirley. "So my Ghost was a temp?" That could explain a lot. Maybe I'd failed at being a Scrooge because I'd had a lousy Lamp. It'd be nice if that was the reason.

Boz nodded. "Why are you suddenly so interested in your own

case? You've never asked questions about your night as a Scrooge before."

He was right; I'd never asked. I hadn't wanted to go there. The past was the past, I figured. There was no point in dragging it out and looking at it. It wasn't like I could change what happened.

"I'm not interested," I said quickly. "I was just momentarily curious."

"Well, you know what they say about curiosity."

I blinked up at him. "What? What do they say?" I asked with false innocence.

He frowned. "It killed the cat."

"I don't own a cat," I assured him. "Plus, I'm already dead."

TWENTY

"OKAY. I'LL START. I AM thankful for all of my truly inspiring coworkers at Project Scrooge," said Stephanie, looking fondly around the table at me and Marty and Grant and three of their nerd friends (who, come to find out, all worked in the Evaluation department at PS, although I'd never officially met any of them before) and even Dave and Blackpool, who'd also accepted her invitation to come to Thanksgiving dinner all crammed in her little apartment, which turned out to be even smaller than mine.

"It really is the best place to work," she added.

From his place beside her, Grant squeezed her hand. "I'm thankful for my beautiful, smart girlfriend," he said, "who never ceases to amaze me." He kissed her hand, and she blushed and kissed him on the cheek.

Vomit. But they were kind of cute together, I had to admit. Even if my Inner Yvonne was telling me that PDAs were rude in formal company. And even if Stephanie was wearing an orange striped dress and a flour-streaked blue apron with squirrels on it. And pigtails.

"I'm grateful for my awesome friends," said Marty, who was trying hard to look happy for the happy couple. (He was a much bigger person than I was. Plus, I'd heard he'd already relocated his affections from Stephanie to some brunette in accounting.)

That brought us to Dave, who raised his bubbling glass of sparkling cider. "I am thankful for my family." This was strange of him to say because a) his family wasn't here, and b) Dave was dead, like I was, so when was the last time he'd seen his family?

On the other side of Dave, Blackpool let out a heavy sigh like this tradition of saying what you were thankful for was unbearably stupid. "I'm grateful that this year is almost over," he said.

Yeah, because this year apparently sucked for Blackpool.

"I can't believe we still don't have the Belle," sighed Stephanie.

Dave shook his head. "No work talk. Not today. Today we're thankful for what we do have."

The three nerds were thankful for: stuffing, the internet, and meeting new people, respectively. I was pretty sure that the last guy meant me when he said *new people*, and he was using the toast to hit on me. Gross.

"So now it's your turn, Holly," Stephanie said cheerfully. "What are you grateful for?"

I took a minute to think about it. "I guess what I'm the most thankful for this year is you, Steph," I answered finally. "I know I was . . . hard on you at first, but you turned out to be not only the best assistant a girl could ask for, but also somebody who I'm glad to call my . . . friend."

Stephanie's eyes immediately went watery behind her purple glasses. "Wow," she breathed. "Thanks, Holly. Just . . . wow." Grant handed her a napkin, and she dabbed at her eyes.

"To Stephanie, the host with the most," I said, and we all raised our glasses and toasted her.

It was true, though, what I'd said. In five years, no one had liked me enough to invite me to anything, let alone Thanksgiving. I usually spent this particular holiday eating cereal and listening to neighbor lady's grown-up children argue through the walls. I don't know how it happened, but somewhere along the line, Stephanie had become my friend. My only friend, if you didn't count Ethan.

"All right, enough gratitude," grumbled Blackpool. "I thought there was going to be pie."

I met up with Ethan later. It was a good night for us to get together, because Boz let almost everybody at PS off to celebrate the holiday. "Relax and enjoy yourselves, people," he'd told us, "because when we get back it's going to be crunch time."

Tonight there'd be nobody tracking Ethan. The whole city was our oyster.

"So your dad lets you go out on Thanksgiving?" was the first thing Ethan asked when he saw me sitting on the bench by my pal, the left lion.

"What my dad doesn't know can't hurt him," I said.

Usually that kind of comment made Ethan smile, like he liked how bad I was, how I so did not care what my parents thought, but not that night. He was obviously thinking about something, his expression distant. And, because it was Thanksgiving, and Thanksgiving was for family, he was probably thinking about his absent family and feeling more alone than usual.

I knew exactly how he felt.

In other news, it was snowing. Winter had fully arrived in Manhattan.

"It's freaking cold," I complained. Once a California girl, always a California girl.

"We could always go inside," he said with a lift of his eyebrows. "I know you're an outdoors sort of girl, but maybe we could go to my place. There's nobody else there."

Oh, I thought. *Ohhhhh.* It was dumb, but I actually blushed. "What about your parents?" I asked, flustered. "Where are they?"

It was like shutters closed in his eyes. He glanced away from me, down the street. "They're visiting my grandmother upstate," he said without even the slightest tell that he was lying, not a lip twitch or a blink or anything. "It'd just be you and me."

He'd asked me to come back to his place before. And I'd said no, of course. Project Scrooge was watching Ethan's apartment twenty-four hours a day. There was no way I could ever go there. But I was running out of excuses.

"Is this the part where you pressure me to move our relationship to the next level?" I asked.

"We've been going out for months," he said. "And you've never seen where I live. And I haven't seen where you live. You know that's weird, right?"

I grabbed his hand. "Look, I know we've been going out for a while."

"Months," he repeated.

"Yes. Months. And that's been amazing. You're the best fake boyfriend and the best real boyfriend I've ever had. I mean it."

"Is this about you wanting me to buy you flowers?"

"No. I'm not a flowers kind of girl."

He smirked like he didn't believe me. "You're not."

"No. I'm just not ready for the heavy lifting," I explained. A blast of cold wind hit me, and I pulled my coat more tightly around me. "If we do that kind of thing, stuff gets heavy, and I like things to be light. Anyway, let's go get some hot chocolate or coffee or something and go over to Rockefeller Center and make fun of the ice-skaters," I said.

"All right," he said, but he was quieter than usual as we made our way up Fifth Avenue.

We were almost to our destination when the impossible happened: I glanced up and saw Ro walking toward us, holding hands with a guy I'd never seen before. Not Captain Bland. A new guy.

My heart gave a little leap at the sight of her. Ro.

Time seemed to slow. She glanced up. She frowned. Her lips formed a word.

Holly?

I turned to Ethan and kissed him; I just grabbed his face and pulled it down to mine, turning us so Ro couldn't keep looking at me. Then I dragged him up the steps and in the door of the nearest building: Saint Thomas Church. I didn't know if Ro had really recognized me or just thought she did. I didn't know if she'd follow me in here, or what I would say to her, how I would explain myself or fix this mess, but I suddenly needed to hide.

"What are we doing?" Ethan said, clearly confused as I towed him into the sanctuary.

"Consider it an adventure," I said breathlessly.

It was dark in there. Good. I led Ethan into a section of pews along the edge of the room, out of sight of the main doors, and sat down, keeping my back to the entrance. I wished in vain for my Hoodie.

"What's going on?" he asked.

"I felt the sudden need for prayer," I said wryly.

He was frowning. "Tori. What the—"

"Don't talk. This is supposed to be a place of quiet contemplation," I shushed him.

He was starting to look mad.

I sighed. "Okay, fine. I saw someone on the street just now who I really didn't want to deal with."

"Who?" he wanted to know. "That girl?"

So he'd seen her, too. I wasn't losing my mind.

"Yes, a girl from school," I said. "She's like the queen bee."

"I would have thought you'd be the queen bee at school," Ethan said.

It was like he knew me. "Right?"

"So she has it out for you? Why? What'd you do?"

"I'm running for student body president, against her," I blurted. "I'm winning, and she is not taking it well. She keeps wanting to confront me all the time. She's accusing me of trying to 'buy' the election, just because my dad is rich." Oh, the lies, how easily they slipped off my tongue. It made me sad. I just kept getting farther and farther away from myself. And I was in a church, lying like crazy. I expected the lightning bolt to come down on my head any second now. "Anyway, I'm sorry to drag you into my drama," I said, looking down at where the Bible was stuck into the back of the pew. "I just didn't want to deal with her today."

I felt like crying all of a sudden.

"Hey," Ethan said softly. He took my hand in both of his and stroked his thumb over the top. "It's okay. I'm glad you told me. It's nothing to be ashamed of, being rich. I'm rich. My name is actually Ethan Winters the third, which means there was an Ethan Winters the second and an Ethan Winters the first, and they were all very, very rich."

"Were?" I said.

He sighed. "I have my drama, too. Stuff I haven't told you. Like with my parents. My dad."

So that was it. He was going to tell me about his dad.

I waited.

"My dad never liked being rich. He could never come to terms with his money. He was always trying to give it away to people, or trying to make it so he could live without it. He was supposed to inherit my grandfather's real estate business, but he didn't want it.

He wanted to go it on his own. He wanted to earn it."

"Nothing wrong with that, I guess."

He laughed, but it was a bitter sound. "Yeah, well. It didn't do him any good. He liked to take the subway and walk to work like the regular guys, but then this one day—at nine oh seven in the morning—he was walking down Lexington Avenue on his way to a meeting. It was just a regular morning. He ate breakfast, kissed my mom and my sister and me good-bye, took the 6 train to 116th Street, paused for a minute and listened to a homeless guy playing a saxophone on the corner of 115th. He gave the guy a twenty, and then continued on Lexington."

He stopped.

"Ethan, you don't have to . . ."

"They were doing construction on the upper floor of the building he was passing. It was a freak accident—that's what everybody called it. Freak. Accident. Like, the guy was goofing off up there—he got fired later—my grandfather made sure of it—and he lost his balance and the hammer slipped out of his hand. And that was it for my dad."

We both sat there in the corner of the empty church with our heads bent. I'm sure we looked like we were praying. I squeezed his hand. For a moment I started to see a memory of that day. When the policeman showed up at their door to inform them that his dad was dead.

"So, he's dead," Ethan said now, almost angrily, jerking us both back to the present. "I lied to you about it. My dad's dead. My mom pretends like it never happened—not the accident, but the whole thing—her getting married, having kids, becoming a widow—all of it. She just started over. So my parents are not happily married, obviously. I don't even live with my mom anymore—I got myself legally emancipated last year. I don't know why I told you my parents were fine. I just—"

"I get it," I murmured. "You don't have to explain."

He looked around like he was finally noticing where we were for the first time, at the Gothic arched ceilings and the rows of polished wooden pews, the stained-glass windows and the carvings of the saints on the walls.

"That's why I don't believe in God," he said, his voice rising like he was challenging somebody. "Because my dad went to church every Sunday. And if he had just come along one minute later—like nine oh eight—it wouldn't have happened. There were so many ways it could have not happened. If he hadn't stopped to listen to the stupid music. If he'd taken a car instead of walked. If the subway had been delayed—it's always delayed, right, so why not this time? If his shoelace had come untied and he had to stop to tie it. One minute. Sixty freaking seconds—that's all he needed. My dad went to church, right? He volunteered—he was in the Big Brothers thing, where he helped this little kid with his reading and took him bowling and did the fund-raisers and everything. He was nice to people, always so freakishly nice. He gave to the poor. But God wouldn't even give my dad one minute."

"I'm so sorry," I said.

He looked up like he'd almost forgotten I was there with him. "Are you religious?"

"No. Church was never a thing in our house."

My mom used to say that she was a spiritual person, but organized religion gave her the creeps. Too much guilt, she'd tell me whenever we'd pass by a cathedral or see an advertisement for an egg hunt at a church on Easter Sunday. She liked to go to Christmas Eve service, though. She loved to hold a candle and sing "Silent Night."

"It's all pointless, because God does not protect you," he said. "He doesn't intervene. For me it's better to think he doesn't exist than to believe that he's up there, watching it all, and he never does anything to help us."

I nodded. God certainly hadn't been watching out for me when I'd been alive. Still, I couldn't help but believe in him anyway, because I was dead, and here I was still. Supposedly making up for my sins.

Ethan stood up. "Do you think she's gone now?"

"Who?"

"That girl you're avoiding. I don't want to be here anymore. Let's go."

"She's probably gone. I'll check." I crept back to the door and peeked out. There was no sign of Ro. I motioned to Ethan. "All clear."

"Do you want to go to Rockefeller Center?" he asked. "Or we could still go to my place. It'd be warmer. We wouldn't have to do anything special. We could just hang out."

I smiled at him. I would have loved to say yes. But I knew that even on Thanksgiving there would be somebody on Dave's team watching the feed on Ethan's home.

"I'm kind of tired, actually," I said. "Maybe I should just go home and crash. My dad's probably looking for me, anyway."

He nodded like he'd been expecting me to say that. "Let me get you a cab."

We walked to a spot farther down the street and I raised my arm to hail a taxi.

"You're mad, right?" Ethan said. "Because I lied to you."

"I'm not mad." I dropped my arm and took his face in my hands and kissed him lightly on the lips. "I promise. I'm not mad."

He tried to smile, but it came off as suspicious. "Why not? I'd be mad, I think, if you'd been lying to me all this time."

I raised my arm again. What I would have given for a cab to come along then to save me from answering his question. But cab after cab was passing me by, one after another. They all already had passengers.

"Victoria?" he said.

I wanted to scream, *My name's not Victoria!* But maybe I could tell him part of the truth.

I dropped my arm again. "I lied to you, too. My parents aren't divorced. My mom died of breast cancer when I was fourteen. She was an actress, and things weren't going well in her career, and—I don't like to talk about her. I should have told you, I guess. Before now, anyway. So that's why I'm not mad. I'm a liar, too."

Finally I dared to look at him, but his eyes were warm, not cold.

"So we're both in the Dead Parents Club," he said.

"Yeah, I've heard that's super exclusive. Lucky, lucky us."

"I'm sorry about your mom."

"I'm sorry about your dad."

"So we're good?" he asked.

"We're good."

"Good."

I smiled. "Good."

He raised his arm, and a cab pulled right up to the curb. He took out his wallet and handed me a twenty. "Is this enough to get you there? Near the Flatiron, right?"

"It's enough. You're always such a gentleman," I teased.

"Even when I don't really want to be." He kissed my cheek, and I slid into the back of the cab. "See you around."

"Later," I said.

He closed the door, and the cab took off down Fifth Avenue.

"Flatiron?" the cab driver asked.

"No." I gave him my real address. I pivoted around in my seat to look out the back window and watch Ethan, who was still standing outside of Saint Thomas Church. Watching me, too.

I felt so close to him then, a connection that I was sure was not just based on attraction or circumstance, not the accumulation of a bunch of fake stories I'd told him. Something we could build on. Something that would last.

I waved to him. Then he was out of sight.

I went home to pick up the Hoodie. Then I took the subway to Ro's aunt's place. Ro wasn't home yet, so I waited. I don't why. I guess seeing her had just jolted me, and I was overtaken by the urge to talk to her. The way we used to talk. While I was standing there across the street from her house, I imagined what it would be like if I were alive. If Ro and I were still friends. "There's a guy," I'd say to her, and she'd grin and say, "Oh, a guy, I see. What's his name?" and I'd say, "Ethan. And I like him, Ro. I really do." And maybe we'd jump around and squeal the way we used to do when we were, like, thirteen. Or maybe we'd be grown-ups and Ro would simply say, "I'm happy for you, Holly. You deserve someone in your life after all you've been through."

After what felt like forever, Ro came home. I smiled when I saw her. She was smiling, too, smiling up at this new guy—Jamie, she called him. They walked up to the fence together and stopped.

"I had such a great time tonight," Jamie said. Again with the holding hands.

"Me too," she said.

"I like you, Ro," he said. "I know we haven't been seeing each other that long, and I probably should play it cool and see where it goes, but . . . I can't be cool. I l—I like you so much it's hard to think around you."

Of course Jamie would have to be crazy or stupid or both not to like Ro.

It started to snow again. First it came down lightly, and then more heavily, in big, wet flakes, almost sleeting. Ro didn't even seem to mind. She just looked up and held her hands out, and then looked over at Jamie and laughed.

"Nice weather we're having," he observed. "So very romantic."

Ro took his hand. "I like you, too," she said. She'd hesitated before she'd said it back to him, but she still said it. She obviously meant it. "I more than like you. Will you . . . will you come inside for a minute?"

"Uh . . . sure," he said.

"I want you to meet my aunt," she explained. "I mean, she's important to me. She's my family here. And I would really like you to meet her."

"I'd love to meet your aunt. My parents live in Jersey, but I'd really like to take you to meet them, too. If that's okay."

She kissed him. She put her arms around his neck and lifted her face up to his, and in the middle of the kiss, she smiled, like she was just so happy to be with him. He smiled back, and reached to cup her face, his palm against her cheek, and he kissed her again. The snow drifted down around them, but they kept kissing. Again and again.

At some point during all of this I started crying. The tears and melted snow mixed together on my face. Ro loved this guy, was what I knew she was really saying. I just stood there cold and shivering, watching them be so happy. And I was not happy for her. I knew it was stupid. I had Ethan. If I wanted to I could kiss him in the snow, and it would look the same. Probably better.

But it had suddenly occurred to me what Ro would really say if I could tell her about Ethan. She'd say, "But he doesn't even really know who you are, does he? How can you build on that?"

And I'd say, "Maybe if I just wait until after Christmas. Maybe then, when the company's not watching him, when it won't get in the way of things, I can tell him the truth."

"And then what?" the Ro in my head asked me. "You'll tell him that you're actually dead, but you like him so much that you couldn't help yourself? You'll tell him, and he won't care? And he'll take that year off before college, but then he'll go to college, and he'll grow up, and you'll just be here, resetting every day, sneaking out to be with him?"

I didn't have the answers.

I had to get away from Ro. I couldn't stand to watch her another minute.

I took a deep, shaky breath. "Bye, Ro," I whispered. I knew she couldn't hear me, but the words weren't for her, anyway. I wiped my face on the sleeve of my Hoodie and turned away, walking off through the snow toward where I could catch the subway home.

TWENTY-ONE

MY DOOR BUZZED. IT WAS Monday afternoon—I'd spent the last four days in bed, basically, feeling sorry for myself. I'd even called in sick to work, which I'd never done before, but I figured I had some sick days saved up after almost six years of slogging away at Project Scrooge. I deserved some time off.

The door buzzed again. I pulled the covers over my head and tried to ignore it, but it kept buzzing, like an angry persistent bee swirling around my head. It wouldn't go away.

"All right," I muttered, and rolled out of bed. I stalked across my apartment and pressed the intercom. "WHAT?"

"Oh, hi, Holly," came a squeaky voice. "It's Stephanie."

"What do you want?"

"I brought you turkey soup. I had so much leftover turkey."

That actually sounded pretty good. So I let her in.

"Oh, you look awful," she commented when I opened the door.

She was wearing a yellow plaid shirt and capris, like a sunbeam determined to pierce the dimness of my world. She bustled into my kitchen and spooned some of the soup—which smelled delicious, by the way—into a bowl. I sat down at my little table and ate it slowly, while she perched on the chair across from me and watched the soup go from the bowl to my mouth like my life depended on it.

"I'm so sorry you're sick," she said. "I didn't know you could get sick when you're dead."

"Well, I'm not actually dead, am I?" I said. Slurp.

"The office wasn't the same without you today. Boz is all freaked out, because we only have a few weeks left until Christmas. He says we're going to have to work overtime if we're going to be ready."

I couldn't imagine how Boz was taking me not coming in to work, even if it was just one day. Or maybe the problem was that I could imagine it. And yet I couldn't bring myself to care.

"We always have to work overtime. That's the company norm," I said. Slurp, slurp. Already I was almost finished with my soup. I wondered if she'd brought dessert.

"So how are you?" she asked. "Do you think you'll come in tomorrow?"

She looked genuinely worried.

"Probably," I muttered. My pity party about Ro couldn't last forever. "Anything exciting happen while I was gone?"

She brightened. "The fire alarm went off in the middle of the day, which has apparently never happened before at the company, and there was this mad scramble for everyone to cover up all the . . .

otherworldly stuff before the firemen came in and were like, *What the—?* And then we all had to stand out on the street for a half hour waiting for permission to go back in, and Boz was pacing back and forth like a crazy person, worried that they'd see something they shouldn't, and then he was saying something about a 'forget serum' that we haven't had to use in years, and anyway, it was all very stressful. And then, when the firemen said everything was okay, it turned out the fire alarm had been caused by Marty making toast with the equipment in the Transport Room."

"Whoa."

She looked at me like, *I know, right?*

"And what did Boz do?" I asked, aghast. The last thing I needed at this late stage in the game was having to find myself a new tech guy. Plus, even though he annoyed the crap out of me, I was kind of fond of Marty.

"Boz said, 'I'm very disappointed in you, young man.' And that Marty owed the whole company a big apology. So at the next meeting in the Go Room, Marty stood up in front of everybody and said he was sorry."

"Oh. Is that all?" That was a bit anticlimactic, but at least I hadn't lost Marty.

"And the vending machines started carrying dried apricots, because someone in records complained about there not being enough healthy choices."

Ladies and gentlemen, my super-exciting work life. Fire drills and apricots.

"Oh, and I almost forgot," added Steph. "We've had a

breakthrough. We figured out who Ethan's Belle is. Dave figured it out, actually. Her name is Victoria."

I choked on my turkey soup. Stephanie patted me on the back while I coughed and coughed.

"How does Dave know her name is Victoria?" I wheezed when I could speak again.

"It was on the audio feed. Ethan said it on the phone with his mom. He told her he had a girlfriend, and her name was Victoria Scott. Dave's been going crazy trying to figure out who she is. There's no official record of a Victoria Scott living in New York City who's, like, younger than seventy. Dave's been spending all his time scouring social media profiles and stuff, but he hasn't turned up anything that works. Ethan told his mom that he met this girl in the club, by the pool, he said, so Dave's petitioning to start monitoring the gym areas now."

I reacted to this news in three ways. First: Oh crap. I was possibly about to be found out. Second: Aw, he told his mom about me. That must mean something. And third: Oh CRAP! Because now of course the company would send me off to sift through Ethan's brain looking for Tori.

Stephanie was staring at me like she'd been expecting an even bigger reaction. "So, it's good news, right?" she said. "There's a Belle after all. We just had to have faith it was all going to work out. So when you come back to work, we'll sift around looking for this Victoria Scott."

I was officially screwed.

I felt sick. "Thanks so much for the soup," I croaked. "That was so thoughtful of you. You're always so thoughtful."

"Whatever I can do to help," she said.

I nodded and tried to walk her back to the door. "Well. I'm sure you can't stay long—I mean, you probably have plans tonight, so thanks again—"

"I don't have plans," she said. "I don't have any homework that's pressing, and I already finished my psychology paper that's due next week, and Grant and his buddies are all on *World of Warcraft* tonight, so I thought maybe you could use some company."

She pulled a DVD out of her bag. A movie. "This one's my favorite. It's about robots."

You'll never guess who the director was.

"I don't have a TV," I said, although now I was kind of bummed about it. I needed to be alone—to think, to try to work my way out of this current nightmare at Project Scrooge—but I also kind of wanted to hang out. Pretend my biggest problem was a head cold. Besides, I hadn't seen that particular movie of my dad's in forever.

"We can watch it on my laptop," she said, pulling that out of her bag, too.

And so it happened that Stephanie and I spent the afternoon curled up on my ratty plaid sofa watching movies—not just one but two, although only the first one was my dad's. In between movies we talked a little. I told her about growing up in California (although I didn't mention that my dad was Gideon Chase because I wouldn't have been able to stand that many wows), and she told me about growing up in Connecticut with her dad.

"We never had much money," she explained. "My dad tried his

best, but he could never seem to get on top of things. Still, we had a lot of love to go around. It was a good childhood."

She was like the opposite of me in so many ways.

"How's it going with Grant?" I asked later, because this seemed like a safe topic of conversation.

She grinned. "Great. So great."

My phone buzzed—a text. From Ethan. It read, *Hey, you up? Want to meet at the lion?*

My scalp prickled thinking that Dave might read these texts. That he was hunting for Victoria Scott, and Victoria Scott was me, and if he found out, I'd be in a world of trouble so deep even the Marleys would probably feel sorry for me.

I can't tonight, I replied. There was no way I could see Ethan now. Not if they knew about Victoria.

And just like that, it felt like it was over. No more Ethan. Deep down I'd always known it was going to happen. My time with Ethan was running out.

"Hey, are you okay?" Stephanie asked, sitting up.

"I'm fine," I muttered, wiping at my eyes. "It's just a lot of pressure this year."

"You're Victoria Scott, aren't you?" she said softly.

Silence. I didn't know what to say. I just stared at her.

"I thought it was too big a coincidence," she went on after a few long seconds. "You tell me that you want to hang out with Ethan in real life, and now he suddenly has a girlfriend. It's you, right? I know it's you."

I sighed. "Have you told Boz?"

She looked offended. "No! Of course not! I promised that I'd keep your secret." She took a deep breath. "I just didn't think it was going to be this big of a secret. This is kind of a big secret, Holly."

"Yeah. I know." I slumped into the couch.

"I know you were trying to help him, but . . ." She bit her lip. "His *girlfriend*, Holly? Are you crazy?"

"It just happened," I said quickly. I was going to have to come up with an explanation, and it was going to have to be good. "I know it's . . . unorthodox, but this relationship I've been developing with Ethan, I really do think it's helping him. Since we've been together, he's been . . . nicer. Better. He's amazing, actually, he's so . . . not like a Scrooge at all. You know, he told me that he's actually become friends with Daniel Denton. He likes the kid now. He likes the Cratchit already. That's good. That's progress, right?"

"Right," she agreed hesitantly. "But what about the Belle? How can *you* be the Belle, Holly?"

"I'm not the Belle. I can't be."

"Well, the Belle always breaks up with the Scrooge, doesn't she? You could break up with him. But . . ."

I was shaking my head wildly. "No, I can't . . ."

". . . what would you do on Christmas Eve? You can't bring him back to revisit memories of you, Holly. He'd recognize you, and everyone would know."

Everyone would know.

"I'm not the Belle," I said faintly. "I can't be the Belle." Was I? For a moment I was utterly confused. I couldn't be the Belle. I couldn't go to Ethan now and play that part the way it always went for every Scrooge, where the Belle accuses the Scrooge of changing and being obsessed with money and says she can't be with him anymore. Because that wasn't the way it was between Ethan and me.

"So what are we going to do?" Stephanie asked.

"We need another Belle," I whispered. "Someone else."

Stephanie frowned, which made the little bumps pop out on her forehead. "There's no time for Ethan to fall in love with anybody now. Although I still think Ethan's too young for someone—anyone—to be the love of his life."

A brilliant idea was starting to take shape in my brain. "We don't need the love of his life. We need a breakup scene."

I jumped up from the couch. "Come on," I said, grabbing my Hoodie off the back of the door. "Get your coat."

"Where are we going?"

"To the office. There's something I need to look into. Right now."

"Okay, people! Let's go over this one more time."

One week until Christmas. Boz, as was his usual style for the last official Project Scrooge meeting of the year, was acting like he'd had ten cups of break-room coffee. He was practically bouncing off the walls of Conference Room A.

"Here's the lineup," he said. "Marley—or, in this case, Ethan Winters the first—is our opener, of course. He warns Ethan that he's about to receive a visit from three spirits when the bell tolls . . . when?"

"One," everybody around the table said at the same time.

"Only there's no real bell, you understand. It's a metaphorical bell. But we do need Mr. Winters Senior in costume, in the Transport Room, no later than eleven thirty. Are we clear?"

Yes, yes, we were clear. It wasn't like we'd never done this before.

"The Marley wears a costume?" whispered Stephanie from her place next to me.

Well, one of us had never done this before.

"Sort of. You'll see." I was saying *you'll see* to Stephanie a lot these days.

"Then we move into Act One," Boz continued. "Havisham. She goes in on her own, introduces herself to our Scrooge, and then moves him through the Portal and into the Time Tunnel."

"Wait, the *Time Tunnel*?" Steph's eyes were huge behind her glasses. "We have a Time Tunnel? How come nobody told me about this?"

"How else did you think we were going to move through time?" I asked.

"I thought we were going to re-create it somehow."

"Well, that wouldn't be any fun. No, we actually go back in time, although we stay in another dimension—one that lies right on top of our own—so the Scrooge can't, like, intervene and change the course of history. Look, but don't touch, that's the rule."

"How does that even work?"

I shrugged. "Something about wormholes and interdimensional planes. I don't do the science. I just play the part. If you want to know how it works, you'll have to ask Grant. And then have a degree in quantum mechanics."

"Ahem." Boz cleared his throat loudly. "Havisham."

"Yes?"

"Are you quite done with your own personal conversation, and ready to tell us about what you have planned for Ethan's journey into the past? Tell me you have something—anything—that you can use with this Victoria Scott."

The moment had arrived. I lifted my chin. "No," I said primly. "There's nothing on Victoria Scott."

Boz actually scowled. "How can that possibly be true? We have to have a Belle."

"It's not Victoria Scott. She's not important to this story."

"How can you say that?" Dave asked incredulously. "Ethan falling in love at this critical juncture is incredibly important. It could change everything we think we know about him."

"For once, I agree with Havisham," Blackpool boomed out. "Ethan can't fall in love. He can't feel love. Not anything true. He's not capable of loving another person. To love, you have to think about more than just yourself. You have to consider the well-being of someone else. From what I understand, Ethan hasn't considered anyone but himself in a very long time."

I tried not to scowl, but I was suddenly furious. I was getting so sick of Blackpool casting his doom and gloom around the office like so much tragic confetti. Of course Ethan could feel love. Ethan was much better than all the hardened old geezers we'd worked on in the years I'd been at PS. Way better. At least he had some time left to live his life. If he lived; that is, if we succeeded in our mission. At least he was still young and had something to live for.

"If he's so bad, then why are we even bothering to try and save him?" I snapped.

The room fell silent.

"I suppose we all deserve a chance to be saved," Blackpool replied coolly. "Even if we don't take it."

God, he was passive-aggressive. It made total sense that he used to be a Scrooge, too. "Did you take it?" I asked. "I guess not, right, because you're here."

Mic drop.

Dave scratched his beard. "But we've noticed distinct changes in Ethan since this Victoria person came on the scene. Surely that's important."

I cleared my throat. "I think we're missing the point. Whatever this thing with Victoria is, she can't be his Belle. The Belle is part of the Scrooge's past—a reminder of an opportunity he missed out on. She's the 'Ms. Right' that he blew his chance with. Victoria, on the other hand, is Ethan's 'Ms. Right Now,' if you get what I'm saying. She's his present, not his past. So she's not his Belle."

"Okay. Let's say that you're right," said Dave. "Are you suggesting that Ethan has no Belle? Have we ever had a Scrooge without a Belle?"

"Never," Boz said softly.

"Oh, he *has* a Belle," I argued. "It's just not Victoria."

"You think it's that girl he saw at the benefit?" Dave asked. "The one in the white dress?"

"No, because she's not his past, either. But I do have a theory."

I nodded at Grant, who turned on the television monitor at the front of the room and then messed around on his laptop until a scene began to play. It was a recorded memory that I'd sifted from Ethan last week.

"Our mistake was getting focused on Victoria Scott. We know that the Belle doesn't have to be a romantic connection, but when we found out about Ethan dating somebody, that was the conclusion everybody jumped to," I said. "But we were wrong. Watch."

In the memory, Ethan was sitting in the dining room of the penthouse, completely alone at this giant gleaming table. A maid set a plate down in front of him and stood back, waiting for him to dismiss her. He took a knife and cut himself a bite of steak. He put it in his mouth, chewed, and then he scowled.

"I said medium rare." He took a napkin and spat the meat discreetly back into it. "This is medium. It's pink in the center, not red. It's overcooked."

The maid went pale. "I'm sorry, sir. I'll tell the cook."

"Tell her she has twenty minutes to make me something edible." Ethan pushed his plate away from him with a disgusted expression. "Make that fifteen."

"Yes, sir." She hurried off.

Dave clucked his tongue sympathetically. "Poor woman. It's not her fault."

"The meat *was* overcooked," said Blackpool.

"Shh," I admonished them. "This is where it gets good."

"Well, that was a move straight out of Grandfather's playbook," came a voice, and Ethan turned to see Jack standing in the doorway.

"Hey, Jacqueline," he said, because no one who knew her ever called her that, and he knew it would bug her. "What's up?"

"Way to be a jerk to the hired help," she commented.

He went back to looking at his phone. "I don't tolerate incompetence."

She took a seat next to him. This time her hair was a bright orange, like a living flame dancing off her head. She even had a tattoo on the inside of her wrist now—a Sanskrit symbol or something. She smiled at him. "Nice to see you, too, little brother."

"What do you want, Jack?"

"I was in the neighborhood and came to see if you wanted to get some dinner. But I can see you already have that covered."

"I can get the cook to make something for you," he offered. "Although I can't promise it will be any good."

"Don't bother," she said. "I've lost my appetite."

He looked up and saw her disgusted expression. "Oh, come on," he scoffed. "She's a cook. She should know how to—I don't know—cook, don't you think?"

"She's a person, Ethan. It wouldn't hurt you to give people a little bit of grace."

"Grace is for screwups." Another one of his grandfather's zingers.

"Nice," she said wryly. "You make me weep for humanity. Seriously."

He sighed. "So that's what you're here for? To give me another 'be kind to your fellow man' lecture? Because there's a morals and ethics class we're forced to take at my school, and I can assure you, I'm getting an A."

She shook her head sadly. "I'm done giving lectures. I just hope you're happy with the life you're choosing here." She stood up. "I know my way out."

"So, what, you're just going to leave now? Until the next time you want to stop by and take the moral high ground?"

Her lips pursed. "There's not going to be a next time, Ethan. I'm not going to come back here again. You've changed. I don't even recognize you anymore."

He scoffed. "Me? You're the one who changes your look, like, every fifteen minutes. You freak."

She gave a sad smile. "Call me if you decide to grow a soul."

I nodded at Marty again, and he paused the video. "You see? This is the breakup scene. She even says some of the lines straight from the Scrooge script. Jack is Ethan's Belle."

A murmur went around the room.

"Jack is Ethan's Belle," Boz mused. "Well, it makes a certain bit of sense. Of course there's no rule that it has to be a romantic entanglement."

"Right?"

Dave looked uncomfortable with the idea, but after a minute he said, "But I still think we need to figure out what's going on with Victoria Scott."

I tried not to roll my eyes. Did I ever mention that Dave, in spite of being the nicest guy at the company, could be, like, mule stubborn?

"I think Havisham is correct in saying that this Victoria person is not important," Boz said. "She was probably just a passing fancy to our Ethan."

Blackpool nodded. "I don't see a real future for Ethan involving anyone named Victoria. But who knows? Perhaps he does have a certain amount of love in store."

He looked at me. He was messing with me now; I was almost sure of it. First with the part about how Ethan was incapable of love, and now that he might have love in his future? What was Blackpool playing at? And—for, like, the hundredth time—what exactly did he know? If he was aware that I was Victoria Scott, he still hadn't told anyone. Maybe he just didn't care. One Scrooge or another, a success or a failure, maybe none of this mattered to Blackpool. He was serving out a prison sentence, like I was. Doing his time.

Or maybe, just maybe, in spite of all of his grouchiness, Blackpool was on my side.

"It's settled, then," Boz said. "We focus on Jack. What else do you have?"

I rattled off the exact dates, times, and locations of the three stops I'd be making into Ethan's past: a moment with his dad from when he was a kid, the Christmas party with his mom, and the breakup scene with Jack. Then my part of Ethan's night would officially be over. For the rest of the night I'd be forced to watch from the sidelines.

"Very good," Boz said when I finished giving him the rundown. "Excellent job, Team Lamp. So then we'll move on to Act Two. Copperfield."

Dave stood up. "So, like Holly, I begin with a brief introduction, and then . . ."

He stopped and glanced down at his notes. He still seemed on edge, which was weird because Dave was usually a pretty laid-back guy. He rubbed the back of his neck. "Then I'll take him to see Dent and his mother—our Cratchits—and then the homeless man on Sixth Avenue, and then on to his grandmother's for the Christmas party."

Good luck getting Ethan to feel sorry for the homeless, I thought. Seeing as how he basically blamed a homeless man for the death of his father.

Dave frowned. "That's all on my end."

"Then he'll be passed along to me," Blackpool said as Dave sat down. "I don't make polite introductions. I'll take him straight to the school, where he can see his classmates cleaning out his locker. Then the Denton house with the heartbroken mother losing her job. And then the mortuary on Eighty-First." He smiled. Blackpool always liked that part—showing the Scrooges their own deaths. I bet he loved that look of pale terror on their faces.

"And then we make him sleep, and get him back to his room, no later than four a.m.," Boz filled in. "Good. It sounds like everything's in place."

Even thinking about Christmas made my heart beat fast. So

much was riding on this one night. In some ways it felt like my entire life (or my entire afterlife, that is) had been leading up to this Christmas with Ethan. Which was silly. This Christmas was just like any other, I tried to tell myself. I just happened to be in a secret relationship with the Scrooge.

Boz surveyed the room like the captain at the helm of a ship. "Let's go get Christmas ready."

We all flooded out into the hall and headed off toward our separate domains as Past, Present, and Future.

Steph trailed right behind me, talking, of course. "I've got a pile of work orders for you to sign when you get a minute."

Ugh, paperwork. "Do you know what the status is on the GCP costume? I haven't seen it around yet."

"They delivered your costume this morning. Do you need to try it on, make sure it still fits?"

I gave her a sharp look.

"Oh, right," she said sheepishly. "Of course it still fits."

"I always have to try it on for the costume department," I said. "They like to change it a little bit every year—add some flair. Call Marie—her number is in my contacts—and she'll set up the time."

"Okay, boss," Stephanie said. "So about these work orders . . ."

"And make sure that Grant's got that lag fixed from last year. That was a bit of a disaster."

"Oh, I think he's got it fixed. He said—"

"Make sure," I said. "There's no room for error here. Just imagine what would happen if we got Ethan into the Time Tunnel and then it shorted out."

She nodded. "Right. I'll make sure. So, the work orders—"

I stopped so quickly she bumped into me. "Okay, okay. The work orders." I grabbed the stack of folders from her hands and started flipping through them.

"Wait, those aren't the . . . ," she started. "The work orders are . . ."

"What's this?" I held up a thick manila folder. It had the word HAVISHAM printed in black marker along the edge.

"Oh. That. It's . . ." She obviously didn't know what to say. Stephanie wasn't a liar, not like me. The minute she tried to think up a lie her blue eyes got all buggy and her voice failed her and she kept licking her lips like the idea of telling a falsehood left her all dried out.

"This is my file," I said. Obviously. The one that I'd found on Dave's desk. I'd been so wrapped up in Ethan for the past few months, I'd forgotten all about it.

"I was just doing some research," Stephanie said.

"On me?"

Her mouth opened and then closed again. She knew. She'd probably known all along, and she'd just wanted to hang out with me in order to—I don't know—study me or something. My brain cycled through all the questions she'd asked me over the past few months: questions about my death, my life, my past relationships, the way I thought about things. It all made sense now.

"Holly—" she tried.

I handed her the folder and turned away.

"Wait, Holly." She grabbed my arm.

I looked at her coldly. "So I was, like, what, an independent study for you? A psychology experiment? A test subject?"

Her hand dropped away from me. "Well, at first of course I was curious about you. You're unique. A failed Scrooge—do you have any idea how rare that is? So yes, I was thrilled to be able to study you. But after a while—"

I let out a sharp laugh that hurt somewhere in my chest. "I actually thought you were my friend."

"I am—"

I shook my head. "It's fine. I'm already over it."

I went back to my office. She followed me, of course. Because it seemed like I was never going to be able to get rid of her.

"Holly, I'm so sorry."

"Don't be sorry." I sat down at my desk and stared out the window. Snow was falling outside. God, I hated snow. I wanted to move to Bermuda.

"I know you must feel—" she tried again.

"We all have our games, right?" I said, waving off her lame attempts to explain herself. "You were just playing yours. It's my fault, really, for thinking it could be anything else. People lie. It's what they do."

"I am your friend," she protested. "I really am."

"Great. You're my friend," I said tonelessly. "So where's this paperwork you need me to sign?"

She sighed and sorted through her jumbled papers for a minute. Then she laid three work orders on my desk in front of me. I scribbled my signature at the bottom of each form.

"There you go."

"Thank you. Can I get you some coffee?" she asked in a wavering voice. "I was thinking of making a run to that shop you like."

I looked up at her. "Just do your job, Dorrit. I don't need anything else from you."

Her head dropped. "Okay."

She turned to go.

"How long is your internship, by the way?" I asked before she reached the door.

"My internship?" She turned back.

"Are you only supposed to work here for this one year?"

"Oh," she answered. "Yes. This one year."

"So it's almost done, then," I pointed out.

"I guess it is."

"Can I offer you some professional advice?"

"Okay," she whispered.

"You need to rethink your wardrobe. I mean, look at you."

She stared down at her outfit. She was wearing a bright red sweater with a Scottie dog on the front and a black skirt and black cable tights and red flats.

"You look like a ninth grader," I observed. "How old are you, nineteen?"

"Almost twenty," she squeaked.

"It's ridiculous. You're working at a prestigious business in New York City. Dress like it. Otherwise no one is ever going to take you seriously. Oh, and get some new glasses, too. Those are terrible."

She swallowed and nodded shakily. "Okay. Thank you."

"Why don't you spend the rest of the day helping Marty set up those cameras we're going to use," I suggested. "I don't need you here."

"Okay."

"Okay," I parroted. "Off you go, then."

It was only after she'd left that I allowed myself to cry.

TWENTY-TWO

THREE DAYS BEFORE CHRISTMAS, SEVENTY-TWO hours before the big night, I took Ethan to the Angelika. It would normally have been too risky, since it was indoors and Dave could feasibly access any indoor security camera in the city, but earlier in the evening I'd used my Hoodie to go around the theater and disable all the cameras. Now they were experiencing "technical difficulties." So Ethan and I were off the grid. Plus, the Angelika was across town from Ethan's usual haunts and the company would never think to look for him there. According to his schedule, he was playing racquetball at the club. And Dave's team had relaxed a lot since we'd officially decided to stop looking for Victoria Scott.

"This is the best theater in Manhattan," I told Ethan as we climbed the steps to the ticket booth. "It's kind of old school and classic, and it always plays the best films. The smaller films that nobody else bothers to see."

Ethan paid for our tickets. To my dad's movie, of course. It was still playing there once a week.

"This is nice," he commented as we went inside, where there was a charming café set up with little wire tables and chairs, like something you'd see on the streets of Paris. "But it's out of the way, don't you think? There's got to be a good movie theater farther uptown."

"But they have the best scones here." I pointed up. "And look."

The ceiling had been painted to resemble a blue sky just before sunset, the clouds all touched with gold. Right in the middle hung a large crystal chandelier that had been highlighted with strips of blue neon so the whole thing gave off a kind of electric-blue vibe. I loved that chandelier.

"It's cool," Ethan said. He seemed uneasy for some reason. Or maybe he was picking up on how nervous I was. "I'm glad you could finally go out again," he said after we loaded up on freshly squeezed lemonade and scones. "We're okay, right?"

He was obviously worried that I was mad about the lying thing. "Yeah," I murmured. Of course I wasn't mad. I'd been in such a funk since the whole episode with Ro. And now Stephanie, who had turned out to be a fake friend. It was good, seeing Ethan. So heartbreakingly, unbelievably good I wanted to grab him and hold on to him and never let him go. But part of me wondered if this would be the last time we got to see each other as Ethan and Victoria. If everything went as planned, Ethan would be spending Christmas joyfully running around telling everyone *Merry Christmas* and trying to make everything right. And then maybe everything would be right. And he'd have his family back—Jack and his mom and his grandmother. And he'd be real friends with Dent. And he'd have a better life.

But I knew it would be a life without me. I couldn't kid myself about it anymore. The point of Project Scrooge was to change someone, inside and out. And when he was changed, Ethan wouldn't be the same. We wouldn't be the same. It'd be over.

"And it was a great idea to go to a movie," Ethan said. "We've never been to a movie together. It's kind of, I don't know, *normal* for you."

"I can be normal." We sat down at one of the little tables and sipped at our lemonade. "I'm amazing at being normal."

"Yeah, you're so humble, too," Ethan said.

"Well, you know, vices are sometimes only virtues carried to excess," I said, another one of Boz's favorite Dickens sayings.

Ethan's eyebrows came together. "Who said that?"

"Some old dead guy."

It was almost time for the movie. We gathered up our food and headed down the escalator to the basement, which was decorated with various artworks that depicted New York City, huge old movie posters, and—my favorite—an old wooden rabbit that used to be part of the Coney Island carousel. The basement was where all the individual theaters were.

Evangeline's Well was in theater two. Ethan wanted to sit in the very back. "So do you have plans for Christmas?" he asked as we settled into our seats.

My heart started pounding just thinking about it. Christmas. Three days away.

"I don't do Christmas," I said. "I refuse to participate on principle."

The corner of his mouth lifted. "You hate Christmas, too, huh? Why?"

"My birthday," I admitted.

He paused with his cup of lemonade halfway to his lips. "Your birthday is on Christmas? How did I not know that?"

"It's the day after Christmas," I corrected. "December twenty-sixth. Which is the worst possible day to have a birthday. It was just awful when I was a kid. Everyone was always so fixated on Christmas, they forgot about me. I never got to have my class sing me happy birthday or hand out cupcakes, and if my parents threw a party nobody ever came, because they all had, like, Christmas hangover."

"Poor baby," Ethan said with a smirk, and I swung at him like I was going to punch him. He laughed.

"Anyway. I hate Christmas."

"I agree," said Ethan, taking a bite of scone. "Christmas blows. It always feels to me like people are playing a game on Christmas—the let's-make-a-big-deal-about-nothing game. They don't know when baby Jesus was really born, do they? No, it's like everything else—it's made up."

"It's not like it's even about religion, anyway," I added. "At least not that I ever saw. It's about the presents and the pageantry and the annoying fricking songs."

He nodded and smiled, glad to have a partner in disliking the holidays.

"So do *you* have plans for Christmas?" I asked him.

Ethan rolled his eyes. "Not really. My grandmother's throwing a Christmas party, as usual. She invited me. But I hate Christmas parties."

"They're the worst," I agreed.

"And my sister's going to be there, so I'm definitely not going to go."

I was quiet for a minute, like I was digesting all of this.

"So . . . you have a sister." I arched an eyebrow at him. "You told me that you were an only child, remember?"

He gave an embarrassed laugh. "Wishful thinking. I haven't seen her in forever."

"Maybe you should go," I said lightly, but of course I knew he wouldn't. Dave would have to bring him there to watch the party invisibly.

He shook his head. "No way. My sister used to be cool, and we hung out all the time, but now all she does is act like I'm a big disappointment to her, because I'm a realist, and I like having money, and I'm planning to take over the business when I'm old enough. And my sister says that's materialistic and she says I'm like my grandfather, and she doesn't really want to have anything to do with that world."

"Hey, there is nothing wrong with having money," I said. "That's what makes the world go round, I always say."

He grinned. "You're a girl after my own heart, Tori."

I know, Ethan, I thought. *I know.*

"But family's important," I said. "It's, like, the most important thing. Believe me, I wish I could spend time with my family again."

"You mean, besides your dad?"

"My dad?" I stared at him for a few seconds before I understood he meant Victoria's dad. Who didn't exist. "Oh. Right. Well, my dad's a piece of work."

"So, what I'm hearing is, you don't have plans for Christmas, and I don't have plans for Christmas," he pointed out. "Do you want to not have plans for Christmas together?"

I leaned over to kiss him. "Why don't we play it by ear?"

"I can never pin you down, can I?" he laughed. The lights dimmed. "What's this movie supposed to be about, anyway?"

I took a deep breath. It was like I was actually bringing Ethan to meet my dad. It felt weird for me to see the movie this way, without my Hoodie, not invisible, sitting next to someone I knew, waiting to see what he thought of something that was so important to me.

"It's about family," I said to answer his question. "It's about how, even when we know it's a mistake or that things are going to end badly, we still choose to fight for the people we love."

"So it's kind of a girl movie, right?" Ethan said. "I get points for taking you to a girl movie."

"I think it's more than a chick flick," I said. "It's a statement about love and life and death and human nature and grief and . . ."

I was talking too much. I shut up. We sat through a couple of previews, and then the movie began to play. The screen faded from black to the opening image: the mayor's daughter, wearing a long red dress, staring at her own reflection in the well. Then the picture changed, shifting to show all the different futures that Evangeline saw when she looked into the water.

Evangeline, by the way, is my middle name.

I glanced over at Ethan, taking in the way that the screen glowed on his face and reflected back in his eyes. It was so unreal: Ethan, watching my dad's movie. My dad's name was up there on the screen, and his company, GCP—Gideon Chase Productions. I shivered.

Ethan put his arm around me.

"See? When she looks in the well, she can see all her possible futures," I whispered close to his ear. "And if you look closely, pay attention, there's a flash where you can see the actual end of the movie. When her father saves her. There, did you see?"

"You just, like, told me the end of the film." He laughed. "Spoiler alert."

"Oh, I'm sorry," I said. We watched for a few more minutes. "But it's kind of obvious, isn't it? That her dad's going to save her? I mean, it's predictable. Not in a bad way, though. It's like it's meant to be. It's all moving toward this inevitable outcome."

"You want to know what's inevitable?" He kissed me. I let him, for a minute. But then I pulled back. "You have to watch this part. Where the monster gets her. The look on her father's face when they tell him, it kills me every time."

Ethan was looking at me strangely. "How many times have you seen this movie?"

"Shh!" An old lady a few rows in front of us turned around and gave us both a disapproving glare.

"Six. No, seven. Seven and a half?" I whispered.

He leaned in again. "So you can stand to miss some."

"No." I put my hand on his chest and pushed him back. "You need to see this."

"Why?" He looked annoyed more than anything else. He'd seriously thought we were only here to suck face in the back row. Boys. Unbelievable.

"Because it's important!" I burst out. This wasn't how this was supposed to go. He was supposed to love my dad's movie. We were supposed to be able to talk about it later. And then we'd actually be talking about my dad. We were supposed to connect about something real. Something that was mine, and not Victoria's.

"You already told me the ending," he pointed out.

"But it isn't about the ending—"

"Shh!" insisted the lady.

"It's fine. I'm leaving." I stood up and pushed my way in front of people's feet down the row. Ethan cursed and followed me out.

"What is wrong with you?" he said as soon as we were out in the hall.

"What's wrong with *you*?" I shot back, fighting tears. And suddenly I couldn't stop thinking about Ro. Ro and her stupid boyfriend meeting her stupid auntie in that stupid little house with their stupid future. All I was ever going to have with Ethan was the present. Tonight. And he wouldn't even watch my dad's movie. He didn't care about it. And I couldn't tell him why it mattered, because I couldn't tell him who I was.

"Tori, stop." He grabbed my hand. "I'm sorry. I don't understand what's going on exactly, but we can go back in there if you want. I'll watch the movie. I'll be good."

I dashed the furious tears off my face with the back of my hand. "No. You're right. It's a girl movie. And you're not a girl."

I grabbed him by the shoulders and kissed him. He was surprised, but kissed me back. Within minutes we'd sneaked into the empty theater next to the one we'd started out in and were full-on making out. I let our hands roam where they may and tried to make everything else go away but Ethan—his lips on mine, his heartbeat thudding under my hand when I laid it against his chest, his clean, sophisticated smell, his soft hair, the way his hand felt on the bare skin on the back of my arm. I tried to lose myself in Ethan while my dad's movie played in the theater next to us and Evangeline and her father played out their tragic story. I kissed Ethan, but I couldn't have him. Not for real. Not for good.

Ethan pulled away. "Whoa. Okay . . . whoa. What the—"

I was crying again. Silent tears were streaming down my face.

Ethan shook his head, stunned. This was the part where I turned into the crazy girl, obviously. "Victoria . . ."

Holly. Holly Holly Holly. I cried even harder.

"Is it that time?" he asked slowly.

"That time?" I sniffled.

"Of the m—"

I smacked him and bolted out of there.

"Tori. Wait. Tori!" he called after me when I was halfway up the escalator to the main floor. He ran up the stationary stairs in the middle and tried to keep pace with me. "Come on! What did I do?"

"So, what, if I'm emotional, I can't have a good reason?" I yelled.

He threw up his hands. "So tell me the reason! Tell me!"

But I couldn't. So I just got off the escalator and headed for the door. "This was a mistake. I shouldn't have brought you here."

Ethan trailed after me. Angry now.

"You never tell me anything!" he said when we got out to the street. "You don't let me take your picture, you don't call me, you don't bring me back to wherever it is you live. Sometimes I feel like I don't even know who you are. I'm not complaining, and I'm not asking to meet your dad, Tori, or get his blessing or anything, but I just want to point out that you're the one who's holding back here. You're the one who doesn't tell me things."

"Says the guy who told me that his parents were happily married, but they just traveled a lot," I scoffed. "You didn't tell me about your dad!"

His jaw tightened. "I did tell you about my dad."

I shouldn't have brought up his dad. I knew it the minute the words left my mouth. "Ethan." I reached for him. My hand brushed his cheek. And suddenly, I saw it. After all that time I'd spent sifting through his memories, trying to crack the dad thing—what his father's death had meant to him—it was there, with no transducer and no lavender mist and no REM state, that I could finally see.

In the memory, he was standing in front of a coffin. It was covered with flowers, and the sweet, overpowering smell of them almost sickened him. His eyes were bleary. He put his hand on the shining wood.

"Dad," he whispered. "Come back."

My throat felt tight with tears, but I couldn't tell if they were his tears or mine. I couldn't tell if this was a memory or part of a dream he was having because of me. The pain of it was indescribable, almost unbearable. His chest felt like it was being cracked open. Some part of him was howling.

A hand with purple polish on the fingernails came down next to Ethan's on the casket. He looked up to see Jack's tear-streaked face.

"Hey, buddy," she said hoarsely.

"Where's Mom?" he asked, but he knew his mother was at the other end of the room, hidden by an ever-shifting group of people and busy doing whatever it was they wanted her to do. "I want Mom."

"I know," said Jack. "You've got me, too, though, you know? You've always got me."

He nodded.

"You. Children. Get away from there," came a voice, and they both turned to see their grandfather in a black suit frowning at them so deeply it was almost a scowl.

"Come," he said. "It won't do for you to hover over the dead."

The dead, thought Ethan. *That's what my dad is now.*

The dead.

"I'm so sorry about your dad, Ethan," I whispered.

Ethan stepped back, breaking our connection. His blue eyes were so cold now he reminded me of Ethan Senior. Like he wasn't looking at me anymore. Like he was seeing Jack when he'd said, "Leave me alone, you freak." He gave me a sarcastic smile. "Like I said, I'm not complaining. You're a beautiful girl, Victoria, and I enjoy the time we spend together, and it doesn't have to be more than that. I'm fine with how it is. It's not heavy, like you said. It's not serious."

"No. It's serious," I argued. "I . . ."

He checked his watch. Like he actually had somewhere to be that wasn't with me. "I should go. It's been fun, but—wait, it really hasn't been *that* fun. It could have been more fun, if you know what I mean."

Now he was over the line. I sighed. "Look, don't be—"

"You've always been this mystery, and at first that was hot. But I'm getting bored. And you're a little, I don't know. Hot and cold."

I closed my eyes. There wasn't anything I could do now. Nothing I could say to fix it. I couldn't tell him the truth. And I couldn't lie.

But it didn't matter, because when I opened my eyes again, Ethan was gone.

TWENTY-THREE

CHRISTMAS EVE. MY HANDS STARTED shaking every time I considered all of the ways that the night could go wrong. The first and most obvious way: Ethan could recognize me. All this time I'd tried to act like that wasn't a possibility, but it had been a danger I'd posed to Ethan's future the moment I stepped into the New York Athletic Club and showed him my face. Still, like I'd told Stephanie when she'd asked about it, the costume was pretty extreme. And I was planning on shining a lot of lights in his eyes.

"You've got some puffiness," remarked Leigh, the hair and makeup lady, as she painted an extra layer of concealer under my eyes. "Have you been getting enough sleep?"

I was getting no sleep, but that didn't matter, because I didn't need sleep. I reset every morning. But I had been doing that crying-into-my-pillow thing for the past two nights. Because it was really over now with Ethan. But it was the right thing, I'd decided.

Inevitable. Victoria and Ethan had always been running on borrowed time.

Marie, who was in charge of costumes for the entire project, bustled into my dressing room with two huge garment bags draped over her arm. "Great job with the hair this year," she said when she saw me. "It's always a work of art, isn't it?"

It was. Leigh had curled my hair and braided the top of it into an elaborate crown, letting the rest fall around my shoulders. Then she'd sprayed my hair with something that made it look white and glittery under the lights. She stuck in tiny sprigs of leaves and holly here and there, like I was a sparkly wood nymph that had wandered out of a snowstorm. For my makeup, she'd covered my face and every exposed part of my body with an opalescent foundation that made me as pale as a marble statue come to life. She'd painted my eyebrows and lids with a layer of shimmering silver, and left my eyelashes bare. As a last step, she'd dusted a final coat of shimmery powder on my cheekbones and lined my lips with a soft, natural pink.

I looked like a totally different person, like a little girl and simultaneously like an ancient primitive force—ageless and ethereal.

"You've outdone yourself," I said.

Leigh smiled. "I could never outdo myself, darling."

Marie hung the garment bags on separate hooks on the wall, and then unzipped one of them and drew out my dress. It was gorgeous—at least I'd always thought so—made of overlapping layers of a semitransparent fabric that looked silver in some lights and so white in others that it almost hurt your eyes to look at it. I took the hanger from Marie carefully and went into the adjoining bathroom to put the dress on.

"Careful of your face," Leigh called through the door as I slid the dress over my head. "You don't want to smear."

"In six years, have I ever messed up my makeup?" I shot back.

"No, so don't start now," Leigh said merrily.

I came out (unsmudged, I might add) and Marie started to orbit around me, fastening the ties in the back and fixing the way the fabric draped around my body. Then she went to the table in the corner and opened a large black box. Inside was a belt that looked like it was made of stars. Even in the relatively low light of the dressing room, it gleamed and twinkled.

A knock came at the door and Stephanie stuck her head in. "Hey. Boz wanted me to see if you're—oh!" She covered her mouth with her hand. "Oh, that's beautiful! You're beautiful, Holly. Wow."

"That's why they pay us the big bucks," Leigh said wryly as Marie finished fastening the star belt around my waist. "Oh, wait . . ."

It was a joke I'd heard before, more than once. Leigh worked that joke in every year, for fun. And I'd heard the same joke from Steph, I realized, not so long ago. I met her eyes. She was wearing a black cashmere sweater and gray jeans with black boots. Her long blond hair was twisted into a simple chignon. Like she'd actually taken my advice about her wardrobe. I wanted to tell her that she looked nice, but I resisted the impulse. We hadn't found much to say to each other since the incident with my Havisham folder, but I preferred the awkward silence to her lame attempts at an apology.

It would take only a few words, a smile, and we could be friends again. She hadn't told me things. I hadn't told her things. She'd used me like I was a science project. But I'd used her, too. I knew that. Me being mad at her was wildly hypocritical. But Stephanie's internship was almost over. She was leaving. So there was really no point.

"What did Boz want?" I asked her.

She seemed to realize that she'd been staring at me, and glanced away. "He wanted to see if you were ready."

Marie hurried over to the other garment bag and lifted out a white fur robe that she settled around my shoulders. It was soft and warm and would protect me from the chills of the Time Tunnel. More important, it would hide most of my face in its hood. I lifted my feet one at a time as Leigh slid on a pair of silver slippers, which were surprisingly comfortable to walk in. I straightened my shoulders. The costume always made me feel powerful. There was just a raw energy to it, like when I was wearing it I became some mythical being made of light.

"Oops, almost forgot the lamp," Leigh said. She opened another black box—this one hat-sized—and set the headpiece carefully on my head. It was like the headlamps that miners wear, capable of shining like a halo all around my head or focusing like a spotlight. The controls for it were hidden in the folds of my robe.

I winced as Leigh drove a few bobby pins practically into my skull to hold it in place, and then drew the hood up and over my head.

"Okay, let's do this." I walked slowly and carefully down the hall toward the Go Room. People lined the corridors to watch as I passed by, whispering and staring.

Steph trailed behind me, as usual, but she didn't talk.

"Ah, Havisham, how glorious," exclaimed Boz when he saw me. "You're a vision. Literally." He chuckled at his own joke.

"So they tell me. I'm ready." I buried my still-trembling hands in my robe and glanced around the room. It was, as always at this point in the Project, crowded. Almost every single employee of the company was required to be here. There were people milling all over the place, fussing over last-minute details, but there were also just your average bookkeepers and pencil pushers, here to see the show.

And there was Dave in his green velvet robes, his head adorned with a laurel of green leaves and his beard decorated with tiny star-like flowers. He looked younger than he actually was right now—it was part of the magic of the night for the Ghost of Christmas Present to appear young when he first arrived and slowly seem to age as the night wore on. How they pulled off that effect, I didn't know, but as he traveled with Ethan his face would become wrinkled and his beard would go silver and grizzled.

I'm the Ghost who will show you the way the world truly is, he'd said to me that night when I was the Scrooge. *Underneath this facade you've built for yourself.*

Uh, thanks, but no thanks, I'd answered. *Freak.*

He'd laughed at my insult. *Well, come with me, Holly Chase, and get to know me better. And through knowing me—and I will admit that I am an oddball—you might actually come to know yourself.*

He turned and smiled at me. "Last time," he whispered.

I may have choked up a little at that. I was going to miss Dave. There'd never be a Ghost of Christmas Present like Dave was—the gentle giant who'd always been so kind to me.

"Good luck," he said.

I reached out and squeezed his hand. "Good luck to you, too, Dave."

I got a flash of Dave standing in his dressing room, his face young the way it was right now, his arms around Steph. She was wearing the same clothes she was wearing tonight. Dave was rubbing her back like she was cold. And then he kissed the top of her head.

Dave let go of my hand. I gasped and stared up into his eyes. I didn't understand. Dave and Steph? But I thought she was with Grant.

"Everything is not always as it seems," Dave said.

No kidding, I thought. It was kind of gross, the idea of Dave and Stephanie. Dave was nice, but he was so old. And dead.

"Places!" came a voice over the loudspeaker. Boz had apparently moved into the control booth and was ready to go.

"Godspeed, Holly," Dave said, and moved quickly away from me to take up his position on the other side of the room.

"Places, please," Boz called. "Marley to the Transport Room."

I turned and nearly bumped into Ethan Senior on his way to the door. He looked frightened, his eyes wide and a bit glassy, like he was drugged or something. Sometimes Marleys looked pretty funky. They were often in various states of decay—Yvonne and her stitched-up neck wound came to mind. But old man Winters had been cremated.

He was thin and pale, his face almost colorless but otherwise normal. Except that he occasionally started smoking—not like cigarettes, but himself, his clothes, his hair. Every now and then smoke would start to rise off him like he was smoldering. I kept waiting for him to burst into outright flames, but he never did. He was wearing a three-piece Armani suit with chains draped over it, and they clanked against each other when he moved.

"Hello, Mr. Winters," I said. Where was Tox? I wondered.

He grabbed at my sleeve. "Tell me the truth," he demanded, his voice like a growl. "How can this possibly save him? I don't know how it can. He never listened to me when I was alive. Why should he listen now?"

"He listened," I assured him. "Believe me, sir. He heard everything you said to him."

"Marley to the Transport Room," Boz repeated over the loudspeaker, more urgently this time.

"You're the past, aren't you?" the old man asked, leaning close to me. "You know Ethan."

He smelled like lighter fluid and old people. I nodded. "I know Ethan."

"All right." He let go of me. "All right, I'm coming!" Tox appeared at his side and started to pull him toward the door, practically dancing with eagerness to get Mr. Winters where he was supposed to be.

"Come on, old timer," she said. "It's time for you to show us what you've got."

"Be quiet," the old man muttered. "Let's just get it done."

It happened the same way for Ethan that it had for me. It all started with three knocks on his bedroom door.

Bang.

Bang.

Bang.

Ethan was out of bed in a flash. "What the—" He crossed to the door and flung it open, but found nobody on the other side. He looked around wildly, prowling from room to room—there was no one, not in the entire house. He was alone.

Still, he made a point of locking his bedroom door that time before he settled back into his bed.

I felt so sorry for him as I watched from the monitors in the Go Room, knowing that he was about to get the ever-living crap scared out of him. I'd been there, done that. I remembered the way the inside of my throat had tingled after Yvonne had shown up in my bedroom and I'd done all of that hysterical screaming.

To Ethan's credit, he didn't scream or shout or anything. When he sat up again and saw his dead grandfather standing at the foot of his bed, he simply froze. He didn't make a sound.

Mr. Winters stepped forward. "Hello, boy," he said gruffly.

Hello, darling girl. I closed my eyes for a moment, remembering.

Ethan didn't answer.

"I said hello," Mr. Winters insisted. "It's polite to speak when you're spoken to, boy. Do you hear me?"

Ethan's back stiffened. "Yes, sir," he mumbled out of habit.

"Good. I don't have much time with you." Mr. Winters straightened his tie. "They won't give me more than a few minutes. So you have to listen now and listen good."

"But you're dead," Ethan said almost stupidly.

"You noticed that, did you?" The old man laughed and then coughed. "Yes. I am dead. All my money and power couldn't stop me from dying, could it?"

"What do you want?" Ethan still hadn't moved. I could practically see the wheels turning in his head.

Mr. Winters sat down at the edge of Ethan's bed. "There's so much that I want," he said. "But it's too late for me now. I'm here to talk about you."

Ethan stared at him mutely. The old man stared right back, his eyes narrowing.

"You don't believe I'm really here, do you?"

"No, sir," Ethan said hoarsely.

The old man clapped a hand down hard on Ethan's shoulder. "So you think this is a dream?" His bony fingers dug into the bare flesh near Ethan's collarbone until Ethan flinched. "How's this for a dream, then?" He squeezed harder. "How's this?"

"Okay!" Ethan burst out finally. "Okay. Stop."

"You believe me now?"

"Fine, I believe you. But what are you doing here? You're dead."

"Yes. I'm dead, and I'm also damned," Mr. Winters said more quietly, releasing his grip from Ethan's shoulder. "I'm doomed to wander around this pathetic excuse for an afterlife, watching the world pass me by. Watching, always watching. Never doing anything, ever again. Just watching. Seeing all that I could have done."

He stood up and crossed to the other side of the room, his chains dragging on the carpet behind him. "I was a fool," he said mournfully. "And now I'm paying for it."

Ethan swung his legs over the side of the bed like he would get up and go to his grandfather, but he stayed where he was. "What do you mean, you're paying for it? What's with the chains?"

The old man picked up a length of the chain and held it out. "I made these," he said. "I couldn't see them at the time, but I was forging them, link by link, all my life." He smiled, showing brown, decaying teeth. "Do you like them? Do they look comfortable to you?"

"No, sir."

"You should pay attention, then, because you're working on your own set of shackles." The old man dropped the chain and pointed a knobby finger at Ethan. "Don't you know?"

Ethan shook his head. "What are you talking about?"

Mr. Winters sighed, which came out as a wisp of smoke. "I wasted my life, boy. I put all of my effort into the wrong endeavors. I valued the money—the little meaningless pieces of printed paper and the investments and the property I came to own—over all else. I let the good things slip through my fingers, and what was I left with when I died? Nothing. Nothing and no one."

"It wasn't nothing," Ethan argued. "You built an empire.

People are still talking about you—the things you did, the way you managed your holdings, your ruthlessness, your genius. You were a brilliant businessman."

The old man coughed. "A businessman. Yes. I was a businessman. But my business should have been in loving my family, shouldn't it? It should have been in improving the state of my city, of my country, of the world. I should have been giving back, but instead all I did was take and take with greedy hands. And now look at me." He raised his arms again and strained against the chains that confined him. "This is my punishment, and it's what I deserve."

Ethan was shaking his head. "No."

There hadn't been a lot of love lost between the two of them. I knew that better than anybody. But Ethan had respected his grandfather. He'd seen the value of how the elder Ethan Winters operated in his life. In the end, he'd wanted to be like him; he wanted to be better than him, even. But now here was this sad old man before him boohooing about love and bettering the world and talking about hell like it was an actual thing.

Mr. Winters approached the bed again. "I've been watching you. It's the worst part, the endless watching. You are making all of the same mistakes." He sat down next to Ethan. "But now I'm here to warn you, so that you can stop all of this now. You still have a chance to make things right again."

"What chance?" Ethan asked.

"You're going to get a visit tonight from three spirits." The old man jumped up again, restless, and started to pace back and forth across Ethan's huge bedroom.

"Wait," said Ethan, his eyes narrowing. "Three . . . spirits?"

He was trying to remember the story. He'd seen it before. He knew it, just like I had known it. He frowned. "Like, ghosts? Like you?"

"Not like me. You listen to them, boy. Do what they say," Mr. Winters said urgently. "They'll help you."

Ethan sat back against his pillows and scoffed. Maybe he could believe that his dead grandfather was somehow resurrected, but no way was he going to believe in three spirits sent to reform him. "Oh, come on," he said with a laugh. "What is this? This is not real. How is this happening?"

The old man rounded on him, went straight at him faster than I thought he'd be capable of moving. He grabbed Ethan by the ear and twisted it until Ethan yelped in pain.

"Are you telling me what's real, son?" he asked. Then he seemed to remember himself. He released Ethan and stepped back. "I'm sorry," he croaked. "I don't want to hurt you. I just want you to see. Before it's too late. You must see."

There was the gleam of tears in his eyes.

"You look so much like your father," the old man murmured, almost to himself. "I loved him, I did. I lost him, but no one can ever tell me I didn't love him. I loved you too, in my way."

Ethan was holding one hand over his ear. He stared up at his grandfather incredulously.

Smoke was beginning to roll off Mr. Winters, starting at his feet and working up his body. In moments the smoke filled the room. He coughed.

"Expect the first Ghost at one o'clock," he rasped, turning toward the bedroom door, which was the transport back to the company.

"Wait," Ethan said.

"One o'clock, boy," the old man repeated wearily. "Pay attention to what they say."

"Havisham to the Transport Room," came Boz's voice over the intercom. "Havisham to the Transport Room. Prepare for Act One."

Stephanie touched my shoulder lightly. "Should we, uh, go now?"

I nodded. "Yeah. Let's go."

My stomach was doing backflips as we made our way down the hall toward the Transport Room. Grant and Marty were waiting for us, grinning the way they both always did on Christmas, like this whole thing was just so unbearably exciting that they couldn't even. Marty handed me the earbud (not the transducer, but just my regular earbud) and Stephanie helped me put it in my ear through my arrangement of hair. We ran a quick test to see if it was working. It was.

"Go kick some Scroogy butt," Marty said as I stepped up to the Portal.

I smiled weakly. "Right."

"You've got this," Steph said softly, like somehow she knew how much I was secretly freaking out.

Bang bang bang went my heart against my rib cage. I nodded curtly at Grant to signal that I was ready. *I'm ready,* I told myself. *I've never been so ready.*

Time to do my thing.

I turned the knob then, and walked through the glowing door.

TWENTY-FOUR

ETHAN HADN'T GONE BACK TO sleep after the visit from his grandfather. Not that I could blame him. I remembered exactly what that had been like when I was the Scrooge—those slow thirty-seven minutes between when Yvonne left me and when the Ghost of Christmas Past appeared in my room.

Wondering if it was a dream or not.

Thinking about the strings of pearls that were her sins, "each one counted," she'd said, "each pearl a person who in life I utterly disregarded."

Wondering if I'd gone insane.

Watching the minutes flit by on my phone until it was finally one o'clock, when all of a sudden my phone had gone dark and then the room had gone so bright.

It was in that light that I stepped forward into Ethan's room, the lamp on my head flaring and making it impossible for him to see my face.

"Who are you?" he yelled, like my light was a noise he could shout over. He put a hand out to shield his eyes. "What do you want?"

I let my light dim a few degrees. The headlamp was still shining, my dress glowing faintly, the belt at my waist twinkling, but now his eyes could somewhat adjust.

My mouth was dry. I took a few steps closer to the bed. Ethan didn't shrink back like some of the Scrooges did. He looked up at me, blinking, his mouth fallen open in a way that was so uncharacteristically uncool that under any other circumstances I would have laughed.

I was struggling to keep my expression neutral as it was, even though he couldn't see my face in the folds of my robe. I held out my hand to him.

"Hello, Ethan," I said in a low voice that I'd been practicing for weeks. A voice that was not my own. A voice he wouldn't know.

"Wait. Is that you, Holly?" Grant said in my ear.

Ethan drew in a sharp breath. God, maybe in spite of everything, he recognized me. I forgot my lines for like sixty seconds before I said, "I'm the Ghost of Christmas Past. The one your grandfather told you about."

"Does Holly have a cold?" Grant said. "Her voice sounds funny."

"What past?" Ethan asked. "What Christmas?"

"Yours."

That answer didn't seem to satisfy him. "Who are you, really?" He moved like he was going to get up and confront me, but then he realized that he wasn't exactly dressed for company. As in, he was only wearing a pair of boxers under there.

"I have a lot of names." I crossed over to his dresser and took out a pair of black sweatpants that he often wore to the club. I knew exactly which drawer they'd be in. "But all you need to know right now is that I'm your friend."

"My friend," he said slowly.

"I am. I've been sent here to help you." I handed the pants to him and looked away while he pulled them on.

"Are you trying an accent or something?" Grant asked me. "Because I'm not going to lie—it's not working."

Ethan stood up.

"Come." I held out my hand again. He hesitated and then took it. I worried that the feel of my hand in his felt familiar to him the way it did to me. I started to lead us toward the door, where we'd be transported into the Time Tunnel and off across time, but suddenly Ethan stopped and grabbed me by both arms.

"Wait," he said. "I'm not going anywhere with you until I know what's going on."

"Uh-oh." I heard Grant's voice in my ear. "The Scrooge is getting physical with the Lamp."

This almost never happened. The Scrooges were usually scared of me—too scared to do anything but what I told them.

"Tell me what's happening," Ethan demanded. "Tell me."

"Ethan . . ."

"Do you need us to tase him?" Grant asked. "Then we'll have to use the forget serum and the time stuff and, ugh, that will be a mess. But we could totally tase him."

"No," came Boz's voice—he was also linked into this feed. "No, just wait."

Ethan shook me a little, and my hood fell back. I turned my lamp up so he couldn't look directly at me. "This is a joke, right?" he said angrily, his fingers biting into my arms. "I know it's not real. What's going on?"

"It's not a joke," I said.

"Wait." His eyes widened. "Tori?" he whispered.

The bottom dropped out of my stomach. I'd been saying all this time that he wouldn't recognize me, that he simply couldn't recognize me in my crazy costume and with my altered voice. I'd told myself that so I could justify hanging out with him. So I could tell myself that I wasn't really jeopardizing my time with him on Christmas Eve. But that was dumb. "We ghosts can appear however we wish," I said softly.

"Say what now?" Grant was confused.

"But you look just . . . ," Ethan began.

"I have chosen this form so that you would trust in me." It was all I could think of to do. I'd pretend I was just wearing Holly like a costume. That kind of thing happened in the movies, right? "I am the Ghost of Christmas Past. Your past," I said again, emphasizing the word *your.*

"You said that already." He relaxed slightly, but I could tell that this was still royally freaking him out.

"Okay, so no Taser?" Grant said.

"No," repeated Boz. "What did you say to him? About trust? I didn't quite catch it."

"Come with me," I said to Ethan.

Ethan's hands dropped away from me. "Fine. Whoever you are. Let me at least put on a shirt."

I waited while he tugged a T-shirt over his head and put on a pair of woolen clogs he used for slippers.

"Do you have a robe?" I asked him. "It will be cold where we're going."

He shook his head. "Where are we going, exactly?"

I took his hand again and pulled him toward the door. It was glowing. He reached out and touched the wood as if he'd never seen it before. It was warm to the touch—like there was fire on the other side.

"Here we go," I said, and opened the door and walked us through.

We were instantly surrounded by a formless, foggy white. The Time Tunnel was like a long hallway, with two ends that could be flipped around. On one side was a waiting area, where I was sure Dave and Blackpool were already hanging out, watching the monitors. On the other side was, of course, an archway that would take us across time. On Christmas we filled the tunnel with fog and snow, so you couldn't really see anything unless you knew specifically that it was there. It was like we were walking through a cloud.

Ethan stumbled, not sure where to put his feet. I stopped and put my hand on his shoulder. "Look at me," I directed, and he did.

"Hold on to my arm, and you won't fall."

"Okay," he said.

We started walking again. Ethan stayed close. I felt the change in the air when we crossed under the archway and the tunnel was activated—a subtle vibration under my feet and an electric hum as we shifted through time and space.

Then we were in a little boy's bedroom. It looked like it was straight out of one of those pricey kiddie catalogs. The walls were painted blue, with a definite astronaut theme—star charts on the wall, a picture of a rocket ship blasting off, a lamp on the bedside table that cast a pattern of stars onto the ceiling. And there was a large letter *E* posted above the bed.

Beside me, Ethan tensed up again. "This is my old room."

"Yes."

"It's just like I remember it." He crossed over to the dresser, which had a fish tank bubbling on it, and two fat black goldfish. "Like, exactly."

"What were their names?" I asked him.

"Sharky and Bones," he answered automatically, and then seemed surprised that he'd still known the answer after all this time.

He turned in a slow circle, drinking in the details of his old life: the quilt with the solar system stitched onto it, the colored balls hanging from fishing line from the ceiling to represent the planets. He stopped when he got to the series of black marks on the side of the closet door frame—a growth chart, going back to when he was three years old. His fingers brushed the marks as he read the dates.

"How is this possible?" he breathed. "We can't really be there, can we? I mean, we sold that place. We moved away."

I could see that he was starting to believe it was real. Stephanie had been right when she'd made that argument. It was the details that made the whole thing convincing. Those details, like Sharky and Bones, that couldn't be fabricated.

The door was suddenly flung open, and a little boy stomped in, scowling.

It was Ethan at age eight. He was mad about something—furious, in fact. He kicked his favorite stuffed doggy out of his way and threw himself onto his bed. He was a miniature version of the Ethan I knew—same cloudy eyes, same way of furrowing his eyebrows, but his dark hair was overgrown, and his elbows were scrawny, and he was missing one of his front teeth.

Ethan stared at him, speechless. Because maybe we might have been able to fake his old bedroom. But no way we'd be able to fake this.

"That's . . . me," he said.

"That's you," I confirmed.

He took a step toward the kid on the bed. "Can he hear me?"

"No." I snapped my fingers next to the little boy's head, but he didn't react. "All that you see here—it's just a shadow of the things that have happened before. The people here won't be able to see or hear us. The point is for us to see and hear them."

He was still staring at the younger version of himself. "I

think I remember this day," he murmured. "It was right before Christmas break, second grade. The day of the science fair. I did a project on—"

"Space?" I gestured around us.

He looked at the floor and nodded like he was embarrassed. "It was a phase. I was going to be the next Neil Armstrong. Colonize Mars. Save our dying world. My science project was on the existence of water on Mars. I worked on it for weeks." He snorted. "My poster said, 'What Happened to the Little Green Men?'"

It hadn't gone well, though, obviously, because the younger Ethan was muttering and punching his fist into his rocket ship pillow.

"I didn't win," Ethan explained. "I got something like an honorable mention. The every-kid-wins-a-prize kind of thing."

There was a light tapping on the door.

"Go away!" said Kid Ethan.

The door opened a crack. "Hey, buddy. I don't want to interrupt you at whatever you're doing, but I thought maybe you'd want to talk."

"Okay," little Ethan grumbled, and the door opened wider to reveal Ethan's dad.

I took a moment to really look at him. I'd seen him before in Ethan's mind, lots of times, but this was different. In this place he was entirely real, not part of a reconstructed memory. He was tall, like Ethan, with the same brown hair and blue eyes—it was the eyes, really, that gave away the family resemblance. He was wearing a suit, but he'd taken the jacket and tie off and rolled up the sleeves to his elbows. His shoes, I noticed, were a little worn and needed a polish. His watch couldn't have cost more than a hundred dollars. His hair needed a trim. Still, there was something warm about him—something approachable and kind.

At the sight of his father, the present Ethan suddenly looked like he'd been given an electric shock. He went completely silent.

"Tough day?" Ethan Winters II asked little Ethan Winters III.

The kid didn't answer. He just punched the pillow again.

"I saw your project this afternoon," his dad continued lightly, coming into the room and shutting the door behind him. "And let me just say, it was awesome."

"It was better than the one about magnets," Kid Ethan burst out. "Who cares about stupid magnets?"

"Magnets suck rocks," his dad agreed solemnly.

"So why did the dumb magnets win first place, and I didn't win anything? Are the judges mental?"

His dad sat next to little Ethan on the bed and ruffled the boy's hair. "I don't know, buddy. It's all subjective, I guess."

"What's subjective?"

"It means that everybody has their own opinion, and everybody thinks differently, so they all come up with different conclusions."

The boy shook his head. "My poster looked way better, anybody with half a brain could see that. Mom bought me the cut-out letters and the spray paint. The one about magnets looked cheap—he just wrote on it in marker."

"Hey, have you heard that phrase, don't judge a book by its cover?" his dad countered. "Sometimes it doesn't matter how much money you spend on something, or how fancy it is. It's what's inside that counts. Maybe that kid had the best explanation of how magnets work that the judges had ever heard. We don't know."

Little Ethan was still scowling. Even back then, he was stubborn.

"Here's what I do know," his dad said. "I know I'm very proud of you for all the work you did. I know that you are now, like, an expert on the planet Mars, and that is so ridiculously boss. That's the point of having the science fair, when you think about it—you get to learn all the amazing things there are to know about science. When you're an astronaut, I bet you'll look back on this day as a turning point in your life."

"I guess," the kid mumbled.

His dad clapped a hand on the boy's shoulder. "You know what would be great? How about you and I go down to the Christmas tree lot after dinner? You can use that sharp scientific mind of yours to figure out which tree would be the best one to put in our living room."

Eight-year-old Ethan brightened visibly at the idea. "Just you and me?"

"Yep, me and you. No girls allowed."

"No girls allowed," the older Ethan repeated softly. "Just me and you. I remember that."

"We should measure how tall the ceiling is," little Ethan suggested eagerly. "So we can make sure not to get a tree that's too big."

Ethan's dad lifted his hand for a high five, and little Ethan giggled and slapped his hand.

"I knew you were the perfect person to be in charge of this very important job," his dad said. "Come on, chief. Let's go help your mom set the table and we'll plan our strategy."

And just like that, they left the room, little Ethan smiling again and his eyes almost glowing with excitement. His bad mood dissipated like a spent storm cloud.

Grown Up Ethan didn't say anything after they'd gone. He just kept staring at the door.

"Your dad was a good man, I think," I said.

He nodded and swallowed hard. "He always made me feel like I could do anything, like I could *be* anything I decided to be. An astronaut. A fireman. A pirate." He wiped his eyes on the sleeve of his tee and turned away from me. "The president of the United States."

Oh boy. I knew everyone in the Go Room would be freaking out over this little remark.

"He died when you were twelve, right?" I asked softly. "A freak accident."

Because God wouldn't give Ethan's dad one minute.

"We should go," I said. "There are other things that you're supposed to see."

He didn't argue. He took my hand again when I offered it and let me lead him back through the Portal and into the Time Tunnel again, where there wasn't even a little bit of a lag before we were swept forward nearly two years, to the Christmas party with his mom and dad and sister all wearing terrible sweaters.

The minute we got there Ethan went straight to his dad and

followed him around, which wasn't a problem, exactly, except that we were supposed to be focusing on his mom.

I understood why he did it, though.

I knew what it had been like for me to see my mother again, even if it was just "a shadow of things that have been." Seeing her had made me remember all that I'd slowly been forgetting, like the shape of her lips when she smiled. The way she smelled like jasmine. That habit she had of clicking her fingernails on the table. All of those things about her had been fading out of my memory, but then suddenly she was right there in front of me, beautiful and vibrant and alive.

"You should redirect Ethan back toward his mother," Boz reminded me through the earbud. "We're getting off topic."

I led Ethan back toward the kitchen. His mom was there wearing her apron and dancing to the song "It's the Most Wonderful Time of the Year" while she poured lime soda into a bowl of fruit punch.

"Your mom liked a good party, didn't she?" I observed.

Ethan's mouth turned up in the corner in that half-amused way he had. "Yes, she did. She still does. And my grandma."

I knew he was thinking about his grandmother's party invitation.

"It seems like a waste, though," I said. "Look at all of this—the decorations, the food, the music and the lights and the fizzy punch—all this time and expense for a few hours celebrating."

This was part of the Scrooge script, actually. You criticized the Fezziwig, called the party frivolous or wasteful, and then the Scrooge always felt compelled to argue on the Fezziwig's behalf. Just a little reverse psychology.

Ethan was no different, apparently. He frowned. "She liked to see other people happy—what's wrong with that? It didn't matter what her job was or where my dad was working or how much money we had—because we didn't have a lot at this point, as you can see. But she'd always go through so much effort so that we could have a good time. She was happy when we were happy."

"She had a generous heart," I agreed. "Back then," I added.

He nodded thoughtfully. "Back then," he said, almost to himself.

The breakup scene, which was what came next, was always the hardest one to get through. Probably because the Belle tends to tell it like it is.

Jack was no exception. "I'm not going to come back here again," she was saying as Present Ethan and I watched from a corner of his grandfather's office. "You've changed. I don't even recognize you anymore. Call me if you decide to grow a soul."

"Oh, come off it, sis," Past Ethan spat back at her. They were in the full-out-fight part of this discussion now. "Like you haven't benefited all your life from our family's wealth. What pays for Vassar? Who pays for you to pretend to be an artist so you can afford to sit around dabbling with paints and moaning about the tragic state of the world? At least I'm honest about it. I like money. I want to make more of it. I want to take what Grandfather built and make it into something huge and indestructible and a legacy for all of us."

But seriously, why am I supposed to feel guilty about having money? I remembered myself saying in my own version of this moment. *The world runs on money. That's just how it is.*

And Ro had looked so sad then, and she'd said, *Do you remember what it was like before, Holly, when we used to watch TV with the sound turned off and make up the dialogue? Or we'd go to the pet store and name all the fish. We'd hang out on the beach and build weird sand creatures. We'd write songs. None of that was about money, remember?*

It was about us, she'd said. And then she'd asked me what happened to that girl. She'd said she'd liked her.

She'd liked me, even when there really hadn't been anything special to like.

I had been so stupid not to understand then what she meant.

I forced my attention back to Ethan. Who was still getting chewed out by his sister.

"You should hear yourself." Jack gave a disbelieving laugh. "You know, you used to be sweet. You were always stubborn, and you always had a temper, but there was this sweet side to you that made up for it. And you were snarky and hilarious and fun to be around. But now you're just this stand-in for Grandpa. It's sad."

"You're the one who's lost your sense of humor."

Jack threw up her hands. "You just pitched a fit over how your meat was cooked."

"Who cares? You're a vegetarian, aren't you?"

"You're unbelievable." She drew herself up until she was

standing as tall as she could and looked him in the eyes. "It's probably better for both of us if I don't see you anymore. You can pretend you disowned me or whatever. Like you're an only child—I think that would suit you. I don't want to be a part of this legacy. Not anymore."

"Fine. Fine, then go," Past Ethan snarled. "You always were a quitter."

I glanced over at my Ethan. He hadn't said anything throughout this entire conversation. He'd just watched it all replay, his jaw set, his eyes distant.

"Like I said," Jack murmured as she moved toward the door, "I hope you're happy in this life. But you won't be."

Then she was gone.

Past Ethan stared after her for a minute, and then swept all the papers and office supplies off his grandfather's desk and onto the floor. He kicked the fancy metal trash can in the corner, leaving a huge dent in both the trash can and the wall, and then he stormed out of the room and slammed the door behind him.

"Are we done now?" Present Ethan asked grimly.

"Almost," I answered. "Have you seen your sister since that day?"

He shook his head.

"She graduated with honors," I informed him. "And she's an art teacher at a middle school not far from where you grew up. Giving back to her community, eating organic, volunteering to read for the blind, even. She's getting married this spring."

"Good for her," Ethan said tonelessly. "*Now* are we done?"

"Ethan, it's important that you—"

"No, I get it," he interrupted. "No need to explain. This was the part where you show me how bad I am. So I'll feel ashamed, right? So I'll promise to be better?"

Well . . . yes.

"I told you, these are just the shadows of things that have already happened," I responded dutifully. "If you don't like it, don't blame me. It's your life."

"Yes. It's my life. It's my business. So why are you butting in?" he asked. "You think I'm some kind of villain who needs to be taught a lesson?"

The Scrooges were always mad at this point. They felt attacked. Exposed. They lashed out. Because they could see, maybe even for the first time, how they were responsible for their own misery. It was a bitter pill. I could still taste it in my mouth even six years later.

"I don't think you're a villain, Ethan," I said. "You're a good person who's had a difficult past, and . . ." I swallowed. "I understand that. Really, I do."

His eyes narrowed. "Why are you doing this to me? What is this?"

I shook my head. "It's your past," I said. "It is what it is."

At that moment I let my lamp flare up again to the level that would blind him. Total whiteout. That was supposed to be my exit. I had to leave him now. This was probably the last time I'd ever see him, I realized, and I was struck by the urge to kiss him—to press my lips to his one last time. But instead I just squeezed his hand and let go.

Good-bye, Ethan, I thought. *I wish you the best life.*

I swallowed back a sob as I fled into the Time Tunnel. I caught just a glimpse of Dave's green robes as we passed each other by.

It was his turn now.

Time to deal with the present. And I was officially in Ethan's past.

TWENTY-FIVE

NORMALLY WHEN MY PART OF the story was done, I waited in the Go Room with everybody else at the company to see how the rest of the night played out. So I would have been there to watch Dave escort Ethan to see his Bob Cratchit, and apparently a homeless guy on Sixth Avenue.

But I didn't see any of that. The minute I crossed back into the Time Tunnel and then back to the present, I ran down the hall to my dressing room. Because I didn't want anyone to notice me bawling my eyes out. That would be considered weird.

My dressing room was empty, thankfully—part of me had been half expecting to find Stephanie in there—so I locked the door and struggled out of my costume, which was no easy task all by myself.

There was a shower in the dressing room bathroom. I only ever used it once a year, and sometimes not even that often, because sometimes I was in such a hurry to get out of the office after Christmas that I just cold creamed my face and went home. But that night—Ethan's night—I took a five-minute shower so I could just cry into the spray of the water. When I got out I did a quick blow-dry and slapped on a regular amount of makeup—so I'd look a little better when I went back out there.

When I got back to the Go Room, Ethan was delivering this touching little speech to Dave on the subject of the homeless:

"Hey, if he's homeless, he should start by getting a job. It's that easy—you work, they pay you, you pay for someplace to live. But this guy doesn't want to work, does he? No. He wants to sit here, and if he sits here long enough, somebody will pay for his next bottle of vodka."

Apparently seeing the Dents and how bad the kid really had it at home hadn't softened Ethan's heart much. He seemed as cool and collected and merciless as ever. Worse off than when I'd left him. Usually, by this point, the Scrooge was starting to soften. To see things differently. To let go of his anger. So Boz was probably a little worried.

I was worried, too, so much I felt sick with it. I'd done my best with the past. I'd tried to show Ethan things that would be meaningful. I'd tried to help him believe, and he'd seemed to; at least for part of it, he'd seemed to. But what if that hadn't been enough?

Dave wasn't giving up on him, though.

"This man is not a drunk," he informed Ethan as they stood before the homeless guy on Sixth Avenue, who couldn't see them, of course, but was mumbling like he knew someone was there. "He is simply a man who's been unlucky in life. Once, this man played the saxophone for one of the most sought-after jazz bands in New York City. He had a beautiful wife and a daughter, and he was more than willing to work, and work hard, every day. But then he was injured while fixing a leak in his roof. After that, there was a series of small misfortunes, one after another, all leading him to this place."

"And how do you know all this?" Ethan asked.

"I can see what's inside him," Dave answered mysteriously. "Right now, what he feels most is cold. Then, hungry. He lost touch with his family—his wife died, and his daughter doesn't even know where to find him. Miranda is his daughter's name. She works at the front desk of the London NYC Hotel just a few blocks from here. She's probably even seen him in passing, but she doesn't really look at him. Nobody really looks at him."

Ethan was looking at him, though. The man was sitting in a sleeping bag and a tangle of raggedy blankets against the side of a building where there was construction going on. He was wearing layers and layers of mismatched clothes: a shirt and a sweatshirt and a coat with a broken zipper, three scarves of different patterns wound around his neck, a faded floppy black hat mashed on top of his strings of shoulder-length salt-and-pepper hair, and a pair of cheap sunglasses.

"If someone would inform his daughter of his whereabouts," Dave continued, "his life would change again. All it would take is a few sentences, and perhaps a pair of warm gloves, to save this man."

Ethan glanced off down the street. "What does this have to do with me? Why are you going through so much effort to show me this one homeless man when there must be ten more just like him in a one-mile radius from here? What, you want me to buy him some gloves?"

"You have a connection with this man," Dave said. "Don't you recognize him?"

"No." Ethan scoffed. "No, I'm pretty sure I've never seen him before."

"Not in person, I think, but he was on the news several years ago—a witness to a terrible accident that happened not far from here. Later he even testified in court."

I could tell when Ethan understood what the connection was because his face went carefully blank. "So this is the saxophone player."

Dave nodded.

"The one my father gave money to that day."

"Yes."

"You think that's going to make me want to help him? If my dad hadn't stopped to listen to this guy, he'd still be alive," Ethan said bitterly.

"That's true." Dave gazed down at the man tenderly. "And it was this man who saw what happened and tried to help him. Your father died in this man's arms."

Ethan took a step back and looked around, like he was deciding to take off and just needed to figure out where to go. "Get me out of here," he said sharply. "I've had enough of this. Please."

I thought the *please* was a nice touch.

"Okay, prepping the tunnel to move them to the party," said the operator from the control booth. It wasn't Grant anymore—someone from Dave's team had taken over his post. He and Marty had taken up their places in the Go Room and were undoubtedly about to start taking bets on whether or not Ethan would fail. My stomach churned at the thought.

Boz was right, I thought. *We shouldn't bet on them.*

The fog and snow machines whirred on. In less than a minute Dave and Ethan came through and the cameras shifted to the party scene—a brownstone apartment in the Bronx. Inside, all the lights were on, and we could hear voices and music—Christmas carols, of course.

"O come all ye faithful, joyful and triumphant . . ."

"This is my mom's place," Ethan said. I'd never seen him look so out of it—the thing with the homeless man had really gotten to him.

"Yes. Shall we?" Dave gestured up the small set of stairs toward the front door.

"Whatever," Ethan said.

It wasn't a big party—about a dozen people or so—but they were all having a great time, from the sound of it. As Dave and Ethan went into the apartment, they could hear someone laughing. It was one of the best laughs I'd ever heard—full and warm and brimming with delight. It just made you feel good, hearing that laugh.

I recognized it. I looked at Ethan to see his reaction.

He stopped when he heard it. "That's my mom," he said. "She always had this contagious laugh."

He was right about it being contagious. Soon everybody was

laughing. Dave and Ethan moved forward toward the sound until they came into a sitting room, which was decorated beautifully for Christmas, with a huge silver tree in front of the window and strands of holly and candles along the fireplace and end tables. Against one wall was a huge, comfortable-looking sofa with several people sitting on it, posing as a man took their picture with a bunch of phones.

"Say cheese, everyone," he said.

At one end of the sofa, Ethan's mother sat wearing a black velvet dress that looked amazing on her. Next to her was a tall red-haired man who I assumed must be the new husband. On his knee sat a little redheaded girl in a green dress—Ethan's half sister. Then an older woman, Ethan's grandmother from his mother's side, who was holding a tiny new baby. Then a young man in his twenties who I'd never seen in any of Ethan's memories. And at the farthest end was Jack—her hair a regular glossy brown again.

"Squeeze together a little," said the man taking the pictures, and they did, which made Ethan's mom laugh again, which made them all laugh. "That's a great one," the man said, snapping off a series of pictures. "That's the whole family, isn't it? It could be next year's Christmas card."

"Not the whole family," Jack said, taking the hand of the man sitting next to her. "We're still missing one. My brother."

"I did invite him," Ethan's grandmother said. "He told me, and I quote, that 'Christmas parties are the lamest of all parties.' And Christmas, he said, was just a stupid excuse to rip people off."

"Sounds like Ethan," Jack said. "He believes it, too. That's what's sad. He's a regular Ebenezer Scrooge."

Everyone in the Go Room burst into a nervous kind of laughter.

Ethan looked out the window, like he was bored and just waiting for the opportunity to duck out.

"Oh, he's not that bad," said the old woman—the grandmother. "He used to be such a sweet boy."

"Used to be," muttered Jack.

"He took your father's death hard, that's all," said Ethan's mom. "It messed us all up, didn't it?" She gave Jack a meaningful glance that said *I know all about what you did during that stage.*

Jack shrugged. "I guess. But Ethan doesn't show signs of snapping out of it anytime soon."

"Where does she get off judging me?" Ethan said under his breath. "Like she's a saint."

"There are two ways to respond when life hands you something unpleasant," the grandmother said, smiling down at the infant in her lap. "You can get soft or you can get tough. Our Ethan has just decided to get tough, it seems. But he'll come around eventually, I think. He's got a good heart under there somewhere. And he has time—God knows, he's, what, seventeen now? He has time to get himself on the right path again."

She was wrong, of course.

"Which is why I will continue to invite him to this 'lame' Christmas party every year," his grandmother said. She was so the Fred in this situation.

"And why I will keep calling him every week," added his mother. "Even though he doesn't want to talk to me. Oh, and that reminds me. You know what?" Her smile was full of mischief, like she was about to spill the best secret ever. "He told me he has a girlfriend now."

Uh-oh.

"Poor girl!" exclaimed Jack. "Who is it? Tell me it's not a Manhattan socialite with an IQ the same size as her waist measurement."

"Her name . . ." His mom paused dramatically. ". . . is Victoria Scott."

"That's a socialite's name if I ever heard one," Jack said.

Ethan's mom reached over and pretended to smack Jack on the back of the head. "He didn't talk about her that way. He called her Tori. He said that she likes to meet in all these obscure places around the city, like the left lion of the New York Public Library—you know the lions? She's a free spirit, apparently."

"Well, perhaps that's just what Ethan needs at this juncture," said Grandma. "A free spirit."

The irony was kind of killing me. I was a spirit, sure, but not exactly free.

"But what kind of name is Tori, seriously?" said Jack.

"Like Jack's such a ladylike name," said Ethan. I smiled. My hero, coming to my defense, even if his sister couldn't hear him.

"Tell me about this Victoria Scott," Dave said suddenly. "I'd like to know more about her."

UH-OH.

"What, you don't already know everything there is to know about me?" Ethan gave him a sarcastic smirk. "You can see inside me, right? Wasn't the ghost wearing her face?"

I was dead. Done for. Doomed. This was it.

"Her face," Dave repeated. "What do you—"

Thankfully they were interrupted by everyone being called to some kind of charades-like game in the other room, which was something straight out of *A Christmas Carol*, too, much to everyone in the Go Room's delight. Ethan went over to watch, and Dave trailed behind him, his question unasked for the moment.

Ethan's mom was up first. She turned to Ethan's stepdad. She lifted her head regally, obviously pretending to be someone else. "I'm like a cat here, a no-named slob," she said in a higher voice than usual. "We belong to nobody, and nobody belongs to us. We don't even belong to each other."

"Holly Golightly. From *Breakfast at Tiffany's*!" the stepdad said immediately.

Jack's jaw dropped. "That was so . . . how did you even get that?"

"We have a psychic connection," his mom said, kissing the stepdad on the cheek. "Your turn, Jackie O."

"We'll see who has a psychic connection," Jack said.

And so they played for a while, back and forth, one team (made up of the little girl, whose name was Grace, and Ethan's mom and her husband, whose name was apparently Richard) against the other (Jack, Mason—Jack's fiancé, and Evelyn, the grandmother), with Ethan's mom's team the clear winner. I didn't fully understand the rules of the game, but it was something like *Who Am I?* They went through a bunch of funny characters, impersonating the person if they could, using well-known lines or sayings. In the next twenty or so minutes they went through George Washington, Katy Perry, Elmo, George W. Bush, Michael Jackson, Kerry Washington, and Harry Potter. We all kind of got into it, even Ethan, who shouted out some guesses even though nobody could hear them.

Then Jack took a slip of paper out of the hat where they'd all put in a clue and read it. Her turn again.

"Grace!" she exclaimed. "Did you write this?"

The little girl giggled. "Daddy helped me write it."

"Okay. Well. This is one I should be able to do." She folded the paper back up and put it aside. Then she stood up and stared coldly at the group. "This party is so lame," she said in a low, boy-like monotone. "Christmas parties are the lamest kind of party. I like money. Do any of you have lots of money? Well, then, you're not worth my time."

It was quiet for a minute. Everyone knew the answer.

"It's Ethan." Jack's fiancé scratched the back of his neck. "I mean, I haven't met him, but we were just talking about him. Mr. Scrooge," he said with an uncomfortable laugh.

Everyone in the Go Room giggled.

"Yes, that's my brother." Jack tried to smile. "He just does what he wants, and the rest of us can go to hell."

I glanced at Ethan. He was looking intently at the floor now, like he was counting the fibers in the carpet. We all waited to see how he'd react. With Scrooges it was generally about fifty-fifty at this point. Half of them were seriously seeing the error of their ways. And half needed Blackpool to give them that extra little push.

"Shall we go?" Dave asked Ethan quietly.

Ethan looked up. I could tell immediately that something had changed in him, and not for the good. Something like what had happened with me on my night as the Scrooge. He'd taken a turn.

"Sure," he said sardonically. "Why not? I can't wait to see your next setup."

"Our setup."

"This is a scam," Ethan said. "This isn't about my character. It's about my money. Right?"

"No," Dave said firmly. "This is about your soul."

Ethan laughed. "My soul. Right. My precious soul."

"It is precious."

Ethan sighed. "If I just write you a check, can we be done now? Honestly, I would pay a lot if you'd just return me to my home. I won't even press charges."

"This isn't about money," Dave said.

"It's always about money." Ethan held a hand up as if to say *Just give me a number.* "No? Okay, then, let's go. Before the flowers in your beard wilt. Seriously, dude. Who puts flowers in their beard?"

I could tell by the look in his eyes that we'd officially lost him. Ethan didn't believe anymore. The same way that I hadn't believed.

He'd decided that he wasn't going to play along. Which meant that he wouldn't repent. He wouldn't be saved. He'd die.

I didn't know what to do. I could only stand there in the Go Room helplessly as it all played out, watching and waiting like everyone else. Some people even had popcorn. Like this was a freak show, and Ethan was the freak.

Stephanie popped up at my elbow. "There you are, Holly. I've been looking for you. Your performance was inspiring, by the way. I think you really made an impression on him." She lowered her voice. "And I'm sure that one-on-one time you spent with him made a big difference, too."

It had made a big difference. Maybe it had made all the difference. I swallowed.

"So," I said numbly, "has it been everything you thought it would be?"

She looked at me blankly.

"This. Christmas." I pointed to the monitors, where Ethan and Blackpool were standing over the homeless man on Sixth, who was lying there completely still, his face a pale blue. Blackpool was the towering phantom now, faceless and silent. I shivered and tried to focus on something other than the memory of my body going numb, limb by limb. "It's your first time seeing it all play out in real life—*A Christmas Carol*, American version 173. Is it, like, blowing your mind?"

"Oh. Yes. It's changing the world," she said, but for once she didn't sound that stoked about it. "Hey, can we go to your office for a few minutes? I want to talk to you about something."

I sighed. "Look, Steph, if this is about you researching me, I told you, I'm over it. It's fine. Don't make a big deal out of it."

I meant it, I realized. I wasn't mad anymore. I couldn't feel anything in the moment. I was so done.

"I got you some Chinese takeout," she added. "I thought you'd be hungry after your big performance. Do you like egg rolls?"

I happened to love egg rolls.

Part of me wanted to stay and watch Ethan, but a bigger part of me wanted to run far, far away now. I knew that Blackpool was going to last at least another hour—he had to take him to Danny Denton's still—the Cratchits'—and there was a scene at the school where the boys there cleaned out Ethan's locker and stole his stuff. Then, according to the itinerary, Blackpool would take him to the mortuary.

I didn't know if I could stand to watch the mortuary scene.

So Stephanie and I went back to my office, and found it all laid out on my desk: little white containers of fried rice and chow mein and sweet and sour chicken, and oh yes, egg rolls.

Stephanie got out a couple of paper plates from a drawer in my desk, but then I found I couldn't eat anything.

"Are you okay?" Stephanie asked. "I've never known you to pass up egg rolls."

"He's going to fail," I said miserably.

Weirdly, she didn't seem surprised by my assessment. "He might."

"He's already decided." I bit my lip. "I know him."

"It will work out the way it's supposed to."

"Stop saying that!" I burst out. "No, it won't!"

"It will," she argued. "Besides, if he fails, he'll just end up working here, right? Like you. That's not so bad, is it?"

She wasn't making any sense. "What?"

"If Ethan fails, he'll die. This morning?"

This morning. Six fifty-six a.m., on Broadway. God, it was only hours away. I needed to sit down. I sank into my chair.

"And then he'll wake up here just like you did," Stephanie said. "And he'll be the new Ghost of Christmas Present."

My mouth opened. For a few seconds I just stared at her. "The Ghost of Christmas Present," I repeated stupidly.

"Da—Copperfield's replacement." She sighed. "I think the company actually knows Ethan's going to fail. Blackpool does, I'm pretty sure—all that stuff about Ethan's hazy future. His future is probably not that hazy. It's just that it would be so discouraging, you know, if he came out and told everyone that Ethan was going to fail."

"The Ghost of Christmas Present," I whispered again.

"Yes." Stephanie gave me a little smile. "So it would be okay, you see?"

I immediately tried to picture Ethan as the Ghost of Christmas Present. If he let his hair grow out and grew a beard . . . and then I remembered that as well-preserved zombies, our hair doesn't grow. But hey, that's what wigs and fake mustaches are for, right? We had a stellar costume department. And Ethan was tall. Not like Dave, not Jolly Green Giant tall, but still. Tall enough.

He'd make a great Ghost, I decided.

The idea was so great, so amazing, so incredibly awesome that I got up and started to pace around my office. If Ethan failed, then the company could give him his own crappy apartment, his non-smart phone, his pitiful hundred bucks a month, and he'd spend some time being super mad about it—I remembered those days, how furious I was underneath everything, like a pot about to boil over. But then he'd start to accept it, like I did. He'd be fine. We actually could be together.

I was smiling now. I couldn't believe I'd never thought of it before. *Ethan was going to be the Ghost of Christmas Present.* It was like a dream come true.

Then I began to picture other things, too, like Ethan and me in our Hoodies walking down the streets of NYC together. Making jokes about the losers we worked with. Holding hands. Kissing. I'd have some explaining to do, sure, about the whole Victoria Scott thing. But eventually he'd understand, wouldn't he?

We'd have a future. Something that lasted past Christmas. Maybe even forever.

"How do you . . ." I couldn't catch my breath. "How do you know for sure he'll become Dave's replacement?" I was thinking about what Boz had said all those months ago, about how a Ghost seems to become mysteriously available at just the moment one is needed.

"He told me," Stephanie said.

"He?"

"Copperfield."

And then I suddenly remembered Dave's vision of hugging Stephanie. Kissing her head. I shuddered. "Ew, that's not right. I'm sorry, but . . . ew."

"Ew?" Now it was Stephanie's turn to be confused.

"You and Dave together. And you still call him Copperfield? Weird. So weird. And I thought you were with Grant now. Grant's awesome. And Dave's, like, old enough to be your father."

Her eyes widened, and she covered her mouth with her hand. At first I thought she was crying, and I felt bad. I mean, age is just a number, right? Who was I to judge? But then I realized she was laughing.

"Wow," she said after a minute. "You always end up surprising me, Holly." She laughed again, then took off her glasses and wiped at her eyes. "Dave *is* old enough to be my father."

I threw my hands up. "Ew!"

"He's not only old enough to be my father. He *is* my father." She set her glasses on my desk.

"What!"

"He's my dad." She took a breath and let it out. "Wow, it feels good to get that off my chest. Sometimes this year I felt like I was going to explode. And why not tell you tonight? You're done with your Christmas Past stuff. It's the last night of my internship." She said the word *internship* like it was a code word for something else. "It's a night for revelations."

"What?" I felt like this was the only word I was saying in our entire conversation.

"You're not the only one with secrets, Holly. I've got a few. Big ones."

Obviously.

"Secrets?" I was sure I didn't know what she was talking about, me having secrets. But suddenly I got the feeling that she knew things about me beyond what she'd read in my file. "Like what?"

I couldn't imagine what else there could possibly be.

"Like I'm not actually majoring in psychology." She closed her eyes for a minute and then rushed on, like she wanted to get this out before she lost her nerve. "I really do feel like I'm your friend. You've got to believe me, Holly. I always felt like we were going to be friends someday, even when—gosh, this is so much harder than I thought it would be. My dad, he thinks I should wait until it's all over and then write you a letter or something, but I think we deserve more than that, right? Because we're friends. We might be the weirdest friends ever, but we're friends."

"You're not a psychology major?" I was still stuck on this.

She acted like she hadn't heard me. "But that's what's so great about it, because before, you couldn't be anybody's friend, not really. You weren't capable of it—you were so self-involved. But that's changed. It took a while, but now you've learned how to think about other people. You know how to be a friend now. Not a great friend yet, but you're getting there."

I was so lost I needed a map for this conversation.

She sighed. "Sorry, I'm not making sense."

"No," I said. "You're totally not."

"Okay. Let me just get it out." She plunked down in the chair across from my desk. She took a deep breath and released it, then leaned forward so we were looking into each other's eyes. "I'm the Ghost of Christmas Past."

My heart started to pound. It was exactly what I'd always been afraid of, the minute that this girl had walked in the door at Project

Scrooge—that she'd been brought in to replace me.

"Okay, whoa there. Calm down." Stephanie reached across the desk and grabbed my hand as I started to hyperventilate right there and then. "It's okay, Holly. Trust me."

"How can you even say that?" I gasped. "What's going to happen to me? Where will I go?"

Her eyebrows lifted. "Wait. You think . . . No. No, Holly. You've got it all wrong. I'm not going to replace you." She smiled tentatively. "You replaced me."

I stared at her. "Huh?"

"I was *your* Ghost of Christmas Past. Six years ago. I'm not surprised you never recognized me. I was almost fourteen, but Leigh and Marie tried to make me look like I was even younger. They had this vision of the Lamp as a little girl." Her big blue eyes were full of amusement and concern.

I was shaking my head, I realized. It was too much.

She frowned, and her eyebrow bumps appeared. "Holly? Say something."

"How? Why?" *Oh good,* I thought dazedly. *I'd moved on to other one-word questions.*

"My dad was a Bob Cratchit once, a single parent just trying to make ends meet, and I was the Tiny Tim. It's a long story, but essentially the Scrooge that year failed to be rehabilitated, and my dad died later in an accident, and Boz felt so bad that he brought us both here afterward, where they gave us the option of working for the company instead of my dad moving on. So then my dad became the Ghost of Christmas Present, and I became the Ghost of Christmas Past. As an interim, of course. The real Ghosts have to be dead, and I'm alive."

"But—" My head was spinning. "But you said you were almost fourteen when—"

"I was eleven, actually, when I started working here. Almost ten years ago."

"You've been working for Project Scrooge for *ten years*?"

"I've been on a leave of absence, so to speak, for the last six," she explained. "But, yes, I worked here before. That's part of why my dad and I decided to take this job. Because then I would get to spend time with him while I was growing up. I got to live with him. I wouldn't have to lose him or go into foster care. Anyway, as you know, this is my dad's last year, so I came back to help him out. I wanted to spend more time with him before . . ." Tears popped up in her eyes. "Okay, it's pretty emotional, finally losing my dad after all this time, but it's the right thing. Being a Ghost is not being alive. It's like being a shadow. You're not fully part of the world. It's time for him to move on and join my mom."

"Does Grant know?" I blurted out. "Does Marty?"

She blushed. "I told Grant a couple weeks ago. He was pretty shocked. He and Marty didn't have a clue about me being the Lamp before. Like you, they thought I was new here."

I sat back, pretty shocked myself—probably more shocked than I had ever been in my whole life.

"Anyway. I've always wanted to tell you that I'm sorry,"

Stephanie said. "For failing you, I mean. I've always been able to see the good inside of you, and the good you could do in the world—so much good, Holly, that you could have accomplished in your life. And you were so young—you were the youngest Scrooge we've ever had in Project Scrooge history. Did you know that? Not just for the American branch, either, but for the world. I was so excited to work on your case. But then I wasn't able to save you. I couldn't convince you that it was real. I failed. And you deserved better." She looked down at her hands. "I'm sorry, Holly. Being the Ghost of Christmas Past is an enormous responsibility. You know that as well as I do. It takes patience, and a cool head, and quick thinking, but more than that—it takes real empathy. You have to understand deep down what the Scrooge is feeling in order to know what will affect him. Or her," she added sheepishly. "Which is why you're such a great GCP. You understand the Scrooges better than I ever could."

"So you're not a psychology major," I said again.

She shook her head. "Too much reading."

"Do you even go to NYU? Is your name really Stephanie? Was any part of this real?"

"All of that's true," she said quickly. "I do go to NYU—I'm going to graduate in two years, if all goes according to plan. I'm a theater major, actually. I have this dream about being on Broadway one day, but that might be a pretty big ambition. And yes, my name is really Stephanie. But you can call me Steph. If you can forgive me, that is."

"Uh-huh." I searched inside myself and found that a part of

me, maybe even a big part of me, was definitely furious that she'd been stringing me along all this time, playing the wide-eyed newbie when in fact she'd been a veteran of this place. She'd totally had me fooled. But there was another part that just . . . accepted it. Steph and I were connected now, and we always would be, like we were sisters or something. We'd both worn the lamp.

I thought about that little blond-haired, blue-eyed twerp who'd taken my hand and tried to show me my life from a different perspective. She'd believed in me. And no matter how she felt like she needed to apologize, I knew the truth: I was the one who had let her down.

"Okay, I forgive you," I said after a minute. "If you can forgive me for being such a stuck-up, horrible little brat."

"Which time?" She grinned. "Back then or this year, when you kept sending me on all those crazy errands?"

"Shut up," I said, smiling in spite of myself. "Both, I guess?"

"I forgive you for being a stuck-up, horrible little brat," she said. "Both times."

"You're a decent actress, in my opinion," I said. "And I'm qualified to know."

"Wow, thanks, Miss Havisham," she said in her squeaky voice. She laughed, and then glanced at her watch. "Holy smokes, is that the time? Grant's waiting for me. He wants to watch the final scene together."

"Don't make him any bets," I advised. "He always wins."

"I know. Especially this year." She held her hand out to me. "It's been a pleasure spending time with you, Holly. I mean it. Thank you."

I shook her hand, and she walked around the desk for a quick hug. I didn't resist. I even hugged her back a little.

"I'll see you in there," she said. "Oh, and Holly? I hope everything works out with Ethan. Then you won't have to be so alone all the time."

I stared at her.

"A loving heart is the truest wisdom," she murmured. Then she was gone.

I should have returned to the Go Room with her, since Boz would be expecting me at this point, but I stayed in my office for a few minutes, thinking about everything Steph had said.

Thinking about Ethan. I was still trying to get my head around the idea that him failing meant that he'd become the new Ghost of Christmas Present.

My Christmas Present.

I wanted to laugh and sing and dance around, it was such an amazing, wonderful turn of events. No wonder Blackpool had been so cranky. Because he'd known all along. He'd known I was going to get a happy ending after all. I deserved to be happy, didn't I?

But then what about what Ethan deserves? said a little voice in the back of my mind.

I felt the elation drain out of me. I couldn't help but think about all the things Steph had just said to me about the responsibility that came with being the GCP. Then I tried to tell myself that it didn't matter. Everything was going to work out for Ethan—he'd get *me* out of the bargain, after all. And death wouldn't be so bad as long as he had me, right?

A loving heart is the truest wisdom.

I loved him, I realized. I loved Ethan Winters. It hadn't been just a game I was playing because I was lonely. I'd fallen in love with him. His heart had spoken to mine.

I loved him. That's all the counted, right? That's all he needed.

Wrong, said the voice.

Wrong. Wrong. Wrong. I knew it was wrong.

Like Steph had seen in me, I could see the good inside of Ethan. All of the bad habits and apathy and coldheartedness he sometimes showed came from hurt, and I knew that he could overcome that hurt, he could change, he could live his life in a different way and be happy in it, if only he had the chance.

I loved him. But if he failed, I'd be the one responsible for damning him to hell. If he failed now, I would have taken away his chance. Steph was right. Being a Ghost wasn't really being alive. If he died today, Ethan would become a shadow. Like me.

What kind of love was that?

But even if I wanted to fix it, what could I do about it now? Now it was too late to get it all back on track. The damage was done. Ethan was playing out the final scene as I sat there with my Chinese food. I spotted the little wrapped fortune cookie on my desk. Sugar sounded good—time to eat my feelings. I unwrapped it, broke it open, and fished out the little slip of paper.

My fortune read, *It's never too late to become what one could have been.*

I stood up. I grabbed my Hoodie from the hook on the back of the door and put it on.

I knew what I had to do.

Even if it was going to cost me everything.

TWENTY-SIX

INVISIBLE, I RAN ALL THE way to the Time Tunnel, praying with every step that it wasn't all over, that I wasn't too late. No matter what my fortune cookie said, there would be a time when it was too late. But when I got there, I saw on the monitors that Ethan and Blackpool were still at the mortuary.

Thank God.

The tunnel was open in preparation for their return journey. I ran down it as fast as I could possibly go.

In the back room of the mortuary, Ethan was standing at the foot of a metal table, staring down at a body that was covered up with a sheet.

His body.

Blackpool was lurking a few feet behind him, letting him soak in the horror of it all, but I knew that in a minute he'd pull the sheet away so Ethan could see his own lifeless face. Then the mortuary guys would come in and put the body into the oven, and Ethan would watch himself burn.

That was how the script went, anyway.

Still breathing hard from my run, I took off my hood.

Blackpool turned to look at me. I couldn't see his face because of his own hood, but he didn't seem surprised to see me there. But then it was Blackpool's job to know the future. It was impossible to rattle Blackpool's cage.

"Can I talk to him for a minute?" I rasped. "I really need to talk to him."

Blackpool nodded and stepped back to give us space. Which I appreciated more than I was ever able to tell him.

"Hi," I said to Ethan as I came up beside him.

He didn't look surprised to see me, either. He kept staring at the figure on the steel table. Something jerked in his throat.

"So this isn't real?" He smiled, relieved, because he'd been almost convinced that this horrible scene before him was possible. But now he was sure I was going to tell him it was all a prank.

I swallowed hard. The Go Room was undoubtedly in full freak-out mode now, seeing me here. I wasn't wearing the costume. Clearly I was here as Holly, and not Havisham. Not the Lamp. Me.

"It *is* real," I told Ethan. "It's your real future."

He shook his head. "It can't be—" He turned to look at me. "You're scamming me, right? All along, since the very first day I met you, you've been scamming me . . ." He bent his head.

"I wasn't scamming you," I said. "I was lying to you, but I wasn't trying to get anything like that. I just wanted to be with you."

He looked up and met my eyes, his eyebrows drawn together, totally confused. "I don't understand what's going on."

I glanced up at one of the cameras. "I'm sorry. I have to tell him. It's the only way. And you know what Boz always says: 'There is nothing so strong or safe in an emergency of life as the simple truth.'" I turned back to Ethan. "Here's the truth, as simply as I can give it to you. There's a company here in New York that tries to save one person every year. One person who has gone astray in life. One person who, if they would turn themselves around, could make a big difference in the world. And this year that one person is you."

Ethan closed his eyes and kneaded his forehead like he had a massive headache. "A company? What company?"

"It's been around for almost two hundred years. I work for them. It's my job to be the Ghost of Christmas Past, to show you the things about your past that made you into who and what you are, so that you finally see yourself clearly and decide to become something else. That's my job, but . . ." I bit my lip and lowered my head, so ashamed that I couldn't meet his eyes anymore. "This year, when I saw you, I . . . I just felt drawn to you like I hadn't with the other Scrooges." I sighed. "So I went to meet you, and then things just kind of spun out of control from there. That's why I always had to sneak around, why we couldn't go back to my place, why I didn't call you. This isn't going to make any sense to you, I know, but that's it. That's the truth."

"Tori," he started.

"My name isn't Victoria Scott. I made that up, because I wasn't supposed to meet you face-to-face until tonight. My name is Holly. Holly Chase."

He still looked skeptical. "Wasn't Holly Chase some famous person?" he asked.

I almost laughed, and I almost cried. After all these years, walking around this city without a soul recognizing me, *now* he'd heard of me?

"I wish I could explain everything, but I can't. Not right now. There's no time. You just need to know that this whole thing tonight *is* real. It's not a dream, or a prank, or someone trying to scam you. It's real, and it's your life. Trust me, I know. I was a Scrooge once, too. Just like you. Only I'm worse than you, obviously. Way worse. I may come in a pretty package, but I'm, like, rotten inside. Pretty much everything I've done, I've done for selfish reasons. I didn't believe it when this was happening to me, either, by the way. The company tried to show me. They tried to tell me, but I wouldn't listen. So I missed my chance. And then I died."

I glanced down at the body on the steel table. Even under the sheet I could recognize Ethan's swimmer's shoulders and the shape of his face. My eyes flooded with tears. "You don't have to die. Not today. All you have to do is choose a different path. Choose to be different. Choose love instead of hate or disdain or apathy or whatever. You can do it, Ethan. I know you can."

Behind us, at the back of the room, Blackpool pushed back his hood. He had the strangest look on his face, an expression I didn't know what to make of—not anger, like I'd expected, not disgust or condemnation. It was more like solemn acceptance.

"Give her one more minute," he said softly. "Please."

He wasn't talking to me.

Then he nodded. One more minute. I had one more minute.

I was shaking again. Terrified about what was to come. Would it be like the first time, when Blackpool put his arms around me and then I stopped being able to feel? Would it be blackness and nothingness again, or worse—would I have to travel in chains? Or be caged somewhere and left to burn? Would it hurt?

I had to keep my focus on Ethan, I told myself. He was what was important.

"Tori . . . or Holly, or whoever." His hand in mine was trembling, too. "What's going to happen now?"

I put my hand on his arm. "That's up to you. Be brave, Ethan, and decide to be different, and everything will change. I promise."

I could tell by his expression that he believed me, and I was so relieved my knees felt weak. "Will you try?" I asked.

He swallowed hard, and then nodded. "Okay. I'll try. I don't understand it all, but I'll try. What about you? Are you going to be okay?"

"Don't worry about me," I said. "This is about you. I am so, so sorry I didn't see that before. I'm sorry, Ethan."

"Holly." Blackpool cleared his throat. He sounded more like his irritable self. "Boz says I have to take him home now. Say good-bye."

A tear burned its way down my cheek. I wiped it. Nodded. "All right." On impulse I reached out and hugged Ethan tightly for a few seconds. "Bye," I whispered against his ear. "Be good."

Then Blackpool led him away. They stepped through the door and disappeared. Gone. Just like that. I'd said good-bye to him for good this time. I waited for a few minutes, crying and shivering, and then I went back, too.

To face my fate.

The halls of Project Scrooge were full of people as I made my way to Boz's office. The first person I saw was Tox, her eyes red, clutching a tissue that she was sniffling into. It was so unlike her that it made me feel even more unsettled. Everyone was staring at me, totally silent, and I could tell some of the others had been crying, too, and some of them were angry—gazing at me with accusation in their faces like I'd done something terrible.

I felt like I was going to the firing squad.

Boz's office door was closed, but somehow I knew he was in there. Waiting.

I knocked.

"Come in."

I slipped inside and shut the door behind me.

Boz was sitting at his desk, his head in his hands, his dark hair sticking out between his fingers. I couldn't see his face. I thought he would tell me to sit down, because that's what he always told me, but he didn't. He didn't say anything. He just sat there until I thought I would go crazy and start screaming. Finally, he straightened up and looked at me. He cleared his throat.

"I'm sorry," I blurted out immediately.

"I know."

"Did Ethan . . . ?"

"He's sleeping now. We'll see what happens when he wakes up."

"He'll change," I said. "I know he will. I know him."

"Oh, Holly," Boz sighed. "What am I going to do with you? I don't even know what to say about this. I'm speechless."

My breath froze in my chest. He wasn't talking about a slap on the wrist. I'd blown everything. I'd compromised the Project. I'd ruined his Christmas.

My chin lifted. "Whatever you need to do, Boz. I'll take it."

He ran a hand through his hair to smooth it and straightened his tie. "You should go home. We'll sort this out later. I think it would be better for everyone if you weren't around right now."

"But Ethan—" I protested.

"—is not your concern anymore."

My eyes filled with tears again. Who knew that a well-preserved zombie could cry so much?

"Leave the sweatshirt of invisibility here," he said as I moved numbly toward the door.

I took off the Hoodie and draped it over the back of the red leather armchair. I went out. The halls were empty again. Everyone had gone back to the Go Room to see Ethan's big finish.

I'm right about him, I told myself. He'd change. Then this would have all been worth it.

I ran into Dave by the dressing rooms. His beard had returned to brown again. He smiled at me. "That took courage," he said. "I'm proud of you."

"You were always so nice to me. Thank you," I choked out, and then went into my dressing room before I totally lost it and started bawling my eyes out right there in the hall.

It was quiet on my way out of the building. I walked the halls alone. Rode the elevator to the main floor alone. The doorman didn't even glance up at me as I pushed out of the rotating glass doors and onto the snow-covered street. A white Christmas. It was early morning, and the street was empty.

It must be close to 6:56, I thought. Ethan was probably just now waking up in his apartment. He wasn't anywhere near Broadway. He wasn't going to be hit by a car. He was going to live.

I smiled. I walked across the street in my shirt and jeans—no coat, because before I'd had my Hoodie. But I wasn't cold. It was snowing in big beautiful flakes. I lifted my head and looked up as it drifted down around me. I put out my hand, and a flake landed in it, and then as I watched, it melted away. Here and then gone. Somewhere in the distance I could hear music. *A Christmas carol,* I thought. I strained to hear it. I closed my eyes and listened. I got a flash of a memory—my own memory, my mother—standing in a red coat on the steps of a church with a little candle stuck in a paper cup in her hand, smiling in a peaceful way as the music rolled over us. She reached and smoothed her hand down the back of my hair.

Silent night.

Holy night.

All is calm.

All is bright.

"Holly!"

I opened my eyes. Steph was standing just outside of the Project Scrooge building on Broadway, panting like she'd been running. "Holly, wait! Don't go yet!"

Maybe she knows about what happened with Ethan, I thought. Maybe she'd tell me. And I was so glad to see her—my friend, my only friend now, if she was still willing to be my friend—that I stepped off the sidewalk to cross over to her. I didn't look. I stepped right into the path of a taxicab that was rushing down Broadway.

I heard brakes, a scream.

I was lying down somehow. Snowflakes were landing on my cheeks. Faces moved over me. Steph's face. I thought she might have been holding my hand.

"Don't go anywhere, Holly," she said. "Don't die."

"Silly," I murmured. "I'm already dead."

I felt dizzy, the way I did sometimes when my body reset. Lighter. Like I wasn't made of meat and bone anymore, but was completely spirit now.

Like I could float away.

And then everything went white.

TWENTY-SEVEN

I WOKE WITH A JOLT, choking for air. It was dark again. I sat up. I was in a bed—but not my bed, not the lumpy twin mattress I'd been sleeping on for the past six years. This was at least a queen. Soft. The sheets felt smooth and cool against my skin. I was wearing silk, which was weird. I didn't own a pair of silk pajamas.

I swung my legs to the side of the bed and looked around. There was a lamp on the bedside table. I turned it on. Light flared, and it hurt my eyes. But when I could see again, I gasped. Which was understandable.

I was in my room. Not my room in my walk-up apartment, but my room from before, in the house in Malibu. There was a familiar white vanity against one wall. I stumbled over to it and sat down in front of the oval-shaped mirror. My own eyes looked back at me—brown and wide and a little freaked out. What had just happened?

I thought I'd . . . died. Again. Hit by a car. Again. Which hardly seemed fair.

Still, here I was, in my old room. I leaned forward to look at my face.

The pimple—the one that had been hanging out just below my mouth for six long years—was gone. I couldn't stop staring at that little expanse of smooth skin. It was gone.

I could hear the hush of the ocean outside. My window was open, and my curtains were fluttering slightly. I could just make out the black outline of the palm tree near my window, swaying in the breeze against a peach-colored sky. The air was warm and sweet with the scent of flowers and fresh-cut grass. The sun was coming up.

Something chimed. A phone on the bedside table. I grabbed it. It was 9:00 a.m., on the dot, December 25. Sixty-eight degrees in Malibu, and sunny. I'd gone back somehow, to my own Christmas. The morning after I'd been the Scrooge, six years ago.

I was home. I'd been given another chance.

Somewhere in the house someone was whistling a Christmas song. I gasped again. Elena. "Elena!" I screamed. "Elena!"

She came running—she must have thought I was being murdered or something, the way I'd screamed her name. "Miss?"

I threw my arms around her. "Oh my God, Elena! You're here!"

"Yes . . . I'm here." She was totally stiff as I hugged her. I pulled back.

"You shouldn't be here! It's Christmas! You should be with your daughter! Nika! Nika—oh my God. You should be with Nika. Right now. You should be with her all week. Take two weeks. Take until February first, if you want. I can handle myself for a month. What's important is that you should be with your family."

"So I'm fired," she assumed.

"No! You're not fired! I was a total jerk before, is what I'm saying. I should never have asked you to work on Christmas. You're the best housekeeper, like, seriously, and I should have appreciated you. God, your cooking is amazing, did you know that? I've been dreaming about your cooking for six years. Hey, maybe you could go get Nika, and come back here, and we could roast a turkey for Christmas." I finally looked at her shocked face. "No. This isn't about me. No turkey for me. You should have the day off, though. Be with your daughter. We'll sort the rest out later."

I walked Elena out. She was still looking at me like I'd lost my mind. Which I was pretty sure I had. "I'll talk to my dad about giving you a Christmas bonus. And a raise. Because you're the best, like I said. I'm sorry for the way I've been treating you."

"All right," she said numbly, like she was expecting people with cameras to pop out any second.

I hugged her again. I couldn't help it. I wanted to hug, like, everyone. "Merry Christmas, Elena."

"Merry Christmas, miss."

I'd also just remembered there was risotto in the fridge. Which I wanted to be wolfing down, like, now. I went back to the kitchen and heated it up. It was as amazing as I'd remembered. I was at the kitchen counter shoveling it into my mouth in big spoonfuls when I got a text. From my dad.

You up yet? Can I call you?

I wiped my mouth with a napkin. My fingers trembled as I responded.

Yes. I'm awake.

I was so very *awake*. I could feel my heart beating fast and the air going shakily in and out of my lungs, and my neck was stiff, like I'd been sleeping in the wrong position, and my stomach hurt, because I'd eaten the risotto way too fast. But pain had never felt so good. It meant I was alive. I kept telling myself that this was real—it must be real, but it was hard to get my head around it. I was really home.

The phone rang. I picked it up on the first ring.

"Dad?"

"Hey, sweetie."

I blinked back tears. "Hi. Where are you?"

"I'm at the hotel," he said. "I sent the actors home for the holidays, but there are some details I need to work out here on the editing."

"It's Christmas," I said. "You should be—"

"Yes, I'm sorry," he said, like I was accusing him of something. "And it's your birthday tomorrow. I didn't forget. I thought maybe . . ." He hesitated.

"Maybe what, Dad?" I loved the way the word *Dad* felt when I said it—like he was mine again. My dad. Mine.

"I thought maybe you'd like to fly out for a few days. Hang with your old man. I know you probably have plans, but—"

"Yes. I'll fly out. I'd love to hang out." I didn't have any idea where he was or what he was working on, but I couldn't think of anything better than seeing my dad again. It was like the very best present I could think of, to spend my—how old was I going to be tomorrow? Seventeen. My seventeenth birthday. With my dad.

"Okay." He sounded surprised and happy. "I'll get my assistant to work out the details. How about today, if she can book a last-minute flight for Christmas Day?"

"Today would be amazing," I said. "I've missed you, Dad."

And then I was full-out crying. Again.

"Oh. Hey. Sweetie, I've missed you, too. So much," Dad said. "I can't wait to see you."

I wiped at my nose, still sniffling. "And we should totally watch *It's a Wonderful Life* together—it's always on TV at Christmas, right?"

He chuckled. "I thought you hated that movie. You said it was 'the cheesiest cheese,' if I remember correctly."

"Maybe it's grown on me. Besides, you like it. We should watch it because you like it."

"All right, who are you and what have you done with my teenage daughter?" he laughed.

"I'm just growing up, I guess."

"Well, don't do that too fast. I couldn't stand it."

"Okay."

After we hung up I walked around my room for a while just

touching things and remembering: my ragged stuffed bunny named Ears. My pretty clothes and shoes. My jewelry box that revealed a ballerina when you opened it, dancing in a circle to "Clair de Lune." I opened the vanity and found the torn pieces of the picture of Ro and me that I used to have taped to the edge of the mirror. A selfie on the beach. I leaned forward to look at it. In the picture, we had our arms wrapped around each other. My hair was brown and slightly frizzy; Ro had the same long black hair, which had dried into beachy waves. We were both smiling. Happy.

I touched her smile with my finger. Ro.

I picked up my phone and called a cab. Fifteen minutes later I was standing outside Ro's house. I knocked on the door.

"Hey, you," I said when Ro answered.

"Holly?" She of course was completely confused because—in her timeline, anyway— we hadn't talked in more than a year. For me it'd been like seven.

"I need to talk to you."

"It's Christmas morning, Holly."

"I know. I know." But honestly, it felt like I couldn't wait. I had to make things right with everyone I possibly could, as soon as I possibly could. Starting with Ro. "But this is like an emergency. I'll just take up five minutes of your time. I promise."

She sighed. Then she came outside and closed the door behind her. "All right," she said warily. "What do you want?"

I was trying not to stare at her—Ro at sixteen, still kind of skinny and with her hair cut in the pixie do she'd had back then.

"You look awesome," I said. "That haircut is so flattering. But your hair looks good long, too. You lucked out with the hair."

"What's going on?" she said.

I just smiled. "So much, it would take forever to explain. And even then, you'd never understand. I got to reset myself. And this time, I'm not going to screw it up."

"Yeah, well, you said it was an emergency." She sounded annoyed.

"It is. You've been my best friend for my entire life."

She was already shaking her head. "Holly," she sighed. "Come on, don't do this to me."

I grabbed her hands. "You can't stop being my friend, Ro. It's impossible. You're always going to be my best friend. It's not actually up to you."

She tugged a hand through her short hair. "Look, we just grew apart," she said. "That happens to friends all the time. I can't do this again. I told you before. I can't hang out with you. I'm sorry if you're feeling lonely or whatever. But I—"

"Oh, I understand why you broke up with me. I mean, you know, what you said last year. I heard you. I totally get it now. And you're right," I agreed. "We grew apart."

She frowned, clearly surprised that I'd admitted that. "We didn't live in the same world anymore. We never really did."

"I don't care that you're a T-shirt and sneakers girl," I said. But then something occurred to me. "Well, actually, I do care. That's who you are. But I don't care about money anymore."

She shook her head. She obviously didn't believe me. She looked around like she was searching for the real Holly, who would jump out from behind the bushes any second now and start making fun of her.

"Do you remember what it was like before?" I asked her. "When we used to watch TV with the sound turned off and make up the dialogue? Or we'd name all the fish at the pet store. We'd build weird sand creatures on the beach. We'd write songs together. Do you remember?"

"Of course I remember."

"None of that was about what clothes we were wearing," I said. "It was about us, right?"

"Right," she said hoarsely. "But—"

"I'm sorry I lost sight of that. I changed, I know I did. My mom died, and Yvonne showed up and whispered all this junk into my ear, and I got a little lost. I've been a total brat, not just to you, but to everyone. I have been. I'll admit it. I've been selfish and shallow and pretty much a horrible human being."

She smirked. "You're not *that* bad."

"The thing is, I'm still that girl you knew. She's in here somewhere." I put my hand on my chest. "And you being my best friend didn't change, even when I changed. That's what I should have said last year." My voice wavered, and I looked away from her. "You're the best person, Ro. You're awesome. You're so smart—I love the way you love books—and you're funny and you're honest and you're kind. And I'm not saying you don't have flaws, because you do. You're too sarcastic sometimes, and you have a short temper, and questionable fashion sense, and you don't like Indian food. But you are like the best. Person. Ever. I'd be crazy to not want to be your friend. I've missed you so much. I love you. I know that sounds weird, coming from a friend, maybe, but it shouldn't, really. You're like the best friend version of the love of my life."

And then I started crying. Again. It'd been an emotional twenty-four hours. Or six or seven years, however you want to count.

Ro was staring at me, dumbstruck. "What happened to you?"

I kept staring at my feet, sniffling. "So much."

"Holly, hey. Look at me," Ro said.

I wiped my face. "So here's my big emergency. I'm kind of hoping that you'll forgive me for being an idiot, and you'll be my best friend again. Unless . . ." I took a deep breath. "Unless you feel like you really can't stand to be around me anymore, which I will try to understand. But I'd really like another chance."

"Okay," she said. She didn't even hesitate.

I looked up. Her dark eyes were twinkling. "What?"

"You can have another chance."

All the air left my lungs. "You mean it?"

She smiled. "Nobody's perfect, right? We can work on our flaws together. We learn. We grow. Maybe instead of growing apart, this time we can grow together."

She was going to say more, but I hugged her. I couldn't wait one more second. I threw my arms around her neck and hugged her like there was no tomorrow. She hugged me back, and I was filled with something that could only be called joy.

"I love you, too, you know," she said. "I have to go inside, because it's Christmas morning and my little sisters are desperate to start opening presents, but I'll call you later, okay?"

"It's Christmas," I realized yet again. "It's Christmas Day."

"Yes, it is. Merry Christmas, Holly Chase," she said softly.

I laughed. "Merry Christmas! Merry Christmas, Ro!"

She hugged me again. "And a happy new year."

TWENTY-EIGHT

WELL, OBVIOUSLY THAT'S THE PERFECT ending to the story. But I'm thinking that you might have some questions. And so did I.

First of all, you'll never guess, not in a million years, where I flew to meet my dad that night.

Or maybe you *can* guess.

It was a good Christmas, and the best seventeenth birthday I could have imagined. Dad and I hung out at his hotel and watched *It's a Wonderful Life*, just like I'd promised, and we laughed and ordered cupcakes from room service and talked, and I felt closer to him than I'd ever felt before. Like we were going to be a real family again. And when he had to go back to working on his film, I decided to stay in Manhattan for a few days. You know—just because.

"I love New York," I sighed as my dad and I walked through

Central Park a couple days after Christmas. Our hotel was right across from the park, and it was so beautiful that winter, full of snow and lights, a place of magic and hidden dreams.

"You love New York?" He looked at me sideways. "Since when?"

"Since . . . now, I guess? There's always something new to discover here," I said. "And the snow is so pretty."

He put his arm around me. "You've changed, young lady, since the last time I saw you. You even look different somehow."

I flipped my newly colored hair over my shoulder and batted my eyes at him. "Why, thank you."

He laughed. "No, not your hair, although that is great. You look like your—" He stopped and cleared his throat. "It's you that's different. I think you were right."

"Which time?"

He laughed again. "When you said that you're growing up."

I nodded. I was technically a very old and wise seventeen-year-old girl, and that was fine with me.

Dad checked his watch. "So I have to go back to the studio, sweetie. Are you sure you're going to be all right on your own?"

"I know my way around," I assured him. "I have a great day planned that may or may not include the Empire State Building and a Broadway show. I'll catch up with you later."

You can guess what I did then, and it wasn't a Broadway show. I took a cab straight to 195 Broadway. And I made sure to look both ways before I crossed the street this time. I had so many things I wanted to say to Boz, to Dave, to Blackpool, even. And so many things I wanted to know.

But when I went into 195 Broadway, it didn't look the same. It was all newly remodeled, with glass and metal and comfortable-looking couches in the lobby. There was a new security desk just inside the door, and the guard there told me I couldn't go up in the elevators without approval. And there was no business listed as Project Scrooge anywhere in the building.

It was like they'd never been there.

I didn't know what to do with myself after that. So I walked to the movie theater—the Angelika, of course—and I watched a film there one last time. One of my dad's, it turns out. It kind of blew my mind wondering if he'd ever make those movies now that he'd made after I died, or if I was the only person in the whole world who would ever remember seeing them.

Thinking like that will drive you crazy. That's the thing about messing with time.

It was after the movie was over, when everybody was shuffling out, that I spotted Boz sitting at the back of the theater.

"Hello, Havisham," he said warmly.

"Am I still Havisham?"

"You'll always be Havisham to me."

I sat down next to him as the credits rolled in the dark. He was wearing that tweed jacket of his, the one with the leather patches on the elbows, and I kind of loved him for it.

"You changed your hair," he commented.

"I was sick of blond," I said. "So I dyed it back. Trying out a new look."

"It suits you."

"Thanks."

"And it seems that's not the only thing that's changed." His eyes were sparkling. I hadn't seen him look so happy before except for the time when he found that first-edition record of Bing Crosby's "White Christmas."

"I'm trying. I'm really trying, Boz. I am. I won't let you down this time."

"Oh, Holly." He reached over and patted my arm. "You never let me down."

I stared at him. "Never? Not even when I was totally messing up your entire company?"

He shook his head. "It all went according to plan, as far as I'm concerned. Although I have to admit you gave me a scare now and then."

My mouth had dropped open. I closed it. "You knew?"

He chuckled like this was the best prank ever. "You didn't really think you'd get something like that by us when Blackpool could see your future and Copperfield could read your mind."

Well, yeah, I'd wondered about that. But they never said anything. They never tried to stop me. "But then why did you let me—"

"You had to come to your own conclusions," he interrupted. "That was the most important part in your rehabilitation."

"My rehabilitation."

"We never give up on a Scrooge, Holly," Boz informed me

cheerfully. "And we didn't give up on you. We've been working on your case for years, hoping to find a way to reach you. And this year, with Mr. Winters, we saw an opportunity for you to succeed. And here we are."

"So all along, it was about me?"

"Not all of it."

"How's Steph?" I asked. "Is she . . ."

"She's our current Ghost of Christmas Past. A job that she enjoys, I think, and will continue to do for a while, until it strikes her fancy to try her hand at something else. Like high school."

"And what about Ethan?" I would never hear the name Ethan ever again without feeling something powerful and protective rise up inside of me. I'd always wonder where he was, and what he was doing, and if he was getting by okay.

"Ethan is a twelve-year-old boy at the moment," Boz said. "He's fine."

I thought for a minute, and then all the pieces seemed to fall into place. "He wasn't a real Scrooge, was he? You made Blackpool choose him, for my sake?"

"You always were a clever girl," Boz answered. "I can see the future, too, at times, although not as often or as predictably as Blackpool. I saw the potential in where Ethan Winters might lead you. It was a great sacrifice on Blackpool's part. He hates telling any kind of falsehood—he thinks it damages his credibility—and he had to stretch some truths in order for things to go our way in this case. But he, too, could see where our clever schemes might lead you. He also foresaw that Stephanie could return and be part of your resurrection, so to speak."

"Poor Blackpool." I arched an eyebrow at Boz. "Are there cameras on us right now?"

He nodded and pointed to a corner.

I stood up and waved at the camera. "Thank you, everyone. Dave. Are Marty and Grant there yet? I guess not. Well, hello, Marie and Leigh. Tox. Even you, Blackpool—Arthur. I owe you all so much." I blew them a kiss. "And Steph. You won't get this, because I don't think you'll remember, but we're friends, you and me. Real friends. So shoot me an email, okay?"

Boz stood up, too, and brushed off his pants. "That was very nice, Holly. I'm sure they appreciate that. Especially Stephanie."

"I need to thank you, too, Boz," I said. "I don't even know how to tell you how grateful I am."

"I did my part—no more, no less." He coughed. "But I suppose I should be going now. I have work to do back at the office."

"What? It's after Christmas. Don't you get a day off once in a while?"

"A day wasted on others is not wasted on one's self," he said. "Besides, this is a world of action, and not for moping and droning on."

Which was when I noticed there were tears in his eyes. He was going to miss me.

"I think I'm going to miss you most of all," I said, giving him a quick hug. He smelled like he always did, like peppermint and tobacco and a hint of Douglas fir.

"Well, now," he said with a cough. "Life is made of ever so many partings welded together."

I pulled away. "Hey, can you stop quoting Dickens? I'm getting a headache just trying to figure out what that even means."

He patted me on the head like I was a little girl and he was my doting grandfather. "Good-bye, my dear."

I nodded and made my way across the aisle to go out of the theater, but then I thought of one last thing and turned back. "What about Ethan? What's going to happen to him?"

Boz gave me a sly smile. "Anything's possible, I suppose. It's a wonderful fact to reflect upon, that every human creature is constituted to be that profound secret and mystery to every other."

"So you're saying you don't know?"

"What I do know about Ethan is this: he's twelve right now, and everything in his world is what it should be. For now."

For now.

I gasped. "Boz, what day is it?"

"You're asking *me*?" he said. "Gracious, I could barely tell you what decade I'm in."

"Come on, Boz. Use the earbud. Ask. Embrace the technology for once."

He listened for a minute, then nodded. "It's December twenty-eighth."

"December twenty-ninth," I murmured to myself. "When Ethan is twelve."

"No, I said . . ."

"I should go." I kissed Boz on the cheek, which he did not expect. "Wish me luck."

"Godspeed, Holly," he said, smiling again, and then he vanished into thin air.

And so it happened that the next morning, December the twenty-ninth, at precisely 9:00 a.m., I was standing on the corner of Lexington and 116th Street, listening to a homeless man play the saxophone.

All I had to do was wait.

And wait.

At exactly 9:03 (which felt like it took for freaking ever), up the street strolled Ethan Winters II. Ethan's dad. He was wearing a gray wool coat and a red plaid scarf, and he looked just how I remembered—like an older, happier version of Ethan. He was whistling as he walked. And then he stopped and listened to the homeless guy play.

"How's it going, Steve?" he asked after a minute.

"Same old, same old," the sax player replied. "It's been cold, though. I'm hoping not to freeze to death."

"You should head over to the Cecil," Ethan's dad said. "They'll have a bed for you there. You can take a cab on me." He gave the man a twenty, and Steve said, "Thank you much, sir. I just might."

"Stay warm." Ethan's dad smiled. Then he started off down Lexington.

It was time for me to do something. Right here. Right now.

"Wait," I called. "Please, um, sir, can you help me?"

Ethan's dad stopped immediately. "What's the matter?"

"Oh, nothing, nothing's wrong," I explained quickly. "It's just, I'm trying to find the Bikram East Yoga Center? It was supposed to be on 116th Street, but I couldn't find it. I have a terrible sense of direction."

It was a lame excuse, I'll admit, but it was the best I could think up on short notice. Plus, I really was wanting to get in some yoga later. I liked yoga when it didn't literally kill me.

"Sure," Mr. Winters said. "I haven't heard of that place, but I can look it up for you." He took out his phone and messed with it for a minute. "Yes, here it is. It's on 116th, but back that way, toward Madison. You must have passed it."

I darted a glance at my watch: 9:06. I still couldn't let him go onto Lexington, just in case. "Back that way?" I frowned. "What side of the street? Are you sure?"

He checked his phone again. "Left. It should be two blocks, on the left." He leaned out to look. "It's that awning there that reads BEYC?"

"Well, now I feel stupid. Thanks. I don't know how I could have missed that."

The homeless guy was eyeing me strangely. I kept my attention on Ethan's dad. I had to keep stalling him. "You look familiar to me. Do I know you?"

He smiled. "I have one of those faces, I'm afraid."

"Me too," I said, nodding. "Everybody always thinks they know me. But, really, I think we might have met before. Do you have kids that I might know?"

"I have a daughter about your age, actually," he answered. "I bet you'd remember if you'd met her. Her name is—"

"Jack," I finished for him.

"Yes." His smile widened. "Jacqueline, but it's always been Jack, ever since my little boy couldn't pronounce her name. We tried to get her to go back to Jackie once, and that did not work out. She's always known her mind, that kid. But I love her for that."

"I like Jack. She's amazing. We, uh, go to school together."

"Oh, you're at New Utrecht?"

I smiled and nodded. "She likes art, right?"

"Yes, she's always sculpting something or cutting stuff up and reassembling it. It drives my wife a little crazy, but we try to understand that it's her artistic soul that needs feeding."

"That's cool of you," I said. "Taking an interest."

"What are you interested in?" he asked.

"I have no idea." Which was the truth. I was still coming to terms with the idea that I was going to have an actual future. "I used to be into fashion, but I've broadened my horizons now. Who knows?"

"Well, you're young," he said. "You have time to figure it out."

"Exactly." I checked my watch again: 9:08.

He was in the clear now. I breathed out a sigh.

"Well, say hi to Jack from me," I said.

"Okay. I will."

He was still standing there, like he was waiting for something. "But to do that, I'd have to know your name?"

"Oh. Right. My name. My name is Victoria. Victoria Scott," I said.

"Victoria Scott. I'll remember."

"Thanks for your help with the yoga situation."

"No problem. See you around, Victoria."

And then he was off. I walked the other way for a minute, and then ran back to check on him. He'd made it safely all the way down Lexington and disappeared into a building. After a minute I saw a guy in a hard hat come out onto the sidewalk and bend over to pick something up.

A hammer.

I may have done a little happy dance right there in the street. For Ethan. For the future he might have now. And then I might have cried a little, too.

"Girl, you've got something going on," said the homeless guy. "I don't know what it is, but it's something good, I think."

"It's very good," I agreed. "Hey, come with me, okay?"

His eyes were instantly wary. "I thought you said you had to go to yoga. What is that, stretching?"

"Yes. Stretching. Lots of good stretching. But I want to introduce you to someone first. Someone who I think you're really going to want to meet at the London NYC Hotel."

"I don't know anybody at a hotel," he said.

"Trust me. You'll know her."

He packed up his saxophone and let me help him to his feet. We walked a few steps, and then he stopped and touched my arm.

"Hey, you're not an angel, are you?" he asked me.

I smiled. "Maybe I'm something like that today."

So that's the story of my afterlife, and now the real story, the one involving my actual life, has finally begun. And if you're wondering if I changed—if I really and truly became a better person than I was in the beginning—I'll tell you that I have good days and bad ones, of course, like everybody else, but I'm growing. I'll get there.

I still have dreams about New York sometimes, and I miss the weirdest stuff, like the sound of neighbor lady's TV and cereal for dinner and the convenience of a Hoodie that makes a person invisible. But I have an excellent life, and I try to be as good a friend, as good a daughter, and as good a *person* as it's possible for me to be.

I can tell some of you want to be upset because this is a story where the girl doesn't end up with the hot guy. You were shipping me and Ethan. I get it. I do. I'll always think about him, for the rest of my life and probably beyond it, about those few months that didn't happen for anyone but me. I miss him. I love him. But love doesn't always have to be about the happy ending. Love can be about beginnings, too.

Anyway, I didn't see the people from Project Scrooge again, but sometimes I feel like someone's watching me, and not just watching, but looking down on me fondly and wishing me the best, especially when December rolls around. I don't hate Christmas anymore, for obvious reasons. I always get a little thrill when that time of year arrives, and everyone starts decorating and hustling and bustling around, getting ready to enjoy not just the holiday but one another.

Because that's what it's all about, right? Connection. Togetherness. Love.

Plus, I always know that there are people hard at work trying to make this world a better place through this one night on the twenty-fifth of December. Which makes me feel like the world *is* a better place, every single year.

And now I'm going to say it—so listen up, because I'm only going to say it this one time. Because I think you deserve the proper send-off.

Here it goes:

God bless us, every one.

Which I think means that Grant owes me a twenty.

ACKNOWLEDGMENTS

THIS BOOK IS THE PRODUCT of many individuals working behind the scenes (just like the employees of Project Scrooge!), all trying to bring this particularly bratty Ebenezer's story to the happiest possible ending. I have so very many people to thank:

My unstoppable team at HarperTeen, starting with Erica Sussman, my brilliant and insightful editor, who spent so much time on the phone with me discussing Holly and her world. (You're always right. It's kind of annoying. But you're right.) Also, a huge thank-you to Stephanie Stein, who is the best Stephanie. Also a big thanks to Elizabeth Ward in marketing; Gina Rizzo, my rocking publicist; Jenna Stempel, who designed this knockout cover; and my copy editor, Alexandra Rakaczki.

Katherine Fausset, my agent. You're a rock star. Thanks for always having my back.

Jolyn Dunn, my Bonneville High School theater teacher, who

cast me as Fan in *A Christmas Carol* all those years ago and instilled my ever-burning love for poor old Mr. Scrooge.

Leslie Hammond, who's been a friend ever since we both played elves in another Christmas play—*Reckless*!—at the College of Idaho. Thanks for helping me wrestle with this novel for the past two years. Your insights were so helpful, and your excitement about Holly and her story was so encouraging.

My Boise friends: Amy Yowell, who's the greatest friend and cheerleader in the whole world; Wendy Johnston, who made me a great Christmas mix tape to inspire me when I was working on the book in the middle of July; and Lindsey Hunt, who always wants me to read my stuff to her.

My Janies: Brodi Ashton and Jodi Meadows. It's awfully hard to write a book without you two, but even when we're not working on the same project, you're so supportive and inspirational and fun. Thanks for talking through plot with me and for letting me drag you over the bumpiest cobblestone road ever (with our suitcases!) to visit the Charles Dickens Museum in London.

Victoria Scott, for letting me steal your name. You're the best.

My students. Thank you for reinvigorating my love of teaching, for your hard work, for your good writing, and for always being excited to hear about how this book was coming along.

My mom, Carol Ware, and her husband, Jack. For all the immeasurable ways you support me and lift me up, both as a writer and as a person.

My dad, Rodney Hand, and his wife, Julie. For always believing I can do what I set my mind to. And for taking the kids on long

ATV rides so I could work.

Will and Maddie, the little people. Thanks for being so patient with this never-ending process of writing books. And thank you for still wanting me to snuggle and tell you stories at the end of the day. I'm so excited that you're learning to read, so someday I can tell this story to you.

Mr. Dickens. You're one of the Ghosts, now, but even so, you continue to inspire me, not only as a writer, but as a writer who tried to make a real difference in this troubled world. You wanted people to see as Scrooge saw, so that they might change as Scrooge changed. I love you for that. And I hope my story can haunt my readers half so pleasantly as yours.

Speaking of my readers—thank you, thank you, with all my heart, thank you. Over the years you have been the best support and most unexpected friends. Bless you, every one!

Also from *New York Times* bestselling author

CYNTHIA HAND

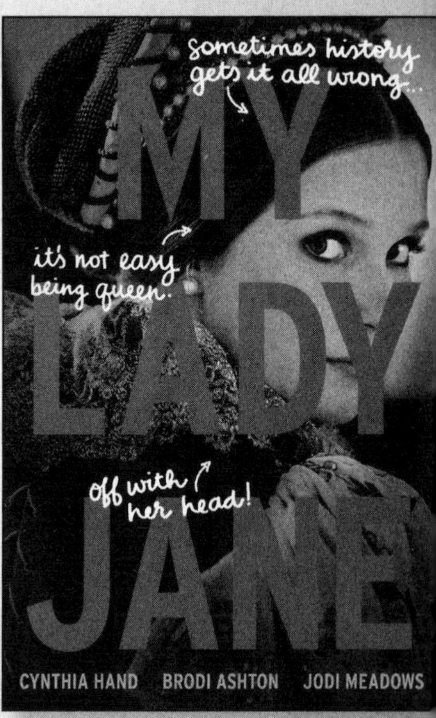

READ THEM ALL!

"Utterly captivating. One of the most addictive books I've read in a while."
—Richelle Mead, bestselling author of the VAMPIRE ACADEMY series

DISCOVER
your next favorite read

MEET
new authors to love

WIN
free books

SHARE
infographics, playlists, quizzes, and more

WATCH
the latest videos

www.epicreads.com